Fly by NIGHT

Fly by NIGHT

FRANCES HARDINGE

MACMILLAN

First published 2005 by Macmillan Children's Books

This edition published 2018 by Macmillan Children's Books
an imprint of Pan Macmillan
20 New Wharf Road, London N1 9RR
Associated companies throughout the world
www.panmacmillan.com

ISBN 978-1-5098-4233-9

1 3 5 7 9 8 6 4 2

A CIP catalogue record for this book is available from
the British Library.

Typeset by Nigel Hazle
Printed and bound by CPI Group (UK) Ltd, Croydon CR0 4YY

To my inspirational grandfather, the author H. Mills West,
and to Rhiannon, Mosca's godmother

CONTENTS

NOTE – THE FRACTURED REALM

❧ PARLIAMENT ☙

Responsible for setting up the Committee of King-makers, established to decide who is truly destined to wear the crown. But as the decades have passed and no decision has been reached, a fractured realm has been born. The Capital follows Parliament still, but every other fragment flies a flag to a different possible king or queen.

❧ THE GUILDS ☙

With the Realm shattered and no one king or queen to look to, the various guilds of skilled working men have grown stronger. They maintain an uneasy, though jealous, alliance with one another – and so keep a kind of common order throughout the Realm.

• *The Company of Locksmiths – a guild of key- and lock-makers, led in Mandelion by Aramai Goshawk. No door can be locked against a skilled Locksmith. And their power grows in the light of this knowledge.*

• *The Company of Stationers – a guild of printers and book-binders, led in Mandelion by Mabwick Toke. Masters of the printed word and all printing presses. If a text does not bear the Stationers' seal, it is heresy and must be burned.*

• *The Company of Watermen – a guild of boatmen, policing the river and those that would travel upon it.*

❧ DUKE OF MANDELION, ❧
VOCADO AVOURLACE

Rules in name in Mandelion, and petitions for the Twin Queens to be returned to the throne. Lady Tamarind is his sister.

❧ THE BIRDCATCHERS ❧

Once custodians of all sacred texts, until they found the White Heart of the Consequence . . . then followed the Bad Time. But now all the Birdcatchers have been killed and the Stationers have burned their books.

❧ THE BELOVED ❧

From Goodman Palpitattle, He Who Keeps Flies out of Jams and Butterchurns, to Goodlady Prill, Protector of Pigs, these are the gods that the people of the Realm make their berry and bread offerings to. Days and hours are sacred to the different Beloved – babies are named according to the Beloved they are born under and people favour the Goodman or Goodlady of their choosing.

PRELUDE

HISTORY FOR THE HOUSEFLY

'But names are important!' the nursemaid protested.

'Yes,' said Quillam Mye. 'So is accuracy.'

'What's half an hour, though? No one will know she wasn't born until after sunset. Just think, born on the day of Goodman Boniface, a child of the Sun. You could call her Aurora, or Solina, or Beamabeth. Lots of lovely names for a daughter of the Sun.'

'That is true, but irrelevant. After dusk, that calendar day is sacred to Goodman Palpitattle, He Who Keeps Flies out of Jams and Butterchurns.' Quillam Mye looked up from his desk and met the nursemaid's gaze. 'My child is a bluebottle,' he said firmly.

The nursemaid's name was Celery Dunnock. She was born on a day sacred to Cramflick, She Who Keeps the Vegetables of the Garden Crisp. Celery had every reason to feel strongly on the matter of names. Her eyes were pale, soft and moist, like skinned grapes, but at the moment they were stubborn, resolute grapes.

Quillam Mye had a most meticulous brain. His thoughts were laid out like the strands of a feather, and a single frond out of place he felt like a tear in his mind.

His eyes were dark and vague, like smoked glass.

The twin grapes looked into the smoked glass and saw a mind full of nothing they could understand.

'Call it Mosca and have done with it,' Mye said. Mosca was rather an old-fashioned name for a fly-born, but better than Buzzletrice or Caddis. He returned his attention to the task of writing his treatise. It was a history of the times in which he, and now his infant daughter, lived. It was entitled 'The Shattered Realm: A Full and Clear Account of Our Kingdom of Rags and Tatters'.

The door closed behind Celery, and Mye was dimly aware that the level of annoyance in the room had diminished. He was alone. But no, he was not alone.

From the wall a pair of eyes watched him. At the moment they were blue, but one of them already showed a peppery speckle which told Mye that one day they would be as black as his own.

The nursemaid had bound the baby in swaddling clothes as tight as an acorn in its cup, so that it could not learn to be wrigglesome. When the baby was nothing but a linen cocoon with a surprised little head peeking out, she had strapped it to a board to give it a nice straight back. The board was hung from a hook on the wall to keep it out of the way.

For the last month, for all the attention Mye had paid to it, the suspended baby might have been a picture hung upon the wall, albeit a picture whose eyes followed one around the room rather more convincingly than one might like. Now, however, it had a Name, and Names were important.

She had a name.

Mye was suddenly sorry that the girl would not have green eyes, like her dead mother. If he had thought about this for another moment, he might have regretted spending so much time among his books, writing of the fates of nations, while those green eyes were still open. However, he very sensibly caught himself in time and decided to think about something else.

But what would he do, now that his sight was weakening? He had always thought that in years to come dear Jessamine would help him with his papers.

Those wide, pepper-speckled eyes, watching from the wall . . . what a pity the child was a girl, and not a boy to be schooled!

'Well, you will have to do. If you had died along with your mother, I would have taught the cat to read.' Mye felt a brief qualm at the idea of turning his daughter into a freak by teaching her letters, but it could not be helped.

The baby watched as he stooped over his manuscript once more and picked up the quill. The study was so quiet and lonely, snug and sealed like a ship's cabin against the rain-blasted world. Once, while he still lived in the city of Mandelion, Mye had longed for such quiet, an escape from the distractions of horse-clatter and hawker-cry. His exile to the remote village of Chough had left him weary of stillness and the dismal, eternal trickle of water outside his window.

Mye laid down his quill again. He had no idea how to speak to a baby, he had no stories for children, and he was embarrassed by the fact that, just for once, he wanted – or rather needed – to talk.

'Well, I suppose if you are to be of any use to me, then I had better start putting sense into your head before foolishness can blot the page.' Mye searched his pipe bowl for inspiration, and then thoughtfully fingered the dry wove of his manuscript. In it he had tried to make sense of the last thirty years of the Realm's history. It was hardly a bedtime story for a child.

But perhaps, told another way . . .

'Perhaps . . . we had better start with a story.

'Once, in a day that some still remember, there was a king who spent a lot of time devising beautiful gardens and thinking clever thoughts about the stars. He meant very well, and ruled very badly, and in the end they cut off his head, and melted down his crown to make coins.

'The Parliament ruled the country after that, and all the people who still thought there should be a king went into hiding, or retreated to the hills, or fled to other countries. The Parliament's leader ruled very like a king, but no one called him a "king", because names are important.'

Mosca, the newly named Housefly, offered no comment.

'The dead king had a son, whom loyal servants rescued and carried abroad. The boy prince travelled afar and became a man prince. He spoke with other kings, some of whom promised to help him win back his throne. He learned the etiquette of court, and found out which princesses were worthy to be his queen. And then, while he was visiting a far-distant king in a land of burning sands, his camel unexpectedly bit off his nose. The prince took a fever and died the next day, through surprise as much as anything else.

'Those who thought there should be a king or queen now argued among themselves. Some thought the old king's daughter should rule, some his sister, some his cousin's son.

'Twenty years passed in this way, and the Parliament fell out with one another as well. They were too busy squabbling to notice their power being stolen away by a clever new enemy.'

Mye hesitated. Like everyone else who had lived through that time, he carried his share of terrible memories and once again he felt them stir, like the breath of a tiger against the back of his neck.

'A Bad Time came upon the Realm. For ten years . . .' Mye halted, looking up into his infant daughter's face. There was still a great deal of blue in her eyes. A fancy struck him that if he spoke aloud of the tortures, the mass gibbets, the screams from the pyres, he would see inkiness flood his daughter's eyes, to leave them as black as his own.

'Perhaps I . . . will wait until you are older before I talk to you about the Years of the Birdcatchers.

'But the Birdcatchers were overthrown and the Bad

 5

Time did pass. Afterwards, the monarchists and the Parliamentarians resumed their struggle for power. Each group of Royalists gathered an army and prepared to snatch the throne for their monarch of choice. Parliament was frightened and prepared their own armies for war.

'And then one day, to their surprise, the leaders of the Parliament found themselves drinking tea with a group of quietly insistent men in very clean but well-used overalls who explained to them that they were not going to do anything of the sort. The Parliament were surprised, for these men were the heads of the guilds, the leaders of the watchmakers and locksmiths and stationers, and other skilled working men.' Mentioning the Stationers, Mye felt a tiny sting of bitterness, but he continued, '"If you go to war," said the guild heads, "you will suddenly find that there are no boots or coats for your troops. You will find that there are no flints for your pistols and no shot for your muskets."

'"No matter," said the leaders of the Parliament. "Our troops will be so inspired by their cause that they will fight in their shirts and their socks, and will use swords and stones if they cannot have guns." "Perhaps," said the guild heads. "But in the meantime even you will have no tea or marmalade for your breakfast tables, and no tailors to darn your robes of office when they tear." And so the leaders of the Parliament went pale and asked for time to think about it.

'Meanwhile, on their own lands, the Royalist supporters prepared to march on the Capital. But each and every one found themselves, one day, talking to a group of quietly insistent men in very clean but well-used overalls who explained to them that they would do nothing of the sort. "You will promise loyalty to the Parliament," said the guild heads, "or your cityfolk will have no flour for their bread or slate for their roofs."

"'Our cause is so just," said the Royalist leaders, "that our people will hold out against a siege even if they are hungry and the snow piles up in their beds." "Perhaps," said the guild heads. "But in the meantime no one will set your wives' hair into ringlets, and your horses will be ungroomed." And so the Royalist leaders trembled, and said they would give an answer next day.

'The next day, the Parliament said that a monarch would be no bad thing, and set up a Committee in the Capital to look into it. One by one, the Royalist leaders came to join the Parliament, and waited to find out who was destined to take up the crown and return the nation to its remembered glory.

'That,' said Quillam Mye to his daughter, 'was seven years ago. Today the Realm still awaits the Committee's Decision. Shall I tell you what has happened since then? I will show you our nation. It is . . .' He reached for his supper plate. 'It is *this biscuit*.'

The Housefly stared at the biscuit obediently, perhaps trying to imagine that the ground beneath her was crunchy and full of almonds.

'Our "kingdom" is like *this*.' Mye brought his fist down sharply on the biscuit, fracturing it. 'See? It still looks like a whole biscuit, but it is cracked beyond repair. Every fragment flies a flag to a different king or queen. You see this?' He picked out a butter-browned fragment. '*This* chunk is the Capital and its lands. And *this* piece –' a piece crested with a large nut – 'is Galdspar. *This* is Mandelion, and *this* is the counties of Amblevetch. But there is no biscuit any more. The biscuit where we once lived is dying . . .'

Familiar pains were throbbing behind his eyes, and he paused to let them pass. Little pale points came and went before his sight, as if a giant cat were kneading the tapestry of the world and letting its claw tips show through the cloth. He sighed, swept away the crumbs and dipped his quill to continue with his writing, then looked up at the baby one last time, as if she had said something to interrupt him.

'Well, if you are to help me with my work, you had better get used to stories without endings. True stories seldom have endings.'

Quillam Mye's great treatise on The Shattered Realm was never given an ending. Eight years later the historian Quillam Mye was dead, and his books had been burned. Twelve years after the night she was named, his daughter could be found hiding inside a dovecote, with a goose tucked under one arm.

A IS FOR ARSON

It was often said that only divine flame could persuade anything to burn in Chough. Many joked that the villagers cooked their dinners over marsh-lights.

Chough could be found by straying as far as possible from anywhere comfortable or significant, and following the smell of damp. The village had long since surrendered to a seeping, creeping rot. The buildings rotted from the bottom upwards. The trees rotted from the inside out. The carrots and turnips rotted from the outside in, and were pale and pulpy when they were dug out.

Around and through the village, water seethed down the breakneck hillside in a thousand winding streamlets. They hissed and gleamed through dark miles of pine forest above the village, chafing the white rocks and learning a strange milkiness. Chough itself was more a tumble than a town, the houses scattered down the incline as if stranded there after a violent flood.

By day the villagers fought a losing battle against the damp. By night they slept and dreamed sodden, unimaginative dreams. On this particular night their dreams were a little ruffled by the unusual excitement of the day, but already the water that seeped into every soul was smoothing their minds back to placidity, like a duck's bill glossing its plumage.

One mind, however, was wakeful and nursing the black flame of rebellion. At midnight the owner of that mind could be found hiding in the local magistrate's dovecote.

This dovecote was large, and from the outside its conical roof bore a remarkable resemblance to a castle turret. At the moment, the dovecote was remarkably free of doves and remarkably full of twelve-year-old girl and oversized goose.

Mosca wore the wide-eyed look of one who is listening very carefully, and she chewed gently at the stem of her unlit pipe as she did so, feeling the splinters working their way up between her teeth. Her attention was painfully divided between the sound of approaching voices and the pear-shaped silhouette of a single dove against one of the little arched doorways above her. Trying to balance her weight on the slender perch poles with an agitated goose under one arm, Mosca was already regretting her choice of hiding place.

Each time a bird appeared at one of the openings, Saracen hissed. If the doves seemed to be hissing, this might make someone curious enough to investigate and discover Mosca hiding there at midnight with someone else's goose. Mosca had excellent reasons for not wanting to be dragged back home to face her Uncle Westerly and Aunt Briony. She had plans of her own, and none of them involved the sorts of punishments that would be waiting for her if she was caught on this night of all nights.

'We're much beholden to you, sir. If you had not chanced by and warned us, the fellow might have been fleecing our gullible housewives a month hence.' It was the magistrate's voice. Mosca froze.

'It was not entirely a matter of chance.' A young man was speaking, his voice gentle and reassuring, like warm milk. 'When I changed horses at Swathe someone mentioned that a man named Eponymous Clent had been staying here for the last week. I knew him well by reputation as a villain and swindler, and your village was only a little out of my way.'

'Well, you must delay your journey a little longer, I fear. You shall stay the night and let me thank you in broth, beef and brandy.' The snap of a snuffbox opening. 'Do you indulge?'

'When it is offered so hospitably, yes.'

The dove stared. It could see something crouching among the tangle of perches. Something big, something dark, something breathing. Something that gave a long, low hiss like skates across ice.

Mosca kicked out, and the toe of her boot caught the dove just beneath the snow-white plum of its chest, causing it to tumble backwards into flight.

'Is something amiss?'

'No, I just thought for a moment . . .'

Mosca held her breath.

'. . . I thought I could smell smoke.'

'Ah, the snuff does have a touch of brimstone in it.'

'So . . .' The younger man sniffed once, twice, to clear his nose, and then spoke again in a less nasal tone. 'So you will no doubt keep Mr Clent in the stocks for a day or two, and then have him taken to Pincaster for further punishment?'

'I believe we must. Chough has a magistrate but lacks a gibbet . . .'

The voices faded, and a door clicked to. After a time, the faint orange ache of candlelight in the nearest window dulled and died.

The roof of the dovecote stealthily rose, and two sets of eyes peered out through the gap. One pair of eyes were coal beads, set between a bulging bully brow and a beak the colour of pumpkin peel. The other pair were human, and as hot and black as pepper.

Mosca's eyes had earned her countless beatings, and years of suspicion. For one thing, they had a way of looking venomous even when she held her pointed tongue. For another thing, her eyes wielded a power that was beyond everyone else in Chough except the magistrate. She could read.

Everybody knew that books were dangerous. Read the wrong book, it was said, and the words crawled around your brain on black legs and drove you mad, wicked mad. It did not help that she was daughter of Quillam Mye, who had come to Chough from Mandelion amid rumours of banishment, bringing city thoughts crackling with cleverness and dozens of dark-bound, dangerous books. Mosca might as well have

12

been the local witch in miniature.

After her father's death, Mosca's eyes had at least earned her a roof over her head. Her uncle, the older brother of her dead mother, was glad to have someone to take care of his accounts and letters. His niece was useful but not trusted, and every night he locked her in the mill with the account book to keep her out of trouble. This evening he had turned the key upon her as usual, without knowing that he was doing so for the very last time. He was now snoring like an accordion amid sweet dreams of grist and fine grain, with no inkling that his niece was loose yet again and embarked upon a desperate mission.

Mosca wrinkled her pointed nose in a sniff. There was a faint hint of smoke on the night air. Her time was running out.

A week before, a man named Eponymous Clent had arrived in Chough and talked his way into every heart and hearth. He had bewitched the entire village with an urbane twinkle. That afternoon, however, Chough had fallen out of love with him just as quickly and completely. Word had spread that a visitor to the magistrate's house had exposed Clent as a notorious trickster and cheat. Dusk had seen him shackled in the stocks and almost friendless.

Almost, but not quite. Since the burning of her father's books, Mosca had been starved of words. She had subsisted on workaday terms, snub and flavourless as potatoes. Clent had brought phrases as vivid and strange as spices, and he smiled as he spoke, as if tasting them.

His way with words had won him an unlikely rescuer.

The magistrate's house had originally been built on a raised lump of land with two deep cracks cut around it on either side, providing a channel for the water. This had been all very well, until the water had enjoyed one of its wild nights, in which it pulled the hillside into new shapes and threw boulders like dice. In the morning, the magistrate had found a hill of white silt and rubble piled up against the back of his house, and the sweet spring sunlight gleaming upon the streamlets as they poured across his roof and dripped in diamonds from his thatch.

In an attempt to snatch the magistrate's vegetable garden from the domain of the ducks, a local carpenter had constructed a simple shaduf, a long pole which seesawed on a central strut and had a bucket on one end to scoop up the water. The base stood on four wheels so that it could be moved around the garden.

Mosca slipped to a window of the magistrate's house, slid a knife into the frame, and levered the window slightly ajar. Against the opposite wall of the darkened parlour hung the magistrate's ceremonial keys.

Champing furiously on her pipe, she pushed her handkerchief into the bottom of the pail, then manoeuvred the long arm of the shaduf in through the window. The machine proceeded in jolts, as the wheels caught on rough ground, and the bucket swayed dangerously, now nearly rattling a pewter plate, now nearly chiming against a warming pan. A jolt forward, another jolt . . . the ring of keys was nudged off its hook and fell into the bucket, its clang muffled by a handkerchief. The metal bucket gonged gently against the window frame as Mosca drew it back, and a moment later the magistrate's keys were in her hand. The key to his chest of silver plate, the key to the village's tithe box . . . and the keys to the stocks.

Mosca pulled off her boots and slung them around her neck, then hitched and pinned her skirts. Like many of the younger girls of Chough, she wore knee breeches under her skirts, to make wading easier.

She stooped to scoop up Saracen once again. Anyone else taking such liberties would have staggered back with a broken arm. However, Mosca and Saracen shared, if not a friendship, at least the solidarity of the generally despised. Mosca assumed that Saracen had his reasons for his persecution of terriers and his possessive love of the malthouse roof. In turn, when Mosca had interrupted Saracen's self-important nightly patrol and scooped him up, Saracen had assumed that she too had her reasons.

Beneath them, the white roofs of lower Chough glimmered under a bright moon as if they had been iced.

The milky water of Chough left white bathtub rings on the sides of stream beds. Plants that trailed in the flow grew chalky, until they dabbled in the water with leaves of stone. A sock left in a stream would petrify, until it seemed that a careless statue had left it there after paddling.

Children of Chough were told that if they misbehaved they would be hung upside down by their ankles beneath the drip, drip of a waterfall, so that in the morning they

15

would be stone children, their mouths still making whistle-shapes from spitting out the water.

There was no escaping the sound of water. It had many voices. The clearest sounded like someone shaking glass beads in a sieve. The waterfall spray beat the leaves with a noise like paper children applauding. From the ravines rose a sound like the chuckle of granite-throated goblins.

The goblins chuckled at Mosca as she scrambled down the slicked roof of Twence the Potter's hut. She realized that she would never hear the sound of their chuckle again, and to her surprise felt a tiny sting of regret. There was no time for hesitation, however.

The next house down the slope belonged to the Widow Wagginsaw. Mosca misjudged the leap on to the domed roof, and landed heavily. Her bootsoles slithered, and she fell to her knees.

Below, a sleep-choked voice quavered a question, and a tinderbox hissed and spluttered into life. Here and there across the cracked surface of the roof, Mosca saw veins of dim, reddish light appear. Someone was moving slowly towards the door with a candle.

Mosca hugged herself close to the chill, wet stone, and started to wail. The wail started deep in her throat, soared like an off-key violin, then dropped into a guttural note. She repeated it, and to her intense relief it was answered by a choir of similar wails below, all tuned to different pitches.

The Widow kept cats – thin, bedraggled creatures that looked like weasels and wailed at anything.

The Widow would often wail as well, and because she was the richest person in Chough no one ever told her to stop. If the Widow thought there was a thief on the roof, Mosca knew that her wails would be heard all over Chough. But the Widow had been wailing all afternoon, ever since she had learned the truth about Clent, and perhaps that had worn her out. After a few minutes the veins of light dimmed and vanished. The Widow thought it was one of her own cats on the roof, and had gone back to bed.

A clamber down the waterwheel of Dogger's Mill, a scramble across the roof of the Chide household, and then Mosca was wriggling through the fence that separated Lower Chough from the Whitewater plain. The fence was little more than a row of spiked iron railings driven into the rock, to let out the water and keep in the children and chickens, both of whom had a way of falling into the rapids, given half a chance. The metal spokes bled rust-trails across the white stone around them, and pointed outwards like spikes around a fort. They were spiked to discourage wild dogs and poachers.

Emerging from the fence, Mosca rubbed the rust from her cheek. There was thistledown fear in her throat, her chest and the centre of her palms. The spikes were also meant to keep out Brackle and Grabspite.

Brackle had a chest like a barrel and skin that looked as if it might have belonged to an even bigger dog, with great black jowls that wobbled when he barked.

Grabspite had a long, low lope, as if he had learned it

from watching the wolves. He had a wolfish look about his narrow muzzle and he could outrun a deer.

The two dogs belonged to the magistrate, as far as they belonged to anyone, and protected the lower border of Chough during the hours of the night. Mosca had seen them by daylight any number of times, but somehow it was very different to know that one or another might suddenly bound out of the woods and bear her down in a flash of teeth.

What was that? A bush dipping a curtsey, or an animal crouching low to watch her? Was that a lean, pointed face with a long jaw?

Mosca cupped her hands under Saracen's weight, and lifted the goose up above her head. Startled, he cycled with his feet, the rough but clammy webs chafing against her arms. His great wings spread wide as he tried to find his balance. When Mosca lowered him again, the wolfish face among the trees was gone.

In Chough, Brackle and Grabspite were regarded with superstitious terror. The villagers feared the bullying of the blacksmith, who feared the wailing of the Widow, who feared the might of the magistrate, who, in his own dry-as-parchment heart, feared his two terrible dogs.

Even Brackle and Grabspite, however, were afraid of Saracen.

The throaty roar of distant waterfalls was now audible. Another faint trickle of sound could also be heard, a dismal, whimpering string of words.

'. . . starved, robbed of my dignity and laid bare to

the ravages of the elements . . .'

The greatest boulder on the shingle plain was known as the Chiding Stone. It stood ten feet high and was shaped somewhat like a saddle. Over the centuries, countless nagging wives and wilful daughters had been chained there and mocked. Their names were etched into the stone by the magistrate of the time, along with a description of their crime. 'Mayfly Haxfeather, for Reducing Her Husband to Shreds with the Lashings of her Tongue', and, near the main dip of the saddle, where centuries of bottoms had worn a rounded hollow, 'Sop Snatchell, for Most Wilful and Continual Gainsaying'.

The Stone's sides were pockmarked with strange dimples and bulges, and easy for Mosca to clamber up. From the top of the Chiding Stone the moonlight showed her a clear view of the rocky pedestal five yards beyond, and the man sprawled upon it.

He was plump, in a soft, self-important way. His puffed-out chest strained the buttons of his waistcoat. They were fine buttons, though, and much polished, as if he took a pride in his appearance. His coat was a little crumpled and disarranged, but this was hardly surprising since he was suspended upside down, with his feet locked into a set of moss-covered stocks. A beaver hat and periwig lay sadly in the stream below, sodden and weed-strewn.

Since there was little he could do about his situation, he seemed determined to strike as picturesque and dramatic a pose as possible. The back of one hand rested despairingly across his forehead, while his other arm was thrown wide in a flamboyant attitude. The only part of his face visible, therefore, was his mouth, which was pursed and plump, as if the world was too hot and coarse for his palate and he felt the need to blow it cool. The mouth was moving, spilling out long, languorous sentences in a way which suggested that, despite his predicament, the speaker rather enjoyed the sound of his own voice.

'. . . before even the Travesty in Three Acts had seen print . . .' The speaker sighed deeply, and combed his fingers through his dishevelled hair before placing his hand back across his eyes. '. . . and this is to be the end of Eponymous Clent, left out in the wilderness to be devoured by the savage geese and weaselly faced imps of the forest . . .' The flow of words stopped abruptly. Cautiously he uncovered his eyes once more. 'Are you human?'

It was a fair question. Rust, grime and lichen covered Mosca's face like warpaint, and dove feathers still clung to her hair and arms. The unlit pipe in her mouth also gave her an other-worldly, young-old look.

She nodded.

'What do you want?'

Mosca swung her legs over to sit in the 'saddle' more comfortably, and took the pipe out of her mouth.

'I want a job.'

'I fear that adverse circumstances have deprived me of all monetary advantages and simple luxuries and . . . did you say a job?'

20

'Yes.' Mosca pointed to the stocks. 'I got the keys to those, but if I let you out, you got to give me a job and take me with you.'

'Fancy,' Clent said with a faint, desolate laugh. 'The child wishes to leave all this.' He glanced around at the dripping trees, the bone-white stones and the cold colours of the distant village.

'I want to travel,' Mosca declared. 'The sooner the better,' she added, with an apprehensive look over her shoulder.

'Do you even have the first idea of what my profession entails?'

'Yes,' said Mosca. 'You tell lies for money.'

'Ah. Aha. My child, you have a flawed grasp of the nature of myth-making. I am a poet and storyteller, a creator of ballads and sagas. Pray do not confuse the exercise of the imagination with mere mendacity. I am a master of the mysteries of words, their meanings and music and mellifluous magic.'

Mendacity, thought Mosca. *Mellifluous*. She did not know what they meant, but the words had shapes in her mind. She memorized them, and stroked them in her thoughts like the curved backs of cats. Words, words, wonderful words. But lies too.

'I hear you told the Widow a story 'bout how you was the son of a duke and was going to marry her when you came into your lands, but how you needed to borrow money so you could hire a lawyer and make your claim.'

'Ah. A very . . . emotional woman. Tended to take, ah,

figures of speech very literally.'

'And I heard you told the magistrate a story 'bout how there was this cure for his aches which you just needed to send for, but which cost lots of money. And I heard you told all the shopkeepers a story 'bout how your secretary was coming any day and bringing all your trunks and the rest of your money so you could pay all your bills then.'

'Yes . . . er . . . quite true . . . can't imagine what can have happened to the fellow . . .'

'They brand thieves' hands, don't they?' Mosca added suddenly. 'S'pose they'll brand your tongue for lying. S'pose it stands to reason.'

Everything was very quiet for a few moments except for the rattle of water on rock and the sound of Clent swallowing drily.

'Yes, I . . . I have quite lost patience with that secretary of mine. I suppose I must let him go, which means that I have a vacancy. Do you . . . do you have any qualifications or assets to offer as a secretary, may I ask?'

'I got these.' Mosca jangled the keys.

'Hmm. A practical outlook and a concise way of speaking. Both very useful qualities. Very well, you may unlock me.'

Mosca slid down from her stone throne and scrambled up the craggy pedestal to slot the key into the lock.

'Purely out of interest,' Clent asked as he watched her, upside down, 'what so bewitches you about the idea of the travelling life?'

There were many answers Mosca could have given

him. She dreamed of a world without the eternal sounds of glass beads being shaken in a sieve and goblins chuckling in the ravines. She dreamed of a world where her best friend did not have feathers and a beak the colour of pumpkin peel. She dreamed of a world where books did not rot or give way to greenblot, where words and ideas were not things you were despised for treasuring. She dreamed of a world in which her stockings were not always wet.

There was another, more pressing reason though. Mosca raised her head, and stared up the hillside towards the ragged treeline. The sky was warmed by a gentle redness, suggesting a soft but radiant dawn. The true dawn was still some three hours away.

'Very soon,' Mosca said quietly, 'my uncle will wake up. An' when he does . . . he's likely to notice that I've burned down his mill.'

B IS FOR BLACKMAIL

Mosca was *almost* certain that setting fire to the mill
had not been part of her plan when she had decided
to rescue Clent. She had escaped from the locked mill
through the hole in its roof with the ease of long practice. The malthouse wall, however, had presented more
of an obstacle. She had known she would need Saracen
to frighten off Brackle and Grabspite on the Whitewater
plain, but the wall was too high to climb with a goose
under one arm. It had made perfect sense to grab armfuls
from the gorse stacks which the village used as fuel, and
pile them against the wall. And when she had clambered
up to the top of the wall, ignoring the sweet smell of
dying summer and the stems which prickled against her
face, it had made sense to light an oil lamp.

She did not remember deciding to drop the lamp,
but nor did she remember it exactly slipping from her
grasp. What she did remember was watching it fall away
from her hand, and bounce so softly from one stack to
another that it seemed impossible that it should break.
She remembered seeing the wrecked lamp sketch a faint
letter in white smoke shortly before the dry stems around

it started to blacken and a hesitant flame wavered first blue, then gold . . . and she remembered a rushing thrill of terror as she realized that there was no going back to her old life.

Now, as Mosca and Clent fled Chough, the wind followed them like a helpful stranger, offering them the smell of smoke from the burning mill as if it thought it might belong to them.

At four o'clock the feverish wind sighed and settled. Mosca had always enjoyed clambering the cliff paths at this hour, watching the frogs bulging on their rocky pulpits while the trees lost their roots among the early-morning mist. When their path crossed the track down to Hummel, she halted nervously, but it was too early for any of Hummel's red-scarfed women to be hefting sacks of grain to Chough's mills.

'I suppose there is a good reason why you have paused to take in nature's marvels? Perhaps your goose has entreated a moment to lay an egg for our breakfast?' For one of such portly build, Clent had kept a fast pace along the treacherous path.

Mosca stared at Clent.

'He's a gander,' she exclaimed. She could not have been more amazed if Clent had mistaken Saracen for a cat.

'Really?' Clent pulled a shabby pair of chamois gloves from his waistcoat pocket, and used them to flick a few burrs from his shoulder. 'Well, in that case, I recommend that you wring the bird's neck and have done with it. It would be a pretty pass if our dinner were to get away from us, would it not? Besides, you will find a dead bird easier to carry and simpler to hide.'

Saracen shifted in Mosca's grasp, and made small noises in his throat like water being poured from a jug. He understood nothing of Clent's suggestion, but he resented the way Mosca's arms were tightening around him.

'Saracen isn't dinner.'

'Really? Then perhaps I may venture to ask what he is? Our guide through the mountains, perhaps? A bewitched relation? Or does our route cross a toll bridge where a payment must be made in waterfowl? May I point out that our provisions will be exhausted all the faster with an extra beak to feed?'

Mosca flushed.

Clent turned his head away slightly and examined her sideways along his cheek. Someone lean, clever and watchful seemed to be peering out of his eyes. 'I assume we *do* have provisions? I am sure that my new secretary would not have made fugitives of us without bringing more than an inedible goose? No? I see. Very well then, this way, if you please.'

He led her uphill along a tiny path that ended before a brightly painted shrine no bigger than a kennel. Beneath its sloping roof a wooden statue of a man held out his hands in stiff benediction.

'Mr Clent!' Mosca reached the shrine in time to see her new employer scooping a handful of fat, golden berries from the pewter offering-bowl.

'No need to become shrill, girl.' Clent peeled a piece of damp leaf mould from the side of the statue's head. 'I am merely borrowing a few provisions, which we will of course repay in the fullness of time. This good fellow . . .'

'Goodman Postrophe,' Mosca added automatically.

'. . . Goodman Postrophe is an old friend of mine. He has been looking after some trifles for me.' Clent's large, trimly manicured hand reached into the darkness of the shrine, and reappeared gripping an oblong bundle bound in burlap.

'But . . .' Mosca stopped, suddenly afraid that she would sound childish and superstitious.

But, she thought desperately, *if we take the Goodman's mellowberries, how will he defend the village from the wandering dead? How will he squeeze the juice into their eyes so that they cannot see the way home?* To be sure, none of the bodies in Chough's graveyard had yet done anything as interesting as rising from the ground and returning home to screech down the chimneys. But perhaps, Mosca reasoned, Goodman Postrophe had kept them at bay until now.

'I am surprised to find you squeamish, given your obvious penchant for felony.' Wrapping the berries in his handkerchief, Clent slid them into a capacious pocket. 'Arson, indeed . . . a nasty business. Little better than high seas piracy as far as the courts are concerned . . . Whatever possessed you to start setting fire to mills?'

A series of pictures chased each other across Mosca's

tired brain as she thought of the mill burning. She imagined the string of the old switchbroom that had often blistered her hands burning through and spilling its sticks. She imagined the tapers she had been scolded for squandering souping into a yellow puddle. She imagined her uncle and aunt shrieking as they strove to rescue sacks of bubbling flour from the blaze, without thinking to look for a charred niece.

'It was an ugly sort of a mill,' was all Mosca said.

'I once saw a boy of about ten hanged for setting fire to a schoolhouse,' Clent added in a matter-of-fact tone. 'Everyone pitied him, but, with a crime so severe, what was the magistrate to do? I recall his family wailing piteously as the cart took him to Blitheangel Square.' Clent gave Mosca a calculating glance. 'Of course, arson cases are all tried in the Capital, and when the hanging is over they give the body to the university to be dissected. I hear they cut out the hearts and examine them, to see if they are colder and blacker than the hearts of ordinary men.'

Despite herself, Mosca placed one hand over her heart, to find out whether it was giving off an icy draught. Certainly she felt as if there was a chill band around her chest obstructing her breathing. Was she being racked with guilt? If she was a diabolical criminal, then she must be due for her first rack round about now. And yes, when she thought of jolting her way by cart through hostile crowds, she felt a sickening throb of remorse.

However, when she imagined herself escaping justice

her spirit became quite tranquil again. *Ah*, thought Mosca with grim satisfaction, as she fell into step behind her employer, *I must be rotten to the core*. The truth was, she felt less sorry about the fate of the mill than for giving Clent information he could use against her.

This I will never see again, nor this, nor this . . . It seemed to Mosca that she should take note when she left the paths she knew. However, the moment when *her* woods became strangers' woods was lost in mist and haste. The early birds testing their voices sounded like the cries of distant pursuers.

The path was a troublesome, fretful thing. It worried that it was missing a view of the opposite hills and insisted on climbing for a better look. Then it found the breeze uncommonly chill and ducked back among the trees. It suddenly thought it had forgotten something and doubled back, then realized that it hadn't and turned about again. At last it struggled free of the pines, plumped itself down by the riverside, complained of its aching stones and refused to go any further. A sensible, well-trodden track took over.

'Wait. Raise your chin, madam.' Clent dabbed at Mosca's cheeks, rearranged her kerchief so as to hide the worst of the moss stains on her bodice and sighed. 'Well, there is little that can be done now. Let us hope that the good people of Kempe Teetering do not mistake you for some forest wight, come to bite the noses off their babies.'

'We're going to Kempe Teetering?'

'Yes – everyone will expect us to make for Trambling

Spike, where the main highways cross, then head towards the Capital or Pincaster. They will not expect us to head for a river port.'

'So we're getting a boat then, are we?' asked Mosca.

Clent did not appear to hear her.

The forests were yielding to soft slopes of green, studded with conical haystacks gathered around central staves. Wide, shallow steps had been cut into the hillside to make it easier to farm, so that from a distance it seemed that a giant comb had been dragged sideways through the fields.

Mosca was fascinated by the leather waistcoats of the farming men, their broad, black-buckled hats and loose, shabby white shirts. The women all wore coarse print frocks, far fuller than Mosca's sand-coloured dress. Over their white mob caps they wore wide straw bonnets, tied under the chin with ribbons of different colours. Like all the other women and girls of Chough, Mosca wore a tight-fitting cap of waxed linen which smelt of old fat but kept most of the water out. It seemed strange to her to wear two hats instead of one but, to judge by the way the farm girls tittered at her, they thought quite the reverse.

Kempe Teetering could be heard long before it could be seen. At the heart of the wind's bluster there was a throaty fluting, like a hundred people blowing into the necks of bottles. There was a *click*, *clack*, *clatter* like loose machinery. There was a keen and steely yodelling.

The hills fell back, and the tumbling tributary which

the people of Chough had always thought of as The River joined the *real* river. This was no shallow treacherous bandit of a river, ragged with foam. This was a sleek and powerful lordling, some thirty feet wide. This was the Slye.

Across the Slye, rippling and fluttering like a carnival carriage, stretched Kempe Teetering.

Most of the town was built across the great two-tiered bridge, the little shops and houses flanking the main thoroughfare. Rope ladders trailed from window and rooftop, and wooden stairways zigzagged between bridge and jetty. A web of clothes lines criss-crossed every available space, so that Mosca's first impression was of a flutter of brightly coloured cloth – saffron, mauve, sky blue, mint green. It was the first real town Mosca had ever seen, and it seemed too big and bright and busy to hold in her head all at once.

Above, the gulls spun and floated like tea leaves in a stirred cup. They followed each boat along the river, tearing off narrow strips of sound with their sharp beaks. They squabbled over spillages, and tried to scare the errand girls into dropping something. Every roof was decorated with a brightly painted wooden windmill, or a whistle in the shape of a bird, or clattering dolls on strings, in a vain attempt to scare away the gulls.

And the boats! Grim, old barges being loaded to the waterline with bales and boxes, while the hauliers bellowed laughter and spat tobacco juice into the water. Coracles like a row of turtle shells, keel-upwards for careening on the waterfront. Sculls and wherries, some with great kites reclining on their decks, each emblazoned with the colours of the Guild of the Watermen.

Clent led the way up the wooden steps to the bridge proper, and paused before the door of a shop.

'We shall call here briefly,' he remarked over his shoulder. 'Within lies a dear friend of mine whom I have promised to visit, and who will be invaluable in our state of extremis. May I stress that silence is a fine quality in a secretary?'

He ducked through the doorway, and Mosca followed.

The inside of the shop looked rather as if an excitable gorgon had run amok. On table and sill were clustered stone feathers, stone briars and stone flowers. Two bird skeletons hung against the window, so that their delicate bone structures could be seen against the light. There were crumpled and crumbling caps and sandals, stone pennies, scarves and ribbons stiff as the robes of a mausoleum angel. Mosca recognized all these strange ornaments as oddments petrified in the waters of Chough.

'Here we are . . . Ah – Mistress Jennifer Bessel!'

Mistress Bessel was sturdy and sun-browned, and she brought a glow of warmth into the room as she entered. She had a dusting of flour on her bare arms, and under her cap a thick plait of hair was twisted like a bread swirl. Curiously, her hands were hidden in a pair of fingerless muslin gloves.

'Mr Clent!' Mistress Bessel's smile widened still

further, and her dimples became wells. 'So my sweet friend has not got himself scragged after all.'

'No, no – there is no man, god or beast that could prevent me keeping an appointment with you, dearest Jen.'

Something in Jen's laugh suggested that she did not believe him.

'Ah . . . and this is my niece, from . . .'

'Chough,' Jen finished promptly. 'My dear bumblebee, look at her eyebrows!'

The little Chough bonnet was all very well for keeping one's hair dry. Eyebrows were a different matter. The Chough water turned them so pale that they were almost invisible, making everyone from Chough look very surprised all the time. Mosca was no exception.

'Still as sharp as a gimlet you are, Jen.' There was a slight note of annoyance in Clent's tone. 'Yes, she has been staying in that unpleasant little village. Chough has left our clothes so chill and damp I fear the child will perish any moment. Jen, my sweet plum, I was hoping you might spare us some clothes that are a little less . . .'

'Recognizable?' asked Mistress Bessel.

Mosca was rapidly coming to the conclusion that Mistress Bessel knew Eponymous Clent rather well.

Clent lowered his lashes and smiled winningly at his hostess's top button.

'Well, I'll take your old clothes in payment, then,' declared Mistress Bessel. She turned to Mosca. 'Listen, blossom, take that door, climb the ladder to the loft and you'll see a leather chest right in front of you. There's a gown of grey stuff which'll do for you, and you can try on a couple of the bonnets and caps. Don't go touching anything else, mind.'

Mosca obediently climbed to the attic and hunted out the chest of clothes. Then, her new clothing draped over one arm, she much less obediently sneaked back down the ladder, so that she could listen at the door while she changed.

'Rather young for you, isn't she?' asked Mistress Bessel.

'Ah . . . a very sad case. I found her starving on the village outskirts, and no man with any feeling could have left her to—' Clent's sentence broke off with a sudden squawk. Peering through the crack of the door, Mosca saw that Mistress Bessel had playfully taken a pincer-hold on his nose with the sugarloaf cutters.

'Now, Eponymous, when I want a story from you I'll pay for it. Speaking of which, do you have any thieves to sell me this month?'

Mosca felt her mouth go dry. Could Clent really mean to sell her out already?

'Of course, Jen. Four of them. An angler, a diver and two knights of the road.' From reading the more lurid chapbooks, Mosca knew that 'anglers' were thieves who sat on roofs and used long, hooked poles to tweak bags from the top of coaches. A 'diver' was a pickpocket, and a 'knight of the road' was a highwayman.

Mistress Bessel reached out eager hands and received a bundle of rough pages, printed in large type. Each bore a large seal of red wax, the seal of the Company of Stationers. Mistress Bessel was too busy slowly and silently mouthing out words to observe the corner of another packet of papers jutting from Clent's burlap package. Clent noticed it, however, and pushed it back into hiding with a furtive urgency. The moment was not lost on the secret watcher.

'Ooh . . . I do like to keep abreast of news in the profession, even now.'

'I thought you would like to see this one, Jen.' Clent extracted a particular sheet and began to read. '"An Account of the Ingenious Crimes and Stratagems of the Gang led by Rosemary Peppett, otherwise known as Lady Lighttouch . . ." Here we are . . . "not since the time of the infamous Mistress Fleetfinger have we seen such Craft and Courage in a Female Breast, and such Cunning use of her Sex's softer charms that the Victims might even count themselves blessed . . ."'

Mistress Bessel gave a wistful laugh.

'Slop and feathers!' she exclaimed. 'Softer charms indeed – I never made use of my looks as Mistress Fleetfinger. I could have done though.'

'That you could, Jen,' Clent said gently.

The corners of Mistress Bessel's mouth drooped slightly, and she thoughtfully smoothed the back of her gloves. Then she gave a sniff and looked up at Clent with a forced brightness.

'So – what kept you?'

'I fear I made myself rather popular in Chough, so

 35

much so that they could not be persuaded to part with me. Indeed, when I finally tried to depart, they . . . put me in the stocks.'

'Ah, your taking ways. So how much *did* you take before they caught you?'

'I was not caught,' Clent declared in an affronted tone. 'I fancy I was betrayed – I know that a stranger stayed in Chough with the magistrate last night. And . . . ah, perhaps I am growing old and fearful, but I have been feeling a shadow at my back since I left the Capital.'

'The gallows casts a long shadow,' murmured Mistress Bessel, 'and sometimes it cuts out the sun. I got tired of feeling the chill of it on the back of my neck, which is why I turned respectable. That, and these.' She held up her hands. There were dark shapes on their backs, faintly visible through her light gloves, each in the shape of a 'T'. *Felon's brands*, thought Mosca. *T for thief.*

'It is not the fear of the gallows, my inestimable Jen. My shadow is flesh and bone and walks on two legs. Jen . . . I cannot linger here. It will not be long before the rabble of Chough work out where I have gone.'

'Eponymous –' Mistress Bessel sounded quite serious – 'what devilish soup have you got yourself into? We were in fellowship once, and now you will not even tell me who you have been working for so secretively this last two years.'

There was a long silence. Clent chased a chapbook around the tabletop with a fingertip. Finally Jen gave a short, bitter sigh. 'Your girl's been gone a long time,' she remarked. 'She's got long fingers, I noticed that. If I miss anything from upstairs, you'll be floating away downriver, but not in a boat.'

Mosca decided that this was a good moment to re-appear.

Mistress Bessel turned a motherly smile upon her as she pushed open the door. 'Ah, now, that's better, my blossom.'

'Mosca,' Clent interrupted quickly, 'we will need a few things from the west bank.' Mosca was quick enough to catch the purse tossed at her head. 'A loaf of bread, some cheese – and an apple or two, if it will not ruin us. And, child –' Mosca halted in the doorway – 'we have yet to find a way of disguising the goose.'

Reluctantly Mosca relinquished Saracen, and ventured on to the Kempe Teetering thoroughfare. She was well aware that Clent might be looking for a chance to abandon her, but it seemed less likely that he would decamp without his purse.

On the far bank, Mosca glimpsed a soft slate-blue dome, and felt something cold slither across her heart like a toad across a stone. She halted, and was butted in the calves by a wheelbarrow of whelks.

Unsteadily, half willingly, she turned her steps towards the church. If she was likely to be hanged for arson, then this was as good a time as any to scrub at her stained soul.

Until now she had visited only the parish church at Hummel, which was little more than a barn sheltering a cluster of shrines. Visitors from a large market town would not have given the Kempe Teetering church a second look, but to Mosca it might as well have been a cathedral.

Several centuries of gull droppings on the domed roof created a white tracery like an ivory fretwork. The great, carved-oak doors were a foot too tall for the entranceway, and leaned against the door frame, leaving a gap for visitors to squeeze between them. Although Mosca did not know it, they had been plundered during the civil war from the wreckage of another church further upstream.

Mosca slipped into a darkness as chill as a funeral morning, and found herself surrounded by the Beloved.

Each shutter was carved with the figures of saints, stiff and identical as playing-card kings. Painted Beloved elbowed for room in the rafter-high murals. Wooden Beloved peered from the pulpit and the altar screen. Stone Beloved bulged like pompous fruit from the trunks of the stone pillars. A goodman of straw had been pulled apart by rats, and a goodlady with a turnip body and potato head was rotting quietly in a corner.

Mosca stared about her, not sure where to offer her confession. She found Goodman Postrophe high on one rafter, but he seemed to be busy talking to Goodlady Prill, Protector of Pigs, so she felt that she would be interrupting. In addition, the carving of Postrophe made him look a little like her uncle Westerly, which gave her pause. Goodlady Prill was plumper than her aunt Briony, but had the same mean, short-sighted sort of stare.

'I told you,' Mosca imagined Prill saying in Aunt Briony's voice. 'I always told you the girl was a wasp in your pocket, and would sting you when she had the opportunity. Small wonder, though, with a father like *that*. The books spoilt her. I have never known such a *knowing* child.' Her tone made it plain that 'knowing' was something that no self-respecting child had any business doing. Mosca's fingernails dug into her palms.

She looked around for a carved face resembling that of Quillam Mye, but none of them wore pince-nez, or was bowed over a book. It would have driven him to distraction, she thought suddenly, being trapped on a carving where the Beloved crawled over one another like bees, droning about meal and chaff, when to pick apples, saving candle ends, and mending chicken coops.

Palpitattle? Ah, there he was, carved into a shutter. The fly-saint grinned like a mantrap, and his great eyes bored right through the wood and were flooded with sky.

''S like this,' he rasped in the voice that Mosca always gave him. 'That Mr Clent's got you by the scruff, now he knows 'bout the mill. You got to get the dirty on 'im. Somink *big*. What 'bout those papers he hid from Mistress Bessel? Hid 'em in the shrine before, din't he? Don't want 'em seen, do he? Printed, ain't they? Maybehaps they ain't got the seal from the Company of Stationers. That'd be enough to buy him a rope cravat.'

If books were feared, the Stationers were feared more. They had started out as simply a guild of printers and bookbinders but they had become much more. By now

 39

they were masters of the printed word, with the right to decree any book safe to be read, or damn it to the flames like a plague carcass. The law gave them full licence to crush anyone who trespassed on their rights by printing books, and they exercised this right ruthlessly.

In Chough it was said that the Stationers had special spectacles which let them read books without harm and decide which were safe for other eyes. In Chough it was said that if the Stationers caught you with a book that had not been made legal by a Stationer seal, they took you away and drowned you in ink. In Chough, the only person who never talked about the Stationers had been Quillam Mye, despite the fact that in Mandelion he had once been a Stationer himself.

In Chough there had always been rumours that Mye had been expelled from the Stationers. Within a day of his death, in fear of that ruthless Guild, the villagers had ransacked his shelves and made a bonfire of his books and manuscripts. In Chough it was said that as the books burned, twisted letters were seen fleeing the blaze, like spiders scrambling out of burning logs.

This memory filled Mosca with a bitterness beyond bearing. Most of her father's books she had never read. He had always promised that she could look through them when she was ten, 'when her brain was no longer soft enough to take a careless thumbprint'. They should have been her legacy. Instead, all her father had left her was an inauspicious first name, the ability to read and an all-consuming hunger for words.

Nonetheless, despite their fear of the Stationers, most people regarded them as a necessary evil. *Better the devil we know*, they thought, *than the devil we have known . . .*

The devil we have known. Mosca tipped her head back, one hand holding her bonnet in place. A heart-shaped gape of sky stared back at her.

The Heart had been the reason for the bloodiest ten years the nation had ever known.

It was said that there had always been many religions, one for each Beloved. But one day, according to legend, a glowing heart had appeared in the chest of every Beloved shrine icon and beaten three times. From that day, all the little religions became one, and everyone believed in a strange, faceless spirit that joined the Beloved together, and which they called the Consequence.

Every church was built with a hole high on one wall, into which was fitted a heart-shaped birdcage, a-flutter with newly captured wild birds. The throb of their wings gave the Heart a beat, to remind the people of the Consequence. The priests who captured these birds daily were known as the Birdcatchers. In time they became custodians of all sacred texts and devoted their lives to staring into the White Heart of the Consequence in order to understand it.

Afterwards it was hard to be sure exactly when the sublime light had dazzled their minds and driven them mad, since they went insane with such calm and dignity that nobody noticed. However, among themselves they secretly started to tell a different version of the story of the coming of the Consequence. They said that those with true vision had seen the Heart glow and beat, then blossom into flame and consume the old Beloved icons completely, so that only the Heart remained. In time, they said, everything should return to the Heart and become a part of its searing light. The highest destiny of any worldly thing was to burn. The highest duty of any person was to become like flame.

On one side of the nave Mosca noticed a narrow arch across which a metal grille had been nailed. Behind the grille, stone steps spiralled steeply into darkness, and she guessed that they had once led to a Birdcatcher library.

Aside from the Stationers, the Birdcatchers alone held the right to print. Later, their extraordinary books became a matter of whispered legend. Words printed in a spiral, like a whirlpool that drew in the reader's mind and never let it escape. Incantations in strange languages which, if read, opened boxes in the mind and let out the imps of madness. Phrases so beautiful that they broke your heart like an egg.

The Birdcatchers' rise to power had been insidious. Amid the turmoil of thirty years of civil war and rocky Parliament rule, nobody had really noticed how many of the powerful men had been taught in Birdcatcher schools, or how many had been converted by the clever Birdcatcher books. At last, when the Realm was thrashing around like a feverish invalid, the Birdcatchers had stepped forward like doctors to lay a cool hand on its brow and calm it. Mosca had seen old men weep when they remembered the day the Birdcatcher priests took power. *Ah*, they whispered, *how joyful we were! We knew they would bring us peace, they would unite the people and the Beloved in happiness, they would put a bit in the mouth of the Realm and rein it tame . . .*

Then the Birdcatchers began killing the Beloved.

First the new rulers had declared Goodman Criesinthedark a demon. Everybody had been very shocked to learn this, but Criesinthedark had very few worshippers, so there had been little outcry when they were whipped in the marketplace and the Goodman's shrines burned. *Ah*, sighed the old men, *how relieved we were that we had found out about Criesinthedark in time!*

But the next month the shrines of Goodlady Jobble were in flames, and her worshippers were being branded above the eyebrow. A month after that, Goodman Haleweather was also declared a demon. His church icons vanished, never to be seen again . . . and so did his worshippers. *That is the last of it*, everybody had told each other. *The Birdcatchers have saved us from these demons, but that is the last of it . . .*

But the nightmare continued, and day after day the people were told that another of the Beloved was really a demon in disguise as they watched their neighbours being led away in chains. It took most of them years to face the fact that the Birdcatchers meant to stamp out belief in the Beloved altogether. *The worst of it*, said the old men, *was the feeling that the gods themselves were helpless and frightened*. The Birdcatchers had spies everywhere,

43

and people grew afraid to pray, to speak, to think . . .

. . . and then, after ten years of terror, something changed in the hearts of the chidden population. The fearful murmurs of protest became a buzz like summer-maddened bees, and then a hurricane roar of outrage. Heedless of menaces and musketfire, the people of the Realm had risen up and driven the Birdcatchers into hiding, into the sea, into the prisons and execution yards.

After the fall of the Birdcatchers, the Stationers had made it clear how much of the madness had been spread by the Birdcatchers' books, their terrible, poisonous books. These books had been burned, and the Heart had been ripped out of every church in the country, leaving an empty hole.

Perhaps the Heart would have given a sense of oneness and completeness that the rabble of reinstated Beloved did not provide. The Heart would have given one the chance to lose oneself in staring away and away into a brilliant nothingness. Perhaps that would have been something worth believing in, Mosca thought dangerously, giddy with her own treason.

A thin wind blew through the gap and chased straw in circles around the floor. Mosca gave a sharp wriggle of her shoulders, and shrugged off her unease. She pulled out the purse, felt it for weight, and then opened it. A moment later she was running from the church, banging her shoulder against the door in her hurry.

The purse contained only a farthing, two pieces of

slate and a jumble of metal scraps and mellowberry pips. With the keen instincts of the unloved, Mosca knew that Clent had contrived this errand so that he could abandon her in Kempe Teetering.

C IS FOR CONTRABAND

Mistress Bessel looked up quickly as Mosca clattered into her shop, and did not seem surprised to see her agitated and out of breath. She peered down at the jumble of oddments in Mosca's palm and tutted.

'Well, that was a mean trick to play. I thought he would at least leave you with a little money in your pocket. Still –' she sighed in a motherly way – 'you're not far from home, so I dare say you can make your way back to Chough having learned a lesson, and no harm done.' Mistress Bessel's shrewd blue eyes moved across Mosca's face as if she was itching to ask whether any harm *had* been done.

Mosca clenched her mouth shut, biting back the words that were buzzing to be released.

'There now,' said Mistress Bessel, mistaking Mosca's silent rage for distress. 'Has he . . . taken something from you, blossom?'

Mosca gave her a dark, furtive glance, came to a quick decision and nodded.

'Well, that is a little too bad of him, but you should have known better than to put your faith in a scapegrace like Eponymous Clent. Did you really mean to traipse all the way to Mandelion at his heels?'

So, Clent *did* have a destination in mind . . . he had sent her away so that he could make his arrangements . . . and he was headed for Mandelion, the very city where her father had once lived . . .

'He's taking a boat downriver, then,' Mosca said, her hot, black eyes fixed on Mistress Bessel's face, 'an' he won't want to hire a Waterman.'

The Company of Watermen, originally a guild of boatmen carrying passengers, had long since taken on the task of policing the river. If Clent was nervous enough to change his clothes, he would probably avoid the Watermen.

'You know which boat he means to take.' Slowly Mosca uncurled her fist again, and separated the farthing from the other scraps.

Mistress Bessel watched with a smile that was still indulgent, but the warmth had drained from her eyes.

'You had a pipe when you come in,' she said evenly. Mosca tugged the pipe out of her pouch, and slapped it into Mistress Bessel's waiting hand, along with the farthing.

'Well, I told you nothing, mind, and you chanced on him by your own good luck. He's taking passage with the *Mettlesome Maid*, a barge fastened on the near bank. She flies a flag for King Hazard – you cannot miss her.'

Mosca took a couple of rapid steps towards the door, and then halted. Something was missing.

'Where's my goose?'

'The goose?' Mistress Bessel whistled through her teeth regretfully. 'Eponymous said it was his. I give him the names of some contacts in Mandelion and told him a place where he could stay, and he give me the goose in exchange. You better take the matter up with him when you find him.'

Mosca clenched her fists, and bristled like a cat.

'Saracen!' she screamed at the top of her lungs. 'Foxes!'

Around the doorway a muscular white neck curled questingly. Into the shop proper came Saracen with his sailor's strut, making a sound as if he was swallowing pebbles and enjoying it. Mosca knelt and reached for him.

'Farthingale!' In answer to Mistress Bessel's sharp cry, a young man with an armful of stone nettles put his head around the door. 'Take that goose away and keep it under control, will you?' Farthingale wiped his free hand on his apron, and went to obey.

Rather a lot of things happened in quick succession. Since most of them happened after Mosca had ducked under the nearest table and pulled her new bonnet down over her face, she could only guess at their nature. However, they were loud, and violent, and sounded as if they might be expensive.

'Throw a rug over it, boy, and grab it!' she could hear Mistress Bessel shouting.

Farthingale must have followed her instructions, since a moment later there was a hoarse cry of pain and a sound like the counter breaking. To judge by his yelling, though, Farthingale was still alive, which relieved Mosca. He was bellowing a great many words that were new to Mosca and sounded quite interesting. She memorized them for future use.

At last she raised the broad bonnet brim and gazed cautiously out into the shop. The floor was awash with the chalky shrapnel of shattered leaves and shivered ribbons. Through the debris swaggered Saracen, trailing a hessian rug like a cloak, a sprinkling of stone dust across his orange beak. Farthingale had taken refuge behind the wreckage of the counter, and was cupping one hand over his bloodied nose. Mistress Bessel had scrambled on to a rickety chair, her skirts hitched. The wood beneath her portly weight creaked nervously as the goose strutted barely a yard from her feet.

Mosca emerged, carefully grabbed an armful of goose, and bobbed a hurried, inelegant curtsey to her hostess.

'I am very sorry, Mistress Bessel,' she explained hurriedly. 'Saracen has an antipathy to strangers.' She had long treasured the word 'antipathy', and was glad of a chance to use it.

She left the shop at a weak-legged walk. It surely could not be long before Mistress Bessel sent a constable after her anyway, but if she ran the woman might think to shout 'Stop, thief!', and then she would have the whole street at her heels.

*

Amid the forest of swaying masts, she spied a yellow flag upon which rippled the Grouse Rampant, the heraldic device of King Hazard. The *Mettlesome Maid* was a hayboat, and a heavily loaded one at that. The crew were doing their best to cover the bales with sacking, while the gulls tugged and scattered the hay across the deck.

Pulling her mob cap down to hide her white eyebrows, Mosca struggled through the crowd of impatient hauliers. A heated discussion appeared to be taking place on deck.

'. . . a degree of haste would be appreciated.' Clent's tones were unmistakable.

'Not for that price. After all, I run the risk. If the Watermen find out I'm carrying passengers 'gainst their rules, they'll hole my boat as sure as rocks.'

'Uncle Eponymous!' squeaked Mosca, and reddened as a number of tanned faces turned grins upon her that glittered like hot tar. 'I spoke to the wherry captain and he'll take us for your price . . .'

The captain of the barge looked a little taken aback, but this was nothing compared to Eponymous's start at being greeted by his 'niece'.

'Your niece?' The captain seemed to be reckoning the odds of losing his passenger. 'Well, can't leave a lass standing on the wharfside wi' these villains. Your price, then, and sixpence more for the girl, and we'll leave it at that.'

Mosca was handed aboard, and delicately seated herself on a bale next to her 'uncle'.

'How resourceful of you,' he murmured under his breath. 'I was just arranging our . . . er . . . I see you have your . . .' His eyes dropped to Saracen.

'Mistress Bessel decided she didn't want him after all,' Mosca said carefully. As she spoke Mistress Bessel's name, she recalled the interesting words she had heard Farthingale yelling at the top of his voice. 'Mr Clent,' she asked meekly, 'what does "pixelated" mean?'

'Deranged. Having had one's senses stolen by the fairies,' Clent replied promptly.

'And pyewhacked feathrin?'

'I believe that is meant to suggest a bird possessed by the devil.'

'And chirfugging?'

'Ahem. I think I shall tell you that when you are a little older.'

For the first mile or so, Mosca sat tensely among the bales, expecting every moment to hear cries from the bank. She felt sure that the barge would be ordered ashore by the river police of the Watermen's Guild, and she would find herself dragged back to Kempe Teetering for arson and goose-theft and hanged without delay. Clent, she had no doubt, would sell her out immediately to the constables if they were apprehended.

Somehow, though, as the barge eased its way through the lapping leagues, the sun started to seep into her head, and it began to seem possible, just possible, that she would not end the day dangling from the Kempe

Teetering bridge as a new scaregull. It was probably the new clothes, she decided. She felt as if she had borrowed somebody else's body and somebody else's life, and would probably find herself back in her own before very much longer.

The sun pricked holes in the weave of her hat and danced from ripple to ripple as the *Maid* eased its way through a haze of midges and a chase of jewelled damselflies. As the barge approached, moorhens abandoned their gossiping in mid-river, and in the green darks among the nettles coots crouched and stared down their white beaks.

Each vessel they passed flew a flag proudly announcing its royal allegiance. In theory, everybody in the country agreed that the Realm needed a monarch again, and was on tenterhooks to discover who the Committee of Kingmakers would choose to fill the throne. In practice, the Committee had been on the brink of a decision for twenty years, and many of the would-be kings and queens waiting in exile had died and handed on their claims to their children. In the meantime the Realm had broken up into a series of smaller city-states, each avowing allegiance to a different distant monarch, and leaving only the Capital truly under the control of the Parliament.

In theory, Chough lay in an area where everybody supported King Prael. In practice, Mosca knew nothing about him except that all the carvings of him looked rather old, and gave him a long chin.

As she watched, a barge painted with the Weeping Owl heraldry of King Cinnamon the Misjudged passed by a wherry that flew the crossed crimson swords of the Parliament. To Mosca's slight disappointment, everybody seemed more interested in hauling ropes than engaging in naval warfare. Each crew made a brief offensive gesture towards the other boat, but no one seemed to have their heart in it.

Mosca was also fascinated with the hauliers of the *Mettlesome Maid*, partly because she had never been able to watch anyone hard at work without being expected to do her part. Compared to the water-whitened villagers of Chough, they seemed tawny and terrible as tigers. Sun and sweat had left them hard and conker-brown, and they seemed to think nothing of the python-thick ropes they dragged as they strained their way along the bank. The jokes they exchanged were like clods of earth thrown at the face, meant good-humouredly – but meant to bruise as well.

The captain was a grim-smiling river-king named Partridge. There was something crooked in the make of his right wrist, as if it had been broken and never quite healed, and something crooked in the corner of his smile, as if that too had been broken and put back together slightly wrong.

'I could never have stomached one of the Watermen's little passenger wherries,' Clent remarked, waving a dragonfly away from his face. 'They are always in such a hurry, and one finds oneself rubbing elbows with so many undesirables.'

For a mad moment, Mosca almost believed that she and Clent had deliberately chosen the barge as the most elegant way to travel, and not because they were fugitives from the law. He seemed so comfortable and glad to have her company that she almost believed that he had not meant to desert her after all, that there had been a mix-up with the purse, that Mistress Bessel had lied about the goose . . .

Clent offered her some of the mellowberries, and she took them. Leaning over the edge of the boat to spit pips at the ducks, she caught sight of Clent's reflection as he watched her with that queer, lean, calculating look she had seen on his face before. The taste of the berries bittered in her mouth, and she knew that he still meant to leave her or sell her to the authorities at the first opportunity.

For a savage moment, she thought of slipping ashore with his mysterious burlap package when the boat moored, and running away on her own. But she knew that she needed him. She had never been further than five miles from Chough – without a guide she would do little better than a tumbled fledgling. A twelve-year-old girl travelling alone, furthermore, would be an easy mark for footpads, gonophs and conmen. She had no contacts, no money, no friends. All she had was a homicidal goose . . . and Eponymous Clent.

In Mandelion, things might be different. Mosca squinted at a blurred memory. She had a recollection of her father talking about a 'ragged school' in Mandelion, and over the years her wishes had painted the memory with a false clarity. Surely he had said that the school never turned away a clever child? Surely he had said you could turn up with nothing but a shilling and a hunk of bread in your kerchief, and if you could read six fiendish pages without a slip of the eye they would welcome you in for the tiniest fee . . .

Mosca gave Clent a wide, friendly grin, which seemed to unnerve him, and took another mellowberry out of his hand. Of course, if she turned 'evidence' against Clent, perhaps they would give her a reward, and then she would at least have some money. But what could she tell them about him? Nothing much, nothing as bad as arson. And he would just unroll his tongue and talk his way off the gibbet, leaving her to take his place . . .

So . . . how to win the advantage again? Mosca's eyes dropped for a tiny second to the package that sat between them. Somewhere inside lay the little packet he had been so eager to hide from Mistress Bessel. Perhaps later, if she and the parcel found themselves alone . . .

The sun slid to rest, and the western sky gleamed like a copper kettle in firelight. Mosca, watching the sun's last gleam, saw it split by the flight of a buzzard, which seemed to douse the light in that instant with its black wings before swooping away to land on top of a haystack. Without warning, the hills which had been sunning themselves like so many contented dogs closed in, black and ragged as wolves.

As the wind became chill, the hauliers' grumbles rose to an ominous level.

'We'll take our sup at the Halberd,' Partridge declared. 'Ye'll dine with us.'

The Halberd had once been a little watchtower set up to prevent pirates sailing up the river from the sea and attacking inland towns. During the war, brimstone had bitten off its roof like the crust from a loaf, and pushed out one of the walls. The rubble remained, now moss-covered, and a rough roof of thatch had been used to shut out the sky.

The crew made the *Mettlesome Maid* fast, and all but two accompanied Clent and Mosca to the tavern's door. Inside, the air was thick with pipesmoke and the moist scent of the earth floor and the cloying smell of over-cooked tripe. To judge by their clothes and sunburned faces, most of the customers were boat crew or hauliers. They were, of course, all men. The tables were a jumble of upturned coracle wrecks, and long deck planks rested on barrels to serve as trestles. The seats were bales of greying straw. Against a far wall huddled a handful of straw mattresses, on each of which a man lay sleeping in his shirtsleeves.

They sat themselves at one of the wider coracles, Mosca noticing with a hungry pain beneath her ribs that a plate of small loaves and a jug of water were already set upon the table. She was also intrigued to notice that when he took up his ale, Partridge first swayed it over the loaves for a moment, before drinking. In Chough, everybody always waved their drinking cups over a jug of water to show that they were drinking a toast to King Prael, the 'king across the Tosteroy Sea'. However, she knew that Partridge's gesture was in honour of King Hazard, the 'king across the Magora mountains', as represented by the loaves.

At the next table a haulier spilt a little water on the table and wafted his cup over it, in honour of King Galbrash, the 'king over the Fallowsmere Lake'. His friend seated opposite waved his tankard over the fingers of his own left hand, to show his allegiance to the Twin Queens, 'the monarchs beyond the Jottland foothills'. A dozen or so royal allegiances seemed to be represented in the Halberd, and yet none of them showed any sign of leaping at each other's throats amid a flurry of ale foam. The business of kings did not seem to be a fighting matter.

Mosca did not know it, but she was staring at a sign of changing times. The days when followers of rival kings would exchange blows or musketfire on sight were long gone. Every town now accepted with a sigh its share of the different allegiances, and every barkeep carefully laid out a jug of water and a bowl of little loaves on each table so that his customers might toast any monarch they chose.

A captain from a lighter joined their table, and was soon deep in conversation with Partridge.

'So – what news in Mandelion?' Partridge asked, stooping to light his pipe at the candle.

'Well, the Duke's worse each day. Did you hear about the new Spires of Prosperity?'

Partridge crooked an eyebrow.

'*Twin* spires, would they happen to be?'

'That's it.'

'Still pairs with him, then?' Partridge sighed, and shook his head.

Amid the stream of strange names, Mosca sometimes lost the thread of the conversation. There was a lot said about a group called 'the Locksmiths', which sounded like the name of a guild, but one she had never heard before. The lighter captain said they were growing stronger in Mandelion, which was something he had hoped never to see. Partridge said it was all right, the Duke's sister would never let them take over Mandelion the way they had taken Scurrey. If the Locksmiths were just a guild of lock-makers, Mosca could not imagine why people looked so grim and frightened when they talked about them.

The beer in Mosca's cup seemed as weak as river water, and tasted much as if a hundred ducks had been washing their feet in it. But after a while Mosca started to feel a warm and empty buzzing space near the back of her head. When she tried to understand the conversation, it was like trying to pick up a thread with Saracen's webbed foot instead of her own fingers.

'Your niece is looking a little dusky around the eyes. Better put her to bed before she falls off her chair and into the fire.'

'Bed' proved to be one of the straw mattresses by the far wall, set somewhat aside from the others. Mosca dared not undress, and she lay down fully clothed, with her bonnet tipped forward to shade her face. From under the brim, she watched Clent brush down his own mattress with fastidious care, remove his coat for use as a blanket, and lay himself down. To her disappointment, he tucked the package under the mattress first.

For the next five hours Mosca stared into darkness, listening to the crunch and rip of Saracen tearing her mattress apart. She had no intention of letting Clent slip off without her again, and she dug straw stems into her palms to keep herself awake. But, exhausted as she was, it was impossible not to doze off, and she was shaken awake at dawn.

'Shake a leg, there.' Partridge grinned down at her, not unkindly.

She followed him out to the boat, her stomach raw and green from lack of sleep. Clent was sitting not far from the stern, peeling a boiled egg with his fingers. There was no sign of his parcel.

As Mosca sat down beside him, she became aware that he was observing her narrowly. He took a bite ou of his egg, stared thoughtfully at the deck for a moment, then looked back at Mosca.

'My dear, I hope you have slept well?' Clent's tone was courteous, but as cold and crisp as the morning. He paused for a moment to pick at his teeth with his little fingernail. Only when Partridge had moved out of earshot did he continue. 'Has it struck you that the river is rather . . . higher this morning?'

'Didn't hear any rain.' Mosca stared out at the river, which seemed as languid as ever.

'I do not mean further up the banks, child, I mean further up the sides of the boat. We are lower in the water than we were yesterday, and I think we cannot put all of that down to the beer and bread in our bellies.'

'You mean . . . they got us off the boat so we wouldn't see 'em loading up with something else?' Mosca squinted about the boat. 'Is it hid among the bales?'

'No,' answered Clent, a little too quickly. 'No, I think not. Cast your eyes upon the deck. The planks beneath us keep the cargo from bruising the barge's belly, but in this case I fancy they are fulfilling another purpose.' Like most barges of its type, the *Mettlesome Maid* had no hold, and the hay bales were piled up on the deck. The deck was a flat layer of planks some little way above the barge's elmwood bottom.

Mosca noticed for the first time that some strands of straw were clamped between the deck planks, as if the planks themselves had been removed and then replaced. She looked up at Clent, her eyes wide with a question.

'Now, under that canvas awning is the place where the crew sleeps. There will be no one there now, and if you were to say you wished to rest there for a while, no one would object. Then you need only lever up one of the planks, slip into the belly of the boat, and we shall have our questions answered.'

'But—'

'Come now. The powers that be have saddled me with a ferrety-looking child, and as far as I know ferrets have only two uses – poor-quality fur trim, or sending down holes after rabbits. Pray be a good ferret, and be quick about it.'

Mosca mimed a yawn, and picked her way along the deck towards the stern. At the gunwale Partridge rested a lazy hand on the great tiller, his eyes on the river ahead. He paid little attention as Mosca pulled up the awning, and slipped into the darkness beneath.

Prising up the planks was no mean feat. Mosca's fingernails were short, and the planks were solid oak and a foot wide. She eventually found that she could slide one of the scraps of metal from Clent's pouch between the planks, and after some painful minutes one rose out of its groove.

Mosca reached deep into the hole, and the flat of her palm struck the grooved wood of the barge bottom. She waved a hand through the darkness, and something knobbed batted at her fingers. Grabbing it, she lifted it into the half-light. It was a small, heavy, wooden figure of Goodman Greyglory, He Who Guides the Sword in Battle. Was there a whole tribe of icons, ripped from their shrines, huddling in the darkness like captives in the hold of a slaveship? And why would anyone be secretly transporting them down the river?

Biting her lip white with caution, she lowered the Goodman back into darkness, and replaced the plank.

She pushed the canvas aside, and emerged on hands and knees, and began crawling alongside the hay bales on the side furthest from the bank, and from Eponymous Clent.

The secret cargo was not hidden among the bales, but she was fairly certain that something else was.

Why had Clent hidden the parcel of papers? Perhaps he was afraid that a waterman's scull might slip alongside the barge and he might be forced to open it. Where had he hidden it? Somewhere out of sight, but easy to reach in a hurry if he had to make a quick escape.

If Mosca had not been looking for something of the sort, she would never have noticed the string trailing from between two bales. Simple, but effective. In an emergency, he could pull the string, and . . .

She drew on the string, and the parcel slid out from its hiding place. Taking the bundle binding in her mouth, she cat-padded her way back on all fours, and dived into the darkness beneath the canvas awning.

When she had dragged off the string and pulled away the burlap, Mosca found herself with a lap full of printed papers. Most were chapbooks of criminals' lives, the pages roughly stitched into their cloth covers. Some were large loose pages, or 'broadsheets', most of which had ballads printed upon them. All bore the seal of the Company of Stationers. Between them, however, was the packet Clent had laboured to hide. It opened to Mosca's eager fingers, and she was at first disappointed to find that it seemed to be a letter of introduction, '. . . Testifying that Eponymous Clent is acting upon the behalf of the Company of Stationers in investigating certain illicit . . .'

The page suddenly became a great deal easier to read as the canvas awning was twitched back, and Eponymous Clent pushed his head into the little cave.

His smile slid away like water off a candle, and his plump face became absolutely expressionless in a way that told Mosca that he was very angry. She stared back, her black eyes burning with triumph.

'How did you find those?'

'You're working for the Stationers? You're a spy?'

'You can read?' Clent stared at her in disbelief as he struggled into the makeshift cabin.

'Full of surprises, me,' whispered Mosca savagely.

At this moment the awning was flung violently aside and, as one, Mosca and Clent jumped to sit on the papers, landing with a thump, hip to hip.

Partridge was stooping at the opening, the crooked corner of his mouth flexing and relaxing like an angry fist.

'Are you people trouble to me?' he asked hoarsely. 'Only there's five or so Watermen wherries blocking the river up ahead, and it looks to me like they're searching boats.'

D IS FOR DAYLIGHT ROBBERY

Mosca and Clent exchanged glances, and silently settled a single matter between them. They were on thin ice, on the brink of disaster, but for now they were also on the same side.

'Ah, now, it would seem that we have an interest in common,' Clent began quickly, turning back to Partridge. 'You do not wish the Watermen to discover that you have been taking passengers illegally, and we . . . we are in no hurry to be found. So let us hurry to an understanding, and, ah . . .'

'And what? What exactly do we do, you lily-handed sack of suet?'

In answer, Clent reached down and knocked once on the planks of the deck, which answered hollowly.

'What, stow you below boards and risk your bootnails inside the belly of the *Maid*? I'll see you gull food first. Dotheril!' The head of another crewman appeared at the opening in the awning. 'I think you'd better hail the Watermen and tell 'em we've just this minute found a couple of stowaways. Doesn't it look that way to you?'

'I'd say so, sir,' agreed Dotheril coolly. 'Guess they must

have crept aboard while we was docked at the Halberd.'

'If you give us up,' hissed Mosca, 'I'll tell them about the other stowaways already down there. *They* don't seem to be hurting your boat none. More of holiness than holes down there, I'd say.'

Clent rallied well, considering that he had no idea what Mosca was talking about.

'Yes, I fear the secret is out. We know that your boat, like many other "maids", hides a secret in her belly. My niece, you see, has an enquiring mind and, while I have tried to damp her desire to peek and pry, it is her nature and there is little I can do about it. Well, Captain, I am at *my* wits' end – have you decided what is to become of us all?'

'We cannot dally long,' whispered Dotheril. 'We could nudge the bank and buy time that way, but if we did that, there might be a rattling in the . . .' His eyes dropped pointedly towards the deck.

Partridge's mouth twitched once, twice, as if he was trying to crack a tiny nut between his teeth.

'Take up the planks,' he ordered in an undertone. 'But if either of you makes a sound, I'll nail the deck in place above your heads, seal the cracks with pitch, and leave you to your prayers.'

They had to lever up three planks before Eponymous Clent was able to squeeze through. He disappeared into darkness with a muffled squawk.

'Quiet!'

'Merciless Fates! I would like to see you hold your

 65

tongue if you had just taken Good Lady Shempoline in the eye—'

'Silence!'

Mosca followed her employer into the cramped darkness below the deck. The darkness was almost absolute, apart from a few strands of light visible above between the deck planks. She raised her hand and felt the coarse wooden underside of the deck and wished she hadn't. It was like finding oneself inside a wooden coffin.

The voice of the water was now far louder. Here you could hear the thoughts of the barge, how it clicked its tongue in annoyance as the wavelets slapped its flank, how it boomed and droned with effort as it strained against the ropes of the hauliers, the drag of the current.

A crickle, a crackle. Somewhere not far from Mosca's head lay Clent's fistful of papers. Somewhere among them lay the Stationers' letter. Even the few lines Mosca had read were enough to prove Clent a Stationer spy. This was her chance to gain something that might give her a hold over him. 'Somink big,' Palpitattle's voice echoed in her head. Her long fingers reached out stealthily and touched a papery corner.

'. . . elcome aboard . . . seems to be the probl . . .' Partridge's voice from on deck.

'. . . orders of the Duke . . .' Long-suffering tones from a stranger. 'Nay, there's no need to uncover all o' the bales. If we search every inch of every boat we'll not see our wives tonight . . .'

Mosca carefully gripped the paper corner between thumb and fingertips, and started to pull at them. Almost immediately her knuckles took a sharp blow from what felt suspiciously like the knobbled features of Goodlady Agragap, He Who Frightens the Harelip Fairy from the Childbed.

'. . . what are you looking for?'

'. . . oofprints.'

Mosca's free hand closed around a bust of Mipsquall, the Patron of High-pitched Winds, and a moment later the saint's twin horns were jabbed firmly into Clent's clenched fist.

'. . . what?'

'. . . orders of the Duke. On account of the highwayman Clam Blythe. His Grace has made it known that *his* loyal people would never harbour such a rogue –' there was a wealth of weariness and cynicism in these words – 'so Blythe must be a-comin' from lands across the river, an' we're to stop all boats to look for signs that they've given him an' his men an' their horses passage across to Mandelion. Hoofprints, dung, signs of horses where there should be none . . .'

Below deck, stealthy move and countermove had disintegrated into a stifled tug of war. A faint rattle told Mosca that Clent had lost his grip on Goodlady Agragap, and was scrabbling for a new celestial ally. She lashed out, too slowly to prevent him snatching up St Whillmop of the Peaceful Dream. As St Whillmop's bland and loving features struck Mosca painfully above the eyebrow, she could not help uttering a stifled mewl.

The conversation on the deck hushed, and feet stirred above, quietly, carefully. The two fugitives froze in the darkness.

'Just the goose puttin' in his farthing's worth,' Partridge declared coolly. Saracen's flabby steps were just audible above.

There were a few more affable murmurs, the slap of palm in palm, and then a cry to the hauliers to take up their ropes. The *Mettlesome Maid* swung back into the current.

Ten minutes later there was a whisper of foliage against the barge-side and a protest of ropes. Two deck planks were levered hastily, revealing a banner of blue sky and two scarlet faces.

'Out,' said Partridge.

The hidden passengers clambered on to the deck, Clent triumphantly clutching his mangled papers to his chest, Mosca gingerly feeling the tender place on her forehead.

'Off,' said Partridge.

There was a duet of protest. The land around was a featureless moor of gorse, without even a dirt track to be seen.

'The route's swarming with Watermen. Ye'll pay what ye owe now.' Partridge watched as Clent grudgingly placed a few coins in his hand. 'And some more for this trouble, now.'

Clent looked around him at the unsmiling hauliers,

and he seemed to be reckoning the odds. His mouth grew as small and round as an unripe plum.

Before Mosca could react, he had seized her around the middle, pinning her arms to her sides.

'Keep the goose,' he called over his shoulder, and he bodily dragged his young secretary from the barge, ignoring her kicks and spirited attempts to break his fingers.

Mosca had time to see Saracen lifting his head quizzically to observe her unceremonious departure, before her bonnet fell over her face again.

It was five minutes before her weight wearied Clent's arms, and his ankles tired of her accurate kicks, and he dropped her in a heap amid the bracken. When she found her feet, the wincing sunlight, the ragged gorse and the slow-blinking wings of the moths were witness to an epic Trade in Exotic Terms.

Mosca's opening offer was a number of cant words she had heard pedlars use, words for the drool hanging from a dog's jaw, words for the greenish sheen on a mouldering strip of bacon.

Eponymous Clent responded with some choice descriptions of ungrateful and treacherous women, culled from ballad and classic myth.

Mosca countered with some from her secret hoard of hidden words, the terms used by smugglers for tell-alls, and soldiers' words for the worst kind of keyhole-stooping spy.

Clent answered with crushing and high-sounding

 69

examples from the best essays on the natural depravity of unguided youth.

Mosca lowered the bucket deep, and spat out long-winded aspersions which long ago she had discovered in her father's books, before her uncle had over-zealously burned them all.

Clent stared at her.

'This is absurd. I refuse to believe that you have even the faintest idea what an "ethically pusillanimous compromise" is, let alone how one would . . .' Clent's voice trailed away as his eyes fixed on something beyond Mosca's shoulder.

They could hear the racket of crude wheels over rough stones. In the distance, beyond the banks of gorse, could be seen the tottering crest of a high-loaded cart.

In an instant, the pair abandoned use of their tongues and took to their legs. Through thick grass and ragged brush they plunged after the cart, Mosca with her skirts scooped thigh-high, Clent whistling to catch the driver's attention.

The cart was little more than a family of creaks on wheels, bound together with rope. The driver, a tiny, tanned imp of a man, was champing on a piece of bread, leaving the reins slack and trusting his ponderous-looking bay to follow her own head.

'Lookin' for a lift to Mandelion, are you? Clamber on up if you can find a space. Go easy, though – my wares has teeths, they does.'

Drawing back the covering cloth, Mosca's gaze was

met by two dozen metal grins, as if the false teeth of a dozen iron beasts had been stolen while they slept.

'Traps. Any kind of traps you needs, I got. Traps for taking the toes off a trespasser, traps for taking the nose off a badger.'

Mosca replaced the cloth, and nervously clambered up to sit on the assembled heap, hearing the occasional spring sing and jaw snap.

Traps in Clent's bed, Mosca thought. Traps in Clent's soup. She hugged herself into bitter thinness, and said nothing. A Stationer spy would have enemies, she was sure of it. She would bide her time until Mandelion, and then *somebody* would pay good money for what she knew about Clent. And then a purse for her belt, a shilling to buy back Saracen, a fee for the school and a trap, a trap for the Stationer spy . . .

'I makes them all myself, you know. Traps for the belt, in case someone tries to fork you of your purse . . .'

'How ingenious,' Clent remarked. 'Have you thought of having posters made? Perhaps making it clear that this is a limited opportunity to buy, since a Coalition of Criminals has declared you their Mortal Foe due to your Effect upon their Livelihoods . . .'

The little trap-pedlar started to laugh, with a sound like a cat coughing up furballs. 'Ah now, I does like the way you talks in capitals,' he remarked. 'It's as good as . . . well, now, will you look at that? It's another of 'em fell foul of the Trollhole.'

Ahead, the road took a sudden dip. The dip had clearly

been rather too sudden for the large wheels of the biggest and most elegant carriage Mosca had ever seen. It blocked the road, tilting in a fashion that could only mean a wheel had come off. Two white horses grazed upon the gorse while two white-clad footmen were stooping to examine the damage. The white box of the carriage perched in fringed splendour on a frame of curling metal tendrils so slender that it almost seemed to float in the air on its own. The entire equipage looked far too fine and fairy-like for the real world, Mosca thought, and the rugged road clearly thought so too.

'Bit of business,' smiled the pedlar, and lowered himself off the cart.

The little pedlar, it seemed, fancied that he had the tools to fix the wheel. The footmen were glad to hear this, and agreed with him that he should be paid handsomely for such a service. There was some disagreement as to what constituted 'handsome', however. The discussion of the attractiveness of various sums looked set to continue for some time.

Mosca sighed and Clent blinked as a single raindrop tapped him peremptorily between the eyes. They clambered down from the cart and approached the bargainers.

'For five minutes' work? That's daylight robbery!' the carriage driver was exclaiming.

'Ah,' Clent intoned ominously, 'better daylight robbery of this consenting sort than something bloodier, would you not say? After all, you would hardly care to be stranded out here come twilight, what with –' he paused dramatically – 'Black Captain Blythe on the loose.'

'Who?'

'Ah, I dare say you know him by a different name. The Widowmaker, probably.'

'Or the Devil's Friend,' Mosca added quickly. A number of eyes turned to her questioningly, two of them belonging to Clent. 'Yeah, he's so uncanny with the things he knows, some people say he's got an imp given him by the Dark Gentleman, who tells him things. Like, when he attacks he always seems to know who's carrying a pistol, and he shoots them before they can draw.' She had the satisfaction of seeing the carriage driver and one of the footmen go white. 'Right through the gullet,' she added cheerfully.

Clent raised his eyebrows slightly, and gave the tiniest nod of approval.

At the carriage window the breeze set a curtain of fine lace quivering as if in alarm. The movement caught Mosca's attention. A single muddy droplet hung from the top of the window. The wind rolled it gently to and fro, then it became too self-important, and fell. It sank greedily into a sleeve like snow, leaving a spot the colour of coffee. A white handkerchief appeared in a slender, white-gloved hand and smoothed at the stain, smoothed and smoothed until it was no more. Mosca's gaze followed the glove as it withdrew into the shadow of the carriage, and she looked in on a world of white.

Until this moment Mosca had thought she understood white. White was old, white was ugly, white was something that had been left in the water too long.

Until this moment Mosca had thought that she understood riches. Riches was the smell of goose fat, riches was a red roll of fat on belly and jowl that kept out the chill.

This strange new world held a multitude of clinging raindrops, but each drop was a pearl.

Mosca had never seen pearls before. And there were so many of them, playing ring-a-lilies across fields of spotless silk, hanging in long strings from the wrist and throat of the carriage's single occupant.

A face hung in the darkness, porcelain-pale and perfect. Above it rose an intricate mound of whorls and curls, pinned in place and powdered until the whole might have been carved out of marble. If there had ever been any warmth or expression in the face, it had long since been smoothed away and stifled with powder. And Mosca suddenly understood that real riches was not a roaring fire or a red woollen cloak. Real riches was snow.

'Heatherson, what is wrong?'

The words were cool, soft, feathery, and Mosca suddenly realized that the woman behind the marble face was young.

'Heatherson, what is happening?'

The woman leaned forward a little to give herself a better view of the road, and Mosca saw that on the gleaming surface of the lady's cheek lay a faint lacework of an even more brilliant white. It was a scar, splaying like a snowflake across the lady's right cheekbone.

'My lady, I think that we might have to . . .' The driver's voice trailed away in a sick little hiccup. '. . . I think we might . . . I think . . .'

The discussion around Mosca had stilled. The pedlar no longer chirruped, the footmen no longer grumbled, Clent's delighted tones no longer painted pictures in the air. The driver above her had raised his hands above his ears. His face was as white as the lace curtain.

Some four or five men had risen from their hiding places among the gorse. Each held a pistol, carefully trained upon the group around the carriage.

E IS FOR EXTORTION

Mosca had never seen a pistol before, but she had jealously bartered for *Hangman's Histories* and *Desperate Tales*, and had seen woodcuts of highwaymen and murderers. She was a little surprised at how small their pistols were. They had always been drawn large in the pictures to make it clear what they were.

How strange it was to look down the barrel of a pistol! It was not exactly fear, more a soft shock, like being hit in the stomach with a snowball. She seemed to be able to think quite clearly, but at the same time her thoughts seemed to move so slowly that she could watch them trundle past with a feeling of disinterest.

Most of the men were young, she noticed with a frosted calm. One of them kept swallowing, as if he was nervous, and adjusting his grip on the pistol. His head kept twitching, as if he was trying to avoid peering over his shoulder, and a moment later she heard what the robber had already heard, the sound of horses' hoofs. None of the armed men seemed alarmed by the noise. They seemed to expect it.

A raindrop fell unexpectedly into her eye, and she

instinctively reached up to brush it away before she had time to consider how the robbers might react to such a sudden gesture. She froze, her fingers still on her cheek, pins and needles running through her chest in preparation for a hail of bullets. The robbers did not seem to consider the twelve-year-old girl a mortal threat, however. Half of their attention was trained on the coach's attendants and half upon the man whose head and shoulders now became visible above the bracken, beyond the road's bend.

A few moments more, and a sturdy-looking grey turned the corner, dappled like slush. To judge by its panting, it had come some way.

The rider of the grey was neither tall nor of Fine Athletic Build. Mosca looked in vain for any sign that he was carrying a flageolet or wearing a claret-coloured cape. But no, he was not even wearing a periwig.

A round-brimmed hat was pulled low on his brow, keeping the wind from his ears. Beneath this, a faint attempt had been made to tie back his ragged hair into a pigtail, but many strands had mutinied. A rough cloak of hessian was flung around him, over his greatcoat.

His face was a fearful sight. It was a good few moments before Mosca understood the meaning behind his reddened eyes, his drawn-back upper lip and the occasional puckering of his face, and she realized that the highwayman was suffering from a streaming cold.

'Black Captain Blythe,' Clent muttered wearily under his breath.

 77

'Take those men off the coach,' Blythe ordered his men, 'and turn out their coats.'

He did not sweep off his hat in greeting.

'Get the passengers out of the coach where we can see them.'

He did not pass elegant comment on their predicament.

'Take their purses. And their boots. And their wigs.' His eye did not twinkle. Mosca started to wonder if he was a real highwayman at all.

As the coach driver and footmen clambered down to be searched, Blythe's eye passed questingly over his other prisoners. The quivering trap-seller received a glance of contempt, and Blythe's gaze slid off Mosca, to rest on Clent.

'You. Open the carriage door and hand the passengers out.'

Hesitantly, Clent laid his hand upon the carriage door.

'My lady,' he murmured softly through the window, 'I fear your presence is required.'

There was a pause. The moon-like face bloomed into view behind the curtain.

'Do they mean to search us?' There was no hint of outrage in the woman's tone. It was simply a question.

'I . . . think so. The captain has many men to pay, and seems too desperate to be nice.'

'Unacceptable.' The voice was soft, almost childish, but chill with resolution.

'Unavoidable.'

'Anything is avoidable. I have a pocket watch crafted in the shape of a pistol. If I give it to you along with my purse, you might take my money to the brigands' leader, and then hold the watch against his head until my men are given back their pistols. You would be well rewarded.'

Clent opened his mouth until it would have taken in a potato, then closed it again.

'My lady, when a man takes a bullet, all the gold thread in the world will not sew him whole again.'

'I am carrying an object of personal value with which I do not intend to part.' Her face was now so close to the curtain that the lace left a fretwork of shadow across her cheeks. 'Do you know who I am?'

Clent gave a nod. Mosca saw that he was looking at a signet ring on the lady's hand, and she was astonished to hear his next words, low and hurried.

'My lady . . . if I can persuade the man not to have you searched, will you be willing to find employment for myself and my . . .' he glanced at Mosca and visibly relented – 'my secretary? We are poets and wordsmiths of no mean standing.'

'Very well.' The porcelain face receded from the window. 'Let us see how you work your will with words.'

'Pass me your purse, then, my lady.' A pouch of purple silk slid through the window into Clent's waiting hand.

'Can you do it?' hissed Mosca under her breath.

'No.' Clent took a shaky breath. 'I need a moment to think.' He pouted skywards for an instant, smoothing rain up his forehead and into his hair. After a few moments

 79

he gave Mosca a smile of slightly haggard hilarity. 'Yes. Now I believe I can do it.'

Blythe had been supervising the searching of the footmen, but now he gave Clent an ugly look of impatience.

'What are you waiting for?'

'There is no one within but a solitary lady – an invalid. She is taken with a fever, and is hurrying home to prevent it becoming dangerous. She has begged that you spare her the cruel humours of the evening air, and allow her to stay out of the rain. This is her purse –' Clent raised the pouch above his head and advanced carefully – 'and she says you are welcome to it, if you allow her the blessing of her health.'

'The sooner she steps out and takes her place with the rest,' Blythe muttered through chattering teeth, 'the sooner she can be on her way.'

Mosca advanced by Clent's side, and was paid no more attention than if she had been a hedge sparrow.

'I think you speak not as you mean. I have heard many stories of Captain Blythe, but nothing that would lead me to believe that he would let a defenceless flower of a girl suffer a lingering death amid agues and delirium. Those words were spoken by the bitter rain, by the holes in your boots, and by the bigger hole inside your belly – not by Captain Blythe. The man before me is too tall for such words.'

Looking into Blythe's face, Mosca suspected that he had never heard himself called a 'captain' before. She thought this might be because Clent had conferred the title himself.

'May I speak quite freely?'

'If you can speak both freely and briefly,' was the highwayman's curt response.

'I thank you.' Clent advanced closer. 'I could not trust myself to hold my tongue while I could see you throwing away such an opportunity. What could you hope to gain by dragging that poor suffering girl out into the rain and cutting the buttons off her gown? Perhaps your men hope to cut off her hair as well and sell it to a wigmaker, and leave her quite shorn and cold?'

'What do I stand to lose?'

'Ah!' Clent raised his forefinger significantly before his nose. 'I am very glad that you asked me that. You stand to lose something of great value, something which I am in a position to offer you. But first I must ask you a question. How often have you had your boots cobbled?'

'What?' The young highwayman was obviously now utterly perplexed. His red-rimmed eyes flitted this way and that as if he was glancing between the unanswered first question and the perplexing second.

'You do not need to answer,' Clent cut in helpfully. 'I can do that for you. The answer is: not as often as the holes merit. I can see a hole the size of a sovereign where your big toe is pushing out its head to test the wind. And why? I can answer that too. When your pockets are merry with coins, do you scurry first to the cobbler, and then to the tailor, and have yourself stitched and made watertight? No! That first night you and your comrades find a tavern, and you drink to every king or queen that has ever been toasted, and then you drink to kings that rule only the lands of your own imaginations, and then you drink until you *are* kings, and no laws can touch you.

'And the next day you must be poor and prudent again, and cannot afford to cobble your boots. But that night!' Clent spread his arms wide, embracingly. 'What a gesture! You are shouting to the world, *I may be wicked, but I will not be mean; I may be wild, but I will not be small; the mud may creep in at my boots but it will not stain my soul . . .*'

After a moment's dramatic pause, Clent let his arms drop.

'I am a writer of ballads – I value gestures. I understand them. I know what I can do with them. Let us suppose, for example, that you allowed this young woman to stay in her carriage, handed her back her money, and wished her and her people godspeed back to Mandelion so that she could find a physician who might save her life – ah, what I could do with that!'

Blythe's eyes asked silently what Clent could do with that.

'I could write a ballad which would make proverbial the chivalry of Clamouring Captain Blythe. When you rode the cold cobbles of a midnight street, you would hear it sung in the taverns you passed, to give you more warmth than that thin coat of yours. When you were hunted across the moors by the constables, hundreds would lie sleepless, hoping that brave Captain Blythe still ran free.

'And when at night you lay on your bed of earth under your dripping roof of bracken, with no company but the wind and your horse champing moss near your head, you would know that in a glittering banquet hall somewhere, some young lady of birth would be thinking of you.

'*That* is what you stand to lose.'

Blythe was as wide-eyed as a sleepwalker. He made several attempts to speak before he managed to get the words out. At last he cleared his throat, and took the purse out of Clent's hand, tested the weight of it, and then returned it to him.

'We are in the business of relieving men of their money, not girls of their health. Let her keep the purse to buy a physician.' He looked a question at Clent, as if to ask whether these words would work well in the ballad. Clent nodded kindly to show that they would do very well indeed.

Clent was halfway back to the carriage when Blythe called him back.

'Do you . . . do you think it would be good for the ballad if we helped them fix the wheel?'

A starry look of suppressed glee entered Clent's eyes.

'Yes, I think that would help a great deal.'

F IS FOR FAIR MARK

It was impossible that Mosca the Housefly could be sitting in a carriage on a cushion of white watered silk. It was impossible that the highwaymen should be letting them leave – she could hear Blythe outside telling the carriage driver what secret signals he should give if other men in the same gang accosted the coach. She felt sure that at any moment Clent's words would slide off the highwayman like magic dew, leaving him clear-headed and choleric.

The coachman gave the horses a long, looping whistle. The carriage rocked on its wheels, then rumbled into motion. Someone thumped goodwill and a farewell into the wall by Mosca's head, making her jump.

It was impossible that she and Clent were to arrive in Mandelion in a carriage, flanked by footmen, cushioned in white velvet like two horse chestnuts in down-lined shells. No doubt the pair of them would wake up and find themselves sleeping under a sycamore sacred to Dorace of the Whimsical Dream. Or the carriage would try to cross running water, and would collapse into a pile of dandelion seeds while their hostess spread swan's wings and took to the sky.

Two pearls were watching her. In the lap of the lady in white lay an embroidered box, the lid adorned with a stuffed ermine stoat whose arched back served as a handle. Instead of glass eyes, small pearls had been placed in the sockets. As the rain lashed the lace curtain, the lady gently stroked at the fur along its back with a gloved fingertip, as if it was a living pet.

'Remarkable.'

The lady did not raise her eyes, and for a moment Mosca thought she was addressing the stoat. It was a moment before Clent found his voice.

'Ah, it was of course a labour of delight to be of service to Your Ladyship, and, if I may say so without offence, my oratory was inspired by the thought of one whose beauty might, ah, give voices to the very pebbles . . .'

There was something about Clent's hopeful expression that made Mosca uncomfortable. His beaver hat offered little complaints as he bent the brim this way, that way.

'Really? I thought that you were inspired by the prospect of employment and preferment. Come now, sir. Make your requests plainly.'

'I had hoped, Lady Tamarind, that you might hire me to write an epic tale of your family's fortunes. The rise of the dukes of Avourlace, their wise rulership of Mandelion over the centuries, their tragic exile during the war and the Years of the Birdcatchers, and then your brother's triumphant return to reclaim his ancestral rights . . .'

Mosca's eyes became round as she realized she was staring at the sister of the Duke of Mandelion.

'Very well.' Lady Tamarind's words were soft and as crisp as a fox-print in snow. 'You shall write it, and you shall be paid for it. I assume I need not read it.'

'And . . . ah . . .' Creak, crick went Clent's hat brim, his eyes bodkin-eager. 'Ah . . . I would request a letter of introduction, that I might mix with the, ah, better sort of personage.' Mosca felt immediately that the letter meant more to him than the money.

'In Mandelion the high and the fashionable may be met with in the Honeycomb Courts, which surround my residence in the Eastern Spire.' Lady Tamarind paused, as if considering. 'I shall send you a letter vouching for your character and advising that you be allowed into the Lower Honeycomb Courts. I will do no more for a man I know so little.'

Clent gave a little exhalation of satisfaction.

Silence followed. The rattle of rain and the crack of stones under the wheels had no power to keep Mosca awake. Her eyelids drooped.

She tried to plan ahead, but thoughts gave under her feet and became dreams. She dreamed that she had found her father in Mandelion. He had been running a school there for years, and had not really died at all, and it turned out that Mosca had lots of brothers and sisters, and they were all studying at the school and waiting to meet her. It was time for her to attend her first day at that school, but Mosca was terrified, because when she tried to touch anything it burst into flames. She knew that there was a pair of white gloves that she had to wear which would make her safe, but Clent had stolen them, and she could not find them. She tried to explain everything to her father, but he would not look at her or speak to her. Instead, she ran to Clent and demanded her gloves back, but he sat there, smirking and smoothing the white gloves over his large hands, until she itched to grab him by the jowls and char him to a cinder.

The carriage wall rapped reprovingly on the back of Mosca's head, and she found herself staring at the deeply sleeping Clent, the dream so vivid in her mind that she felt sparks might leap from her eyes and settle on his cravat.

'Hate has its uses, but it will serve you ill if you wear it so openly.'

The quiet voice jarred Mosca into wakefulness. Lady Tamarind was looking directly at her and, snatching for a fistful of her wits, she struggled to explain.

'He—'

'Your grievances do not interest me. Your master's request does. Why is he so keen to mix above his station?'

Sparks of hate crackled in Mosca's mind.

'Spying,' she hissed recklessly. 'He's a mangy old nook-gazin' spy. 'S got papers, signed by the Stationers – I *seen* 'em.'

Lady Tamarind's immaculate mask of a face hung in the dusk of the coach and looked at Mosca. For several moments her features showed not the slightest motion. Perhaps she disapproved of Mosca's indiscretion. Perhaps she did not believe her.

'A Stationer spy,' she murmured at last, very quietly and without rancour. 'What is his name?'

'Eponymous Clent.'

'Eponymous Clent.' There was an odd, distant note in Tamarind's voice that Mosca did not understand. 'How a name changes everything!' Her gaze never moved from Mosca's face. 'A man's face tells you nothing,' Tamarind continued in her usual tone, 'but through his name you . . . know him. Eponymous. A name suited to the hero of a tall tale. But such heroes are seldom to be trusted. And you – are you a spy, like your master?'

'Not me, he din't even mean me to see them papers.'

Mosca stiffened as one of Clent's snores became a nasal hiccup. Then his sonorous breathing resumed, and she relaxed again. 'I'm jus' his secretary till I got something better. I'm going to school,' she added. 'I can read.'

Now Lady Tamarind's arctic stare held real interest. When she spoke again it was in a softened, urgent tone that reminded Mosca of velvet rubbed the wrong way.

'You seem interested in my pearls, girl. Would you like to have one?'

Mosca suddenly felt that to win just one of them she would willingly burn down Chough in its entirety, mill and malthouse, kiln and kitchen. She wanted to keep it, stare into it like a tiny, eider-grey crystal ball, and understand this strange new whiteness before it slipped out of her life again. She shrugged, not meeting the lady's eye.

'If you do something for me, and do it well, you may

have a pearl, and perhaps "something better". How much courage do you have, girl?'

'Enough to pluck the tail of the Devil's horse, but not enough to ride 'im.' Mosca whispered the old Chough adage automatically.

'What is your name?' The lady sounded as if she might be pleased.

'Mosca Mye.' As soon as the words were out of Mosca's mouth she remembered that she was a fugitive from justice. But how could she refuse to answer this snow queen? Giving a false name was unthinkable. Nobody ever lied about their name. Names were what you *were*. 'And . . . you're Lady Tamarind. The sister of the Duke. The Duke of Mandelion.'

'I am. What would you say if I told you that even the sister of the Duke has powerful enemies? Dangerous enemies.'

Mosca remembered the conversation in the Halberd.

'Locksmiths!' she breathed excitedly. Lady Tamarind's fingertip paused in its stroking of the stoat's forehead. Mosca hurried on, 'Heard the bargemen talking at the Halberd. Yestereve, when they thought I was drowsed. 'Bout how the Locksmiths wanted to take over Mandelion . . . like they did Scurrey . . . but how you'd never let 'em. Who are the Locksmiths?'

'Probably the most feared guild in the Realm,' said Lady Tamarind, after a hesitation. 'Once they only made locks and strongboxes, but all the guilds have grown stronger and more powerful since the days when there was a king. Tell me, child, have you ever heard of the Thief-takers?'

'Yeah.' The Thief-takers had been mentioned in many of the *Hangman's Histories*. 'They're the ones what you call in to catch thieves when the constables can't find 'em, aren't they?'

'That is only a part of the truth. Listen well, girl. The Thief-takers are no better than the villains they seize. All Thief-takers answer to the Locksmiths, and their real task is to make sure that there are no criminals at large . . . except those that work for the Locksmiths themselves. The Locksmiths run the criminal underworld in four major cities, and are a rising force in the others. Do you understand now why I say I have dangerous enemies?'

Mosca's jaw fell open.

'If you are to work for me, you must speak of it to nobody, and we can never be seen together.'

Mosca nodded.

'Good. The Locksmiths are on the rise, and if I cannot stop them, Mandelion will be theirs. I must know if others mean to act against the Locksmiths. The Stationers, in particular.' Tamarind leaned forward and dropped her whisper, so that it was scarcely more than a tingle on the eardrum. 'I cannot be seen to be plotting, but I must know their plans.'

'You want me to spy on the Stationers?' Mosca sanded her lips with a dry tongue-tip.

'You will stay with your master, and find out more about him. He will bring you into contact with other

Stationers, and can probably find you a place in a Stationer school. And once you have been schooled properly . . . it will seem less remarkable if a person of eminence should choose to employ you. When you have information for me, seek out the city Plumery. You will find a patch of pheasant feathers planted in front of the statue of Goodman Claspkin. Hide your letter inside the quill of one of these, and place it back in the earth. It will reach me.'

Mosca blinked hard, trying to commit everything to memory.

'Now listen, for your own safety's sake. Beware men who wear gloves even indoors and at luncheon. Keep a close guard on your pockets and purse – the Thieftakers sometimes serve an enemy by planting stolen goods upon them. And, girl? If you think that you are suspected . . . beware of accidents . . .'

Clent drew a long, waking breath. His eyes fluttered open, and stared unseeing and glassy at the carriage roof. Tamarind drew back against her seat with impeccable composure. Mosca curled away from Clent, closing her eyes and feigning sleep.

It seemed to Mosca that she had spent barely five minutes leaning against the window frame and counting her employer's breaths when the carriage lurched and woke her. The woman in white was staring out of the window, the scar dead white in the stony light. Mosca wondered if she had dreamed the strange conversation.

Mosca dozed, and woke, and found that villages had

 91

sprung up at the roadside. She dozed, and woke, and found that the road was running alongside the river, and above the bristle of sails quivered some half-dozen craft-dragging kites which bore the insignia of the Watermen, a silver pond-skater against a black background. She dozed, and woke, and found that the sky was dim and a harsh crosswind was flattening the curtain against the roof.

The carriage was crossing a bridge. Houses clustered along the bridge-side as if to peer back at Mosca, and between them Mosca glimpsed a stretch of water so wide that at first she took it for a lake. But no, there were the far banks, curving away to clasp hands at the horizon. This was still the River Slye, and on the far side of the bridge the city of Mandelion smoked and sprawled and scored the sky with spires.

Helpless with excitement, Mosca wriggled to the edge of her seat, leaning out through the window for a better view. To the east and the west two spires rose above the rest, and the city stretched between them. Behind a long piecrust of crumbling wall clustered a mosaic of roofs, and a great dome that seemed in the dull light to be as glossy and ethereal as a soap bubble. To the west along the waterside unfinished ships bared ribcages of stripped wood to the sky. The creak and crack of the shipyard was as faint as a cricket orchestra.

The wind roared with an estuary freshness. It carried the smell of sandflats and sea-poppies, and the pale wails of wading birds, and the clammy, silver-eyed dreams of fish. Although she had never known the coastlands,

Mosca felt with a thrill that somewhere beyond the edge of sight the ocean hugged its unthinkable deeps and dragged its tides in shrug after monumental shrug.

The carriage reached the end of the bridge, and now the tallest buildings Mosca had ever seen flanked the road. Evening had swallowed their black timbers and left their white plaster faces floating in the air like flags. To Mosca it seemed that they must in some fashion belong to the lady in the white dress, for they too were white. The gleaming white sails on the river had to belong to the lady. The fat white moon, sitting on a sliver of cloud like a clot of cream on the blade of a knife, had to belong to the lady.

'Tell the driver where you would like to be set down, Mr Clent,' remarked Lady Tamarind.

'I believe our, ah, friends reside in East Straddle Street, my lady.' The carriage steered around a squabble of hansoms and took a riverside road, the gleam of water occasionally visible between the buildings.

At last it drew up alongside a shuttered shop. Unwillingly Mosca let Clent guide her out on to the street.

'Your Ladyship, the, ah, the, ah, letter . . .'

'. . . will be sent to you at these lodgings shortly.'

There was a chill finality in the childlike tones as the porcelain face faded behind the curtain. The carriage lurched back into motion. Clent, hiding his disappointment, turned to knock at the door of the shop.

Mosca stared up at the hanging sign above the door. It

depicted a man's hand clasping that of a woman.

'Mr Clent . . . why we stoppin' at a marriage house?'

Before Clent could answer, the door was opened by a man as squat as a pepper pot, wearing the broad-brimmed hat of a chaplain and an expression that seemed to be a compromise between piety and a suppressed sneeze. A few whispered words from Clent, however, and the man's face broke into a broad, badger's grin, revealing a fine array of caramel-coloured teeth.

'Ah, Mistress Bessel give you my name, did she? If you're a friend of Jen, come in and be welcomed by Bockerby. You must take a pinch of snuff with me before you sleep.' His every sentence began in a deep, sonorous, church-bell voice, and ended in a chatty, rough-cut tone like a pedlar's shamble.

Mosca and Clent were led through a cramped, ill-swept corridor into a cramped, ill-swept parlour. The tabletop was crowded with vases. These were filled not with flowers but with bunches of dried, branching honesty plants, crowned with glossy seedpods the size of sovereigns and the colour of jaded paper. On a stand stood a name-day book, so that each couple who came to the marriage house could see if a match between their names was auspicious.

A host of tiny Beloved idols sat in rough-cut recesses in the wall, rather as if the little gods had gouged out their own homes like nesting birds. Many of the Beloved shown were unfamiliar to Mosca, but with some apprehension she recognized Goodlady Mauget of the Almost-Truth,

Goodman Happendabbit of the Repented Oath, St Leasey, He Who Lends His Cloak to the Sly-in-the-Night, and Goodlady Judin of the Borrowed Face. The largest shrines were to Leampho of the One Wakeful Eye, a goodman who according to legend would smile upon contracts and unions that Torquest the Joiner of Hands would not touch with the tiniest finger of his steel-gloved hand.

Mosca knew that all respectable weddings took place in church, but for couples with too little money or too much to hide there were the marriage houses. Girls with child, forbidden love matches, would-be bigamists, anyone who did not want their affairs boomed to the congregation – all of these could creep with their sweethearts to a marriage house, and have a licence for a handful of shillings. To judge by his outfit, Bockerby served as cleric and master of ceremonies for this establishment.

Bockerby had fetched a mahogany box from the mantel, and now he offered it to Clent, who placed the daintiest pinch at the base of his thumb, before lowering his nose to his wrist and taking an energetic sniff.

'So –' Clent settled in a large rocking chair and gestured Mosca towards a stool by the wall – 'what news in your brave city, Mr Bockerby?'

'Been here before, sir? No?' Bockerby gave a one-shouldered shrug and drew in a pinch of snuff, creasing his brow into a map. 'Ah . . . truth is, Mr Clent, you find us in a bit of a hubble-bubble.'

'I noticed your city wall was badly burned.'

'Mostly old fires, Mr Clent. Yus, Mandelion's a battered old nell.'

'The old war?'

'The old war. And then . . . the Birdcatchers. We was hit bad, worse than most. I was only about eleven when they took over, but I remember it, clear as clarion.'

Mosca waited for Clent and Bockerby to glance at her and drop into vagueness, but to her surprise neither of them did. Somehow, without noticing, Mosca had become old enough to hear about such things.

'First thing they did was ban the whelkmaids' dances on St Squeakle's Day. Any they caught "devilish frolicking", as they put it, had their toes tied together so tightly they could hardly walk. Then came the purges. I remember seeing whole family pews empty, and no one telling me why.' Bockerby laughed, and Mosca wondered why so many people laughed at memories, even the ones that weren't funny. 'Right little clinger I was when it came to questions then. Real little crab.' He made stubborn pincer-motions with his thumb and forefinger. 'What I remember clearest is stealing off to fish downriver by the Leaps, and coming home in the dark. No moon, all pitch.

'The windmills along the bank all tick and creak different as their sails turn, so I always used the sound to tell my way, but this one night I could hear not so much as a click to guide me. I was just starting to think I was witched and would never find my way home when I saw two little lights a-bobbing, and I realized it was the lantern of a link boy crossing the Ashbridge over his reflection. I was so blanched by the dark and the silence, I stayed on the bridge till morning, and when the dawn came I saw why the windmills were silent.

'From the sails of every mill wooden birdcages were hanging, each the size of a puncheon, but full of people instead of ale. Men, women, children, all dressed for the festival of St Jarry. The Birdcatchers had surprised them during the midnight candle-walk, wrung their necks, and winged them.'

'Winged them?' Clent asked cautiously.

'Perhaps they never did that outside Mandelion. See, they put long pins in the quills of feathers, and then they stuck the sharp ends of the pins into . . .' At last Bockerby seemed to remember Mosca, glanced at her, and gave a small gesture as if pushing away a memory. 'You can imagine how glad everyone was when the present Duke came back from Jottland with his sister.'

'How is the Duke?' Clent asked carefully, as if asking after an illness of a delicate nature.

'He's . . . not what he was.' Bockerby seemed to be choosing his words carefully. 'When he first come back from exile, seventeen years past, just after we'd kicked out the Birdcatchers, we was all flags and smiles and thrown hats. Then a couple of years later there was that rumpus during the Year of the Dead Letter, when the Stationers were fighting among 'emselves. The Duke put those riots down hard, an' nobody saw him the same way after.

'Now we got new riots, folk fear he'll put musketmen out on the streets again. I don't speak against him, mind.

 97

His . . . funny little ways get funnier every year, but that's all trim for a duke. Show me a man with blue blood, an' I'll show you a man with a bonnetful of bees.'

Clent sighed. 'Well, Beloved preserve the wits of the mighty, and spare the skins of the small! Good Mr Bockerby, I fear we droop upon sleep's altar. If you might show us our rooms . . .' He flicked sharply at Mosca's nose to rouse her to alertness.

Bockerby took the candle and led them from the parlour. Mosca shambled after Clent through another corridor to a little chamber with a desk, a closet, and a smell of long-forgotten mouse-adventures.

When Bockerby had gone, Mosca gratefully collapsed into a truckle bed at the foot of the main bed, but her mind was no longer quite ready for sleep. Strangely, her betrayal of Clent's secret to Lady Tamarind had taken some sting out of her hatred. Too much newness had broken like a wave against her mind and, odious as he was, Clent's presence was almost comforting.

'Is the Duke pixelated, Mr Clent?'

Clent shuddered. 'That is a judgement upon me for seeking to extend your vocabulary. If I hear you using such words to describe a duke in my hearing again, I shall put you on a diet of dry verbs and water until you have learned to speak more wisely. In Mandelion, an ill-chosen word in the wrong company may cost you your neck.'

'Well, if he's not pixelated, what's all this 'bout bees an' bonnets an' *pairs*, then?'

'Ah,' Clent said significantly. '*Pairs.*' He settled himself comfortably on the sill. 'The Duke's love of *pairs* dates from his sojourn with Queens Meriel and Peri. You have heard of the Twin Queens?'

'They're granddaughters of the last throned king?'

'Very good. And do you know why their portraits always show them in long, trailing sleeves?'

Mosca, who had never seen a picture of the Twin Queens, shook her head.

'All twins are born together, but the Twin Queens were born *hand in hand*. The outside edge of Meriel's right hand was joined fast to the edge of Peri's left. Between their little fingers grew an extra finger, which both sisters could move at will.

'When they were five, it was decided that this strange bond had to be broken. Meriel was allowed custody of the extra finger, but ever since they were divided the queens have taken to wearing gloves and long lace sleeves to hide their difference. The superstitious say that both sisters can still move the finger, even though it grows on Meriel's hand.

'Our current Duke of Mandelion, Vocado Avourlace, and his sister, Lady Tamarind, were born in exile in Jottland, where their family had loyally followed the Twin Queens and their mother. As a youth he spent much time in the company of the young queens, and when he came of age he began wooing them with zeal. The problem was that he was unmistakably courting them both, for in truth there was little to choose between them.

'At last the sisters made it clear that he must pick one bride. He chose Peri, and at first there was general rejoicing. However, Peri wanted to know why she had been chosen, and the Duke admitted that he had chosen Peri because Meriel's extra finger frightened him. After this confession, Peri ended the engagement. Some say that she was angry at the slight to her sister, but others say that she still felt the finger to be part of her, and would not marry a man who could not accept it.

'Even now, back in his homeland, it is said that the Duke spends every waking moment dwelling on thoughts of the Twin Queens. At mealtimes he arranges his chicken bones and cherry stones into pairs, and he sighs over the coins that display the queens' identical heads: Meriel on one side, facing right, Peri on the other, facing left. And he still dreams that if he rebuilds Mandelion with a beautiful symmetry worthy of the Twin Queens, they will forgive him, and come to rule the Realm with Mandelion as their capital.'

'Will they ever come to Mandelion, do you think?' Mosca asked.

'Perhaps, on a day when the sun turns to soup,' Clent remarked drily. 'In the meantime, it looks ill for the Duke's line, for he will marry none but they.'

'But Lady Tamarind might have children! Is she married?'

Clent gave Mosca an astute glance, and she blushed, fearing that he would see how the noblewoman had left her spellbound.

'No, nor can I find that she has any suitor or favourite.'

'Why? Is it because of her scar?'

'Lady Tamarind wears her scar like a flower,' Clent said softly. 'If she is unwed, it is because she would have it so.'

'Where did Lady Tamarind get her scar?'

'That I do not know, though I believe she was already marked when she came back from Jottland as a child of thirteen.'

Lady Tamarind was at that very moment nearing the end of her long journey home from the Capital to Mandelion's Eastern Spire. She had disembarked from her carriage, and a sedan now bore her through the Honeycomb Courts towards the spire. Although she was quite unconscious that she was the subject of fascinated discussion in the marriage house, her thoughts also happened to be focused upon the scar that marked her cheek.

The scar was not something she could easily ignore. On the few occasions when she smiled, it pulled taut against her cheek, as if trying to pull her back into solemnity. In winter she could feel the cold through it, as if a real snowflake had landed on her skin. The nearest she knew to fear was a throbbing flutter behind her scar, and as she recalled the events of the carriage ride she could feel it, like a moth's wing beating at her cheek. *Ah*, she thought without emotion, *I suppose that episode must have frightened me.*

As one footman handed her from the sedan, his fellows busied themselves with unfastening the six great locks to the door of the Eastern Spire.

'My business in the Capital is concluded,' Tamarind explained. 'Kindly send a letter to Mr Kohlrabi's lodgings, telling him that I require his presence as soon as he is back in the city, then bring me a dish of tea, the latest issue of the *Gazette* and a bag of dead cats.' Five minutes later her ladies-in-waiting were at her side with the requested items, and together they entered the spire.

One by one the locks slid to behind her with smooth, liquid clicks. The great locks bore the Guarantee of the Locksmiths. This meant that they were of the very finest quality. It meant that if they were broken, the Locksmiths would pay a small fortune in recompense. It meant that word had been put out across the underworld that the Eastern Spire was a no-go area, so that no clear-thinking thief would consider milling the locks, in case the Locksmiths' dreaded Thief-takers were sent after him.

All of this might have reassured Lady Tamarind, if she had been hoping to lock out anyone but the Locksmiths themselves. She had resorted to other measures to make sure that the Locksmiths could not wander into her apartments and search them at will.

As she climbed the stairs she slid on a long leather glove that reached to her shoulder. At the door of the salon she paused, then drew out one of the dead cats by the tail and carefully flung it towards the middle of the floor.

There was a rasp, like the hiss of sand through a straw, and a low, leatherbound river of wickedness snaked out from the darkness below the harpsichord. Its jaw opened impossibly wide, like a lean book crowded with teeth, and caught the cat before it could touch the ground.

The two ladies-in-waiting stayed at the door while Tamarind advanced to examine her pet. With satisfaction she noted its distinguishing features, the dirt-coloured dent above its left eye, and one flattened tooth jutting out from its fellows.

Originally her rooms had been guarded by a Shrieking Foxhawk that would lunge for the eyes of any but herself. One day she had returned to find the hawk strangely docile, and slightly larger than before. Next, she had bought a savage wolfhound to keep intruders from searching her apartments, but she became aware that there had been another switch when Tartar unexpectedly bore puppies. It had taken longer for the Gravyscale Python to be replaced, and after that she had resorted to ever more exotic animals. By the look of things, the Locksmiths had not yet succeeded in finding themselves a substitute crocodile.

As the animal snapped at the carcass with a soft rip like a spade biting through turf, Tamarind settled herself on the window seat and opened her stoat-handled embroidered box. The signet ring she had brought all the way from the Capital was still within, safe from the bloodied hands of highwaymen and the gloved fingers of Locksmiths. The ring had been expensive to fashion in secret. She was all too aware of the consequences, should it be discovered in her possession.

Below her window, Mandelion spread itself like a butterfly of brick and slate. Even from this angle the extraordinary symmetry of the city's design was obvious. The Eastern Spire had its match in the west, where the Duke of Mandelion kept his quarters.

The thought of her brother's obsession caused a pulse to flutter beneath Tamarind's scar. *I must be feeling something*, she thought. *Could it be fear? No, it is not fear.* She moved to another window and gazed down towards the pillory and gibbet in the yard.

Far below in the courtyard, a man was on his knees. The constable was selecting a long branding iron from the fire, and considerately dipping it in water before pulling the felon's hand towards him. Maybe the brand was a 'T' for thief, or an 'F' for forger. *It would be quicker and simpler to hang them outright*, Tamarind reflected. *Brand a man as a thief and no one will ever hire him for honest labour – he will be a hardened robber within weeks. The brand does not reveal a person's nature, it shapes it.*

With a tip of one long finger she traced a tiny circle around the snowflake on her cheek. *Could it be fear? No, not fear.*

The house in Jottland where she had been born and spent her childhood had looked over a glade that was set aside for badminton. Too clearly she recalled the last time she had ever played the game. She remembered the glistening of the rain-stricken garden as she dragged her elder brother by the sleeve with all her thirteen-year-old might. She had only hazily understood how deeply his rejection by Queen Peri had cut him. However, she had known that it could not be good for him to sit for hours in his closet, staring at coins, or at two faces in a locket. She had known that it was her task to distract Vocado and draw him out of himself.

Her brother had winced as if the birdsong gave him toothache, and had swiped at the shuttlecock, first listlessly, then so savagely that the fronds enmeshed themselves in the strings of the racket. Tamarind had run to help him disentangle them, but he had shaken off her hand. At her feet, water was puddled in the hollows of the lawn and her reflection had regarded her with delight and surprise.

'Look, Vocado!' She had pointed at her reflection. 'I have a twin!'

A twin. Nothing could have triggered Vocado's anguish like those innocent words. She had looked to her brother for a smile, just as his racket completed its savage swing at her face . . .

Down in the courtyard, the constable was lifting his brand away from the felon's hand, and turning to face the judge. In the spire room one could hear no screams, feel no heat, smell no burning, but Tamarind knew that the constable would be speaking the traditional words as he displayed his handiwork to the gathering.

'A fair mark, my lord.'

G IS FOR GENTLEMAN'S AGREEMENT

'Hoi!'

Mosca shifted from sleep to waking in her usual way, flinging out her fists to left and right. On this occasion, she bruised her knuckles on two close wooden walls, and was shocked into total clarity. Above her an unfamiliar set of rafters was looped with long, dusty, cobweb banners. The sound of water nearby made her think herself back in Chough for a moment. But this was a watery voice of a gentlemanly sort, each lap like the idle slap of a horsewhip against a calf.

'Hoi!'

Mosca's head was turned to one side at an awkward angle, and her pantaloon-clad knees were hooked over a wooden footboard. Below the rafters was a single window, the grey pre-dawn sky sliced into diamonds by the window leading. Somewhere beyond the window, someone was trying to shout under their breath.

Mosca heaved herself out of the truckle bed, and pulled the window open. Below, a woman with a fat yellow pigtail and a wide, frog-like mouth was hauling her gentleman companion to his feet, her strong, plump arms around his middle.

'Hey! You up there!' The woman was using the hoarse, hushed call of one who is trying to rouse the house without waking the neighbours. 'You does marriages, right? We wants to get married. Don't we?'

'Bwuzzug,' her friend agreed, and smiled at the bottle in his hand.

A little further along the wall, another window opened and a head of wild red hair appeared.

'You need a marriage done quick?' The voice was young and as sharp as a thorn. 'You got three shillings, and sixpence for the late hour?'

'Right here in me purse.' The strain of holding her fiancé upright was starting to show in the colour of the plump woman's face.

'I'll come down and let you in, then,' declared the red-haired girl. 'You'll have to guide his hand when you're signing the register, though, looks like.'

Somewhere in the house, a tinder scratched and heavy soles flapped on wooden boards. Then the front door opened and swallowed the woman and her drunken friend.

Five minutes or so later, the other window swung wide again. The red hair had been pushed roughly under a mob cap, and there was a wise, pale face the colour of uncooked pastry beneath it. The face's owner scanned the windows until she spotted Mosca.

'Sorry for you bein' woken, ma'am, I hope you an' your husband will have no more trouble.' Mosca could

 107

only assume that the other girl could not see her face properly. It was strange to be called 'ma'am' by someone who looked two years older than her.

'I'm not here for marriage – we're just stayin' here, that's all.'

'Oh.' The red-haired girl relaxed and grinned. 'What are you here for, then? I'm the Cakes.'

'What?'

'I does the Cakes. For after the nuptyals. What you here for?'

'I'm a secretary.'

'Oh.' The Cakes' face fell as if she did not think she had been told the truth, and then she shrugged as if to show that that was Mosca's business. 'See you at breakfast, then.'

While the sky silvered behind the distant spires, Mosca tried to patch the tatters of her plans. The slumber-bewitched conversation with Lady Tamarind had changed everything. Had it really taken place?

Thinking of Lady Tamarind, Mosca felt her stomach twist. It was excitement – but excitement of a not entirely pleasant sort. Rather, it was a sudden awareness of something she lacked, something she had sensed in the rich otherness of the lady in the coach. The lack ached, like a hole in a tooth.

To work for Lady Tamarind! Sooner or later Lady Tamarind's strange white wealth and power must surely rub off on Mosca like powdered snow . . . and Mosca would become . . . she could not clearly see what she would become. The thought seemed to pass on soft wings behind her, close enough to stir her neck hairs with the breeze of its passage. There was the faintest sensation of little golden drops of venom trailed across her skin, like those bled by a bee after the sting.

At six o'clock the market bell rang, and hawkers gradually filled the streets. With a sense of infinite luxury, Mosca gazed down at the step to watch pewter being polished by someone other than herself. By the time she followed a carefully spruced Clent down to a late breakfast, she could not imagine why she would wish to be anywhere else. Bockerby greeted them in the parlour with a new wariness and crispness that made Mosca realize he had been drunk the night before.

'Ah, yes – I recall you saying that you are a friend of Jen – how is dear Jen?' Bockerby asked as they all sat down.

'Brown and bonny as a wren, and becoming quite the mistress of means. She is growing plump on it, and has taken on two apprentices.'

'Ah, plump now, is she? She always had a hungry wit – I was surprised to hear she'd retired. Ah, all of us respectable nowadays . . . even Jen.'

'She lost a taste for the profession after a magistrate . . . gave her a strongly worded letter, you might say.' Clent gave a wince of a smile.

Bockerby grinned mirthlessly, and touched each of his teeth in turn with his tongue-tip, as if counting them.

 109

'That'd be a letter "T", then,' said Mosca through a mouthful of bread.

Bockerby looked at Mosca as if she had appeared from nowhere. After scrutinizing her briefly, he looked sharply to Clent. 'Is this one flash?' he asked, nodding towards her.

Clent inclined his head in something between a nod and a shrug. 'Safe enough, for immediate purposes.'

Bockerby gave a wordless murmur of dissatisfaction.

'How old is she? Ah, it cannot be more than thirteen years . . . a bit green, a bit green. Still –' Bockerby hacked himself another piece of bread – 'if I were you I'd marry her anyway. They're often more pliable, you know, once they bear your name.'

'Have you traded your sense for pence?' Clent's outrage was deafening. Somewhere beyond the fragile wall, the drone of a marriage ceremony halted briefly, before continuing more hesitantly. 'I am little enough pleased to find myself having to think for two, without shackling myself in perpetuity.'

Bockerby shrugged and wafted his glass over the jug before drinking, in honour of King Prael.

Mosca could only conclude that she had suddenly become invisible. She decided that, if this was so, it was probably a good time to steal all of the bread and cheese left on the table.

'Well.' Bockerby watched Clent shrewdly over his meaningless grin. 'You must do something about her sooner or later, you know.'

'Yes, yes, I know . . .'

'Mr Bockerby?' The red-haired girl pushed her head around the door, and blew a stray ringlet off her nose. 'Need you in the east chapel, Mr Bockerby.'

'Well . . . to work. Beg pardon.' Bockerby stood, and slapped his broad-brimmed chaplain's hat on his head. 'My sacred duties call me. Now, my friends, as you return to your rooms, do remember you are set up in apartments usually set aside for our customers, so if you pass anyone in the corridor, pray try to look . . . blissful.'

Mosca was not quite sure how to manage 'bliss', and Clent clearly had something on his mind, so it was perhaps just as well that they encountered nobody in the passageway.

When they were safely in the privacy of their rooms, Clent slid the bolt to.

'Sit down. No, over there by the desk.' He rummaged through his bottomless pockets, and drew out a few objects, each of which he put down on the desk in front of Mosca. 'Ship's articles,' he declared.

Mosca stared down at a roll of unused paper, a bottle of ink, and a slightly mangled quill.

'Are they?'

'If you must interrupt,' Clent responded tersely, 'you might at least do so intelligently. Ahem. Sometimes two privateer ships may be forced to sail abreast for a time. They may have a common aim, or a common foe, but, for whatever reason, to squabble is to founder. In such circumstances these gentlemen of the waves are accustomed to draw up a list of articles – of rules – to be observed by all parties. Do you understand now?'

Mosca understood that a truce was being proposed. She chewed on her cheek for a few moments, but she had promised Lady Tamarind to hold with Clent for now. What was more, without Saracen, Clent had become her only link to the world she understood.

'Do I write them down, then?'

'You are my secretary, are you not? Take these down and write small – paper is dear. *First, that Mosca . . .* ah . . .'

'Mosca Mye.'

'*Mosca Mye . . . will serve Eponymous Clent in the capacity of Secretary, obeying all Reasonable Instructions without Question, and in exchange Eponymous Clent will provide for the said Mosca Mye's meals and lodging . . . and . . . ah . . . twenty shillings per annum to be paid at the end of each year.*'

'*. . . and a pipe . . .*' Mosca added, with a bitter emphasis. *And a goose*, she wanted to add, but she did not dare to think too hard about Saracen.

'What? Oh, very well, but if you require tobacco you must find that for yourself.'

'*. . . and clothes . . .*' Mosca continued stubbornly.

'*Adequate clothing*,' Clent amended. 'And for the moment your current apparel seems to serve very well.'

Without looking up from her writing, Mosca extended one foot to show the worn state of the shoe. The flat soles of the shoes she had found in Mrs Bessel's chest had been walked to ruin by some younger child.

'Let us not be delicate about this, your shoes will serve

very well for a few— Songs of the celestial, child, are you wearing breeches?'

Mosca pulled her feet back under her skirts.

'They're wading breeches,' she explained defensively.

'My dear frog, you are no longer living in a puddle. Now I dare say that you could pass for a measly kind of a boy, but right now you are neither fish nor fowl. Take this down. *Second, Mosca Mye will choose one gender and stick to it.*'

'*Third, Eponymous Clent promises not to take things what are Mosca's, or use 'em to pay for things, or run off sudden.*'

'Oh . . . if you please.' Clent waved one hand airily, as if the idea of him doing anything of the sort was clearly absurd. '*Fourth . . .*' Without looking up, Mosca could tell that Clent had paused by the window. She could not be sure whether he was gazing out at the view of the river or watching her reflection in the glass with his clever grey gaze. '*Fourth, Mosca Mye shall not divulge anything of a sensitive nature pertaining to her employer without his permission, nor shall she rifle through his papers or repeat his conversations.*'

'*Fifth, nor shall he 'peach on her neither, nor handle her things.*'

'*Sixth, she shall not hoard information from his attention, but shall be diligent in keeping him informed.*'

'*Seventh, he will keep her wise about stuff what concerns them, and persons what they are working for.*'

'All right, that will do, sign at the bottom.' Clent

 113

added his signature to hers.

'So –' Mosca watched as Clent rolled the paper once more and slid it into his top pocket – 'why we workin' for the Stationers, then?'

'This evening you shall sup full on answers, but in the meantime we both have work to do. I must write the ballad I promised to that cut-throat of the road, and you . . . well, my *last* secretary, for all his faults, always took the greatest care that my boots were kept clean – I believe that there are some rags beside the ewer. Furthermore, the sorry state of my coat currently reflects badly upon your diligence. And . . . for goodness sake, before we go out, do something about your eyebrows.'

Clent retreated to the little closet, and Mosca pulled a bit of charred wood out of the fire and, using her reflection in the window, carefully drew herself new eyebrows with the charcoal tip.

The rest of the day Mosca spent removing gorse spines and travel dust from Clent's cloak, darning the seams, and cleaning his boots. From time to time Clent himself would explode from his closet, gripped by fits of poetic rage.

'St Bibbet lend us light! Why must the man have a name so unsuited to verse? I have already used "lithe", and unless I use "writhe" I shall be forced into repetition.' He would smooth his hair as if combing his thoughts, then return to the closet.

A little after supper he finally emerged, scanning a

scribbled paper like a mother looking for signs of sickness in a newborn baby.

'It must do, it must do.' He glanced at Mosca's new, coal-black eyebrows, and gave a thin, despairing 'hhssst' through his teeth. He donned his coat, picking and preening over it with hands that trembled. 'And thus,' he murmured in apprehensive tones, 'must we brave the gaze of Mabwick Toke.'

'Who's he then?'

'Mabwick Toke is the head of the Stationers' chapter in Mandelion. He can quote the whole of Pessimese's "Endeavours", from Amblebirth to Aftermath, in the original Acrylic. He can speak twenty languages, half of them living, including two from the Aragash Heights, and one that can only be spoken with a coin under the tongue. When he travels, his carriage is lined with shelves so snug with books that the very breeze must squeeze for entry. He once uncovered a league of subversives by identifying a single silken thread in the paper weave of an opera ticket. If wits were pins, the man would be a veritable hedgehog.'

'If he's so sharp, what do they need *you* for?'

'Because there are delicate matters afoot, and they require a Special Operative who is not too obviously linked to the Stationers. I am an Unknown Quantity, and may pass through Mandelion Like A Ghost.'

To Mosca's mind, Clent did not look as if he had haunted anything but a pantry, but she managed not to say so.

'When do we go see Mr Toke the hedgehog, then?'

'Now. Put on your bonnet and follow me.'

Mosca snatched up her bonnet, slipped her outdoor clogs over her leather indoor shoes, and clattered after Clent.

Out in the street, Mosca's sharp eyes were dazzled by a hundred sights. The sound of hoofs on cobbles was deafening, and Mosca started as a horse's head appeared directly in front of her, blowing through its nose with a sound like a broken bellows.

'My good fellow, where might I find the *Telling Word*?'

A tinker paused in response to Clent's cry and stared skywards, as if judging the position of the sun.

'The *Telling Word*? You'll find her on Morestraws, just outside the Papermill.'

Clentstrode across the cobbles, paying little attention to his secretary, who followed him at a hop, still fastening the buckle of one clog as she struggled to keep up with him.

At last he halted outside a large building with a mighty mill wheel which jolted Mosca with the memory of Chough. From within came a vigorous *whoomp! whoomp! whoomp!* as if many pairs of giants were playing battledore at once. Several men, stripped to their shirts, were hurrying to and fro with barrows, some full of white rags, others full of coloured rags, rope ends and scraps of sailcloth. This was clearly the Papermill, and the rags were destined to be shredded and pulped and thumped into paper.

Peering through the open window of an adjoining building, Mosca saw two rows of women sorting scraps of cloth with quick, practised fingers, cutting them into pieces and slicing off buttons. Fascinated, she scampered to the next window.

And here, criss-crossed by the diamond-pane light from the window, was a Stationer printing press, its square-shouldered wooden frame standing up straight like a gutted dresser. A large man in his shirtsleeves lowered paper gripped in a hinged frame on to a blackened tray of type, then pushed the tray on rollers into the heart of the press. A mighty heave on a lever, and the machine stressed and pressed the paper down on to the type. Mosca could almost feel the flexing of the metal, forcing words into the world. The lever was raised, the tray dragged out, the frame lifted and the printed page tweaked free. A second man dipped the ends of what looked like fat drumsticks into a pot of ink, and slathered the mix over the type again, in readiness for the next page. The two men glistened with heat and effort. The press glistened with lamp-black and varnish. On the other side of the room an elderly, fox-faced man scanned each page carefully. In one hand he held a stick of wax, which he softened in a candle before drawing a molten splotch in each page corner and stamping it, using a ring with the Stationers' seal.

Mosca nearly broke her neck turning her head upside down to read the drying sheets. They were posters in big, crumbly-looking capitals, advertising 'Clashes between the Heraldry Beasts of the Many Monarchs', to be held at the Grey Mastiff Inn.

Clent, meanwhile, had approached a smaller building across the road, flanking the river. It was unlike anything Mosca had ever seen before.

She knew it was a coffeehouse, for the sign above the door bore the image of an elegant Eastern coffee-pot. Even with her limited knowledge of the world, Mosca had heard of the coffeehouses of the big cities. Many men chose them as a place in which to relax, or cut deals, or talk of high matters with the like-minded. Each coffeehouse had its own character, and usually its own loyal band of customers, close knit as any club.

The walls of this coffeehouse, however, were almost completely hidden under a jostling patchwork of sun-bleached, slantwise posters and printed snippets. Along the guttering, newspaper cuttings fluttered loosely like scarecrow rags. Each page bore the red blot of the Stationers' seal, so that the coffeehouse seemed to be suffering from a slight case of measles.

'Eponymous Clent, poet,' Clent declared airily, brandishing his scrawled poetry at a quiver-cheeked man at the door. 'Here to speak with Mabwick Toke.' The door swung back, and Mosca followed Clent into the *Telling Word*.

They entered a large square room filled with tables that bore a startling resemblance to writing desks, complete with ink splashes and glass quill stands. Several customers, indeed, had their own writing boxes open before them, quills and steel pens nestling on the green felt lining. Coffee fumes mixed with the metallic scent of ink, and instead of brisk tavern chatter there was the deadened murmur of voices hushed through habit.

Mosca's eyes were helplessly drawn to the sheaves of words pinned here and there on the walls, and the advertisements behind glass. Words, words, words. This was her gingerbread cottage. The smell of ink, however, seemed to be dizzying her. From time to time she could swear that the floor was gently dipping and rising.

Mosca and Clent were led to an unsmiling little man of fifty with a gnawed, yellow look like an apple core. The little man's mouth was a small, bitter V-shape, and seemed designed to say small, bitter things. His wig frightened Mosca; it was so lustrous and long, so glossy and brown, one could think it had sucked the life out of the little man whom it seemed to wear.

'Ah . . . Master Printer Mabwick Toke? Ah, I am honoured to meet a man so celebrated among the Stationers—'

'What I would like to know, Mr Eponymous Clent, is why you have chosen to meet me at all,' Toke interrupted sharply. 'We have agents of our own in Mandelion. Our whole reason for bringing you here was our wish to use someone who was not obviously connected to us.'

'Assuredly, assuredly.' Clent spread his plump hands reassuringly. 'However, as a poetic practitioner it would be strange if I did not approach the Stationers about publishing my works. On this occasion –' he passed his scroll of paper across the table – 'I have taken the precaution of preparing an excuse for my visit.'

Mabwick Toke ran a quick eye over the ballad, droning the words to himself in his throat. Absent-mindedly, he caught up a quill to jot and correct, occasionally licking at the nib to wet it. This was clearly a habit of his, since the tip of his tongue had become as black as that of a parrot. *He drinks ink*, thought Mosca, looking at his black tongue. *He eats nothing but paper*, she added to herself, noting his dry, pale lips and the crumpled-looking skin of his face and hands.

'Fair. A little florid, but it will sell. Your invalid lady is not named, but that is no great matter. You paint your highwayman in colours too bright for his craft perhaps. It lacks moral instruction. Could you add another verse to say that he has gone to the gallows, but that he repented his wickedness at the eleventh hour?'

'With respect, my good sir, I hardly think so. The fellow still lives . . .'

'Too bad. Well, I suppose we must print the ballad as it stands until this man Blythe has been caught and hanged.' Toke rolled the ballad carefully, and laid it inside his mahogany writing box.

'Good sir –' Clent cleared his throat – 'the truth is, without this man Blythe we would never have reached Mandelion so soon or so safely. It has been the only stroke of good fortune in a journey otherwise blighted by calamity. To relate the details would be to tell a tale of hazard, indignity, betrayal and misfortune . . . for which, ah, you are clearly too busy. Suffice to say that since leaving Long Pursing I believe that I have been followed. In Webwyke I heard that a well-spoken man had been asking for me by name, and in Lampgibbet he enquired after me by description. I tried to shake him off by taking the narrow roads, and took lodgings in a dismal hovel-stack called Chough, but I fancy he found me out even there. Some gentleman arrived there unexpectedly, I know that much, and spent hours talking with the magistrate. That very afternoon I was dragged from my tea table by a howling mob and clamped into the stocks. If I had not proved ingenious, I think his slanders might have seen me hanged. Master Toke, someone meant to prevent me reaching Mandelion.'

A gentleman arrived unexpectedly . . . Mosca suddenly remembered the conversation she had heard from the dovecote, between the magistrate and the man with the voice like warm milk. But she was already biting her tongue to stay mum and secretary-like, and she wasn't sure she could capture her tongue again if she stopped holding it.

'Mr Clent, were the seals on the letters I sent you intact?'

'Letters? Good sir, I received only one letter, calling me to Mandelion and recommending secrecy.'

'Two letters were sent. The second, which gave further details, has clearly been intercepted. I would assume therefore that *someone* knows all too well why you are here – and that you yourself have not the slightest idea.'

Clent ruefully inclined his head.

'Very well, the reason for summoning you is this. There is an illegal printing press in Mandelion.'

A silence fell across the room, as if everybody there had expected his words but had hushed out of respect for the gravity of the announcement. One or two of the eavesdropping Stationers clutched reflexively at little Beloved talismans on chatelaines for reassurance. Clent raised his eyebrows and pursed his lips in a silent whistle, as if he had been told that Mandelion sat on a layer of gunpowder. Only the child of Chough thought that a printing press did not seem half so exciting after meeting a real live highwayman.

'Caveat! The printed villainy!' The quiver-cheeked young man approached with a step as rapid as a stutter, carrying a mahogany box as if he thought it contained live vipers.

'Mandelion has been flooded with pamphlets.' Toke unlocked the box to reveal a small square of brownish printed paper which seemed to have been torn from some larger sheet. Using a pair of tongs, Toke lifted the fragment and extended it towards Clent, whose eyebrows climbed as he read.

'Madness, and mischief, and menaces of murder,' Clent muttered under his breath. 'Radicals, I assume.'

Mosca had heard a little about radicals from chapbooks about the trials of traitors. She had a fuzzy idea that most radicals shouted a lot, and threw grenadoes at anybody rich or powerful, and tried to stir people with hoes into charging at people with muskets. All the would-be kings agreed that they were mad and dangerous, and radicals could be prosecuted for treason in any part of the Realm.

'It reads like the ranting of a radical,' Toke said, taking back the paper. 'There is the usual canting about equality for all, and suggestions of how many ploughmen's families could be housed in the Duke's private residence. But these pamphlets also reveal the Duke's precise plans for rebuilding the city more symmetrically; for example, the fact that everything from Midmackle Street to The Crockles is to be levelled to make room for a new marketplace. Those streets are now in uproar. When the last pamphlet came out a week ago, there was a riot, sir.'

Mosca remembered what Bockerby had said the night before about riots in Mandelion.

'People are often excitable about losing their homes,' Clent murmured.

'That is not the point. No street-ranter could have known of these plans. Only someone at court, and close to the Duke,' continued Toke. 'I believe that somebody has tried to make these pamphlets *look* like the work of radicals, and has tried too hard. I see the hand of the Locksmiths in this. Aramai Goshawk is in Mandelion.'

The name was strange to Mosca, but she noticed that Clent had gone completely white.

'But . . . I have heard no reports that he had left Scurrey . . .'

'Reports from Scurrey? There *are* no reports from

 123

Scurrey. Since Scurrey became a Locksmith city six months ago, there is a new city gate, solid oak and heavy with locks, and hardly a soul has been permitted to leave or enter.

'Goshawk undoubtedly *was* in Scurrey. His Thief-takers too, secretly hiring half the felons in the city, and claiming rewards for "catching" any criminals that would not work for him.' Toke's bitter little mouth gave a twitch which might have been a smile. 'When Goshawk's tame cut-throats and pilferers were causing enough trouble to frighten the mayor, the Locksmiths came forward and offered to crush the crime wave. That buffoon of a mayor agreed, gave them half his treasury, and signed charters to give them special powers. The next day a boatload of guards in Locksmith liveries turned up with masons to rebuild the city walls. And now, *anything* might be happening in Scurrey, for all we know.

'Now the Locksmiths have sent Goshawk to Mandelion, and he is trying to play exactly the same trick with our Duke. The Duke's dearest dream is to see his beloved Queens ruling Mandelion, and he has a morbid fear of seeing them assassinated by insane radicals. The rogue pamphlets read like something from his worst nightmare – raging against the Twin Queens, and calling them "A Monster of Nature which might Count to Twenty-one on its Fingers". It has thrown the Duke into frothing and fits, and he would do anything to find the people responsible.

'Of course, he first turned to us to hunt down the perpetrators. For the last month we have trawled the city for the press. We arrest anybody found with one of these pamphlets, but it always turns out that they found it pinned to a tree, or pushed through their window. There is no pattern to where these pamphlets appear – east side, west side, the press seems to dance where it will. The paper is crudely pulped and unfamiliar, and we can learn nothing from it. Every few days more scandal sheets from this invisible press appear in our streets, in spite of our efforts. The Duke is fast running out of patience.

'Who stands to gain from all this? Why, the Locksmiths themselves. Goshawk has promised the Duke that if he will call in Locksmith troops and give them special powers, they will find the rogue press where we have failed. I believe that Goshawk himself is writing these scandal sheets, in order to persuade the Duke that there is a radical conspiracy, so that the Duke will call in Locksmith help to crush it. If we do not find this accursed press, and fast, the Duke will agree to Goshawk's terms, and another city will fall into the hands of the Locksmiths.'

Lady Tamarind's words returned to Mosca's mind: *The Locksmiths are on the rise, and if I cannot stop them, Mandelion will be theirs. I must know if others mean to act against the Locksmiths. The Stationers, in particular . . . I must know their plans . . .*

By this point, Mosca was listening so hard that she felt her ears might poke holes in her muslin cap. She did not understand everything that was being said, but three

 125

things were becoming clear. First, her conversation with Lady Tamarind had been no dream. Second, the Stationers did not like the Locksmiths any more than Lady Tamarind did. Third, Clent was heartily terrified of them.

'Ah. Ahem. I must say, had I known that you wanted me to spy on the *Locksmiths* . . .'

'Mr Clent,' rapped Toke, 'you were caught with sixteen illegal burlesque chapbooks of "King Cinnamon and the Milkmaids", hidden in a hurdy-gurdy. You wisely chose to work for us rather than hang. You, sir, are caught between the frying pan and the fire, so you will sizzle and like it.'

Clent visibly wilted and, despite herself, Mosca almost pitied him.

'We chose you as our agent because *we* cannot be seen to be investigating the Locksmiths. We are fighting a strange and secret war here in Mandelion – but it cannot become an open war between our guilds; that would be disastrous for the Realm.' Toke's pale eyes shone. 'Both Caveat and I have been followed everywhere for some time by gentlemen unwilling to introduce themselves. Fortunately they do not dare enter this coffeehouse. For the last four days I have lived here. Caveat has been here for two weeks.'

Caveat nodded rapidly, and twittered faintly.

'I could survive thus for weeks, but Mandelion will not. Do not be deceived by the city's calm, Mr Clent, there is hanging thunder in the air. The last time Mandelion crackled like this, it was just before that terrible Mye trouble, fifteen years ago . . .'

Mosca gave a guilty start, before recollecting that Mye was a common surname, and that anything happening fifteen years before was unlikely to have been her fault. Perhaps it was her nervousness that made the floor seem to plunge and rise again beneath her feet.

Toke finally noticed her. 'Mr Clent – is that girl yours?'

'Ah, yes – it became necessary to retain the services of this child. I brought her that she might be signed up as an apprentice of some sort, so we could bind her to secrecy . . .' So she was to be bound to secrecy again, even after signing the 'ship's articles'. Mosca was getting the distinct impression that Clent did not trust her.

'As you wish. Caveat, fetch the appropriate papers and have her sign articles as an apprentice rag-sorter.'

When Caveat returned, he was struggling beneath two great scrolls of paper. Speaking his sentences piecemeal, in a strange, pouncing, broken fashion, he listed the terrible things that would happen to Mosca if she gave away Stationer secrets, and then pointed to a place at the bottom where she could 'make her mark'. Mosca's pen trembled. What was the 'Mye trouble'? Would the Stationers be prejudiced against her if they discovered her name? She could not sign with a false name. It would sit like a china mask over a real face – everyone would surely see the *join*. Instead, Mosca signed with a cross, as if she was an ordinary country child with no knowledge of letters.

'Does this mean I'll be goin' to a Stationer school, then?' she whispered to Caveat as she handed back the papers. 'I mean, you'll want me lettered up proper, won't you?'

'I dare. Say that if your employer gives. A good account of you it will be considered.' Hearing Caveat was like watching an animal scuttle from cover, pause halfway to look about itself, then continue its low run. He attempted a smile, but eye contact seemed to alarm him, and he scurried away, cradling his scrolls.

Clent was giving an account of his meeting with Lady Tamarind, the promised letter of introduction and access to the Honeycomb Courts.

'Good.' Toke looked more good-humoured now. 'If you learn anything in the Courts, leave your report at the bookbinders in Pellmell Street. Your girl can mingle on the streets, and keep her ears open.' He studied Mosca acutely for a moment or two. 'Have I met you before, girl?' He frowned when Mosca shook her head in bemusement. 'You look familiar. No matter.'

'Come, Mosca,' Clent whispered. Mosca was rather relieved that nobody actually seemed to want to drag her off to sort rags there and then, and she followed Clent back out to the street.

The crowds were sparser now, and Mosca noticed Clent's gaze darting nervously to the remaining dawdlers.

'Mr Clent,' hissed Mosca, as she hurried along beside him, 'how do we know if we're bein' followed by Locksmiths?'

'A true Locksmith will always wear gloves, because the outline of a key is branded into his right palm,' Clent whispered back. 'The head of each secret cell also wears a chatelaine at his belt – with keys on the belt that match the brands of all the men that answer to him.'

'Mr Clent . . . most gentlemen wear gloves out o' doors, don't they?'

'Yes, child, they do.' Clent's eyes darted from one street corner to the next. 'Anyone we meet on the street might be a Locksmith spy.

'Goshawk himself is a shadow among shadows. It is said that his fingers are slender and dainty as a child's, and that he has kept them so by binding them every night in lemon-drenched muslin. He has fashioned keys so quaint that only he can use them, and he can pass through a triple-locked and bolted gate as easily as you or I might walk through rain. He can sense a secret passage or compartment the way a cat's pink nose can scent a crock of cream. We have been commanded to spy upon the Wind.'

H IS FOR HIGH TREASON

The next day, the letter from Lady Tamarind arrived in a whitewood scroll box, and Clent began fussing over his apparel like a dowager before a dance.

'Oh false fates, to leave me without wig powder – child, see that you whisker your way to the kitchens for a spoonful of flour, it will have to serve . . .' And again, 'I cannot go to the Honeycomb Courts without scented gloves . . . pray slip into one of the ten-shilling rooms and borrow a basin of rosewater.'

'What 'bout me?' Mosca scattered flour liberally over Clent's wig, and then brushed the loose grains out of his eyebrows. 'What do I wear?'

'I have let your aspirations climb too hastily,' Clent declared, washing his hands daintily in the rosewater, and examining his nails. 'Because I have allowed you to meet the most eminent Stationer in the city, now you think yourself ready for a debut in ducal circles. I can scarcely walk the Honeycomb Courts trailing some unweaned driggle-draggle.'

Mosca pushed her tongue into her cheek, and tweaked Clent's cravat into shape. Nothing in the unweaned driggle-draggle's manner revealed that her head was buzzing with a dozen furtive plans of her own, and that she was feverishly calculating for how many valuable hours the Honeycomb Courts would keep Clent out of her hair.

'You, madam, have a pair of voracious and inquisitive ears. I recommend that you employ them around the city, and see if they can gather anything of use.' And with that, Clent was out of the door with a swing and swagger.

Five minutes later, his secretary slipped out of the marriage house into the cool of the early morning.

Mosca's plan was this. She would hunt down the 'ragged school' her father had mentioned, and dazzle them with her learning. Perhaps Mr Twine, the schoolmaster her father had mentioned warmly, would remember the name of Quillam Mye and lend her some money, so that she could buy back Saracen when Partridge reached Mandelion. If not, then there was nothing for it but to work for the Stationers and hope that they paid her before Partridge sold Saracen or ate him.

When she thought of Lady Tamarind, her heart tried to tug itself in two. She had promised to report the Stationers' plans to Tamarind, but so much had happened since then. For better or worse, she had signed articles with Clent, and been taken on as a Stationer apprentice. If she gave away Stationer secrets and they ever found out, they would use her hide to bind books. And after all, did she know anything worth reporting? Only that the

Stationers did not trust the Locksmiths.

For a while Mosca walked north with the wind at her back, hoping that it would carry her to a busier thoroughfare where she could ask directions to the Ragged School. When the breeze changed direction, however, Mosca lost her bearings. The river she had left behind startled her by appearing on her right. She could not know that it curved around on itself, the city nestling in the crook of its elbow.

This was disappointing. Irrationally, Mosca felt she should have inherited her father's intimate knowledge of Mandelion. His throwaway comments about the city should have magically meshed in her mind, giving her a faultless instinct for finding her way around.

Eventually she called out to one of the 'ragmen' who poled their laden rafts up and down the Slye, bartering for scraps and discarded cloth. He was glad of a conversation with someone who had travelled beyond Mandelion. Mosca traded him some extravagant lies about life in the Capital in exchange for some drab facts about local geography.

'Don't know that there'll be much there for you, though.' The ragman stared quizzically at her departing figure, and Mosca concluded that he did not think she looked scholarly.

Only as she neared the right street did her self-confidence falter and her insides start leapfrogging. What if the teachers sneered at her grimy muslin or asked about her background? What if they expected her to be able to read Old Acrylic?

She turned the final corner, and stared.

The school's weathervane had been fashioned in the shape of a crouching man with a book in hands, head jutting forward eagerly, and Mosca easily recognized the pointed features of Goodman Whiskerwhite, He Who Searches for Truth.

Unsteadily, Mosca walked forward and prodded the weathervane with her foot. It was half buried among broken, mossy roof-tiles. Raising her head, she looked across at the mounds of rubble shored against the few remaining walls of the school, their gaping windows sad and jagged with broken leads. She shrugged both shoulders like a bird settling itself.

To judge by the advance of the moss and decay, the Ragged School had been dead longer than Mosca had been alive. Only as the dream broke and its shards cut her did she realize how close she had been clutching it. She had not *hoped* the school would accept her, she had *known* they would. At the back of her mind, she had believed that her father had meant her to hunt down the school, had made plans to ensure her future happiness when he was gone . . .

'Daft old dunnock.' Mosca could hardly recognize her own voice. 'What's the point of sending me here? That's it, is it? That's the best you can do?' Quillam Mye's mention of the Ragged School had not been a clue, or a part of some all-wise and all-knowing plan. He had died and abandoned his daughter without making any provision for her future. The ruin of the Ragged School was a devastating disappointment, but it also felt like a betrayal.

Mosca scrambled across the ruined school, her eyes stinging. The demolition was too complete to be a matter of accident or time, and there were no traces of fire. She found a hiding place beneath the lean of a tumbled timber, and hugged her knees there for a while, while ivy tickled the back of her neck.

While she was glowering numbly at her own clogs, she noticed something square-cornered and yellow-white wedged between two nearby bricks. Mosca wrestled it out, and found herself staring at a child's hornbook. Gripping its handle, she shook the dust off it, and raised it up to stare into it like a hand mirror. The layer of horn meant to protect the paper underneath was grimy and cracked, and the weather had blotted the letters of the alphabet almost beyond recognition. The backing board was rotten.

As a child she had spent hours sitting with such a hornbook beside her father's desk, while he wrote and she laboured over her lessons. Not a word or a look between them in an hour, just a strange, silent sense of connection. Despite herself, Mosca glowed with the memory.

This was something, at least, and there might be more treasures to be found. She crawled out of her cave, and began searching through the rubble. She was just starting to conclude that dozens of other looters had stripped it bare, when she looked up and found she was not the only forager.

Two other children were picking over the rubble, one a

girl of fifteen or so in a bent yellow bonnet, and the other a boy of about six, still in his infant gown. They saw her and pulled themselves upright like startled hares. The girl seemed to be holding a steel pen in her hand.

Something rushed past Mosca, and the hornbook was snatched out of her hand. She could only watch as a boy of her own age galloped, goat-footed, away from her across the rubble, his hand-me-down breeches flapping loosely.

'Oi!'

She hitched her skirts and sprinted after him, leaping a fractured chimney in a bound. Too much had been taken from her during her short life for Mosca to surrender a treasure that easily to an opponent her own size. The boy sprinted flat out without looking back, and Mosca matched his speed, her bonnet flapping against her back at its ribbon's limit. Down another alley, and another.

Round a corner, on to a busy thoroughfare . . . and right into a fustian coat and a blow to the gut.

Mosca doubled up and took a step backwards. Her hands knotted into fists and readied themselves at her waist to fend off another blow.

Further down the road, she saw the boy she had chased toss the hornbook to a group of older boys without breaking stride. One of them caught it, and slipped it into his pocket without looking at it. The thief kept running.

Mosca looked up from her crouch to see who had struck her.

It was a boy of about fifteen, dressed in the shabby style of most apprentices, with a pigtail as stubby as a paintbrush. He was arranging rolls of satin across the tables outside a haberdasher's and, to judge by his manner, had no idea of her existence, let alone the fact that his elbow had just found its way into her stomach. Nonetheless, when she advanced a step to move around him, he moved backwards with an insolent nonchalance, under cover of shaking out a length of cobra-green silk. His eyelids flickered as if beneath his lashes he had given her a surreptitious glance. He had a pleasant, pink, rounded face, and the smile of someone who would always find something flattering to say about ugly women's hats.

It is a very terrible thing to be far smaller than one's rage. Mosca felt something enormous swell within the knotted stomach that she hid behind her fists. It seemed it must surge out of her like a wild, black wave, sweeping away stalls and strollers alike and biting the plaster from the walls. However, when her vision cleared, her attacker was standing unharmed and unruffled.

The thief was almost out of sight. Mosca took another impulsive pace forward, and was knocked off her feet as the haberdasher's apprentice stepped quickly to block her. There was a hot ache in her jaw where his arm had hit her, there was a bruised shock in her hip from her fall, there was a prickle of rage about her heart and fingertips. She had no doubt that her attacker was blocking her path so that the thief could escape. On all fours, Mosca crawled away from him, then rose to her knees, wiping the mud from her hands.

It was while she was recovering her breath that Mosca witnessed something rather extraordinary.

The three boys who had been thrown the hornbook suddenly stiffened like dogs at a scent. With an air of purpose they darted across the road, and laid hands upon a young man wearing a chocolate-brown tricorn. They seemed set upon dragging the unfortunate man to the nearest alley, and Mosca assumed that they must be young gonophs determined to strip him of all his valuables. Curiously, however, their victim seemed neither worried nor surprised. He allowed himself to be manhandled out of the street, and disappeared from sight.

Near this alley rose a ragged wall where flints bulged and brandished, where arrow slits showed slivers of sky. Any native of Mandelion would have known that this was the old city wall, breached many centuries before during half-forgotten feuds over blood and money. Mosca knew only that this was something she could climb.

Carts splashed her hem as she slipped across the road, ducking her head so that the clothier's apprentice would lose track of her in the crowd. She wriggled through a fissure in the wall. Blush-petalled daisies quivered in every crack and tickled her fingertips as she climbed.

The wall rose over an alleyway where the young man was recovering his composure. He wore a dusty coat and a wig so misshapen it seemed some absent-minded soul had used it as a tea cosy. He blinked at the world about him through a pair of tiny spectacles tinted the gentle blue of a spring morning. In one hand he carried a walking cane, and under his free arm was tucked a large loaf of bread.

A group of children was playing at marbles in the alleyway. A sharp whistle raised their heads, and their game was abandoned with extraordinary casualness. There was a fumbling in jacket and skirt-pocket, and each fetched out a roll of paper, an inkbottle and a quill. The girl with the bent yellow bonnet was there, wiping rust from her scavenged pen. The last child to join the group was the clothier's apprentice. At the mouth of the alley he paused to cast a glance up the street as if still looking for Mosca, then moved to take his place next to a slim girl with a frayed, white lace shawl over her head.

If any of them had thought to look up, they might have noticed a hole halfway up the flint wall. It had for a time served as a station for a small cannon. Now it provided a crouching place for a short figure who hunched herself against the wind like a starling, frowning with her fierce new eyebrows of coal.

'Ah . . . good morning.' The man in blue glasses adjusted his hold on his bread, and tore it in two. It divided easily, and Mosca could see that a small and battered book lay within the crust. 'From the place where we left off yesterday. Ah, yes . . . *the responsibility of government is to protect the rights of the low from the tyranny of the high and not the property of the high from the desperation of the low* . . . oh good heavens, my apologies, we covered that already, did we not?' He crinkled his nose and adjusted his blue-tinted spectacles as he leafed through the book. Each of the dozen or so children seemed to be faithfully noting down his every word, including his hesitations and self-interruptions.

It was a school, a school! A back-alley school of stolen moments and stolen pens, but a school. Mosca could have wept tears of blood at finding herself forced to watch at a distance. All her life, her bookishness had made her a freak and an outcast, and other children had treated her with scorn and mistrust. Now it seemed clear that she would find no brothers and sisters even among schooled children like herself. She was an outcast still, and if she tried to approach, they would chase her away like a pack of young dogs snarling off an intruding stray.

'Ah, here we are. Ah – *A Colloquy on Truth*, thought to be by the same author.' The teacher cleared his throat and raised his head, and somehow the mist of absent-mindedness seemed to clear behind his little spectacles. 'On Truth.' He started to read.

'Truth is dangerous. It topples palaces and kills kings. It stirs gentle men to rage and bids them take up arms. It wakes old grievances and opens forgotten wounds. It is the mother of the sleepless night and the hag-ridden day. And yet there is one thing that is more dangerous than Truth. Those who would silence Truth's voice are more destructive by far.

'It is most perilous to be a speaker of Truth. Sometimes one must choose to be silent, or be silenced. But if a truth cannot be spoken, it must at least be known. Even if you dare not speak truth to others, never lie to yourself.

139

'In my head I built a room, in which I kept the truths I dared not speak. And in this room sometimes I said, the kings will return no more to the Realm. Nobody dares say this, but everyone knows it is the Truth. In this room I said, it is good that the kings' tyranny is gone forever. Men would hang me for saying so, but their hearts would whisper all the while that I spoke the Truth. And in this room I said that until the ordinary people choose their own leaders they will suffer, and this too is the Truth . . .'

The meaning of these words would have been lost on most children – and, for that matter, on many adults – but the eavesdropper in the cannon nook was Mosca Mye, who had begged and bartered for books and broadsheets all her life. This was radical talk – this dripped treason. The teacher below could be hanged for the words he was reading out. Mosca's eyes glittered vengefully.

'In this little room of the mind the truths grew strong and strident, and I knew that I must speak them whatever the cost . . .'

There was a sharp whistle from somewhere directly below Mosca, and with a shock she realized that the boy she had chased had been standing with his back flat against the flint wall, keeping an eye on the street.

'Class dismissed,' declared the teacher sharply, slamming his bread shut with a small explosion of crumbs.

Five of the children disappeared through holes in the ruined wall, the smallest leapfrogging through on his hands. The eldest boy scrambled up the side of the nearest house, then hung his arms over the roof's edge to pull up a smaller friend. Four others dropped to their knees and silently renewed their game of marbles.

The teacher pulled his cravat loose, and then retied it as he walked back towards the street. By the time he reached the mouth of the alleyway he was pulling it back into its bow, for all the world as if he had simply stepped into the alley to get out of the wind and set it straight. At the street corner he passed a tall gentleman in a full-bottomed wig who had just stepped into the alley, the reason for the lookout's whistle, and nodded to him courteously.

Legs shaking with excitement, Mosca scrambled down the wall, and set off in pursuit of the treasonous teacher. Very soon she was learning a few harsh lessons about spying in a busy city street.

She had long since learned tricks of invisibility. Be still where you can, be as silent as you can, let other small sounds drown your steps. If you cannot fool the eye, then fool the brain – stand where you are not expected and you will not be seen. Keep to the highs, keep to the lows, and avoid eye level if the terrain lets you. But these were tricks for the freckled woodland. Here in the street it was a matter of understanding patterns of flurry and flow. Stillness made one obvious, like a stone in a stream.

Time and again she would knock her bonnet against a swinging milk-pail, or nearly blunder beneath the wheels of a cart. Just to keep the teacher in view she was forced to squeeze alongside walls and between bodies, leaving a trail of trodden toes and murmured annoyance.

Thankfully, her quarry seemed cheerfully unaware of

 141

the world around him, but this too presented problems. At one point he stopped dead and dropped to a crouch to examine a snail whose shell had cracked beneath his boot. While an oyster seller's tray tipped dizzily above his head, he could be seen placing together the fractured pieces of the snail's shell and nudging it gently on its way. By the time he walked away with an oblivious smile, the road behind him was a tangle of tumbled bodies and overturned barrows. Despite herself, Mosca was impressed. The only other creature she had seen cause so much chaos in a ten-second period was Saracen.

She followed the teacher through Riversliver Race, where mackerel shimmered in slick silver heaps, where prawns with gummed black eyes questingly stirred their jointed legs. Through the Hides, where headless turkeys hung over doorways, plucked of all but wispy feather collars and garters, where rabbits dangled like furred gloves. Through a street sickly with the smell of tanners, through a network of alleys and ginnels. Down to the riverside, and in through the door of a coffeehouse.

'Welcome back, Mr Pertellis,' said a coffeemaiden at the door as she took the teacher's hat and coat.

As the door closed behind him, Mosca watched, agape and aghast.

It was not so strange to see the teacher entering a coffeehouse. What Mosca did not expect was for the coffeehouse to judder, grind gently sideways, then abandon the roadside altogether and drift out into the open river.

A violent wind roared in through the newly opened gap, leaving Mosca to wrestle with her ever-rebellious bonnet. The walls of the coffeehouse had been painted cunningly to give the appearance of brickwork, but she saw now that they were wooden. Above the roof swung two broad, square sails. In the sky, at the end of long, strong tethers, tugged six or so diamond-frame kites, most of them only two feet across, but the largest was six feet wide, and was decorated with a twist of laurel on a white background.

'You lose somink, love?' asked a passing stevedore.

'I lost a coffeehouse,' Mosca answered indistinctly. 'It . . . floated off down the river.'

The stevedore peered after the receding coffeehouse. 'Half an hour late, too. 'Spect they were waiting for one of their regulars.' This reply was somehow unsatisfactory.

Mosca tried again. 'It floated away down the river.'

'Wanted to catch it, did you? Well, the *Laurel Bower* stops on Tootle Street for sugar, that's your best chance of boarding her this side of the river. Ye'll have to run, though.'

And so, without pausing to question the strangeness, Mosca darted in the direction of his pointing finger.

She struggled down street after street, her eyes following the white kite above the roofline. And yes, at last, there was the coffeehouse, sliding to a halt alongside the jetty.

The door opened, and several men stepped out into the sun. One of them looked slightly familiar, and as Mosca tried to push past him he stepped forcibly into her path.

143

Mosca was taken roughly by the shoulders, and suddenly her feet were no longer touching the ground. The face of Partridge, the barge captain from the *Mettlesome Maid*, was inches from her own.

'Do you know what I want?' he hissed. The knot in his cheek was tying and loosing itself with frightening rapidity.

Mosca shook her head.

'I want . . . my . . . barge . . . back.'

'We 'aven't got it!'

'No.' Partridge glared into her eyes with an intensity almost insane. 'The goose has it.'

For a moment Mosca had a nightmarish image of Saracen biting through mooring ropes and taking the barge out, perhaps learning to trim the sails by himself . . .

'We plucked up the planks to get out our cargo,' Partridge explained slowly, 'and the goose got down there, and we couldn't get it out. And so we couldn't get our cargo out. And then we sent Dotheril down below deck, and the goose broke his ankle, and now we can't get *him* out. I want my barge back.'

Mosca nodded slightly.

'And I want money – compensation for time and business lost.'

Mosca nodded again, a little uncertainly.

'And you know what else I want for my trouble with the goose? I want your uncle's heart spiked on a boat-hook so I can hear it crackle as it bakes in the sun.'

I IS FOR INFORMER

Mosca looked into Partridge's eyes, judging his gaze and the force of his fingers against her shoulders.

'I'll get yer money! You just got to let me go, an' I'll get yer money! Beloved blind me with brands if it ain't so!'

Partridge stared at her distrustfully, and his grip tightened on her shoulders. There was nothing Mosca had wanted more than to find Partridge and buy back Saracen. However, right now her pockets were empty, and Partridge seemed to have gone a little mad.

'I'll have my money, all right,' Partridge said grimly. 'I'll sell your skin to a drum-maker and have my money.'

Mosca decided that Partridge was not in the right mood for negotiation.

She twisted like a snake and sank her teeth into his right-hand knuckles, all the while tearing at his fingers with her nails. He shifted his grip and she pulled free, hearing a *tick-tack-tack* of snapping seam threads. On impulse, she leaped a mess of mooring ropes and sprinted for the coffeehouse, which was making ready to cast off.

As the sailors on the roof braced long poles against the quay in readiness for pushing off, Mosca jumped. Her hands snatched at a dangling rope, and then her feet found support on the crude wooden rungs nailed to the coffeehouse wall. Winded, she could only cling and pray that the *Laurel Bower* would push off before Partridge's angry hand could close on the scruff of her neck.

It would not have interested her to know that at this very moment she was dangling between two worlds, each with its own laws. Leaping from the shore, she had left behind the city the Duke controlled. On the river, only the free-and-easy rules of the Watermen applied. The coffeehouses of Mandelion criss-crossed the river to escape the shore laws, so that customers could speak freely. Here sedition and wild conspiracies bubbled like the coffee-pots.

Meanwhile, within Miss Kitely's coffeehouse, the *Laurel Bower*, the young teacher in blue-tinted spectacles brightened at the sight of a newly arrived friend.

'Copperback!' The teacher pushed forward to take the hand of a man who had an angry question locked eternally into his brilliant brown eyes. 'I am so glad to see you – I was hoping that we might discuss the matter of the recent . . . that is, aha, hahow. Ow. Er . . . ow?'

Copperback continued to grip the teacher's hand with painful firmness until he had watched a man in a crimson waistcoat reclaim his hat and trip out through the street door with a swing of his cane. When the door had been made fast behind him, and the crockery had rattled with the casting off, Copperback's grip relaxed

146

slightly. Several other men around the room who had been watching the door with earnest interest allowed their shoulders to relax.

'Beloved above, Pertellis,' Copperback muttered at last. 'I thought you were going to spill right in front of him.'

Hopewood Pertellis blinked through his blue spectacles at the room about him, noticing the general tension for the first time.

'Who . . . ?'

'A spy for the Duke's men. I'd stake my eyes on it. What is become of the world if we cannot even talk safely on the river? He came in yesterday and told us he had just arrived in Mandelion from one of the university towns, and wanted to meet other men of letters who "cared for the much-wronged common people".'

'Well, I suppose it may have been true,' Pertellis suggested.

'No, I think not.' Miss Kitely herself had drifted in, carrying a dish of coffee for Pertellis. She was a thin, pale woman whose heavy lids could have been ugly but instead just made her eyes acutely blue. 'He bought coffee for himself, and anyone who would talk to him, and never asked them to return the favour. I had my girl overcharge him, and he didn't complain. Then he started to talk about how interested he would be in reading fresh-written tracts, and to ask whether anyone could show him some.'

'Did anyone tell him anything?' asked Pertellis.

Copperback exchanged a look with Miss Kitely, who

lowered her heavy lids in a slow blink, then raised them again. Copperback traded glances with several others in the room, who nodded slightly or raised their eyebrows expectantly, then he faced Pertellis again and folded his arms.

'And why would you be particularly interested in knowing that?'

'I beg your pardon?'

'Pertellis –are you running this infernal printing press?'

Pertellis paused in lifting his coffee dish to his lips. 'Goodness. Well, that is a question. How would you react if I was?'

Copperback flung his hands up over his head and, finding nothing he could usefully do with them, settled for meshing their fingers and letting them wrestle for a moment, before swinging them down against his thighs with a slap.

'I knew it had to be you. It has your stamp all over it. Pertellis, by Pipshriek, Protector of the Rash, why did you not tell us? You should have given us the chance to shake some sense into you! You will bring the Stationers down upon every one of us – we shall all have our noses cut off at the next Assizes!' Copperback flashed a furious and apprehensive glare round the room.

Every regular at the *Laurel Bower* would have risked arrest as a radical if his papers had been searched and his sympathies investigated. Their views differed, but they shared a passionate belief that the world was arranged unfairly. It was like a broken leg that had healed crooked and would have to be broken again if it was ever to grow straight. They all understood the danger they faced by holding to this belief.

'I see.' Pertellis sipped thoughtfully. 'And how would you react if I said that I was not responsible?'

'Pertellis . . .' Copperback gestured in frustration. 'Pertellis, we've all guessed that it must be you, what with your indomitable passion for circulating tracts. Most of us possess a copy of "Upon the Inequalities of Law" copied out by the children of your Floating School.'

'Yes, I . . .' Pertellis cast a beleaguered smile downwards. 'I think most of my children now write a pretty fair hand.'

'The hand is fair enough, but the words! Pertellis, they write down everything you say. On one page of my copy, a paragraph ends with "Oh dear, class dismissed, out of the windmill in single file, children."'

'Indeed, indeed. A printing press removes all such problems, and saves a deal of time and risk. It seems that it has been decided all round that I am running such a press. I can hardly resist such a weight of numbers, so I shall not protest.' The young teacher's voice rose. 'Would I be ashamed to be throwing sparks into the tinder of men's minds in such a way? No, I would not. Last winter, the over-taxed poor starved so that the Duke could build his Spires of Prosperity. This winter, innocent people will perish on the streets because he has knocked down their houses to make way for more follies. Is it worth speaking out against these things? Yes, it is!'

Copperback made an inarticulate, exasperated sound, and strode back to his table, where he sucked at his pipe so furiously that he swiftly vanished in a cloud of scented smoke. The *Laurel Bower* was dark and windowless out of respect for the window tax, but the sunlight entered the wooden walls through a hundred knotholes, illuminating ghostly swirling spears amid the blue smoke.

Miss Kitely brought Pertellis his own pipe.

'You are too stubborn,' she said under her breath.

'Have I made an enemy?' he asked quietly.

'No, just too passionate a friend. He is worried that he will live to see you on the gibbet.'

Pertellis sucked slowly at his pipe and then gave his hostess a glance that was alive with concern.

'That customer who just left – have you been troubled by many of the Duke's spies since my arrest last month?'

'I can scarcely lock my door against them.'

'No, I suppose not. I had not thought that when they failed to prove a charge of sedition against me, they would turn their attention to my friends. I have put them in danger.' Pertellis shifted his weight from one elbow to the other, so that his face was a little turned away from Miss Kitely's hooded eyes. 'I have been thinking that it was time I found myself a real office instead of coming here . . . perhaps one I could share with the Winnowing brothers . . .'

'I have in store a great many of those little brandy cakes of which you are so fond,' Miss Kitely declared evenly. 'They are too bitter for most tastes, and if you stopped coming here I would probably lose the money for them. I would take that hard, Mr Pertellis.'

Pertellis made a small noise, as if he had drawn in too large a lungful of tobacco.

'The funny thing is,' he continued after a moment, 'I think I would have given up the school a long time ago, but that the children are keener than I. It is all *their* arrangement now – I never know as I walk down the street what corner they will have found and made ready for the lesson. I have explained the dangers to them a hundred times, but they have such a passion to learn. None of them can afford the fees for the Stationers' schools, and even if they could, what would those schools teach them? How to be obedient and useful servants and never question anything, that's all.

'So my school goes on, and it seems that every month there is a new, bright face among the children. Even today, I am sure I noticed a young girl I had never seen before following me. I suppose she must have heard about the school from one of the others. She was too shy to approach me, or I would have talked to her. But I dare say I will be seeing more of her . . . she had that hungry look . . .'

Pertellis's view of Mosca's hunger for knowledge might have changed if he had been aware of the many salty terms her mind had devoured over the years. Most of them were being muttered under her breath at that very moment. A gaggle of small children had noticed her clinging to the rungs and had taken it upon themselves to run along the quayside, pointing out the stowaway at the tops of their shrill voices.

'Oi!' A reddened face appeared above her. 'No passage 'cept to customers! 'Op it!'

'Where do I 'op? I'm not a bleedin' frog!'

'Should have thought of that before. No passage. Watermen's rules.' The sailor straightened, and took a long look up and down the river's broad expanse. 'Take her starboard.'

In the middle of the river rose a pillar of rock upon which stood a bronze figure of Goodman Sussuratch, He Who Preserves the Unwary from the River's Embrace. A little wooden jetty stretched beside it. With much wrestling of kite wires, the coffeehouse was turned to glide alongside the jetty.

'You get off here. Now 'op it! Hail yerself a wherry.' Reluctantly, Mosca released her hold and dropped on to the jetty.

'I hope maggots crawl in through your ears and lick your brain clean from the inside!' she shouted after the coffeehouse as it surged away. She had no money to hire a Waterman.

But what was this, churning softly through the brown water of the Slye like an oversized tea chest? It was another coffeehouse, to judge by the sign swinging above the door, but this was a dingy edifice that seemed to have been stained coffee colour from the inside out. Its kites bore a picture of a stag, and over the door were painted the words 'The Hind at Bay'.

The men on the roof of this coffeehouse had fallen foul of a sudden change in the wind's direction. The boom had jibbed, and all hands were now busy working to bring the boat back into the wind. None of them noticed a short figure scaling the stone steps that spiralled up Goodman Sussuratch's pillar, and then crouching, ready to jump. Their ears were too full of the deafening crack and slap of the slack sail to hear a gentle weight drop on to a corner of the roof.

Thump.

Not a loud noise, but loud enough to wake a man.

The man it woke did not move immediately but lay, frowning, for a few seconds, as if becoming gradually aware of the awkward posture of his head against the chair back, and then he opened eyes the colour of verdigris.

He blinked at the discoloured walls, at the tired faces of the drapers who chatted over the *Tradesman's Companion*, at the copper gleam of the coffee-pots beyond the hatch.

Lapsing back into his chair, he dozed off with the speed of one used to sleeping on the move. Only when the entire room jolted to starboard, causing regulars to lunge with a practised gesture to save their coffee-pots, did his eyelids flicker open again.

A farewell word for his host. He had a pleasant voice, with a reassuring quality like warm milk. A smile for the girl who brought his hat and walking cane. He had a pleasant smile, as frank as a handshake. A few steps

 153

through the door and his hat was knocked from his head as something pale and pointed descended on wings of muslin as if from the heavens, to land a-crumple at his feet.

Mosca blinked up into the sun. The man standing above her seemed young. He seemed startled. He seemed to be wearing a long gentleman's travelling cloak.

She seemed to be sitting on his hat.

Perhaps she could hand back his flattened hat with a curtsey, and make a bolt for it before his surprise turned to anger? She stood unsteadily, and the man instinctively reached out to catch her arm, and prevent her falling through the crack between doorstep and jetty.

'Steady, there,' he said, not unkindly.

Mosca did not answer, but froze, staring past the stranger's shoulder.

'What's wrong?' He turned, and saw what she had already seen, the figure of Partridge on the quay, shielding his eyes to stare at the roof of the coffeehouse. It suddenly occurred to Mosca that, for all their busily swelling sails and struggling kites, the coffeehouses moved at something less than walking speed, and Partridge had probably been keeping pace with her along the shore. The barge captain seemed to have lost sight of her for the moment, but it would not be long before he spotted her. She shrank back behind the man in the travelling cloak, who turned to her to look a question.

He thinks I'm a pickpocket or a stowaway or a runaway apprentice or a murderer . . .

Mosca could only look up at the stranger with terrified appeal, and shake her head.

Partridge stroked his jaw, took a few hasty steps towards the coffeehouse . . . and disappeared, taking the world with him, as Mosca was swallowed by a total blackness. The darkness was warm and smelt of wet roads and grass seeds. It took Mosca several panic-stricken seconds to realize that the stranger had swept his cloak around her.

'Keep pace if you can.' The voice was low and slightly muffled by the cloth. 'Try not to stumble, and maybe he will not notice the extra pair of feet.'

Walking at half a crouch, she tried to stay as close to her unexpected saviour as she could without jostling him. Nonetheless, she was continually bumped and buffeted, presumably by other walkers who tried to push through the billowing slack of the cloak without realizing that it was full of crouching, terrified girl.

The sound of the wind had faded a little by the time the cloak pulled back and returned Mosca to a world of sunlight. She shifted her skewed mob cap on to the back of her head, and blew loose hairout of her eyes. She was standing with the stranger in an alley between a sandstone wall and the cold, high flank of the cathedral.

'So – to what terrible act have I just become an accessory?' Her rescuer smiled, and folded his arms. When he smiled, his eyebrows rose into two neat chestnut crescents, as if they knew the world was destined to surprise them again and again, and were determined to believe in pleasant surprises. *Not gentlemanlike enough*

 155

to be handsome, thought Mosca. He wore no wig for one thing, just his own unpowdered red-brown hair, tied back with black ribbon. Instead of fashionable pallor, his face was tanned to a tea-stain. And yet somehow he did not have a manservant's careful self-importance. He had the modest assurance of someone who carries the world in his watchcase.

Mosca flushed. Some impulse of gratitude compelled her to attempt the truth.

'My goose sort of stole that man's boat, but he didn't mean to – he was prob'ly just frightened. An' now he's angry an' wants to put everyone's hearts on spikes an' cook an' eat them.'

The young man in the cloak pressed his lips firmly together, and stared intently at the ground. He nodded twice very slowly, as if this answer was just what he had expected.

'Mm. I see.' His tone was slightly tremulous, and Mosca realized that he was trying not to laugh. 'Well, I dare say that if you had been setting out to deceive, you would have come up with a story that made rather more sense than that. So I think I must accept your words as the truth. And anyway, even if it is a lie, then I am sure it is a great improvement upon the facts.'

'It's true!' It seemed too hard that on one of the few occasions when she was trying to be honest she should be doubted.

'All right, my apologies. What's your name?'

'Mosca.'

'Pleased to meet you.' He held out a hand. 'Linden Kohlrabi.'

She shook the offered hand, not sure whether she was being mocked.

'You are not from Mandelion, are you? Your accent sounds familiar, but I cannot place it.'

'I just come here with a poetic practitioner. I'm his secretary.' Her declaration was proudly defiant. The corners of his mouth trembled with another suppressed smile. Suddenly she wanted to impress the man before her.

'I'm only doin' that for now,' she added, 'cos soon I'm going to work . . . over there.' Above the sandstone wall and the mosaic of roofs she could see the pale needle of the Eastern Spire. 'That's where Lady Tamarind lives, and I'm goin' to be workin' for her.' She grinned up at Kohlrabi, and was delighted to see that, yes, his eyes had now paled to a startled green. 'I'm goin' to get a place there, an' read her poetry, an' carry in her letters on a tray, and . . .' She lost words as her mind drifted away to a serene cold place where nothing could jostle her and no one could lift her by the collar. 'That's where I'm goin'.'

'What a coincidence,' Kohlrabi answered smoothly, his expression deadpan. 'I was thinking I might drop in there myself – call in upon Her Ladyship, admire the tapestries, and I hear there's a rather fine view from the topmost room . . .'

Mosca looked at his muddy boots and sly smile, and laughed aloud.

157

'You're making fun,' she said. 'You don't believe me. 'S all true, though. You'll see!' She gave the Eastern Spire a wave, and then turned and sprinted away along the alley.

Mosca's good mood carried her halfway home before she remembered the back-alley school. Bitter thoughts stung her again and again, like a wasp in a clenched fist. *I could've sat sentry for 'em up on the wall*, she thought, *I could've lifted pens for 'em from the Stationers*. But then she remembered the clothier's apprentice elbowing her off her feet, and felt the bruises to her limbs and her pride. She didn't want to go *that* school, she'd never wanted to go to *that* school, it was rotten and radical and full of traitors.

But . . . who would pay to learn of an unlicensed school, teaching radical books? The Stationers would. They would give her money, and she would buy back Saracen. They would be pleased with her, and send her to school, the way Lady Tamarind wanted.

By the time Eponymous Clent came home, smelling of wine and wearing an orchid pinned to one lapel, Mosca's mind was quite made up. He gave her a giddy, pink-nosed smile as he handed her his hat.

'Ah, an admirable day. To have my poetry appreciated by persons of quality . . . and means . . .'

Mosca thought that for a Special Operative, Clent seemed rather easily distracted.

'I hope you managed to occupy yourself today, my dear?'

Mosca grinned grimly.

'Shuffle your thoughts snug, Mr Clent. You'll need room in yer skull for everything I got to tell you.'

While Mosca was telling Clent all about her adventures with Partridge and the alley school, Linden Kohlrabi was preparing to make a report of his own. The strange young girl with her wild stories and excitable black eyes had provided an amusing and welcome distraction from this unpleasant duty, but now it could be avoided no longer.

The footmen at the gates to the Eastern Spire had been told to expect him, and he was shown in to meet Lady Tamarind immediately.

'Your Ladyship. I regret to say that Eponymous Clent has evaded me. I traced him, I trailed him, I caught up with him and in a little village called Chough I lost him. He is still at large.'

'I know,' answered Tamarind. 'He is in Mandelion.'

'Already?' Kohlrabi raised his eyebrows. 'I suppose he took a boat downstream?'

'He arrived by coach. My coach. We picked him up the roadside.'

There are a number of things one cannot say to the sister of a duke, and Kohlrabi spent several icy moments not saying them.

'My lady,' he burst out at last, 'if he were not so diabolically dangerous . . .'

'. . . then I would have risked throwing him out of

 159

my carriage as soon as I learned who he was,' finished Tamarind. 'But I have turned the accident to the best advantage possible. I have recruited an agent to watch Clent's every move, so that we are forewarned if he intends any harm. I do not yet know how reliable this agent will prove, but she shows promise . . .'

J IS FOR JUDGEMENT

The next morning, Caveat of the Stationers left the safety of the *Telling Word*, and travelled by sedan to call upon a bookbinder in Pellmell, where Eponymous Clent had been told to leave any reports.

'We've sent two different apprentices to pick up the reports,' Mabwick Toke had declared angrily that morning. 'Neither of them got there. Tittle was jostled under a cart, and is still in the care of the barber-surgeon. We don't even know what happened to Weft. No, this time we'll send a full guildsman – the Locksmiths can't harm him without breaking the Rules, and openly declaring guild war. Even Aramai Goshawk would not dare do that. Caveat! You'll do.' Toke opened the door of the coffeehouse. 'The Clamouring Hour is nearly over, so go quickly while the streets are empty.' The many sects of the many Beloved had very different ideas about how the bells should be rung for worship, and it had become customary to let them battle it out through the metal of their bells for an hour every other day. Every church, shrine and cathedral became a scene of cacophony as bells chimed and clanged and tolled and jingled in every pitch from baritone to baby-chick squeak. Worshippers of more obscure Beloved would sometimes buy bells and hang out of upper windows with cotton in their ears, adding their own music to the general chaos. Most people preferred to hide indoors until the Hour was over, with their windows firmly closed. Caveat sat hunched in the sedan with his fingers in his ears as discordant peals assaulted the morning air of Mandelion.

Mr Toke always. Knows what he is doing, Caveat told himself, as he ducked into the bookbinder's shop. *But how. Can we be sure that the. Locksmiths. Care about the Rules when we have not. Heard from anyone in Scurrey for so long anything. Might be going on in there.*

Two minutes later Caveat emerged on to Pellmell, tucking Clent's report into his waistcoat. Although he stop-started his way through spoken sentences, he could read faster than hummingbird flight, and he had taken in Clent's three pages of curling prose in as many glances. His eyebrows, which had been dancing like frightened caterpillars, were now dancing like excited caterpillars.

'The *Telling Word*!' he called sharply to the chairmen, raising his voice to be heard through their cloth-rag earplugs. He clambered back into the waiting sedan. Short phrases were easier to shout all of a piece. 'Be quick!'

The chairmen obediently set off at a jog. Caveat was just settling back in his seat when there was a thump from ahead, and the front of the sedan swayed and dipped.

'What? What was that?' Caveat was almost sure the

foremost of the two chairmen had called out something.

A series of thuds and crashes came from behind, and a muffled 'Oh!', as if someone had just remembered something very important. The rear of the sedan dropped sharply and bounced on the cobbles, so that Caveat fell backwards, his wig down over his nose and his feet skywards.

Before he could remonstrate, the sedan was lifted smoothly and, as if nothing had happened, the unseen chairmen set off at their obedient jog. A moment later this accelerated to a disobedient canter, and then to a downright rebellious gallop.

While he tried to right himself, his phantom carriers took a left, a right, a left, a left, a right. Caveat could hear more than two pairs of feet clattering on the cobbles, and the echoes spoke of dank, empty alleys and high walls.

Then the echoes were gone, and there was the slap of flat soles on wet wood. Wind's laughter, a fanfare of gulls. The mad gallop halted. The entire sedan swung giddily sideways, then plunged. Caveat struggled himself upright and leaned out of the window, just in time to see the caramel-coloured surface of the river rising to meet him.

A throaty splash. Cloudy water surged in from the cracks around the doors. Caveat lurched for one door, and the sedan tilted, shipping water through the open window. In terror he flung his weight the other way and righted it, not a moment too soon.

As he sat rigidly in the very centre of his seat, feeling the rising water tickle his calves with cold, he heard a

163

loud banging-scrabbling sound not far from his head. Looking up, he saw a black iron claw had hooked itself under the upper frame of one window. Three more bangs and scrabbles, and grappling hooks had secured the remaining windows. The sedan ceased its whirligig, and with a long, dragging gush rose into the air.

After a few minutes of hushed paralysis, Caveat pushed up the lid-like roof of the sedan, and stood. The sedan hung, dripping, from four sturdy ropes in the shadow of a narrow footbridge, the battered boards of which leaked sky through seam and knothole. Inches below his feet, the Slye chewed the city's flotsam like stale tobacco. On the dismal jetty nearby, three men in gloves stood watching.

'Funny sort of a fish,' said one. He had a rippled scar like mackerel markings down his left cheek. 'But you never know what you're likely to hook at Whickerback Point. All kinds of brackle washes up here.'

'You're very lucky we was passing by, Mr Stationer,' his taller companion called, scratching the corn stubble at the corner of his grin. The third said nothing, but blew pipe smoke out through his teeth.

'Perhaps,' halted Caveat. 'You might fetch the. Beadle to help me if so there'll be a. Shiny. Shilling. For you.' The men on the bank could not have seen his guildsman's insignia, and yet they knew who he was. Despite their rough apparel, all three wore gloves of good quality.

'Wouldn't like to leave you a-dangle, sir,' called the tall man. 'What if you was to fall? Notorious for accidents, this place.'

'Acca- acksi- acc-' Caveat's broken sentences disintegrated completely.

Locksmith 'accidents' were infamous. Everyone knew of the sneak thief who had bowsed himself silly on brown ale, boasted of breaking a Locksmith lock, and been found the next day with his skull cloven by the gilded arrow of a fallen weathercock. Then there was the story of the Roaring Bladdiman brothers, two rakes who had kicked in a Locksmith's door to have a conversation with his pretty daughter. The following night at their favourite tavern a stack of barrels had collapsed on to them, rolling them flat like pastry beneath a pin.

'You know what, my dubbers,' said the mackerel-cheeked man, 'I think we'd best try to swing him to shore with a one-two-three.'

'Yeah, and maybe fetch the good cull a nope on the costard and make him easy,' murmured the pipe-smoker. 'Get the nizey to bird us the brittles first.'

Caveat blinked. He knew every dictionary better than his parents' faces, but this was thieves' cant, and he could not tell whether the smiling men on the shore were praising his cravat or plotting to cut his throat.

'If you tumble in the bubble while we're swinging you to shore, we can haul you out, sir,' shouted the tallest man. 'But first you'd best throw us anything you wouldn't want lost in the dunk.'

'No. Need I will be. Fine in fact I was just. Waiting here for a friend.' Caveat's fingertips performed a quick patrol of his pockets, as if he thought the watchers could pluck purses with a glance.

'Right now the best friends you got in the world is those four ropes,' said the mackerel-cheeked man, 'and wise men don't wear out their friends' patience. Else the ropes might wonder why they're bothering with a man who can't look to his own good, and they'll break and give you to the Slye to buss.' There was no mistaking the threat in his voice.

If, as Caveat suspected, these were Locksmith Thief-takers, he had little doubt that they would dare to bring an 'accident' upon a Stationer guildsman. He thought of icy water creeping into his nose and mouth as he fought the current. He imagined his wig soaked and bedraggled on a shoreside, a tug of war toy for gulls.

'Hoi!'

Caveat turned his head and gave a faint twitter of relief as he saw a little rowing boat approaching. A young man with a crooked nose lowered his sculls and stared at the suspended Stationer.

'You all right, mister? You need a lift to shore?'

'Yes! Oh yes! The, ah. Far shore.'

The three men on the jetty watched stony-faced as the little rowing boat glided up to nudge the hanging sedan. The sculler stood up and put out his hands to steady Caveat, who opened a door and gingerly lowered one foot into the boat. Then, without warning, the young man gave the Stationer a vigorous push in the chest. As Caveat fell sprawling backwards into the sedan, the oarsman pushed away with his paddle.

'Sorry, old love.' The youth waved a farewell with the rolled-up papers that his long, gloved fingers had tweaked from Caveat's pocket. 'Can't take passengers, can I? Watermen's rules.' He tossed the papers and Caveat's purse to the men waiting on the bank, grabbed his sculls and plied them. The laughter of the four men faded with their footsteps, and Caveat was left rocking in darkness amid the laughter of the wind, his face in his hands.

Eponymous Clent's report gave a detailed, florid and in some instances even accurate account of Mosca's discovery of the Floating School, and her attempts to follow Pertellis. Aramai Goshawk, the new leader of the Mandelion Locksmiths, read and reread it, turning the pages carefully with his tiny, perfect hands.

Goshawk's 'offices' were never in the same place twice, and today he was holding court in the domain of the gulls. The cathedral roof offered a splendid view of the city, unequalled even by the spires. The great pitted dome shielded his desk and chair from the worst of the wind, and all around him the gulls eddied and perched, angelwing-white in the sun. He was pleased by their cruel raucousness, their symphony of selfishness.

The man who stood before Goshawk twisting his cap seemed less happy. His knees trembled with the height, and he flinched from the gape of the gulls' beaks.

'So –' Goshawk raised colourless eyes to look at him – 'which part of the city does your gang control? Point it out to me.'

167

'Over there, between the river and Cockle Street.' The young thief's face furrowed as he realized how small his territory looked from Goshawk's vantage.

As far as Goshawk was concerned, people were greedy, frightened or both, and that was all you needed to know about them. He preferred them frightened. Greed had probably brought this young criminal to Goshawk to offer his gang's services, but fear would later prevent him changing allegiance. In time, fear would bring a parade of thieves, swindlers, blackmailers, fences, nook-gazers, murderers, magistrates and courtiers, all desperate to make terms with the Locksmiths. Secretly, Goshawk thanked the Birdcatchers for filling the Realm with broken, frightened people. The old anthems to freedom were dead. Nowadays everybody wanted safety, and the Locksmiths offered safety – for a price.

In Scurrey, Goshawk's tactics had been effective surprisingly swiftly. The turning point in his fight for the city had taken place just after he had seized control of the Mawkins gang. Openly attending the funeral of Willet Mawkins in his customary sombre black clothes, he had heard a whisper of fear among the 'mourners' that caused his pitted cheeks to pucker in an almost-smile. The other criminal gangs had decided that Goshawk's victory was inevitable . . . and from that moment it was. They fell over one another in their hurry to join his organization. And now Scurrey was docile, a city of empty, fearful streets and shuttered windows, where everybody paid their tithes to the Locksmiths . . .

The thief before him was by now deeply regretting the mission that had forced him to approach Aramai Goshawk.

'We've a man in the pound,' he was explaining, 'our best sly-in-the-night. His trial's due for the first day of the Assizes, four days from now . . .'

'. . . and you want me to send a pair of plumpers to give him an alibi?' The Locksmiths employed many 'plumpers', men who would perjure themselves for money. 'I can do this. But first . . . I would like to see some evidence of your loyalty to us.'

A plan was forming in Goshawk's mind. His eye slid over Clent's report. In spite of his guild's attempts to intimidate them, the Stationers had not halted their efforts to investigate the Locksmiths. Their interference did not frighten him – but it was an annoying distraction. Goshawk needed all his resources for a battle of wits that he was waging with a very different and more powerful enemy.

For months he had been fighting the Duke's sister, Lady Tamarind, for control of Mandelion. Influencing the Duke was like trying to grab a fistful of maddened bees, but he was sure that he would have succeeded by now, were it not for Tamarind whispering in the Duke's ear. Her network of spies seemed the equal of Goshawk's own. The agents he sent to break into her apartments in search of her correspondence were almost invariably mauled by her monstrous pet collection. Worse still, their battle of wits seemed to have become tavern gossip, and crooks that should have flocked to join him hung back leerily, waiting to see who would win. Goshawk frowned. He could ill afford to let the underworld suspect that he was dancing daggers with the Stationers as well.

'The Stationers need to be frightened, that is all, and they will back down,' he muttered under his breath. 'They are too afraid of an open guild war to risk a confrontation with us. Let us see. Their investigation has led them to this Pertellis, on whom they seem to place great value . . .'

He looked up at the waiting thief.

'Let us see how skilled your men are. By dusk I want you to find a man of letters named Pertellis.'

Meanwhile, blithely unaware how famous he had become in two short days, the young lawyer Hopewood Pertellis spent the afternoon at the Mandelion prison, speaking with a farmer he was due to defend at the upcoming Assizes for non-payment of the Duke's harsh new taxes. He thought of nothing but the case as he walked home, and as he absently munched through the potage that his patient housekeeper left by his elbow.

The rooms of Pertellis's house were unusually dark. In Mandelion, as in most cities, a tax was paid for every window, and only the well-off opted to pay for their daylight. Pertellis worked hard, but the clients he chose were seldom rich, and over the years he had boarded up most of his windows. The cheap candles he used gave off a smoky, sulky light and smelt like a mutton joint that had been left out in the rain. Nonetheless, like many quiet men, Pertellis had a stubborn streak wider than the Slye, and that night found him working late on the farmer's case, squinting painfully in the dim light.

At the moment when his study door opened, he had just taken off his glasses to rest his aching eyes. So it was that, when he raised his head to discover the source of a furtive wooden creak, he saw only five or so dark shapes which were born from the shadow of the doorway and moved towards him without a sound.

At midnight a young linkboy, patrolling the darker docks of Whickerback Point with his lantern in search of someone who might need guiding home, chanced to hear a sneeze. By the light of his lantern he discovered the hanging sedan, and within it the shivering Caveat.

A helpful beadle brought Caveat back to the *Telling Word*. Thus Toke learned of Caveat's ordeal, and the contents of Clent's report concerning Pertellis and the Floating School.

He quickly roused three Stationers in the *Telling Word* from their coffee-haunted dreams, waving aside their reluctance to go chasing teachers in the middle of the night.

'Stop mewling, and find your coats,' Toke snapped. 'Many of the Birdcatchers were teachers too, never forget that. Teachers to the sons of important men, secretly twisting their infant minds. The boys grew up and became powerful, with the seeds of Birdcatchery lodged

 171

in their heads, and nobody knew, until it was too late, how *many* of them there were. No, children must be taught by Stationers or not at all, or we shall have the same problem again in twenty years. When a head is too full of the wrong ideas, there is no option but to remove it – far better to stop the ideas getting there in the first place.'

Once ashore, Toke woke the high constable, who recognized Pertellis's name. The young lawyer had been arrested twice on suspicion of sedition, but acquitted for lack of evidence. His address was included in the records of the trials.

An hour later, accompanied by his three Stationers and two petty constables, Toke stood before the door to Pertellis's house and knew instantly that he was too late.

The locks of front door, back door, closet and writing desk had been picked without leaving so much as a scratch. The housekeeper was found, trussed and gagged, in the metal bath, her muslin cap pulled down over her face. Pertellis was gone. The whole thing had been managed without waking the neighbours, or even the dog that slept in the hallway.

In the pantry Toke found several hollowed bread loaves, with a different forbidden book hidden in each one. The Stationers now had evidence against Pertellis, but no Pertellis.

Mabwick Toke knew a Locksmith break-in when he saw one. But why had they taken Hopewood Pertellis? If Toke was correct, the Locksmiths themselves were responsible for printing the pamphlets vilifying the Duke. But if the Duke believed that *radicals* were running the secret printing press – perhaps the Locksmiths meant to present Pertellis to the Duke in chains as the radicals' leader, and so win his trust and gratitude. Or could it be that the Locksmiths themselves had been using Pertellis as a cat's-paw to run the printing press, and were afraid that he might talk if the Stationers caught him?

'In any case,' Toke muttered to himself, 'if the Locksmiths think him worth grabbing, he *must* be important. And I shall snatch him back, Mr Goshawk, just you see if I don't. I've never sought a war with you, but I won't flinch from one either. I fought the Birdcatchers when they held the country in the palm of their hand, and if *they* couldn't frighten me, Aramai Goshawk, then you shan't.'

He looked around at the pale, sleep-starved countenances of the other Stationers.

'Gape any wider, and you will yawn your faces inside out. All of you, go into the streets and shout out for a linkboy. Bring back as many as you can find!'

Within a short time there were half a dozen linkboys in Pertellis's front hall. Surveying their sly and spotted faces, Toke thought it no wonder that they should welcome the veil of darkness in their nightly work.

Using a little sharp questioning and careful bribery, he soon learned that the youngest linkboy had seen five gentlemen 'helping a friend home'. The boy had offered his lantern, but had been told to 'sling his hook'.

'Followed 'em as far as the Drimps in case they changed their mind,' the boy added, then gave a gap-toothed grin as Toke put a coin in his hand.

On the narrow street known as the Drimps lived a blind tallow-maker who always slept with his shutters open. When Toke visited him the next morning, he was able to recall that, a little after second bell, he had heard half a dozen men moving with haste along the Drimps, and down Strangeway.

Hearing this, Toke's eyes glittered. Strangeway was a crooked, covered alley which led all the way to the city wall, and emerged opposite a tavern called the Grey Mastiff.

The Grey Mastiff was famed throughout Mandelion for the quality of the 'beast fights' held within its walls every fortnight. For some time, however, Mabwick Toke had suspected that the Grey Mastiff was also used secretly as a Locksmith meeting place and safe house. Several known Locksmiths had been seen to congregate there every time a beast fight was held, and Aramai Goshawk's supercilious silhouette had been glimpsed at one of the upper windows.

'They're not taking him to the Duke, after all. Not straight away anyway. This man Pertellis is hidden there, I'd stake my wig on it,' Toke muttered to himself as a sedan took him back to the *Telling Word*. 'But how to tweak him out?'

Toke had no men who could pick a lock or scale a wall

the way Goshawk's underlings could. But did he need them? He had enough evidence to draw up a warrant for Pertellis's arrest. Could he not send his men into the Grey Mastiff with the warrant and have them boldly arrest the man and walk out with him?

Toke's eyes became sharp and hard as a further idea occurred to him.

'The Duke wants to believe in a radical conspiracy against him, does he?' he murmured speculatively. 'Well, let him! I shall make this Pertellis out to be the leader of the conspiracy, the owner of this demon printing press and chief enemy of the Twin Queens, whether he is or isn't. Then I shall have my men march in and arrest him on the night of the next beast fight, when the Locksmiths have their meeting in the Grey Mastiff. I'll make sure my men bring a constable with them, so he'll see the "radical leader" ringed around with Locksmiths. Let's see how much the Duke trusts Mr Goshawk once he hears reports that the Locksmiths have been discovered hiding the leader of the radicals from the forces of justice . . .'

The Locksmiths would be disgraced but, importantly, they would not be arrested. None of them would be placed in danger, and so nobody could accuse Toke of breaking the guildsmen's Rules.

'I shall have to send in Clent and his bold-eyed girl to spy out the place before we act,' Toke resolved. If Goshawk had read Clent's report, he would know the poet's name, but would probably not recognize his face.

In any case, it was better to risk an irrelevant rogue than one of the Stationers' valued guildsmen. 'Casualties of war,' Toke growled, as he picked up a pen to write out Clent's new orders.

That evening, Toke's letter lay on the dinner table in front of Clent, liberally smeared with gravy. Toke had given a sparse account of the night's events, naturally omitting all mention of Clent's intercepted report. Somehow, as Clent repeated this account to Mosca, it became a tale of breakneck chases and exchanged pistol fire.

Mosca listened, wide-eyed. 'So . . . the Locksmiths got Mr Pertellis in this Grey Mastiff, then?'

'Yes – and in three nights' time, the Stationers plan to march into the Grey Mastiff and snatch this radical teacher from Goshawk's very own gloved fingers. Word will reach the Duke that when this firebrand Pertellis was arrested, he was caught in a conspiratorial tableau with the Locksmiths . . . and the Duke will smite his noble brow with grief at his own blindness, and throw off his Locksmith flatterers. Our task is to spy out the tavern beforehand, and make sure that Hopewood Pertellis is within. A simple matter for two fox-witted souls like ourselves.'

The fox-witted souls bickered cheerfully over the last helping of broth, unaware that in another part of the city Aramai Goshawk was rereading Clent's report and peering at the names of Eponymous Clent and Mosca Mye.

K IS FOR KIDNAPPING

'I want my goose back!'

'Mosca, while your affection for your anserine accomplice does you credit, I hardly think—'

'I want my goose back!'

'I can see that your orphaned state has caused you to regard the bird as a family member, perhaps a particularly beaky uncle—'

'Mr Clent, I want my goose back!'

'Have you forgotten that by your own account Mr Partridge is planning to roast my heart in the sun?' bellowed Clent. The conversation had made little progress over the last half-hour and he was starting to lose his temper.

'You could give him money. Bet he wouldn't eat your heart if you give him enough money. Bet the Stationers gave *you* money for what I found out.' Clent had been so delighted with Mosca's discovery of the Floating School that the pair had actually got on tolerably well for two days. However, Mosca had just woken to a gleaming morning, and the sight of Clent trying on a new cravat. Instantly she had guessed that he had been paid without telling her. 'They did pay you, didn't they? That's my money, or near enough anyway.'

'Read through our "ship's articles" again, child, if you have not forgotten your letters as well as your duties. You are bound to obey my orders, and you stand to receive a generous salary at the end of the year. Before this explosion of ingratitude, I had even *considered* recommending that the Stationers grant you a place in a school, as you requested.' It seemed to occur to Clent that their voices had become rather loud given the thin walls of the marriage house, and his voice dropped to a whisper. 'If, of course, you would rather throw away all hopes of bettering yourself in favour of buying yourself a mangled old fowl that seems to be harbouring all the demons of fable within his moth-eaten breast, then so be it. The choice is yours.' Clent folded his arms, and his mouth became an adamant plum.

A place in a Stationer school . . . Somehow Mosca's thoughts were not where she had left them; the idea of school had been so real to her. She had imagined the cool of a slate between her fingers, and had seen herself cutting quills for the younger children. She had even puzzled over how she would stop Saracen eating the inkbottles. Now the school seemed a means to an end, and that end was Lady Tamarind and the Eastern Spire.

Two images flitted before Mosca's eyes.

Mosca saw a woman stepping out of a white carriage, lifting her hem slightly to protect it from contact with the street. Two footmen dusted the cobbles with swansdown brushes so that they could not stain her satin shoes. She swept through a door into a ballroom where the walls were hung with the hides of white tigers. She danced, and, from mahogany tables, stuffed ermine stoats watched her with pearls instead of eyes. She drank from a crystal glass. She was too beautiful to smile or flush, and her eyes were black, black as pepper. They were Mosca's eyes.

Then Mosca saw the darkened hold of the *Mettlesome Maid*. Saracen was scrambling unsteadily over a heap of wooden and leaden Beloved, his leathery feet sliding on ridged faces and graven wings. He gave little chuckling noises in his throat, but his neck drooped with weariness and hunger. He nibbled at the pointed nose of the Kind Lady of Fools, and then shook his head disappointedly. Soon, when he was weaker, the sailors would pull up the planks and come after him with spades and boathooks . . .

'Well?' Clent was waiting with a look of satisfaction on his face. 'Have you recovered your senses and made your choice?'

She had.

'I Want My Chirfugging Goose Back!'

'Well, you can't have it!' Clent snapped, scarlet-faced.

'Then you're a mouldy-mouthed liar an' a cheat an' I'm not doing nuffin' for you no more!' screamed Mosca. Before she had finished the sentence, Clent had stormed from the room, slamming the door.

His boots made a very satisfying thud as they hit the wall. All Mosca's strength was not enough to tear

 179

the sleeves of his coat from the body, so she settled for stamping his new wig flat until it resembled a terrier that had fallen foul of a dustcart-wheel.

As she was standing, panting, her boots dusted with flour from Clent's wig, she suddenly saw with absolute clarity what it was that she needed to do. If she could squeeze no reward from Clent and the Stationers, she could think of only one person who might give her money for Saracen's ransom, and that was Lady Tamarind.

Clent had left paper, quill and ink bottle in the window seat. Snatching them up, she scratched out a quick letter.

Dear Ladyship,

> *The Stationers have an antipathy to the Locksmiths, on account of they suspect they are running a printing press to make the Duke go into fits. This is all to help them take over the city somehow.*
>
> *The Locksmiths are hiding a radical called Hopewood Pertellis who teaches forbidden books to a school in alleys and I seen him do it. They are hiding him in the Grey Mastiff. Tomorrow night the Stationers will go in and arrest him when he is all ringed about with Locksmiths, so the Duke will find out how tricky and toad-spotty the Locksmiths are and slap his head.*
>
> *Mosca from the Road.*

She rolled the letter into a narrow pipe, tucked it into her apron pocket, and hurried from the marriage house with her heart beating.

''Scuse me.' She tugged at the sleeve of a woman with a basket of gillyflowers. 'Can you tell me the way to the Plumery?'

The woman's smile faded. She was of middle age, with a broad, cheerful face that sun and hard work had polished and cracked like wood. She gazed sadly at Mosca as if she had seen a ghost of a dead daughter standing behind her.

'Of course, blossom.' She whispered directions gently, as if she was talking to an invalid, and Mosca left her, feeling more ill and uncertain than before. As she walked, the streets dwindled into alleys, the houses became dwarfish, and then she took a turning into an open square and stopped dead.

Even before Mosca saw the shrines of Goodman Postrophe at every corner she sensed something deathly in the square's stillness. No sheep or goats cropped the central green. Among the grass, their quills planted deep into the earth, nestled thousands of feathers – pigeon, magpie, dove, pheasant, rook. Most were broken-backed from the wind, and ragged from rain. Mosca felt superstitious fear climbing her spine on spider-feet.

Mosca had never seen a plumery before. She remembered a pedlar talking about the Plumery in the Capital:

. . . didn't have room to do it proper, you see, not inside the city walls. 'Sides, most of the time the bodies were shovelled into

 181

the same great pits outside the city bounds, and even after the
Birdcatchers fell, nobody had the stomach to go pickin' through
the bones all jumbled together and working out what was
whose . . .

There would be a similar desolate memorial in every city in the Realm. Each of those feathers represented a grave, a man or woman or child killed by the Birdcatchers. This she had already known, but she had not expected to feel as if she were staring into the city's open wound. Mosca could not guess how many thousands of feathers twitched in the early breeze. There were too many to think about safely, and she decided not to care whether the tiniest downy feathers were children.

She realized that she was not alone. People moved around the green in ones and twos, talking in church whispers or bowing their heads in silence. Some knelt between the feather plots, replacing broken plumes with fresh. The Praymaster chaplains from the cathedral would renew all the feathers on St Berrible's day, but clearly some of the departed had families who liked to keep their graves in fine feather.

On a little pedestal sat a statue of Goodman Claspkin, He Who Carries Our Words to Departed Kin, one hand extended as if to cup the chin of a beloved child. Her knees weak with cliff-edge shakiness, Mosca knelt and reached a trembling hand towards the clump of pheasant feathers at his feet, as if she too had come to renew the plumes on a loved-one's grave.

She tugged at a feather. It slid out, to show a tube of

horn fastened to the feather's stem. Struggling against the urge to look around, she pulled her letter out of her pocket, slid it into the tube, and pushed feather and tube back into the earth. It was done. She had broken the Stationers' oaths of secrecy, and if they ever found out, they would put her in a printing press and crank it down until she popped like a chestnut . . .

She hurried back to the marriage house, thinking that everybody was wearing gloves and was watching her strangely. She opened the door of the room she shared with Clent, and Clent himself turned to stare at her, a queer and unfocused expression on his face.

'What?' Her hands twitched. Had he seen the earth on her knees? Did he suspect her? How could he suspect her? If he did, Mosca just wanted him to say so. 'What?'

'Perhaps . . .' Clent held up a finger, and peered at a point over Mosca's head, trying to stare his thoughts into clarity. 'Perhaps if you truly wish it we will retrieve this winged warzone you call a goose. But.' He waved his finger. 'But. The Goose Must Earn His Keep. If it becomes necessary, he must be considered a . . . an Agent of the Stationers' Company, and committed to their cause.'

Mosca stared at him, uncertain whether to feel relieved or suspicious. Clent seemed to have gone slightly mad, but mad in her favour. Lady Tamarind might not pay her for a day or two – why not take advantage of Clent's change of heart?

'S'pose that'd be all right,' she agreed warily.

'Splendid. Make my wig and coat ready, and we shall brave Mr Partridge after breakfast.'

The wig!

Clent strode down to order breakfast.

A few minutes later, Mosca was knocking at the Cakes' door with a muffled, rapid urgency. There was a tiny noise within that she took to be a call to enter. She had flung open the door and taken two steps into the room before she realized it had been nothing of the sort. The Cakes was on her knees by her bed, a piece of embroidered cambric gripped in both hands and her mouth making a loose, rubbery shape as if she were about to cry.

Apologies did not come naturally to Mosca, so she did not make one. Instead she ruefully held up the wig by way of explanation.

'It's Mr Clent's . . . I . . . stepped on it.'

The Cakes sniffed, and her face sharpened into its usual business-like expression.

'Looks like most of the Mandelion militia stepped on it an' all.' She stood up, biting in both her lips, and walked over, taking the wig from Mosca's hand. 'Here, I got a brush for this kind of thing. We rent out wigs to grooms as can't afford it and you should see the state we get some of 'em back in . . .'

Mosca watched as the other girl made little fussy, twitching gestures with the brush, which somehow seemed to tease curls out of their tangle, so that they sprang back into their intended shapes.

'So . . . Bockerby beats you a lot, then?' As far as Mosca was concerned, crying alone meant one thing.

'What? Oh no, almost never . . . it's just weddings. I always cry at weddings.'

Mosca stared.

'What – at all of 'em? But you live in a marriage house! No wonder you're so thin, you must be all dried up inside with squeezin' out tears.'

'I just like weddings,' the Cakes said sadly. 'I like watching folks write their names in the register – the ones that can write. I like giving 'em the Cakes. I like the happy ones, an' the frightened ones, an' even the ones in their altitudes with gin. I like watching 'em in their best bits of ribbon and their grandfather's smartest waistcoats. I like throwin' the honesty pods over 'em for good luck. I guess I just . . . keep hoping some of it'll rub off on me, somehow.'

The hand holding the brush drooped miserably. Clearly the Cakes had to be cheered up, or the wig would never be salvaged.

'Well, it might rub off. You're not ugly or anything. You're just sort of pointy.' Mosca had a feeling that these encouraging words had sounded better in her head, but as it happened the Cakes was too despondent to take offence.

'Doesn't make any difference. No one's going to want me with my Base Beginnings.' The Cakes gave Mosca a narrow glance, then sighed. 'Oh well, someone'll tell you, I guess. My father meant to marry my mother, but somethin'

185

put it out of his mind and he went to sea instead, and when he came back my mother was dead and I was ten.'

'Didn't he do nothin' for you?'

'Course,' the Cakes answered curtly, then gave Mosca another appraising glance. 'Took me in, didn't he? Gave me a position. Can't say fairer than that.'

'Bockerby's your father?'

'Course. An' he's kind when we're alone, treats me right and everything. I think he's sorry he didn't marry and can't call me his daughter. It's funny really – we write out lots of marriage licences for people, and sometimes if they ask us to, we write down the dates a bit earlier than they should be, so children look like they were born proper and legal after the wedding. But it's too late to do that for me.'

The Cakes pushed up her fists inside the wig and turned it about, inspecting it critically. 'That'll do, I think.'

By the time Clent returned to his rooms, Mosca was waiting for him and polishing his boots. Her expression of unaccustomed innocence seemed to alarm him a little, but he passed no comment, and they walked down to breakfast without further argument.

He was unusually quiet throughout breakfast. Mosca decided that his head was probably full of Schemes, and that if he wished to share them with her, sooner or later he would. Her own head was full of Saracen and the thought of seeing him again.

From Bockerby they learned that most barges and

narrowboats could be found moored on the wharf near the Dragmen's Arches, and after breakfast they set off for the wharf.

The Dragmen's Arches had been cut into the old fortified wall so goods could be unloaded from boats and brought into the city. Mosca and Clent slithered down one of the brick ramps that descended through the arches, covered with wooden slats so barrels could be rolled up more easily.

'There she lies.' Mosca tugged Clent's sleeve and pointed.

The *Mettlesome Maid* had been laid up at the end of the quay, at a slight distance from the other barges, as if, despite her name, she had become timorous or coy. One of her crewmen squatted on deck, twisting and plaiting some narrow lengths of line, the cotton startlingly white against his tanned fingers.

'Indeed. Mosca – I fear it is often incumbent upon a gentleman to prevent injury to the feelings of others, regardless of his own sentiments. At this moment I sense that Mr Partridge must be quite mortified at the way he spoke of me to you. If I were to approach the boat, and he were already in a state of mental turmoil, the sight of me might cause him considerable distress, and he might . . .'

'. . . rip your heart out an' spike it on a boathook an' roast it an' eat it an' throw the bits he didn't like to the seagulls . . .'

'Mosca . . .' Clent glanced at her, then closed his eyes and gave a little shudder, as if he had looked down into a

187

moral well at her benighted soul, and had been gripped by vertigo. He dropped a purse into her waiting hand. 'Take the money. Retrieve your goose. Let us have the matter over with.'

Mosca approached the *Mettlesome Maid* with some trepidation, encouraged only by the fact that Partridge was nowhere to be seen.

'Good morning, sir?' she called out quietly. The crewman glanced up at her, then let his eyebrows rise and his knotwork fall into his lap.

'Blood and breath. Well, that's something. Hey! Dotheril! The Niece is here.'

A mournful, eerie sound rose up from the belly of the barge. It sounded like a cat in a bucket. It might have been a sob of relief.

'Come on.' The sailor stood up and held out a hand. Mosca took it and tripped carefully aboard up the gangplank.

'Is Mr Partridge about?' Best to know the worst quickly.

'No, he's not. I'm hoping you've nothing particular you need to say to him either, for I cannot tell you where he might be found. He went off yesterday, saying that he'd be gone for a while as he had some business to attend to – which I took as meaning business at the Ship Inn. When he was not back by dusk, I knew he'd crawled into a bottle. When he wasn't back by morning, I thought maybe someone had stoppered the bottle before he could get out.' He gave a grim laugh.

'So – you talked to him yesterday evening, then?'

Mosca was frightened to ask whether Partridge had left his men detailed instructions involving her heart and boathooks, after chasing her over half the city.

'No – not since yesterday lunchtime. The captain'll roll back down that ramp like a barrel before long, I'll take my oath, but till then I can't tell you where to find him.' The sailor suddenly glared at Mosca, and gave a slightly menacing motion as if loosening his shoulder. 'Of course, now it comes into my head that perhaps the captain's in a jail somewhere, clapped in darbies. Would you know something of that? Has your uncle decided to blow the widd?'

'No . . .' Mosca bit her lip, not entirely sure what she had been asked, but certain that 'No' was probably the safest answer. She looked about for a change of subject, and gave a vague gesture in the direction of the deck.

'Is . . . is he all right?'

'Not so hearty. A broken ankle, but he'll rally.'

'That's not what I . . .' Mosca stopped short of explaining that she had been enquiring after her goose, not the injured Dotheril.

'What are you waiting for?' There was an echoing wail from below the planks. 'Get-this-thing-out-of-oh-Beloved-above-it's-walking-up-my-chest-again . . .'

The sailor tugged up the edge of canvas, and gestured Mosca under it with a jerk of his head. Three planks had been left out of place, presumably to let air reach the trapped Dotheril. Mosca pulled off bonnet and cap, and swung her upper body down through the crack, head downwards.

The first thing she saw was an inverted Saracen, his white plumage gleaming moonishly in the darkness. Fat little soap bubbles of joy burst in his throat as he saw Mosca.

Another fainter sound from the region of his feet drew Mosca's attention to the object upon which he stood.

'Mr Dotheril . . . 's all right, just don't move. 'S all right, really, he only stands on your face if he likes you.'

'I can't say as my feelings is likewise,' hissed Dotheril through his teeth. There were tight creases around the corners of his mouth, as if he had been doing everything through his teeth for some time. He was bracing his elbows against the shifting beach of graven godlings, and trying to drag himself backwards. One of his hands was tightening around an oaken pedestal.

'Please don't go hitting him with Good Lady Syropia the Forgiver, it's not good for your soul, or your health neither. You'll go frightenin' him. A wild dog tried to bite him once, an' he broke its neck.'

Dotheril's hand faltered, and released the icon.

'C'mon, Saracen, we'll find you barley.'

'Barley!' Dotheril's voice shook with rage. 'It's had bread, and cheese, and biscuits, and strips of mutton – not a scrap could they throw to me without that devil clapping its beak around it, and shaking it down its gullet . . .'

Saracen waddled forward, chuckling solemnly, until

190

Mosca's falling hair tickled over his beak and white neck. She closed her arms around his solid, white weight, and struggled herself upright.

Bonnet back in place, she pushed her way out through the tarpaulin. The sailor who had been waiting nearby suddenly remembered that he had left his ropework near the bow, and nearly kicked bales overboard in his haste to recover it. As Mosca climbed gingerly after him to make her farewells, it seemed to occur to him that light for working was far better at the stern, and he scrambled away from her to find a suitable seat.

'You don't want me to wait for Mr Partridge to come back?'

'No!' The sailor's voice had a tight sound, as if he was trying to hold his breath. 'You just . . . just go your ways.'

'And you don't even want—' Mosca's hand half reached for the money in her pocket.

'No!'

'Right then.' When Mosca's feet had crossed the plank back to the jetty, the sailor's shoulders relaxed a little.

When he saw Mosca approaching along the street with Saracen in her arms, the muddied look of concern on Clent's face suddenly dropped away, and he positively beamed.

'Let us regard this latest recruit in our Grand Objective.' Clent put his head to one side as he pretended to examine the goose, taking care all the while to stay out of reach of Saracen's beak and wings. 'Hmm. Chin rather weak, but

 191

fiery eyes courageously spaced. Shoulders drawn back, chest thrust forward nobly – yes, madam, I think your friend has the makings of a soldier.'

With every step away from the Dragmen's Arches, Clent's mood seemed to soar, and they dragged Mosca's own spirits skyward like a man-sized kite. The smiles he directed at Saracen were so generous and affectionate that she felt a rush of warmth towards Clent. Not enough warmth to make her return *all* the money, of course, but enough for her to tell him that Partridge's men had asked for only a little ransom.

'Admirable – no doubt you sliced their price with that pointed little tongue of yours. There must be celebration, and now –' he tossed his purse three yards in the air and caught it on the descent, to the disappointment of a couple of eagerly watching urchins – 'now we have the means to conduct ourselves properly at the Grey Mastiff tomorrow night. I hear that their wine is a symphony, and that for tuppence they will sell you a cream pudding the size of a bath. Many fine ladies and gentlemen put their powdered noses through the door, and it will do you no harm to be seen there – but first we must prepare to be worth their gaze. Your poor shoes must be resoled, and I fear that we will need a muzzle and leash for our leather-footed comrade – lest he commandeer another barge as he did the *Mettlesome Maid*.'

Somehow Mosca was left with the feeling that they had come into money, rather than just losing less than expected. Somehow it was almost impossible to remember that not very long before, Clent had been arguing bitterly against cobbling Mosca's shoes or retrieving Saracen. Clent simply swept such memories away, with the impatience of someone shoving crockery aside so that he can spread a treasure map across a table. The facts fell to the floor with a fractured tinkle and were forgotten.

The leatherworker refused to cut the price of the muzzle and lead, even when Clent explained that Saracen had once saved Mosca's life by dragging her out of a burning church and he now had to be muzzled to prevent him turning a violent beak upon himself for having failed to rescue the rest of her family. However, the leatherworker said it was a touching tale and that it did him good to laugh now and then. He gave them each a sip of gin, which made Mosca's nose numb and lit a candle behind her breastbone. They bought a muzzle meant for a young foxhound. When Saracen shook his head, it rattled a bit but did not fall off.

The cobbler enjoyed the tale as well, particularly with the addition of two storms and a gypsy conspiracy. Despite Clent's insistence that Mosca had worn her soles thin on a pilgrimage to a hilltop shrine to Goodman Claspkin to pray for her dead family, the cobbler would not cut his price either. However, after he had stitched on Mosca's new soles he gave them half an oyster pie to break between them. They cupped it in their hands and munched it on the way back to the marriage house, the juices running down their chins.

Only as they reached their rooms did Clent's manner sober a little. 'My mind seems alive with ideas this evening, and I must spear them with my quill. I am sure I can rely upon you not to interrupt me.'

After he had disappeared into the closet, Mosca perched on the edge of the bed with her pointed chin resting on her hands, thoughts intertwining behind her black eyes to become a plan. Perhaps a sly, buzzing whisper in Mosca's brain told her that she had a chance to make a useful ally and put someone in her debt. Perhaps, however, a part of her had heard the Cakes' story with a sense of recognition, and guessed at the other girl's loneliness.

It was midnight when Mosca crept to the door of the Cakes' bedroom, late enough for the other girl to be making no attempt to stifle the sound of her sobs. There was a snuffly sort of a gasp when Mosca knocked, and when the Cakes opened the door, her mob-cap was pulled almost down to her chin to hide her red eyes.

'You got something of your mother's?' whispered Mosca.

'What?' The Cakes gave up and lifted her mob-cap frill to see who was talking.

'Your father, he does the marriages sacred to Leampho with the One Wakeful Eye, don't he?'

The Cakes nodded.

'I was remembering . . . back where I come from, there's this old ceremony they do sometimes, when you want to marry someone who's alive to someone who's dead – if they both wanted to marry. I mean, like, if they were just about to marry and then the man got stamped to death by a cow or fell in the rapids. I been thinking an' I think I can remember how it goes. You got something of your mother's?'

'Yes, a bit of lace and a stuff gown. But is that sort of ceremony legal?' the Cakes asked doubtfully. 'I mean, legal enough to put in the register?'

'We can't tell anyone,' Mosca said quickly. 'It's not the sort of thing you can tell about. I mean, it's like Leampho with one eye open and one eye closed, right? Our eyes are open to see this, but the rest of the world has to have its eyes shut.' Mosca almost believed her words herself. 'What does it matter if no one else knows? *You'll know*. Come on, and put the shawl round you. I got one of your father's cravats off the back of a chair in one of the chapels.'

The little chapel Mosca chose bristled with clay vases full of dried honesty plants, the sheer shell pods reflecting the light of the Cakes' candle like so many pale eyelids. The white lace shawl had split a few stitches but, draped over the head of the Cakes, it gave her an other-worldly look and hid her tearfulness. As soon as Saracen had satisfied himself that the cravat was not edible, he allowed it to be tied around his neck without further argument.

'You stand there, and play your mother . . . and Saracen'll be your father.'

Mosca wet her lips, took a breath, and began to speak. She pulled out rags of wedding words she had heard by

 195

listening through the thin marriage-house walls. She patched them with pompous-sounding phrases from her father's books. She stitched the whole together with the scarlet thread of her own imagination.

In an alcove on the wall, a porcelain Leampho stood with one eye closed, as if winking to let Mosca know that he was on to her. The Cakes, on the other hand, snuffled her way through the ceremony, and at the end had to wipe her eyes with the shawl.

'It must be a real wedding,' she said at last, 'or I wouldn't be crying.'

Mosca put the cravat in her hand and left the Cakes to enjoy her tears.

Mosca retired to her trucklebed, where she lay in a state of happy sleeplessness for almost an hour, listening to the brook-like sounds of Saracen chuckling himself to sleep. It seemed that at last things were turning out as they should.

At the very moment when Mosca slipped into sleep, Tamarind was waiting for an audience with her brother. It was a peculiar and unsociable hour for an interview, but the Duke's whims had become more irregular recently. Her face powder hid any sleepless circles around Tamarind's eyes.

Most visitors to the Duke's residence in the Western Spire found themselves trying to blink away double vision, and pinching the bridge of their nose to clear a headache. Every desk, every shelf, every chair, every stair, everything here had its twin. Tamarind, however, was accustomed to the obsessive symmetry, even the window-shaped alcoves painted with matching views in place of the recalcitrant countryside.

'Beautiful Tammy!'

Resplendent in an emerald-green dressing gown, the Duke strode forward to take his sister's hands in greeting. Like many of his line, Vocado Avourlace was a handsome man. When he had first arrived back to reclaim his family's ancient rule over Mandelion, he had seemed the very picture of the hero come to usher in brighter times.

At first only Tamarind had noticed the awkward, disquieting way his expressions changed, as if a puppeteer were pulling wires to move his face muscles, and doing it rather badly. Nowadays she saw the fear in everybody's eyes. Her brother was going out of tune like an old piano, and nobody would come to retune his strings. Dukes and kings may go mad at their leisure, for nobody has enough power to stop them.

'Come and sit down, I have wonderful news.'

Tamarind seated herself.

'Your good news, Vocado,' she prompted him gently, with the same quiet, level tone she used for her pet crocodile. The Duke's eyes were large and brown, but dull and lifeless. He blinked, and for a moment they became very bright, like pebbles licked over by a wave. After a second they dulled again, as if drying in the sun.

'I thought I would never hear from Them again, after . . .' A small palsy passed across the Duke's face. He never spoke directly of his broken engagement to Queen Peri. 'But They have forgiven me.' Reverently, he drew out two identical letters with matching seals, and placed them on his lap. 'Their Majesties . . .' There was a world of awe, ache and longing in the whispered words.

'That is wonderful, Vocado.'

'You never believed They would forgive me, Tamarind,' he added sharply.

'Of course I did.' Tamarind softly stood and moved around behind him so that he could not see her face. Her hands trembling slightly, she lifted his ornate, powdered wig from his head. She took an ivory comb from her hair and ran it through his brown hair, as carefully as if she was calming a dangerous beast. 'What do the letters say?'

'They say that I must find the master of the printing press that profanes their good name. And I shall. I shall make harpsichord keys out of his bones for Their Majesties to play when they come back to rule Mandelion. Little white keys for their little white fingers.' The Duke twisted his head to look into Tamarind's startled face. 'I am joking, Tammy.' He gave a sudden, disquieting smile. 'You never seem to know when I am joking any more.'

It was true. Even Tamarind, who had spent her life trying to govern her brother, was finding him ever harder to predict or understand.

'What else do they say?'

'They advise me on how to know my enemies,' he murmured, then looked at her suspiciously over his shoulder. 'Why are you so keen to know? You have things on your mind, Tamarind. Some day I think I will open up your head to find out what they are.' He stared at her for a few moments, then smiled to show that he was joking. Above the smile his eyes kept staring at her.

Tamarind's gaze dropped to the letters on her brother's lap. With satisfaction she noted the wax seal on each letter, the imprint of the Twin Queens' insignia. It had cost her considerable trouble and expense to have the signet ring made secretly in the Capital, but she prayed the fruits would be worth it.

'And . . . have they helped you know your enemies, Vocado?'

'My mind will not settle.' The Duke gently stroked the letters with his fingertips, as if the paper was living skin. 'Sometimes when I have been reading these letters I look into the clouds for the face of my enemy, and I seem to see Aramai Goshawk staring back at me. But, Tamarind, what am I to do? This radical conspiracy must be crushed – I see their hand in everything – helping highwaymen escape, rousing my people to riot . . . My constables are useless. The Stationers too. Goshawk tells me that he has troops upstream who can be in Mandelion in two days if I give the word. Only the Locksmiths can help.'

'That is not true.' Tamarind circled her brother to stand before him, and dropped to her knees. 'Goshawk is not your only choice. *I* can help. Off the coast a ship stands ready with troops from Jottland – awaiting word from *me*.'

'The Watermen have sworn that they will not permit any troops to be brought along the waterways from the coasts, until the Succession is decided,' the Duke answered dully.

'You might distract them. If you gave them enough money, you might persuade them to go upstream and delay the Locksmiths' ships and . . .'

'Why do you wish to put me at odds with the Watermen, Tamarind?' The Duke scowled, and Tamarind could sense the floor becoming quicksand beneath her feet. It was time to gamble all her gains, and she did so without a tremble.

'You must listen to me, Vocado. The Locksmiths are playing you false. The Stationers have discovered the identity of the man running the radical conspiracy, the master of the villainous printing press. They have not arrested him because he is being protected. The Locksmiths are hiding him, Vocado.'

An ugly sickle curl was developing in the corners of the Duke's mouth. The curl appeared when he was on the brink some cruel or violent act. It had appeared on the day of the fateful badminton match.

'I can prove it.' A frightened moth was a-flutter behind Lady Tamarind's scar. She could not read her brother, or guess whether his current anger boded ill for Aramai Goshawk or for herself. 'Put some men at my disposal, and I will prove it to you by tomorrow night. You . . . will want time to think about this, Vocado. I will leave you.'

She composed herself outside the door. Her scar

throbbed so hard it numbed her cheek. In one instant she had staked everything – her influence over her brother, the fate of Mandelion, her own life. All now depended on the decision the Duke was about to make. Vocado Avourlace was alone with the voices that only he could hear. They murmured from twinned smiles in painting, tapestry and stained-glass window. The words that whispered from the newly arrived letters, however, spoke most clearly.

'We have every faith that you will find the culprits,' whispered the twin voices, 'and when you do, arrest them without hesitation. The law is your lance and you may wield it as fiercely as you see fit in order to crush the evildoers . . .'

'Yes . . .' For days the Duke's thoughts had been circling giddily like tea leaves in a cup. Now at last they were settling, and soon they would form a pattern which would spell out destiny for Mandelion and everyone in it.

L IS FOR LOCK-PICK

To Mosca's delight she was granted the next morning off without even having to ask.

She left the marriage house and immediately turned her steps towards the Plumery. Perhaps there would be a chance to take her own letter back. Perhaps there would be a response from Lady Tamarind. In truth she was not sure where her hopes lay.

Again she walked between the desolate feather lawns, again she knelt before Goodman Claspkin. She pulled up the message feather, and could instantly see the dark roll of her letter through the translucent yellow horn. She was safe, she was in time, she was bitterly disappointed. She pulled it out . . . and discovered that it was not her letter.

'You have done well,' it read. 'Keep me informed of your employer's doings and let me know when you have found a place in a Stationer school.' A tiny object rolled out of the letter into Mosca's palm. It was a seed pearl.

With the pearl wrapped in her handkerchief and hidden deep in her skirt pocket, Mosca sleepwalked back through the streets. She would never sell the pearl. She would keep it forever. She had a piece of Lady Tamarind in her pocket.

She was roused from her trance by the cries of the 'chapmen', pedlars who carried cheap books for sale. It was hard to part with the little money she had slyly won, but she could not resist the sight of a stack of chapbooks, with their rough-cut pages and bright cloth covers.

'You got anything 'bout what happened to the Ragged School?' Mosca asked one chapman, who stooped to search his pack.

'You want something on the Book Riots, do you? Who you buying it for?'

'Me.'

The chapman did not look as if he believed her. 'Bit bloody for a lass – wouldn't you like a nice ballad about Captain Blythe like the other girls?'

'I don't mind blood. I like books with gizzard and gunpowder in 'em.'

'Right you are, then, here's "A Report on the Tumultuous Disorders of the Year of the Dead Letter".' A yellowed, well-travelled chapbook was placed in Mosca's hand.

Soon Mosca was squatting on the grass of a pleasure garden and chewing her way through a penny loaf, eager to devour her new chapbook on the Book Riots.

. . . In Mandelion the Year of the Dead Letter will be forever remembered for the so-called Book Riots, where murders and mischief were committed by a deluded mob, spurred on by the words of one Quillam Mye . . .

Mosca felt as if someone had filled her head with gunpowder and then blown sparks into her ear.

. . . After the fall of the Birdcatchers the Stationers decreed that all books should be hunted out and brought to them. All those that bore no Stationer seal or that smacked of Birdcatchery were piled high in the marketplace and burned while children danced around the pyres with much merriment . . .

. . . a celebrated Stationer named Quillam Mye condemned the Book-burnings. He wrote Pamphlets commanding all free men to defend their books, and made Speeches from atop the Unlit Pyres. Inflamed and deceived by his words, a vast Mob took to the streets, offering outrage to the Duke's men, breaking Windows without number, and bloodily striking down all who would not join them in shouting Mye's name . . .

. . . it is said that Quillam Mye used witchcraft to escape Mandelion before justice could befall him, so that he might spread Birdcatchery and trouble in other cities . . .

'You're all pixelated!' Mosca gasped aloud. 'Witchcraft my socks! If he was a witch he'd have witched us out of Chough in three winks! And as for Birdcatchery . . .'

Her father had hated the Birdcatchers. Of course he had. Hadn't he? It suddenly seemed to her that when talking of the Birdcatchers her father had nearly always given her facts, not opinions.

She desperately tried to remember him ranting against the Birdcatchers the way everybody else did. Instead she recalled that once she had asked him who had started the rebellion against the Birdcatchers.

'Unwise people,' had been his only answer, though he had looked at her with unusual warmth. Unwise people. What did that mean? Her eyes dropped to the page again.

. . . Panople Twine, Headmaster of the Ragged School, had sided with Mye, and after Mye's disappearance the Duke in his wisdom had the walls of the Ragged School battered down. Twine's tears fell as fast as the bricks, and he died soon after of a broken heart . . .

'You broke the school,' she whispered aloud. Somehow this was the only part of the tale that she could feel and understand. Her father had broken the school.

But how could it be the same Quillam Mye? Mosca could not accept it. Try as she might, Mosca still could not imagine her father frothing at the head of a deluded mob. Then again, looking around at the green lawns, the marble fountains, the gentry having their likenesses painted in the Playing-card Makers' pagodas, it was hard to imagine Mandelion the scene of shrieks and blood and discharged muskets. But clearly the city was not as calm and sane as it seemed.

Mosca received a further hint that something was amiss when she got back to find Eponymous Clent making hats for Saracen.

Sensibly enough, he had chosen to keep his distance while doing this. While Saracen gobbled barley from a chipped china bowl, Clent crouched by the door, watching him critically with one eye shut, like an artist judging an angle for a portrait. At arm's length he held up a scrap of yellow damask, as if trying to judge how it would look against Saracen's bulging brow. A few moments later he dropped the scrap, and held up a blue rag.

'Mr Clent . . .' Mosca was for a moment afraid to ask

what he was doing, in case his answer revealed that he had gone mad during the day. Perhaps this was what happened when you stole berries from shrines.

'Ah, you're back. Tell me, do you think your friend Saracen would permit a ribbon or lace to be tied below his, as it were, chin?'

'Probably bite your ears off,' Mosca replied curtly. 'What d'you want to tie ribbons on him for?'

'Mosca, sit down.' Clent's tone was that of a kindly uncle who must break the news of the death of a beloved kitten. Mosca sat, wincing as the broadsheets in her petticoat pocket crackled loudly. 'As you doubtless recall, we agreed that Saracen should pay his way in the service of the Stationers' Company.'

Mosca twisted her mouth to one side to show that she was listening and did not like what she was hearing.

'Now, as you know, tonight we bless the Grey Mastiff with our custom. We are under orders to investigate the tavern, find out where the Locksmiths meet, and make sure Pertellis is there. Unfortunately, the part of the tavern containing the private rooms is barred to everyone but the staff, the Locksmiths and, ah, the trainers for the beast fights . . .'

'No!' Mosca shouted when her breath returned to her. 'You're not puttin' Saracen into the beast fights! I'll set 'im on you an' have 'im give you extra knees where there shouldn't be—'

'Child, child!' A kindly laugh wove through Clent's words like a golden thread. 'I thought we had reached some sort of understanding and were past such demonstrations. Mosca, you must, *must* trust me a little.' He smoothed his hair back with the air of one who is amused but perhaps a little hurt. 'The beast fights are not extravaganzas on the same scale as those in the Capital. Oh, I grant you that the Grey Mastiff's posters boast of "Clashes Between All the Heraldry Beasts of the Many Monarchs" but I understand that the reality is a rather pitiful affair. Newts painted red to resemble salamanders, tabby cats standing in for tigers, calves passing for bulls.' Clent waved the daisy-shaped rag of cloth in his hand. 'How else could we expect to enter Saracen as King Prael's Star-crested Eagle?'

Mosca glanced protectively at Saracen.

'Were not your village supporters of King Prael, anyway? Where is your sense of patriotism?'

'I keep it hid away safe, along with my sense of trust, Mr Clent. I don't use 'em much in case they get scratched.'

'Well, what about your sense of duty to your unfortunate fowl?' Clent changed tack without blinking. 'Is he never to be more than he is? You may be standing in the way of Saracen's destiny – preventing him from becoming the toast of every alehouse, the talk of every drawing room . . .'

'I don't think Saracen cares much about fame, Mr Clent. Maybe that just works on highwaymen.'

'All right, then picture this.' Clent spread his hands and smoothed the air in front of him, as if it was sand and he was preparing to draw in it. 'A darkened alleyway, in which two hardened ruffians squat, brandishing cudgels. There is an unwary step – the pair hearken and tense for attack. A short figure appears in the alleyway. It is an old goose, its neck swinging stiffly as it waddles. The two thieves smile – there will be goose in the pot tonight. But wait! One seizes the arm of the other to halt him. "By my troth," he whispers, "it is the goose from the Grey Mastiff! I shall never forget the time I saw him best that pine marten tricked out as Queen Drizzlesoft's lion." Their eyes mist over, and the cudgels hang forgotten in their hands. They let the feathered hero pass, and their minds fly back to the exploits of their forgotten soldiering days. Noble impulses of their hearts rekindle after long years, and . . .'

Clent's eye fell upon Mosca, and he halted abruptly. 'But why do I persist, seeing that your breast is clearly dead to all sense of duty and compassion? Very well, let me put the matter plainly without frills or ornament.' This sounded so unlikely that Mosca was intrigued despite herself. 'If they are not stopped, the Locksmiths will take over the city. They will place an eye to every keyhole and an invisible knife to every throat. But why should that worry you?' Clent gave Mosca a quick, penetrating glance. 'Perhaps you would like to help Lady Tamarind pack?'

'What?' Mosca sat bolt upright.

'It is no secret that Lady Tamarind has done her utmost to dissuade her brother from putting the Locksmiths in power. If they win, she will have no choice but to flee. Of course . . .' Clent paused in his pacing, then sat down opposite Mosca. 'Of course, if anyone helped Lady Tamarind by exposing the diabolical plans of the Locksmiths, she would owe them a great debt . . .'

Mosca chewed the inside of her cheek for a moment or two, then looked up at Clent with an expression somewhere between shyness and hate.

'So it's just newts an' things, then?' Her tone was blunt but uncertain.

Saracen had nudged his bowl across the floor until it chinked against the skirting board. He straightened his strong, white neck, snapped his beak at the empty air, and looked ready for anything.

Half an hour later, he was waddling fiercely towards the city's East Gate with a star of yellow worsted drooping over one eye and a black ribbon knotted becomingly under his chin. Mosca walked a pace or two behind him with his leash in her hand, jutting her pointed chin and ignoring all the people who laughed and called out to tell her that her dog was bewitched. Clent did not appear to hear the catcalls, but walked with a swing of his cane as if his companions were the most elegant imaginable.

The Grey Mastiff was built up against the old city wall, and set back from the other houses. It gave the impression of lounging against the wall, like a rakish pickpocket watching passers-by. Into the wall were set great iron rings for tethering horses, and half a dozen boys dawdled, ready to rush to the side of any rider and offer to guard his horse for a penny. The stone walls of the inn were the stale colour of old cheese rind, and pitted as if a hundred mice had set their teeth in it. When Mosca got closer she realized that some of the holes were pockmarks left by old musket fire, probably from the civil war, and she noticed that most of the fortified wall was scarred in the same way.

Clent had taken off his gloves, as he always did when he wanted to gesture aristocratically. As he approached the ostler at the door, he used them to flick away imaginary flies. Clent had also hooked his arm so that Mosca could rest her hand decorously in the crook of his elbow. This posed a few problems, since Mosca's other hand was on the leash and Saracen wanted to look at the horses, but after a moment's tug of war she managed to haul in the leash and recover her balance.

'Good evening to you, my worthy fellow. Will you tell me how we might arrange for our Star-crested Eagle to enter the lists?'

The ostler, a hefty-looking man in a white apron, stared down at Saracen. He forgot to chew the piece of straw in the corner of his mouth.

'For King Prael?' The ostler chose a polite tone, perhaps impressed by Clent's confidence, perhaps intimidated by the way Saracen had taken a companionable hold of one of his breech-buttons. 'We'll take sixpence from you then, sir, and you'll take five shillings for every fight your beast wins.'

Clent fished out the sixpence casually, as if it would not leave a hole in his purse to pain him, and the ostler tied a piece of red yarn around their wrists to show that they were trainers. They entered the Grey Mastiff inn, Saracen reluctantly releasing the ostler's leg.

From the high rafters dangled tiny wooden medallions, each with its own royal crest painted on it. Smoke had darkened the earth-coloured murals on the walls, where cream-coloured hounds clustered around a muscled bear on its hind legs. The animals were painted with fearsomely puckered muzzles and glaring, lopsided eyes that looked almost human.

A blackened oak door was flung wide now and again as serving men pushed through, holding great plates of roast pigeons and tartlets above their heads. The air from this door roared with heat and dripped with the smell of roasting beef. Above the door jutted a gallery along which sat a dozen or so figures in daintier dress, their faces and wigs thick with powder, their handkerchiefs held to cherry-painted mouths to keep away the chimney smoke.

For a moment Mosca took one of the ladies for Lady Tamarind, and something clutched at her stomach. The lady's dress was a cascade of foam exactly like the one that Mosca had seen in the carriage. Her wig was styled in the same way as Tamarind's, and a star had been painted on one cheek in the same place as Tamarind's scar. However, her mouth was too large and clumsy, and she laughed too loudly and too often. There was also a black mark on the cuff which Mosca was sure Lady Tamarind would never have tolerated. It was several inches across, and shaped like a heart on a playing card.

In one corner, a little counter with a fringed canopy brimmed with pewter pots and was backed with barrels. Behind the counter a woman darted back and forth like a wasp war-dancing, grabbing pots, filling them, slapping them on counters with little eruptions of foam, and snatching coins from a reaching forest of hands.

'Wattleebeezer?' It took a moment for Mosca to run the woman's question through her head a second time and hear it as 'What'll it be, sir?'

'A pot of three-threads, and half a pot of cider for my young companion.'

'Potthreethreadarfpotcidrcominup.' The woman winked at Mosca. As she did so, her cheek joined in the wink by bunching, like cloth puckered by a tugged thread. 'Thin'else?'

'We are entering this noble animal into the beast fights. Where may we find the training rooms so we can refresh and prepare?'

'Dorntrite.' Only the woman's pointing finger gave her two customers to understand that she had intended to say, 'Door on the right.'

Carrying Saracen so that he would not get trodden on, Mosca followed close behind Clent as he shouldered a path through the crowd. The throng was thickest around a dropped pit, just below the gallery. The pit itself was quite hidden from view by the wall of men, some in velvets, some in wool, some clutching purses, some almost teetering into the pit as they leaned forward to call out abuse or encouragement.

'Forward for King Cinnamon and the Realm!' one gentleman was shouting into the pit, while his gestures with his tankard filled his neighbours' eyes with foam. 'Remember our glorious dead of Lantwich Hill! Grab him by the beak!'

Mosca knew that the beast fights were supposed to let the supporters of different monarchs compete without actual battles breaking out. However, everyone here seemed excitable enough to draw swords and leap into the pit, so she was quite relieved when she passed through the side door and heard it close behind her.

A little passage led to a sequence of small, cell-like rooms. In one, a man in his shirtsleeves squatted beside a chittering cage. He was sipping from his tankard when his eye fell upon Saracen, causing him to sneeze out his mouthful of ale.

'Ignore him, madam,' Clent muttered. 'Anyone would think that he had never seen an eagle before.'

They found a little room, empty but for two stools and the smell of fear-stained sawdust. They had barely settled when a harassed-looking ostler pushed his head around the door.

'Star-crested Eagle? You were just in time; we're drawing tiles to see who's sparrin' with who right now.'

With growing qualms, Mosca helped to coax Saracen into a wooden crate, and she watched fearfully as the ostler carried the crate away.

Clent waited for him to pass out of earshot before murmuring in Mosca's ear, 'Come, madam, let us

 213

make use of our eyes and ears.'

They poked their heads out through the door, then Clent entered the passage one way, and Mosca the other. At the first door Mosca heard a dismal mewling and at the second the contented grunts of a young pig. At the end of the corridor was a buttery full of enormous barrels stacked on their sides. A range of cockspurs and muzzles hung from hooks on the wall. She had just taken down one of the leashes and was wondering whether to steal it for Saracen when the round lid of one of the barrels swung aside like a door, and a man climbed out. Mosca could see that the barrel was little more than the mouth to a dark tunnel behind.

The man was tall. The skin of his face had a slight lumpiness, like rice pudding. His clothes were simply styled from black cloth, but at his belt hung a silver chatelaine from which dangled five finely jewelled keys. Mosca's eyes, however, were fixed upon his hands, which were incredibly small and delicate. His calfskin gloves might have been made for a child.

Goshawk himself is a shadow among shadows, Clent had said. *It is said that his fingers are as slender and dainty as a child's* . . .

Eyes as colourless as oysters rested on her face. Mosca flinched as he raised one hand . . . then watched speechlessly as he removed his hat, handed it to her along with his cane, and walked out through the buttery door. Aramai Goshawk, the leader of the Mandelion Locksmiths, the shadow among shadows, had apparently mistaken Mosca

Mye for one of the Grey Mastiff tavern wenches.

Grimacing in her effort at stealth, Mosca tiptoed after the Locksmith and was in time to see him disappear into one of the trainers' rooms. One undignified scamper later, she was dragging Clent down the corridor to the door where she had seen Goshawk disappear, accompanying the action with much gesturing and meaningful mouthing.

The door was thick and, with both their ears warring for the keyhole, Mosca and Clent could hear little.

'If I knew, I would tell you.' One voice beyond the door raised its tone enough to become clear for a moment. 'But I don't.'

Pertellis! Mosca mouthed at Clent in glee and excitement. *That's Pertellis!*

Eyes glittering, Clent led Mosca back to the door which led to the main room of the inn.

'Quickly now. You must venture out through the street door and drop this handkerchief in a conspicuous manner. That will signal to our friends across the street that we are ready for the final scene in our little drama. I shall wait in the back corridor, ready to show them to the right room.'

Re-entering the main room of the inn, Mosca was almost deafened by a tide of patriotic shouting, interrupted by occasional outraged hooting. She elbowed her way to the door, Clent's handkerchief in her hand. Out in the street, feeling rather foolish, she let the kerchief fall to the cobbles, where a reveller immediately trod it into a puddle. Trying hard not to look around her for

Stationer spies, she pushed her way back into the tavern and towards the pit.

Meanwhile the shouting in the room seemed to have become even louder. A man standing on the wooden stairway to the gallery was trying to make his voice heard above the racket.

'. . . triumphant. The Weeping Owl of King Cinnamon is triumphant. Make good your bets, gentlemen.' The shouting dwindled to a murmur, part grumble and part satisfaction, and coins clinked as they passed from palm to palm. 'And now . . .' The speaker reached into a leather pouch, which rattled as he drew out two ceramic tiles, each shaped like a heraldry shield. 'Now we shall all witness the Struggle of two Titans of the Royal Blood, King Hazard of the line of Wilkfester, and King Galbrash the Dauntless. Gentlemen, in a moment we shall present to you the clash between . . . the Grouse Rampant of King Hazard, and the Grey Wolf of King Galbrash!'

The floor of the pit was some four feet below the level of the floorboards, and was scattered with earth, trampled feathers and spilt ale. While offers of bets were being bellowed all around, a wicker basket and a large sack were lowered down into the pit. The sack, Mosca noticed, was undeniably rather bigger than the basket.

Two boys with long poles reached down into the pit, one to overturn the basket, the other to prod at the sack. Something fluttered out of the basket.

Mosca's view was partly blocked by a fat man's elbow, but she got the impression that the something was dappled brown and not very large.

The sack was trying to stand. It found it could not and rolled around feverishly for a moment. Then a long nose poked searchingly through the neck of the sack, muzzle pulled back from the pointed teeth by the tightness of the gap. The rope at the sack's neck was loose and after a moment a narrow, grey head pushed through, to be followed by powerful shoulders and starveling flanks. The animal was shaking the sack off its haunches when it noticed its opponent.

Mosca did not see exactly what happened next, but she saw enough. A grey shape streaked across the pit, and then there was a sad little explosion of feathers.

'That was a wolf,' she whispered drily. 'A *real* wolf . . .'

'The Grey Wolf of King Galbrash is victorious!' shouted the announcer on the steps. 'But let's drink a toast to the gents who brought us yet another fine grouse – don't worry sirs, maybe some day you'll find one that can rip the giblets from a wolf!'

Applause mixed with shrieks of laughter accompanied the departure of two disappointed-looking men in barbers smocks.

'Now . . .' The announcer reached into his pouch and drew out a new tile. 'The next Spectacular Battle will take place between the Star-crested Eagle of King Prael and . . .' He rattled back into the pouch again.

Please, not a wolf, thought Mosca. *Please, not a tiger or a lion.*

'. . . and . . . the Smiling Civet of Queen Capillarie.'

Mosca had no idea what a civet was.

On one side of the pit a crate had been lowered. Mosca thought she heard Saracen's characteristic chuckling sounds from within. On the other side, a sack slowly descended. It sagged shapelessly, and it was hard to tell the size of the animal inside. Not very much larger than a cat, Mosca thought and hoped.

'Two shillings on the Civet!' shouted the fat man next to Mosca.

'Ten shillings on the Civet!' someone else called out.

Not many people seemed keen to bet on the Star-crested Eagle. Mosca had a clammy feeling that they knew more about civets than she did.

The neck of the sack was prodded open, and an ugly smell seeped into the air. For a moment a set of dull, grey claws appeared through the sackcloth, and then from the darkness inside the sack two eyes glimmered like mother-of-pearl. Then part of a face pushed at the opening, a tapering face mottled in greys like a decaying mushroom.

The lid of the crate was knocked aside with a long-handled pole, and Saracen's head appeared above the rim. His star had slid downwards, so that he now appeared to have a black ribbon bow decorating his forehead and a yellow spiky beard adorning what could loosely be called his chin. The crate rocked on its base as Saracen exploded from it in a lather of white wings.

Saracen was obviously annoyed. Something was tickling his neck, and someone had put him in a crate, and somehow he had fallen into the earth, and now the heavens were bellowing at him and spattering him with ale foam. And there was only one creature in front of him that might be responsible, a creature deftly wriggling from a sack. A brindled animal with a ridge down its back and fur in wet-weather colours. A beast with eyes full of night, and a reek like a rotting forest.

To the delight of the audience, Saracen lowered his head, holding his neck level to the ground, and hissed. There was a cheer from some followers of King Prael.

The civet lifted one paw, as if to wash it like an embarrassed cat, then a thrown muttonbone hit it behind the scruff, and it flattened its ears. It began edging sideways, its head turned to one side. Mosca had seen cats turn their heads that way when angling for a bite.

Beak agape, Saracen made a rapid run at the civet, his neck extended like a knight's lance. At the last moment the civet twisted like a flag in a gust and sprang sideways, landing with its speckled paws spread. It darted forward to bat softly at Saracen, then backed away at a crouch.

The attack looked clumsy and gentle, like a child touching another in a game of tag; but as Saracen steadied himself Mosca saw a red spot the size of a farthing bloom above his shoulder. It had been a long time since she had seen Saracen hurt by anything.

Mosca struggled her way through the yelling crowd to the wooden stairway. She had to tug the tavern spokesman by the sleeve several times before he noticed her.

'Hello, miss – you want to stand on the steps to see better? All right, but only the second step . . .'

 219

'No, I . . . that's my goose down there. I want my goose back.'

'Well, now, can't go interrupting mid-fight, can we?'

'I can give you another sixpence . . .'

'Can't be done. Now look, I have to . . .'ere, Carmine, come and take care of this, will you?' A youth stopped sweeping sawdust and pigeon bones across the floor and hurried over, wiping his hands on his apron. 'This young lady's getting a bit excitable – take her back to the trainers' rooms and let her out when the fight's done, all right?'

Carmine already had one firm hand on Mosca's shoulder, and Mosca already had one foot drawn back to kick him in the shins, when the two of them bothered to look each other in the face. They froze as they recognized each other. Carmine was none other than the clothier's apprentice who had knocked Mosca over in the street, four days before. Clearly he had an evening job.

Mosca took a step in the direction of the pit, which turned into four steps away from the pit as Carmine dragged her into a clear space.

'What are you doing here? More spying?'

'Don't know what you're talking 'bout. You're daft, you are, moths ate your wits instead of your waistcoat.'

'*I* saw you, snooping round after Mr Pertellis. And now he's gone missing. You can't hear it, but the whisper's out about you. We'll spot you wherever you go in this city.'

Mosca's face went hot. She felt scared and confused, and she decided to be angry. Anger was easiest. She was just trying to shape words around her anger when the tavern door swung open again and two Stationers shouldered their way in, flanking a constable in a black-and-green tunic embroidered with the heraldry of the Twin Queens.

Carmine turned his head to follow Mosca's gaze, and his grip tightened on her arm. When his head snapped back to look at her, his face was pale with terror and seemed in an instant to have become painfully young.

'You 'peached on me,' he whispered. He sounded startled and almost hurt. 'You really did – you 'peached on Mr Pertellis, and now you've led 'em to me, so they can take me away and put out my eyes . . .' He turned and plunged into the crowd.

A jubilant cry from the spectators roused Mosca from her stupor. To judge by the uproar, Saracen and his opponent were providing the best fight of the evening. People were standing on chairs and tables to get a view of the pit. There were enough people clustered tip-a-toe on the gallery steps now so that the announcer did not notice Mosca as she squirmed her way in among them. She was therefore in an excellent position to see everything that happened next.

She saw Saracen turning with his wings spread, terrible as storm clouds. She saw the civet with eyes full of firelight, sputtering white feathers. She saw a great number of jostling heads obscuring the pit.

She saw another couple of men in the Duke's distinctive black-and-green livery push their way through the door, then another three. Mosca was not well versed in city ways, but it did seem to her that arresting one radical or even two could hardly require so many guards. However desperate they might be, they could scarcely cause *that* much trouble . . .

A moment later she looked across to a darkened corner of the tavern, and saw Carmine releasing the wolf.

Finding its cage door suddenly open, the wolf was quite willing to skulk along the wall without drawing attention to itself, while still trying to look as much like an oversized dog as possible. However, one portly man in Apothecaries' livery felt fur brush his hand, glared down irritably, and then shrieked like a boiling kettle.

Until now, the crowd had been divided between those shouting for the goose and those shouting for the civet. Now it was divided between those who were still enjoying a fine and ribald night out, and those who had noticed that a large and hungry wolf was wandering through their midst. In spite of the wolf's tactful retreat, however, it could not be long before everyone became aware of the situation. Chairs were overturned; at least one pistol was brandished but, thankfully, not discharged. Suddenly the crowd was divided between those who had decided it was better to jump into the pit with the goose than stay on the level with the wolf, and those who had a ring-side opportunity to see exactly how bad a decision this had been.

The Duke's men completely ignored this havoc. They also showed no interest in Carmine, who, in a tearful frenzy of panic, was untethering hawks, tipping badgers out of crates, loosing owls, and upending a jar to release something that looked very much like a red-painted newt. Instead, the Duke's men progressed resolutely towards the door to the trainers' rooms.

Barely a minute after the door had closed behind them, it opened again, and Goshawk walked out through it. His stride spoke of calm haste, but his pale eyes were opalescent with rage. As he reached the street door he made a small, impatient gesture as if dusting something from his cuff, then he slid a set of manacles from his wrists and hung them over the side of an unattended tankard. He vanished out into the street – without, Mosca noticed, bothering to retrieve his cane and hat.

Two of the Duke's men burst out through the back door and stood on tiptoe, scanning the crowd with expressions of alarm and annoyance. As Mosca watched, two more of them re-emerged, each gripping one of Hopewood Pertellis's elbows. His tricorn and his spectacles were missing. There was a bloodied slit in the corner of his lip. Something plummeted in Mosca's stomach, and the taste of her cider thickened and sickened on her tongue.

Behind this trio followed the rest of the Duke's men, frog-marching a group of startled-looking middle-aged men who all wore elaborate chatelaines at their belts, calfskin gloves, and keys on chains round their necks.

'Mosca.' Somehow Clent had appeared beside the gallery steps. 'Much as I hate to drag you away from these entertainments, I find that they start to pall.' His plump face was glistening with perspiration.

It was a lot easier to approach the pit now, because no

 223

one seemed quite so keen to cluster around it any longer. The civet's owner was leaning over the edge of the pit, while a friend held on to the back of his breeches, and making 'Here, puss' tweeting sounds to lure it out from behind Saracen's crate. Fortunately, it seemed that someone had tried to throw a chair at Saracen at one point, which made it an easy matter for the goose to clamber up on it, and then beat his way through the air to Mosca's waiting arms.

'Gentlemen! Gentlemen!' The announcer could be heard shouting, his voice ragged as Mosca and Clent pushed their way to the street door. 'Contain yourselves, please, gentlemen, no pistols! The fight is called to a halt, but I am glad to announce that the Star-crested Eagle of King Prael has shown the greatest valour, and is the victorious . . .' The door closed behind them before he could finish his sentence.

If Mosca's mind had had room for anything but Saracen's safety, it might have occurred to her that something must be badly wrong if Clent was not claiming the five shillings for his victory. She might have thought it strange that Clent was leading them away through the night streets alone without looking for a linkboy to light them. And if she had looked up from Saracen's tiny cuts to observe Clent's face, white and haggard in the moonlight, she would have realized that the night was only just beginning.

M IS FOR MURDER

By the time the shrieks and clatter of tumbling brass-ware had faded in Mosca's ears, rain was falling, in drops so fine that it was scarcely more than a tickle on the skin. After ten minutes the cobbles shone as if with nervous perspiration, and Mosca's soles began to slither.

'Mr Clent . . .'

'Keep walking.'

'Can we slow down?'

'No.'

They took a left through the Drimps, where the tallow-makers' wares hung behind dusty panes like the pale fingers of ghouls.

Clent at last paused in the empty street and stared up at the moon, which was the clean, startled white of a newly sliced cheese. He blinked as if the creamy light were trickling into his eyes, then wiped his hand up his forehead into his hair. Little panicky stars darted around within his eyes as if trying to escape.

'Catastrophe,' he muttered. 'Utter catastrophe.'

'But we won, Mr Clent!' Mosca could only assume that he had missed the end of the fight. 'Saracen beat the civet and . . . and quite a lot of other people who weren't even *meant* to be in the fight, too.'

'It will be all over Mandelion by morning,' Clent intoned hollowly.

'Looked like half of Mandelion was there tonight already, nobs and guildsmen, and scholars, they all saw Saracen . . .'

'All of them at once . . . one fell swoop . . .'

'Yeah, swoops, and peckings and buttings . . .'

Clent hooked his finger into his cravat to pull it away from his throat, as if he had felt it tightening like a noose. 'There is no doubt about it. It will mean war.'

Mosca stared at her employer.

'What?'

At about the same time, some of Mosca's earlier sentences seemed to penetrate Clent's absorption.

'What?' His gaze was cold, distracted and somewhat annoyed. Then he sighed, and his face took on a look of weary tolerance. 'Mosca, the Duke has arrested all the Locksmiths in Mandelion.'

'But . . . that's good, isn't it?' Mosca asked tremulously.

'No, it is not good!'

Even during his most petulant bellowing, Mosca had never heard him speak so coldly. Once again she felt that she had glimpsed a sharp and knife-like character sheathed within Clent's pompous, ponderous exterior.

'There are Rules, child, Rules! For years, the Guildsmen's Rules have been the only thing stopping the Stationers and Locksmiths ripping each other apart.

That throng we have just left may bellow for this king's grouse or that queen's civet, but in their heart nobody *believes* in the kings or queens any more. The Realm is held together by the guilds, and everybody knows it. And if the guilds fall on each other's throats, heaven help us all.

'Mabwick Toke expected the Locksmiths to be shamed, incriminated even, but not arrested! Beloved above, the Assizes begin tomorrow! Do you know what will happen if an entire chapter of Locksmiths is executed? What was the Duke thinking?'

Mosca shook her head.

'The Locksmiths will assume that the Stationers have deliberately *broken the Rules.* There will be war. Stationers will be locked in their own closets to starve, or strangled with chatelaines. Locksmiths will be stabbed to death with steel pens, or crushed as thin as biscuits in paper mills. Then the Watermen will take the side of the Stationers, so the Hansoms Guild will back the Locksmiths, and all the other guilds will choose a side, right down to the Playing-card Makers and the Milliners. There will be murder and bloody mayhem on the highways and the waterways. The towns will starve, and soldiers turn to banditry. And all the kings and queens who have waited their chance for decades will see that there is anarchy, and they will arrive with their armies all at once. *Does that sound good?'*

Mosca's mouth was dry. She was not sure which she found more alarming: the picture Clent had painted,

227

or the startling intuition that for once he was actually speaking the truth.

'I didn't know . . .'

'No, why would you?' Clent gave her a complicated look, half bitterness, half forgiveness. 'How would you know?' He sighed. 'The worst of it is that I do not think the Locksmiths even *have* the confounded printing press.'

'What?' Everything Mosca had been told about the Locksmiths did a neat somersault in her head.

'I was listening in while they tried to torture Hopewood Pertellis into telling them who was *really* running the printing press. Then they got sidetracked into talking about the difficulty of finding a docile crocodile on the black market, for some reason. Then they started interrogating the spy they had found behind their door.'

'They found a . . .' Mosca's gaze met that of Clent.

'Oh,' she mouthed silently.

'Naturally, when they pulled me in by my collar I told them that I had hunted them out because I had a burning desire to join the Locksmiths. I got no further. They knew who I was. They knew I was working for the Stationers. Before the Duke's men arrived, it became very clear that they knew everything I had written in my last report to Mabwick Toke. Somehow, I know not how, they must have read it.'

Mosca blinked to clear her head, which seemed terribly crowded all of a sudden.

'Does that mean we're working for the Locksmiths now?'

'No. It means that we are leaving. My name was in that report.' He sighed. '*Your* name was in it, Mosca.'

The rain seemed to creep into Mosca's eyes as she ran to keep up, and it tingled at the back of her tongue with a taste that she knew was tears. She did not raise her head, for fear of seeing her beloved Eastern Spire fading before her eyes, stolen by tears and darkness.

'Mr Clent . . . you could . . . you could leave me behind. You could . . . send a note to Lady Tamarind, sayin' how you didn't want a job from her after all and sayin' . . . she should give *me* a place instead. I know you'd like it better that way.'

Clent stopped in his tracks, and stared down into her face with no expression at all. The rain was falling more heavily now, and a galaxy of droplets nestled furtively in his wig.

'No,' he said quietly at last. He loosed the bow of Mosca's bonnet ribbon, which had been working its way sideways, and tied it again. 'No, I do not think I could do that.'

The kennel ditch down the road quickly filled with rainwater which chased mess and market scraps towards the river. With them hurried Mosca and Clent.

At last they found the marriage-house sign swinging above them.

'Mosca, there is a little boat tied at the back of the shop. Bring it round to the ground-floor window – the one shaped like a scallop shell. Wait in the boat.'

Mosca nodded, her eyes and mind so full of rain that

229

she could not speak or swallow. While Clent fitted his key into the lock and turned it carefully, wincing each time the works clicked, she slipped around the side of the marriage shop and clambered over the pile of kindling that doubled as a fence. A pair of sad, rust-coloured chickens crouched under a rotten board and watched as, with Saracen clasped in her arms, she slithered awkwardly down a bank of mud and sodden grass to the water's edge.

The boat was round, like an overgrown coracle, with a couple of splintered sculls wedged inside. The mooring rope had been made fast, thoroughly but not expertly, and Mosca had a sudden mental image of the Cakes knotting it over and over for safety's sake, while her red ringlets bobbed against her nose. Then Mosca imagined the Cakes standing aghast by the waterside in the morning with her scoop of chicken feed drooping from one hand, looking at the place where the boat should have been and starting to cry.

Doesn't matter, Mosca told herself. *She cries all the time anyway.*

Mosca stepped into the boat, put Saracen down, and loosed the mooring. The sculls were clammy and heavy, so she manoeuvred the boat along the wall by grabbing handfuls of ivy and pulling. A stone face of St Marpequet, the Warden against Early Frosts, had been carved into the stone sill of the ground-floor window. He stared upwards as if his mouth was gaping to drink the rain. His impressive and aristocratic nose hooked just enough for Mosca to tie the rope to it.

Mosca had decided that she would leave Mandelion with Clent. She did not notice herself making the decision; rather the decision seemed to have fallen into her head from the rain-laden sky. She hoped that there would be no war, and that in time Clent would bring her back. There was a throb in her mind when she thought of Lady Tamarind, but for now someone seemed to want Mosca with them, and that was too strange and new to be thrown away lightly.

She did not hate Clent for the way he had spoken. For most of her life she had been at the mercy of stronger and more powerful people who cared nothing for her. She had always been afraid, and her fear had made her angry. Now, all of a sudden she began to understand that Clent also spent his days feeling powerless and afraid. Perhaps he too was angry at finding himself portly and past his prime with little to show for it, but still having to use every fox's trick just to stay ahead of the hounds.

What tricks would he be pulling from his sleeve now? He did not want to wake the house, so Mosca supposed he was planning to leave with his pockets padded. Blankets from the beds, probably, candlesticks and scraps from the kitchen . . . in her mind's eye Mosca followed Clent's figure from room to room, and then she nibbled her knuckle as she imagined him snatching the offerings from the little shrines to Leampho, Judin, Happendabbit, perhaps even pocketing the icons themselves to melt down or sell later.

He wouldn't.

Of course he would.

He mustn't.

The scallop-shaped window opened inwards and, by using the thick stems of the ivy as leafy rungs, Mosca was able to scramble on to the sill and tumble through, into the chapel beyond. To be sure, she had not been able to stop Clent robbing Goodman Postrophe's shrine, back near Chough, but this time she felt he might listen to her. He wanted her to come with him, and surely that must mean that everything had changed.

She was in the little chapel of Leampho, where Saracen had married the Cakes' dead mother. She felt her way to the door, glad that she knew her way back to her rooms despite the darkness. By each chapel door she paused to listen, but all was silent. At last she reached the rooms she shared with Clent, and gently pushed the door open. The main room was dark and cheerless, but the closet door was slightly ajar, and through it wavered a timorous hint of candlelight.

Clent had said that under no circumstances should she enter the closet, that he needed the privacy it gave him. But he wanted her to come with him, and surely that must mean that everything had changed.

Mosca pushed open the closet door. There was a candle on the floor, so near the door that for a moment she could see nothing but the brightness of its flame. Without even thinking, she stooped, picked it up, and held it at arm's length to illuminate the closet. Only then did she stare into the room in front of her and see that everything had changed.

Clent was half stooping over the heavy oaken clothes chest by the wall. His face was flushed with effort, and his knuckles white with the strain of lifting what looked like a great bolt of cloth. Peeping above the edge of the trunk was a wig that Mosca had not seen before, a mass of unpowdered brown curls. Then Clent saw her and slowly stood, and the candlelight softly traced the outline of a tanned cheek beyond the wig, and Mosca knew it was not a wig at all.

An arm was hanging over the side of the chest, she now realized, dangling quite casually like a daytripper trailing his hand over the side of a pleasure boat. There was something terribly wrong with the skin of that hand. It was pale, not an aristocratic powder-pale, not a scholarly shun-the-sun pale. It had an underground pallor, like ripped-up roots, or the eyeless things that children of Chough were told lived in the mountain caverns. The colour seemed shocked as well as shocking, and Mosca knew that the owner of the hand was dead.

The wrist was slightly crooked, as if it had broken once and never quite healed.

'I thought . . .' Clent said, handling each word carefully as if testing its edge for sharpness, 'I thought I told you to wait in the boat.'

'I come in out of the rain,' she said in a voice so small that she hardly recognized it.

'Do you have anything you want to say?' There was

 233

something frightening about Clent when he used short words.

Mosca shook her head.

'We will discuss all this later, but for now we must make the best of the situation. Come here and help me with this.'

Mosca hesitated, wondering if she could drop the candle and run.

'Listen, girl, have you any comprehension of the predicament we would find ourselves in if we were discovered fixed in this tableau?'

Well, you wanted something on 'im, the rasping voice of Palpitattle whispered laconically in Mosca's imagination. *And now*, the voice added as she took a few steps towards the chest, *now you're goin' to be an accomplice an' he'll have something on you too.*

Partridge's eyes were closed, at least. He was crammed awkwardly into the chest, as if he had mistaken it for a truckle bed and was determined to sleep there despite all discomfort.

If I run, Mr Clent'll know I'm going to raise the house, and he'll catch me and kill me . . .

She watched as Clent folded Partridge's errant limbs into the chest. He closed the lid, crouched, gripped one end, and then looked up at Mosca expectantly. It took a few seconds for her to understand his meaning, then she crouched and managed to slide her fingers under the chest.

The box was even heavier than she expected, and she

had to drop her end on to her knee. In a shambolic, improvised way the pair of them tilted and wobbled the chest between them until Clent was supporting most of the weight. They proceeded from the room one clumsy step at a time, a strange, four-legged creature with a wooden body, Mosca walking backwards.

At any moment someone would open the door, and there they would be. '*Thieves*', would be the cry. Bockerby would fling open the chest, and the cry would change to '*Murderers*'. Mosca suddenly felt how the cold wind would whip her clothes about her as she stood upon the scaffold. And the universities would cut her heart out to see how black it was.

Please, Mosca prayed silently to each and every Beloved, *please let me get away with this. I'll never ask for anything else, I promise, and if I get away with this, then some day I'll make myself rich and give all the money to the shrines, but please, please, I need to get away with this. Otherwise I'll be strung up, and hung up on a gibbet and ate by rooks and then I can't do nothing for any of you.*

In the shrine of Leampho, Clent bit off bitter words under his breath. 'We will never get the box through the window. We shall have to sit him between us with a coat over his head.'

Saracen stared up from the boat as Mosca climbed down from the sill, and he offered no comment. A moment later, Partridge's dead face appeared through the window, framed by the ivy. Then Clent could be seen with his arms around the river captain's waist, heaving him through the hole.

Mosca tried to slow Partridge's descent, but her hands seemed able to grip only feebly, and in the end the dead man fell into the boat with a crash and a splash. Mosca sank to a crouch to stop herself falling overboard as the boat bucked, and watched as one of Partridge's boots floated away down the river, filling with water as it went.

'Keep your eyes open. Our lives depend upon your perspicacity.' Clent climbed down into the boat, the creeper crackling under his weight. He took up the oars and steered the boat carefully along the wall, dipping the oars silently and drawing slowly. He paused by the bank to scrabble up some slick, fist-sized stones with his plump fingers, and then he heaved on the oars again, and the bank swung away and abandoned them.

For a while the river's current rolled the little boat about, the way a child rolls a marble between his hands. Houses fled away giddily to the left, only to reappear from the right, and the moon circled above Mosca's head like a moth. Fat raindrops hit the dark glass of the river's skin, each leaving a coin-shaped dent with a crinkled edge. The papery sound of the rain was so loud that Clent had to lean towards Mosca to make himself heard.

'The island . . .' He pointed towards the lonely pillar of Goodman Sussuratch in the middle of the river, then gestured towards Partridge. 'Stones . . . in his clothes.' He had to repeat it several times before Mosca understood.

236

The stones were deathly cold, but Mosca dared not speak or disobey. She unbuttoned Partridge's shirt just enough to slide some stones inside, holding them all the while at arm's length. She was afraid that if she leaned forward, Partridge's parted lips would start to whisper.

I want your uncle's heart spiked on a boathook so I can hear it crackle as it bakes in the sun . . .

There were deep creases running down each of Partridge's cheeks, as if twin tears had worn grooves. They joined in a red crease under his chin. Maybe all dead faces looked that way, thought Mosca. Maybe death crumpled you up like a ball of paper.

They were so low in the water that when they finally reached the island the little boat slid right under the jetty, and knocked against the rocky side of the great pillar.

'Now we wait for the mists to thicken,' Clent said quietly.

Peering out from beneath the jetty, Mosca realized that the distant row of houses was already dimming, as a veil of vapour stealthily rose from the river. Feeling the chill of water seeping into her shoes, it suddenly occurred to her that, if Clent wanted her silence, her current position was more dangerous than it had ever been in the marriage house. She kept her breathing as steady as she could, and peered stealthily at Clent. He seemed to be staring out at the mists, but she could see his face only in silhouette, so she could not be sure that he was not stealing glances at her.

Clent's manner had seemed so natural and casual when

 237

he had told her never to enter the closet. He had seemed so kind and good-humoured when he had given her the day off and thus kept her away from their rooms. Had it really all been an act? But Clent had been afraid of Partridge, and sometimes fear made you angry. Perhaps after years anger cooled, like a sword taken from the forge. Perhaps in the end you were left with something very cold and very sharp.

What exactly was it that Clent did for the Stationers? Was it just spying? Or were there times when a quill was not enough, and a knife was needed? Was that why they used him? Perhaps Partridge had bullied his way into the marriage house to find Clent, and found him in the middle of doing something very terrible . . . the way Mosca herself had just interrupted him.

'Now,' Clent whispered at last, 'take his feet.' The jetty was too low to let them stand, but somehow amid the rocking and struggling there was a splash, and suddenly there was nothing left of Partridge except a circle of foam, and his loosed cravat tracing a question mark on the water's surface. Tiny bubbles fizzed for a few moments. Silence followed, and then Clent gave a croak of alarm.

'There!'

Something had surfaced, ten yards downstream, and was gliding away with its wet shirt ballooning on its back.

'Slice the moon, the fellow has shed ballast!' Clent struggled with the paddles, but in his haste one handle became wedged between the planks of the jetty. By the time he tugged it free, the sodden shape had been swallowed by the mist.

Without a word, Clent abandoned their pursuit; he pushed away from the jetty and rowed in silence for some time. At last a bank crept into distinctness, and Mosca saw the marriage house loom into view with a mixture of relief and confusion. Why had Clent returned? Was he no longer trying to escape Mandelion?

She followed Clent up the ivy with Saracen. Obeying Clent's silent signals, she helped him carry the chest back to their rooms. Although it was now empty, her legs trembled, and twice she almost dropped it. When they reached their rooms, they found the candle low in a mess of tallow.

'Why've we come back, Mr Clent?'

Clent gave a bitter little shrug, and dusted off his lapels with a shadow of his usual manner.

'That fellow will be found. If we vanish the same night, the hue and cry would be after us. I fancy we have little choice but to brazen the matter out.' He pulled off his wig and stretched himself out upon the bed without bothering to remove his boots. His lids drooped for a moment with an air of utter exhaustion, and then flicked open once more. 'Where are you going?'

'I . . .' Mosca had taken a few steps towards the door without even thinking. 'I got to see to Saracen. The civet hurt him, an' I got to rub the place with brandy. The Cakes got some.'

'Very well. But do not go far, and be sure not to wake me when you return.'

Mosca took up Saracen's leash in one slack hand, and led him away.

The Cakes opened the door to Mosca's knock. She was wearing a knitted nightcap, and her red ringlets hung to her shoulder. She had been looking pinker and happier since the midnight marriage, Mosca noticed.

'Come in! Are you hungry?' The Cakes seemed pleased and surprised at her nocturnal visitor, although her smile crumpled a little as Mosca pushed through the open door, dropped to a squat, and tucked her knees to her chin. 'What is it?'

Mosca buried her nose between her knees, and stared up at the other girl with big, black, helpless, hostile eyes.

'Mosca . . . what is it?' The Cakes' face started to take on that drooping, beaky look it always had when she was about to cry. 'You're scaring me. Has someone hurt you?'

Mosca shook her head.

'Is it a bad dream? I know how it can be with dreams. You can stay here for a bit if you like.' The Cakes went back to her bed and sat down on it, sensible and big-sisterish. She pulled off her nightcap, and combed her fingers through the ringlet-wrangle on her head. 'There's some pieces of cake there on the dish, if you're hungry; they're a bit stale but still good enough. A couple we had earlier went straight to bed without eating a thing – the bride was so far in her altitudes she couldn't hardly stand.'

The Cakes floated before Mosca's eyes in her halo of candlelight. It seemed to Mosca that she was looking up at the other girl from the bottom of a well so dark that she could not see her own hands, and that the Cakes' world was a tiny, bright bubble drifting almost beyond reach. Mosca wanted to reach out to that world, but it seemed to her that if she did she might burst it, and then she would be left alone in an infinite blackness.

'Was it a dream?' The Cakes wrinkled her nose as a stray hair tickled it.

'Yes,' said Mosca huskily. 'It was just a dream.'

N IS FOR NOT PROVEN

Just a bad dream . . .

Mosca lay in her truckle bed, wondering why it was so dark and why she could hear water clicking against the wood like a great tongue. Her questioning fingers discovered that the bed had a lid, locked shut, half a foot above her face. The air was becoming warm and unbreathable. She beat against the lid until the lock splintered.

The lid swung back, and the white face of the moon stared down at Mosca through the lace curtain of the mist. She sat up, and found that she was sitting in the oaken clothes chest, which was floating past the pillar of Goodman Sussuratch.

Close by, a slender galleon gleamed like mother-of-pearl. High up on the deck sat Lady Tamarind upon an ivory throne. The threads that sang from her white spinning wheel stretched away through the mists to every unseen corner of the city. Other threads intertwined with them and linked them, until Mosca started to fancy that they formed a pattern like a great spider's web.

'I'm trying to get to the Eastern Spire!' called Mosca. 'I don't want to drown in this black water!'

'Catch this thread, and my boat will pull you to the spire.' Lady Tamarind pulled loose a slender thread from the wheel and threw it in Mosca's direction. It touched the open lid of the box and clung there, as if it sparkled with some sugary, sticky essence. Mosca reached for it, then she hesitated and took a moment to pull her sleeve down over her hand. She did so partly because the line seemed too bright to touch with her grimy fingers, and partly because it frightened her with its ground-glass glitter. While she hesitated, the thread peeled loose, fell into the water, and snaked away from her grasp.

'I didn't catch it!' she called out, distraught. 'Please, can you throw it to me again?'

'There is only ever one chance,' answered Lady Tamarind and, above her, white lace sails swelled despite the stillness. The web-threads swung softly over their reflections as the pearl-galleon slid away through the mist. 'Someone wishes to speak with you.'

The wake of the galleon was a ruffled ribbon of white lace, and in its throes bobbed a sodden shape, face down, its hair floating like weed and its wet shirt ballooning on its back. It drifted towards Mosca in spite of the tug of the current and the drag of the galleon's wake.

There were splintered sculls in her hands, so in terror she started to row. The marriage house floated up to greet her, without bothering to bring the shore with it. She clambered in through the scallop-shaped window, and stumbled from room to room. Behind her she heard a dripping and a dragging and the flabby slapping of dead, wet feet against floorboards. She ran into her room and hid in her truckle bed, knowing that Goodman Postrophe could not stop the dead coming home, because she and Clent had eaten all his mellowberries.

And it was in her bed that she awoke, wondering why it was so light, and why she could hear only the lap of the water, and the screech of the gulls, and the sound of a town crier bellowing his news in the street.

'. . . Body found Stabbed through the Vitals with Brutal Force . . . Body found Tangling in the Trout Nets by Whickerback Point . . .'

Mosca clenched her eyes shut, and pushed her fingers into her ears. *Let it be a dream let it be a dream let it be a dream* . . . She gave the Beloved every chance to rearrange the world so that the events of the previous night had not happened, but when she pulled her fingers out of her ears the crier was still shouting.

Perhaps Clent had taken flight in the night? Mosca sat up carefully and peered hopefully towards the larger bed. But no, there he was, his great stomach swelling and falling in slumber, his nostrils widening and narrowing as he breathed steadily.

Saracen's tiny wounds had faded from live-poppy-red to dead-poppy-red, and he was demonstrating his hearty good health by trying to eat the spluttered mess of candlewax. He looked up at Mosca as she swung a leg out of the truckle bed, and if he saw her as a murderer's helpmeet there was no hint of it in his coal-chip eyes. Mosca knew that she could have laid waste to whole cities without losing his regard, and she felt a throb of comfort.

'Mr Clent!' A token knock at the door was followed by the sudden entrance of the Cakes, her pointed face pink and excited. 'The constable has come for to ask everyone some questions an' can you come down to the breakfast room please?'

Clent sat up with impressive if graceless promptness, snatched his wig from a bedknob, and slammed it on his head back to front. Only then did he go about the business of actually waking.

'I beg a multitude of pardons . . . a constable?'

The Cakes nodded, pleased and self-important.

'He says I'm a sharp young thing,' she announced happily, 'on account this morning I noticed our coracle was tied under the window not to the tree how it always is. And I run down to report it to the beadle, and they says it might have something to do with a body they found this morning. An' the constable thinks maybe it's a gang of wandering cut-throats and robbers, who might have tried to get in to our house to steal from the shrines and kill us in our beds . . .'

Clent and Mosca had remembered to return the clothes chest to its place. They had forgotten about the coracle.

Oh sweet Beloved Spare us Sores, thought Mosca. *Look at us, we're thieves, and mill-burners, and spies, and one of us is a cut-throat as well. We're Criminals of the Murkiest Hue, and we're not even very good at it.*

'We would of course be delighted to speak with your admirer, madam,' Clent assured her with haggard courtesy. 'Perhaps you will allow us a few minutes to refresh and make ourselves respectable.' The door closed behind Cakes, leaving Mosca and Clent to furious whispering.

'Yer wig's on back to front!'

'And your eyebrows are smudged down over your nose! And where by the feathered head of St Minch are my . . . oh, there they are. Turn your apron inside out. The right side looks as if you have been chasing rats up chimneys.'

'Yer boots are all over mud, Mr Clent . . .'

'And a hundred men's boots will be so in this weather, calm yourself. Wait – bring the ewer and bowl to me. Stand still . . .'

Mosca's shoulder blades knotted themselves as Clent dipped his handkerchief in the bowl and dabbed at her face. It took all her willpower to avoid flinching from his hand, as he wiped away her coal-dust eyebrows and carefully drew on a new set with a pencil, his own eyebrows waggling with concentration as he did so.

'We returned from the beast fight and went directly to bed,' he muttered as he added the final touches. 'Nothing woke us, we heard and saw nothing. If we both hold to this, I think we shall brave the storm without capsize.'

Mosca followed Clent down the passage with her heart bursting. Goodlady Syropia regarded her with pitying wooden eyes. Goodman Trybiscuit hardly dared watch her through his painted fingers. *Please I need to get away with this please please please* . . .

The constable was a man in his forties with ragged red hair and tired-looking eyes that drooped downwards at the corners. A bottle of gin stood on the table, suggesting that the Cakes had added a nip of comfort to his coffee to take away the chill of his morning walk. He was playfully tossing his hat from one hand to the other as he talked to her, and his laugh only faded into formality when Mosca and Clent entered the room.

'This is the gentleman who lodges with you regular, then?'

'I am Eponymous Clent, and the honour is mine. I fear I am unlikely to be of help to you, sir, but any trifling assistance I can offer you is indubitably yours.'

'That's very gentlemanly of you, sir.' The constable seemed a little flabbergasted by Clent's manner. 'But I do not know why you should feel you cannot be of help.'

'Perhaps I have misunderstood,' Clent began again, quickly. *Too quickly, Mr Clent, careful, Mr Clent* . . . Mosca was horrified to find herself trying to advise a murderer to caution in her mind. 'I apprehended that some blackguards tried and failed to rob this house, and cut the throat of some other poor devil later in the night. I fear that I was in too profound a sleep to have heard anything of use.'

'Well . . . I don't see that they can have failed to get in, sir. There was a boat tied up by the window, you see, sir, and if they didn't get in that way . . . then how did they get back to the bank? There's another thing, sir –'

the constable reached out and broke off a single husk of honesty, and rubbed its papery disc between his thumb and forefinger – 'there were lots of these in the dead man's collar and hair. You don't get them growing round here, not till you're way downriver to Fainbless. I think our poor devil was in this house not so long ago.'

There was a small noise like a trodden fledgling. Mosca wondered at it for a moment until she realized that she had made it. The constable did not seem to have heard, but Clent gave her a wary glance.

'Then it would seem that I have tumbled into misapprehension,' he said with a smile, lowering his weight into a chair and resting his elbows on the table, where his hands began nervously tearing pieces of crust and arranging them in lines. 'I am of course solicitous to answer your questions, but perhaps I might send the girl away. Her years are rather tender for matters of mortality, and she has her errands to perform.'

Too clever, Mr Clent, too wordy. People don't like you when you're too knowing.

'Can I ask what errands are so urgent that she cannot pause to help track down a murderer?' The constable's tone was cold.

Inspiration suddenly bit Mosca like a gnat.

'I got to deliver a message to Lady Tamarind.' She spoke reflexively, just as she might have slapped at an insect's bite. 'Mr Clent works for Lady Tamarind.'

'Lady Tamarind . . .' The constable was shocked back into courtesy. 'Can you prove this, sir?'

Clent went pale, then he evidently remembered Lady Tamarind's letter introducing him as a poet in her employ, and sent Mosca to fetch it. The constable's face relaxed as he read it, and soon he was wearing his jovial expression again.

He rolled the letter carefully and handed it back with a new respect. 'Well, good sir, make no delay for me, I would not have Her Ladyship kept waiting on my account.'

'Then I shall write the message – if you will excuse us a few minutes, good sir.'

The constable nodded, affable once more, and Mosca followed Clent back to their room.

'Lady Tamarind, Lady Tamarind,' Clent murmured to himself. 'It is a thought, a chance at least. I cannot stay here, waiting for the Locksmiths' men to trace me. If we can only find sanctuary in the Eastern Spire before the storm breaks . . .'

Mosca fetched paper, ink, pen and sealing wax and stood behind Clent while he wrote.

'Your most esteemed and radiant Ladyship,

I enclose the first stanzas of your epic, and hope against hope that their humble worth summons your smile for at least an instant, if only in magnanimous pity for my efforts and struggles of the soul.

My lady, I must trespass further upon your good will. The payment you have so generously offered I do not claim, but rather ask that you may find occupation and accommodation within the Eastern Spire for myself and my secretary. Our situation has grown precarious, and my lodgings ill-suited to one blessed with your patronage.

In the name of gratitude I implore you to consent, knowing as you do how this fickle world can knock both high and low on to their axles, and leave them reliant on the assistance of strangers.

Yours in awe and admiration,

Your servant Eponymous Clent

Mosca watched as the hot wax sealed the letter, her heart beating in her ears. As soon as the letter was in her hand she made for the door, blowing on the wax to cool it.

She stepped into a world washed clean, full of newly woken smells. A nervous wind of stammering gusts broke the clouds like bread. The rain had varnished every street sign. Everything promised newness.

Mosca ran. She ran to outpace her ill luck. She had to reach the spire before Clent had time to guess at the treachery in her head. If she could only use the letter to get inside the Honeycomb Courts! Once there, by hook or by crook she would find a way to speak with Lady Tamarind. She would tell the noblewoman the truth about the events at the Grey Mastiff, and beg to be hidden in the Eastern Spire, safe from the Lock-smiths . . . and from Eponymous Clent. If only she dared tell Lady Tamarind about the murder of Partridge! But Mosca herself was steeped too deep in that.

The slouching shops of the riverside yielded to square-shouldered houses with gleaming porticoes. Tall windows arched as if raising their eyebrows to see Mosca run past.

She reached the edge of a broad and busy thoroughfare. On the far side, a row of tall, iron railings held off the curious crowds. The wrought-iron gates were decorated with the outlines of two young women who seemed to be holding hands at the place where the bolt fastened the gates. The Eastern Spire rose from a broad, square sandstone building, braced with columns and teetering with statuary.

When she approached and tried to speak to one of the guards at the gate, he nodded her in the direction of the tradesmen's gate.

The tradesmen's gate merited only two footmen, who saw no reason to stop playing cards as Mosca approached.

'Letter for Lady Tamarind from Mr Eponymous Clent. I was told to come in and wait. Lady Tamarind'll want to see me.'

One of the footmen took the letter and used it to scratch his ear as he looked Mosca up and down.

'Better follow me, then.'

A door painted with the heraldry of the Twin Queens opened into a corridor of tapestries, musty from too many damp winters. Another door opened, and there was a clean rush of cold air as they stepped out into a wide rectangular courtyard, surrounded by a sheltered colonnade.

'Wait here. Don't wander off.' The footman left Mosca in a darkened archway, and hurried off with the letter.

The courtyard was paved with great, six-sided tiles, glazed in creams and shades of caramel. Across it extravagant figures lolled in sedans, or strolled idly like sun-struck drones over a giant honeycomb. Along the darkened colonnade, footmen paced briskly in cloth-soled shoes, and serving girls tripped with baskets of dry lavender, beating them with pestles to fill the air with its scent.

Mosca stood nervously cleaning out the dark crescents from under her fingernails and tucking stray hairs under her mob cap. Eventually one of the lavender girls noticed her and approached. She was about fifteen, Mosca guessed. She had a plump prettiness, a narrow waist, and her flouncing frock looked very becoming on her. Her nose turned up enchantingly, and from time to time she would smile down through her lashes and admire it.

'Were you looking for the servants' quarters?' she asked as she drew level with Mosca.

'No, no, I'm here to see Lady Tamarind. She's going to give me a job.' *Lady Tamarind would see her, they had an understanding, a connection, Lady Tamarind would see her.*

'So what are you meant to be, then?'

'I'm a secretary,' Mosca announced with angry uncertainty.

'You don't look like one. Secretaries are men.'

'I'm different – I'm secretary to a poet.' Mosca was almost feverish with nerves. 'I got a practical outlook an' a concise way of speaking. We're wordsmiths of no common order.'

The chambermaid looked her up and down.

'Your bonnet's on funny.'

'It's . . . it's fashion!' Mosca flashed back defensively.

'It's not. I work in the chambers of Her Ladyship, and have the handling of her wardrobe. There's nothing I don't know about fashion – I see her gowns before everyone in the town copies them. Sometimes –' she bent forward confidentially – 'sometimes some of the ladies pay me to tell them how she will be wearing her kerchief tucked to the next party, or whether she'll be wearing a mantua gown. And when she gives me her cast-offs, the ladies will pay next to anything you like for them.'

'She gives you her clothes – just gives 'em?' *When I work for Lady Tamarind she'll give me dresses, ones I can cut down to my size* . . .

'Lots of them, yes. Good clothes too, but Her Lady-ship cannot abide wearing anything with a smudge or a spot on it, even if it's as small as a pinhead. Sometimes I get her damaged stoats as well.'

Mosca must have looked impressed, since the chamber-maid's haughty expression thawed a little.

'Here, you can't see anyone like that.' With a superior air, the maid pulled Mosca's bonnet ribbons loose, looped them across through a set of hooks under the crown, doubled them back and tied a bow beneath Mosca's chin. 'There. *That's* fashion. Now you won't look a disgrace when you meet the housekeeper to give her your references.'

'I'm not here to meet the housekeeper! It's got to be Lady Tamarind!'

'She won't see you. She won't see anyone today.' The lavender maid gaped at Mosca's ignorance. 'Today's the first day of the Assizes. She's getting ready right now to walk with the Duke to the Courthouse for the Grand Opening.'

The lavender girl walked away, while the ground beneath Mosca became a raft and bobbed on a hidden sea.

The Assizes. Mosca had forgotten about it. The chiaroscuro image of Clent stooped over the body of Partridge had driven everything else from her mind. She had forgotten the pale-eyed Locksmiths, nursing vengeful thoughts in their prison cells. She had forgotten the guild war, and the disaster stalking Mandelion.

Lady Tamarind would not see her. The footman would return and show her back to the gate. She would have to return to the marriage house and Eponymous Clent. If she tried to run away now, it would look like guilt, and the constable would send the hue and cry after her for Partridge's murder. Mosca felt as she had in her dream when the glistening thread had snaked away from her through the black water, taking all hope with it.

No. If the Lady would not see her, she would find the Lady. Peering out cautiously from her appointed post, she slunk from column to column, scanning the gilded multitude.

Excited snatches of conversation reached her ears.

'. . . rather a pity to waste such a charming refrain on that miscreant, but all of a sudden it seems that every song is dedicated to Black Captain Blythe . . .'

' . . . how terrible that the treason trial of the Locksmiths takes place in the second week, when I am promised in Pincaster . . .' Indeed, here nobody seemed to be interested in the murdered body at Whickerback Point. In the Courts the story of the moment was the arrest of the Locksmiths.

Suddenly, beside the fountain, Mosca saw Lady Tamarind.

'Your Ladyship!'

The woman turned. She had bulldog jowls under her white powder. Age creased her neck like an accordion. It was not Lady Tamarind.

Out of the corner of her eye, Mosca saw the footman who had brought her through the gates hurrying towards her with a look of thunder. She snatched a snuffbox from the hand of a passing notable, and flung the contents in the footman's face. As she ran, she heard the false Tamarind squawking in outrage at the black spattering her gleaming gown.

Mosca sprinted through a gilded arch on to a slender lawn where Playing-card Makers were painting portraits of court ladies. And there, adjusting the lily in her elaborate coif, was Lady Tamarind! But no, this Lady

Tamarind had a weak and dimpled chin, and she gawped when Mosca grabbed her arm.

Tamarind after Tamarind bewildered Mosca's vision as she ran. Every other lady aped the brilliant white of Lady Tamarind's attire. Every other cheek was painted in imitation of her scar. Mosca wondered if they would be so eager to imitate her if she had lost an eye.

Ahead of her, a lady was passing through a gate. Her bombazine gown had enormous 'panniers', so that her hips stuck out two feet on either side. Crouching behind this prodigious dress, Mosca managed to avoid detection for long enough to slip through the gate; then she pelted away. As near as she could judge from memory, she was heading towards the spire.

She reached a dead-end courtyard, bordered by a stone lattice wall in which the faces of many Beloved were carved. Through the holes in this wall she could see another courtyard, its hexagonal tiles gleaming with white marble and gold paint.

'Vocado, I must entreat you.' It was the voice of Lady Tamarind. 'Let me send for my men.'

Peering through an aperture, Mosca glimpsed a woman in an immaculate white mantua gown. She had vividly envisaged finding Tamarind dressed as in the coach and in her dream, and for a moment she thought that this was yet another lady imitating Tamarind's style of dress. The next moment she saw the scar shaped like a snowflake on the woman's cheek.

Beside her stood a storybook prince. He seemed taller

than any mortal man, aided by the raised heels of his wine-red shoes and the stately proportions of his gold-dusted wig. His floor-length frock coat and waistcoat were patterned with eyes like those on butterflies' wings. It could only be the Duke.

'Goshawk has escaped,' Tamarind continued in the same level, urgent voice. 'He has almost certainly sent for that boat of Locksmith troops waiting upstream. The Watermen have agreed to delay them, but that buys us only a little time. The ship with my troops is some distance down the coast, and the roads to the ocean are slow and overgrown. Even if we send a messenger now, it will take ten days for the ship to reach us. Vocado – we must send for them *now*.'

'Very well, Tammy. I shall sign the order.' The Duke's voice was light and musical, but somehow a little off-key.

A young man tripped forward and held out a scroll while the Duke signed it. Mosca was just wondering why he looked familiar when two strong arms seized her round the middle.

'Your Ladyship!' Mosca hooked her fingers into the stone lattice and hung on in a quicksilver rush of madness. 'Your Ladyship!' Everything she wanted was beyond the wall.

The Duke turned to look at Mosca, and her stomach jolted as she met his dead brown eyes. She remembered a fox she had once seen flopping about in a strange sickness. *Don't go too close, it'll bite yer . . .*

257

'A radical spy,' he said, in a tone with the same meaningless music to it.

'No.' The white lady gazed into Mosca's urgent, contorted face with eyes the colour of mist. 'Merely an errand girl. She wants to bother me for money. Give her a shilling and throw her out.'

The young man beside Tamarind raised his gaze to look at Mosca, and his chestnut eyebrows rose in surprise. Although his hair was now brushed and carefully fastened into a pigtail, and though he now wore a smart but simple coat of dark blue wool, Mosca immediately recognized Linden Kohlrabi, the man who had helped her by hiding her under his travelling cloak.

Mosca's fingers lost their strength. The footman dragged her from the wall and carried her back the way she had come. She had no spirit to fight. She did not blame Tamarind for the way she had spoken – how could she? Instead, she hated herself with a leaden anguish. Tamarind had been busy with something really important, probably something to do with saving the city from the guild war and the Locksmiths. Mosca had blundered in, shouting like a lunatic in front of the Duke, in spite of Tamarind telling her never to seek her out. Talking to Tamarind had seemed like her only chance, but now she realized she had spoilt everything. Lady Tamarind would never forgive her.

'It's all right.' A quiet voice behind her. 'You don't have to throttle the girl. She'll be coming with me.' Mosca was lowered to her feet, and she reached up a trembling hand to straighten the ribbons the lavender girl had tied so carefully. She did not look into Kohlrabi's face, but she fell into step with him as he walked back through the gates to the thoroughfare.

There was a great crowd in front of the Honeycomb Courts and Courthouse, but beyond them the streets were all but empty. As the crowd thinned around them, Mosca stole a glance at Kohlrabi.

'You work for Lady Tamarind.' Mosca had not intended it to sound like an accusation.

'And you, it would seem, work for Eponymous Clent.' Kohlrabi's tone was tired and a little wary.

'She told you that?'

'Lady Tamarind told me that I was to see you safely outside the gates, and tell you that she could not be seen speaking to you, but she would arrange an interview with you once the Assizes had run their course. Until then, she says you should continue as before.'

Mosca's felt a small surge of hope. She had not been abandoned after all, perhaps. Could she and Clent survive until after the Assizes?

'I do not know what your dealings are,' Kohlrabi continued, 'but I know that Her Ladyship seldom does anything without a reason. Why did you come to the Courts, Mosca? Did Eponymous Clent send you?'

There was a hint of sharpness in his tone, and Mosca gave him a narrow look.

'You don't like Mr Clent.'

'No. I know too much about him to like him. How

much do *you* know about your employer, Mosca?'

Mosca nibbled at her fingertips and stared at him mulishly. 'I'm just working for him right now, that's all. I don't know nothing about him, and I don't look to.'

'Mosca . . .' Kohlrabi stopped, closed his eyes for a moment, and sighed. 'You may not believe me, but I am duty bound to warn you – Eponymous Clent is a very dangerous man. I know what I am talking about – I have spent the last month trailing him from post to post, observing the disaster in his wake.'

Mosca's eyes widened as a memory stirred. Suddenly her nose was filled once again with the smell of damp, and rot, and dove-droppings, and wind-blown smoke. Suddenly she knew where she had heard Kohlrabi's name before, and she remembered words spoken by a young voice, a reassuring voice like warm milk . . .

'You were in Chough, talkin' to the magistrate!' The words were out before she could stop them.

'Dry Stones and Thistles,' Kholrabi murmured. 'I wondered where I had heard your accent before. Chough. How could I be so stupid? Of course – you must be the little girl who burned down the mill.' Mosca must have looked terrified, because he put out a hand soothingly and gave a slight laugh. 'It's all right, it's all right. I have no thought of handing you over for your most heinous crime. But in the name of the most holy, Mosca, of all the people you could have taken up with, why Eponymous Clent?'

Because I'd been hoarding words for years, buying them

260

from pedlars and carving them secretly on to bits of bark so I wouldn't forget them, and then he turned up using words like 'epiphany' and 'amaranth'. Because I heard him talking in the marketplace, laying out sentences like a merchant rolling out rich silks. Because he made words and ideas dance like flames and something that was damp and dying came alive in my mind, the way it hadn't since they burned my father's books. Because he walked into Chough with stories from exciting places tangled around him like maypole streamers . . .

Mosca shrugged.

'He's got a way with words.'

'You caused quite a sensation, disappearing like that. For a while they thought you had burned to death in the mill, until they found the magistrate's keys missing and Clent gone. You should go home, you know – I'm sure your family will understand that the fire was an accident. They'll just be glad to have you home again.'

Mosca gave a little crow-cough of a laugh.

'You didn't meet my uncle and aunt, did you?'

Kohlrabi studied Mosca's face.

'No, I didn't.' He didn't ask her any more about her family.

They had come to a halt at the edge of a square in which a gibbet dripped sullenly and a set of scaffolds swayed their ropes in the breeze, a patient motion like the swing of a cat's tail as it waits by a mousehole.

'What's wrong, Mosca? You look ill. Come, the wind is chill, and we should get indoors soon anyway, before the Clamouring Hour.'

As they approached, the landlady of the nearest ale-house had fastened her shutters and was closing the door, but she took pity on them and let them slip inside before she barred it closed.

There was very little conversation in the alehouse, partly because all the patrons had pushed little wads of linen or leather into their ears.

From some distant bell came a series of rapid chimes, not unlike someone sounding a dinner gong.

'Ah, that sounds like Goodlady Winterblossom's fanfare,' Kohlrabi murmured. 'She always likes to get her word in first. The others won't be far behind. Well, I suppose we have privacy of a sort. No one is listening.' Kohlrabi smiled at Mosca. It felt oddly exciting to be part of a little faction daring enough to leave their ears unblocked.

'So why were you followin' Mr Clent?'

'I was in Long Pursing on an errand for Lady Tamarind when I first heard his name. He had vanished overnight, leaving ruinous debts to about a dozen tradesmen. That same night the landlord he owed two months' rent apparently fell into his own well and drowned. I promised the dead man's son that I would listen out for word of Clent, and that promise has led me a ragged route from hostelry to hamlet, following his trail. I lost track of him in Chough . . . only to find when I returned to Mandelion that Clent was already here.'

Mosca thought of herself snatching Clent from beneath the nose of the patiently pursuing Kohlrabi, and little prickles came and went across her face.

'There is blood on that man's hands,' Kohlrabi added quietly. 'I haven't found proof yet, but I don't doubt it is there to be found.' Mosca could not speak, but watched him with eyes as hard and shiny as obsidian coins. Kohlrabi leaned towards her. 'Mosca – do listen to me when I say this. No one is as they seem, particularly in Mandelion. You may see them day after day, until their every gesture becomes as familiar as the song of the birds, but still you do not know them.

'Perhaps I can explain what I mean with a story. As you know, twenty years ago the Birdcatchers were chased into hiding, and those that were caught were hanged or burned. In one parish the congregation gathered every year in their church to celebrate their victory over the Birdcatchers. One night, when the celebration was at its height, someone smelt smoke and found that the church was on fire. No one had time to do anything about it, though, because a moment later the flame reached the gunpowder stored in the vault. Later the few survivors worked out that the man they had hired to sweep out the crypts had been buying and smuggling in gunpowder for over four years. He was a Birdcatcher waiting for vengeance, and no one had guessed.' Kohlrabi smiled wryly. 'I . . . tend to remember this well. My father was lost in the explosion – you might say that it was rather a formative incident.'

'*My* father just died one day. He went into his study sayin' he had a headache, an' then when I brung in potage he was dead, so I went an' hid in the Chimes' kiln. I would have stuck there in the study if I'd thought everyone was goin' to burn his books. All of them . . . all. I'd never even had the chance to read most of 'em.' Mosca frowned to keep her face from crumpling.

'Do you have anything of his?'

'I had his pipe.' Mosca sniffed, thinking regretfully of the much-chewed pipe in Jen Bessel's hand. 'I used to chew on the stem, cos then I could taste his pipesmoke. I couldn't make his voice in my head. I mean, if you know someone well, you can sort of make them say things they'd say in your head, an' I can do Palpitattle any time I like, but I can't do my father. Still, when I could taste his pipesmoke, it was sort of like he's there at a desk next to me, an' we're both too busy to talk, but I'm there in the study with the books an' I can think clearly . . . He didn't like Chough, I know he didn't.'

'It wasn't much of a place for a scholarly man, if that's what he was.'

'He was more than that.' Mosca gave Kohlrabi a sly, wary look. 'He was Quillam Mye.'

'QuillamMye!' Kohlrabi's eyebrows climbed. 'Quillam Mye's daughter!' He sat back in his chair and stared at her, while in the city beyond the door bell after bell raised its voice in excitement.

'"I had to leave Mandelion because of an altercation" – that's all he ever said about it to me,' Mosca said, feeling shy and alarmingly important.

'I saw him once!' Kohlrabi leaned forward again.

Outside was a chaos of metal tongues, and he was forced to shout. 'The height of the "altercation", Mosca! I was ten years old, and running with a crowd through the streets, because we'd heard that the Stationers were sending men to arrest Quillam Mye. Hundreds of us, you could not breathe for the press of bodies.'

Mosca leaned across the table, hands cupped around her ears to funnel his words into them.

'His windows were dark, he had sent his servants away so they would not be arrested. And when we got there, a Stationer carriage was at his door. He came out with no fear on his face, and climbed into the carriage, but we . . .' Kohlrabi gave a flinching smile and half-covered his ears. Mosca could only hear snatches of his words now. '. . . knew they would take him to his death . . . crowd swarmed the carriage . . . hurled off the driver, detached the horses . . . dragged the carriage through the streets ourselves . . . to safety . . . and I saw his face at the window . . . Hundreds of us, Mosca! Hundreds . . . all shouting his name . . .'

Her father, a hero then, drawn through the streets of Mandelion. Her father, dying amid the dull hostility of Chough, where nobody knew what he had been.

Outside the doors of the tavern a thousand strident bells argued like an army clashing their shields. Kohlrabi's words were swallowed, but Mosca could see him still shouting and gesturing, his eyes bright with excited memory.

'I'm sorry!' she shouted, knowing that Kohlrabi could

 265

not hear her. 'I want to tell you everything, Mr Kohlrabi, I want to, but I can't!'

Kohlrabi was still speaking, more sombrely now, an earnest and rather sad light in his eyes, as if he had noticed some of the anguish in her face.

'It's too late!' she went on. 'I didn't know 'bout Mr Clent's wolfkin ways, an' now I'm in blood up to my wading breeches.'

Kohlrabi ceased speaking, gave her a wincing laugh, and covered his ears.

'An' I can't bear to tell you now, not when I might get away with it, not when maybe you don't ever need to know what Quillam Mye's daughter done. I'm sorry, Mr Kohlrabi, I'm sorry, I'm sorry . . .'

She sat staring at Kohlrabi while the bells' clamour waned. When Goodman Boniface's deep chime signalled the passing of the 'Hour', she took her hands from her ears and stood up.

'I got to go back to Mr Clent now, Mr Kohlrabi.'

'Mosca . . . if you learn anything of Clent's plans, or if you need my help, then for Daylight's sake come and find me at my coffeehouse, the *Hind at Bay*. Do not try to ride this out alone.'

Mosca could not look into Kohlrabi's face. The secret of Partridge's murder seemed to have bound her to Eponymous Clent more surely than if Bockerby had wed them. She walked out of the tavern in silence.

O IS FOR OATH

For three whole days after her conversation with Kohlrabi, Mosca felt less alone. It was a strange and shiny new feeling, and she decided not to think about it too hard, in case she wore the paint off it.

It was a difficult time. Clent seemed uncomfortable in Mosca's presence, but unwilling to have her far away from him. He sent her on countless errands and snapped at her to hurry back quickly. If she was gone for long, he would be pacing by the time she returned. If she came back before he expected her, he would look annoyed, and his fingers would start playing rapid sonatas on imaginary harpsichord keys at the table edge.

Mosca had nothing sharp to say to him now. She lived in fear of him, and slept with Saracen on her chest for safety. Hour by hour she thought of running away, but she was sure he would come after her to silence her, or somehow blame her for the death of Partridge. Furthermore, she could not flee without Saracen, whom Clent now kept in the closet during her errands 'for safety's sake'.

'We will lie low here for now,' Clent said each day, 'and wait for Her Ladyship's response.' And Mosca, who secretly knew that no letter would arrive, was sent out into streets that fizzed and buzzed with gossip about the Locksmiths' arrest and Goshawk's escape– excited, frightened, doubtful and scandalized by turn. She brought back broadsheets so that Clent could scan them for signs of the guild war.

One morning, every sheet roared of a fire that had broken out at the Papermill the night before.

'Aramai Goshawk's first move,' muttered Clent. 'It is a warning shot over the Stationers' bows, I fancy. As I thought, he blames the Stationers for the Locksmiths' arrest – and he means to frighten the Stationers into arranging their pardon. Fruitless, fruitless.'

Days passed, and the date of the Locksmiths' trial approached, with no word of a pardon for them. 'Run down to the kitchen,' he would say from time to time. 'I am certain I heard the front door slam. Find out if the constable is visiting again, and if he is, pray stretch those voluminous ears of yours and try to catch a word or two. And . . . hurry straight back.'

And Mosca would slip down the corridor and huddle behind the kitchen door, ready to dodge away if she heard steps. Usually there would be no sound but the clatter of plates as the Cakes made cakes, while singing a snatch of something that sounded very much like Clent's ballad to Captain Blythe. Sometimes Mosca would feel a draught and realize that the front door was open, and hear the Cakes' voice as she haggled with a hawker from the ragman's raft.

Mosca spent hours tucked into the window, watching the parade of nervous, drunken or excitable couples approach the door. Some of the brides looked rather round-bellied, though they usually tried to hide the fact under their cloaks.

'Run down to the chapel,' Clent would say, when the door was opened to another pair, 'and see if any of them keep their gloves on even to the exchanging of the rings,' and Mosca knew that he was afraid of the Locksmiths coming after him.

But one day, when she had been sent down for the thirteenth time to listen at the kitchen door, Mosca did indeed hear the constable's voice, asking questions about strangers in the marriage house.

'Oh, some folks come to the door to ask after nuptyals,' the Cakes was explaining, 'but no one gets into the house without they're gettin' married. An' the back rooms, they're all for happy couples to stay in after the ceremony.' She clearly thought this the most romantic thing imaginable. 'All their names are safe down in the register, an' you can be sure that no one else has been in the house 'cept Mr Bockerby and me.'

'And your regular lodgers,' the constable added.

'Oh yes, 'cept them.' There was a silky, slopping sound, as if the Cakes was whipping up a syllabub for her guest.

'Tell me . . . these guests of yours, do they have a goose?'

'Why yes, that they do, a fine, white, fat one. I never see one so big. Why?'

'We've had a bit of excitement this morning, that's all.

 269

Did you ever hear the pair of 'em mention a man called Partridge?'

'Not to my face that I remember,' the Cakes said slowly, 'but I do start to think I might have overheard the name once, while I was passing their door. I keep my ears folded shut, mind, and I don't go eavesdropping, but I can't be held to blame if they will go shouting at each other all the time. But they might have been talking about a partridge to put in a pie, or something.'

'Do you often discuss recipes so loud you can be heard in the next room?'

'Well, no . . .'

'Is Mr Clent in the house this moment?'

'I think so – he stays in most mornings.'

'Then I think I'd like to talk to him.' There was a sudden scrape of chair feet against the floorboards, as if someone had risen to their feet quickly. 'What was that? I thought I heard a rustling outside in the passageway.'

'Oh, that'll be nothing but some bundles of honesty I hung to dry in the Chapel of Goodman Pulk the Tardy. They make quite a din when the seedheads pop.'

Sure enough, when the constable pushed open the kitchen door and cast a curious glance up and down the corridor there was no one to be seen, and no movement but the gentle swinging of a row of honesty bundles in an unfelt draught. He walked the length of the corridor and knocked on the door at the end. A voice answered in calm tones, and when he pushed the door ajar he found Clent alone. Clent was reposing in the window seat in a pose suggestive of poetic abstraction, a roll of paper curling across one knee, a quill delicately imprisoned between the tips of his thumb and forefinger, his gaze adrift above the city as if the clouds were sharing their secrets with him.

When his gaze fell upon the constable, he rose and offered a gracious bow, blinking slightly as if he needed to refocus his eyes in order to look upon ordinary, worldly things.

'A welter of pardons, my good sir. I thought you were Bockerby's girl servant with a dish of tea. Do take a seat.'

The constable sat himself down on the room's only chair.

'Your own girl's not about?'

'Ah, no, I sent her to buy ink.'

'Too bad. It was the girl I particularly wanted to speak to. No matter. I can tell you now that we have discovered the name of the dead man found at Whickerback Point. Have you heard the name Halk Partridge?'

Clent raised his eyebrows, and seemed to consider for a few moments.

'The name is faintly familiar, but the hook floats free and will not catch upon anything.'

'The Watermen were worried that the poor cove we found in the nets might have been knifed by a spider boat working the quays, so they put out a description of the dead man to see if anyone recognized it and could put a name to him. The river water made this hard, since by the time they pulled him out he was tending to the blue and bilious, if you see my meaning, sir. But he had a little kink in his wrist, just here.' The constable pulled back his cuff, and rubbed at the knob of his wrist bone. 'A most particular kind of a kink, and one of the porters on the jetty remembered seeing a barge captain with just such a kink.'

Clent wore a patient and polite expression, as if the high matters of his poem were calling to him and he was trying not to hear them.

'So we went down to Dragmen's Arches,' continued the constable, 'and we found out that barge skipper had not been seen for about a week, and we heard his first mate was bowsing at the Wide-eyed Kipper. So we searched the mate out at the Kipper, and one of my men laid a hand on his shoulder to get his attention. And quick as you can blink, the fellow looked up, saw us in the Duke's colours, and threw his stew at my head. He was a right dog for a fight, and it was only when we had three men sitting on his chest that we got any sense out of him.

'He had it in his head we'd come to arrest him for smuggling, and swore his own soul black as a kettle, laying curses on the pair he thought had cackled on him. A pair of passengers the barge had taken up at Kempe Teetering, was how he put it. I think his exact words were, "a bloated viper with a lawyer's pretty manners, and a ferrety-looking girl with unconvincing eyebrows".'

Clent shifted uncomfortably at this unflattering description, and for an instant his eyes did have a furtive, viperish expression.

'He also mentioned a goose.' The constable looked

meaningfully at the floor, which was strewn with tiny white feathers from Saracen's grooming and the pale blots of his droppings.

'Invaluable birds,' Clent smiled brightly. 'Far better for guarding one's domicile than a mastiff.'

'Mr Clent.' The constable leaned forward, resting his hands on his knees. 'I hope you can understand my position. I have no wish to harass a gentleman in the pay of the Lady Tamarind, or to risk a scandal which might besmulch her name, but I cannot be in any doubt that you know this man Partridge, and know a good amount about his dealings. This whole business has become too serious to ignore.

'And so, Mr Clent, I have to ask you a question, and I think you know what it is going to be.' The constable sat back, folded his arms, and peered at Clent's carefully blank expression with narrow dislike. 'Who has been melting down gods to make gunshot?'

Clent's poker face broke down at this unexpected question, and he simply boggled.

'I entreat your pardon . . . perhaps you could elucidate . . . I find myself a little . . . What?'

'Once we had the first mate in darbies, we tracked down the rest of the crew. Most of them stayed mum, but the youngest got leaky, and told us they'd dropped off their smuggled cargo at a potter's on the waterside. We turned the place over, and found nigh on a hundred and forty god statues under the floorboards. As you know, most god likenesses have a core of lead in them, so they

273

won't get blown over in their shrines. They're about the only source of lead that wasn't melted down during the war to make shot. And there under the floorboards, sure enough, was a set of bullet moulds and smelting gear. It is no secret that our noble Duke is seeking the ringleaders in a Diabolical Radical Plot against the Twin Queens . . . and we suspect that these bullet-makers may be part of the plot.'

'Good sir, I can assure you that I know no more about this than the greenest pea fresh-popped from its pod. It is true that my secretary and I did travel from Kempe Teetering by barge for a time, and if you say the captain's name was Halk Partridge I will not gainsay you, but if the first mate fancied that we were aware of his dark doings I can only tell you that he was deluded . . .'

The constable gave a slow nod, but not as if he was satisfied.

'Very well, Mr Clent.' He stood to leave. 'You may realize that you remember more about our friend Partridge, and when you do I hope you will tell me about it. And when your secretary comes back, I'd thank you to bring her to the watch house to answer some questions. You see, she was seen climbing aboard Partridge's boat the day after he disappeared, and talking to one of his crew.'

Clent remained motionless as the constable left the room, and he stayed so until the front door slammed. Then with tiptoe haste made absurd by his bulk, he tripped silently to the window to peer into the street. Only when he was satisfied that the constable really had left the marriage house did he tweak his coat off his bed, revealing the crouched form of Mosca, who had been listening to the interview with some confusion, and watching through a buttonhole.

Clent's eyes were very bright. There was a vague smile on his face, and Mosca feared that he had gone insane under the pressure and might try to murder her at any moment.

'Do you see it?' he asked, holding up one finger.

Mosca looked at his finger then back at his face. She glanced up at the ceiling, to which the finger seemed to point, then back at Clent.

'It is a glimmer of light. It is the faintest promise of escape from the dark caverns we have been walking. It is, I think, a Way Out. Give me a moment of absolute silence, and I shall find it.' He closed his eyes, and his hand moved slightly, just as if he was really feeling along a rocky wall for a crack or a hole.

Mosca bulged her cheeks full of air and held her breath, not daring to move in case her skirts rustled.

'I have it.' Clent's eyes flicked open again. His expression was wild but jubilant. 'The fissure is narrow, but I believe that with will and courage we can squeeze through it. We shall feel the sun on our faces again. Listen – a week ago you saw Hopewood Pertellis polluting the minds of children with his treasonous teachings, yes? Afterwards, being a good and loyal child of your nation, you followed the villain to see where he went, and you saw him enter conversation with our friend Partridge, give him a purse of money, and walk away with him.'

'But he didn't . . .'

'How do you know? Something like that may have happened – it probably did. If Partridge was not selling the leaden bullets to Pertellis himself, then he was probably selling them to one of Pertellis's confederates. Have faith – this story is perfect, it ties up everything for the best. Let us say Partridge was murdered by radicals when he tried to blackmail them. The constable can preen himself on uncovering a radical plot and solving a murder at once, and we will be safe.'

'But Mr Pertellis—'

'Is a radical. He probably spends his nights dreaming of roasting baby princesses like chestnuts.'

It did not seem likely somehow. Mosca thought back to Pertellis's baffled, spring-blue gaze, and tried to find the words to explain her doubts.

'He tries to put squashed snails back together,' was all she could say.

'Then he is clearly insane,' Clent answered confidently. 'Anyway, what does it matter? The man is due to be hanged for high treason – one little murder will not make his situation any worse. Our position is too precarious to be nice about such things.'

Clent's words did have a ghastly sort of logic. Mosca was lost for an answer, and offered no protest as Clent put on his coat and steadied his periwig.

'Now, that is a solemn face to be wearing when our salvation is within reach. Child, I quite understand your reservations, but trust me – no one will be able to disprove your story, and I doubt they will even try. Come now. If we tarry, that will look like conspiracy.'

Mosca followed Clent through the streets like a sleep-walker. After all, would it be such a big lie? And besides, what choice did she have? If Clent hanged, he would see to it that she hanged beside him. Suddenly Mosca wished that she had told Kohlrabi everything after all.

'Look at that,' Clent murmured under his breath, ges-turing with his cane at a ballad-seller near the bridge. 'I write one ballad on Captain Blythe, and now every penny-a-page scribbler has a song about him. If they are to be believed, our poor friend Blythe spends his every working hour defending young maidens from unwanted advances, and giving money to starving beggars, and helping unfortunate farmers to escape from the beadles who would drag them to debtors' prison. And apparently all the while he is a perfect picture of a gentleman with gallantries for every lady – I wonder where he finds the time to groom his horse and practise his gavotte.'

Clent's mood seemed to have recovered miraculously.

'Mosca, you must remind me to pick up some fresh quills on the way back. I have a mind to compose that letter you requested, recommending you to Lady Tamarind's employ. Would you prefer to be painted as a loyal character with a soul as pure and true as diamond, or an able-witted, adaptable, quicksilver sort of animal? No matter, I am sure I can contrive a union of the two. You know, it is the most curious thing, but . . . I believe I shall actually miss you, Mosca.'

By a potter's brick kiln, a waif-faced boy with a knuckle-shaped coal-smudge on his cheekbone paused to watch Mosca go past, a glowing pot gripped forgotten in his long tongs. His face was narrow and unforgiving.

'It is strange to admit it now,' Clent continued, 'but there was a time when I felt that your companionship would be something of a burden to me. I was entirely mistaken, I confess it – you have proved a worth far beyond your years and the limits of your education. If your mind were not so set upon working for Lady Tamarind . . . ah, but I know that in that lofty castle dwells your dearest dream.'

The grey Eastern Spire rose in the distance like a finger admonishing silence. In the dark doorway of a wigmakers' a young girl in a bent yellow bonnet imitated the gesture, bidding her younger brother be quiet with a finger to her lips, and then pointing across the street at Mosca and whispering.

'As for myself, I feel a yearning to see the Capital again. It is all very well to be such a notable figure and so sought after, but sometimes it is more relaxing to be just one minnow in a great iridescent school. And when you are well established with Her Ladyship, as I have no doubt you shall be, you must persuade her to take you with her to the Capital to see the Crystalcourt. Every one of its million windows is thinner than your finger, and filled with a shard of glass cut cunningly so as to throw tiaras of rainbow colour upon the floor. Some of the ladies have trains so long that whole legends of days past can be embroidered scene by scene along their lengths. And when your mistress can spare you, I shall show you the Dizzyfeather Club, where one may sit beneath a green-fringed canopy and sip wine as dark as blackberry juice from glasses narrow as thorns. And there is no sight to equal the gilded barges along the Pettygall . . .'

There was no sight to equal the grim swing of the gibbet as rooks nipped at its links. Or the old watch house, round and battered-brown as a peaked pie, with the high walls of the jail behind it. In front of the watch house the red-headed constable shared his pipe tobacco with a tall man in Watermen's colours, but when he saw Clent and Mosca his eye darkened, and he muttered a farewell to his smoking companion.

'You found her then?' he called out.

'Fairly found, safe and sound, and filled with a tale which will gladden your heart, I think, sir,' Clent called back cheerfully. 'Might we step inside?'

'You might.' The constable was clearly somewhat perplexed by Clent's change of mood.

They followed him in through a heavy oaken door into a poorly lit room where a tousled deerhound lay upon the stone flags, its flanks twitching in sleep. The room smelt of cold suppers and boredom. Mosca had never realized before that boredom smelt so much like egg custard. The constable ruffled the hound's belly with his booted toe, and leaned back against the wall, his pipe bowl cradled in his palm.

'Go on, then.' He looked expectantly at Mosca, and she

 279

found she could not speak. Not that it mattered much, for Clent was uncurling the coloured ribbons of his story before she could draw breath.

'Perhaps you are unaware of it, but a week ago this child was the Undoing of a Wild and Notorious Radical, known as Hopewood Pertellis. It was she who first reported him to the Stationers, having witnessed him presiding over the Infamous Floating School, where he cast Seeds of Evil into minds as pink and innocent as baby clams. It was she who informed them where they might find his Forbidden Books of Infamy. For you see, this man Pertellis—'

'I know about Pertellis.' The constable's face did not look so tired now. He had an alert look as if he had glimpsed something round and white inside his oyster.

'Very well, then. Overcoming the fluttering frailty and fears which belong to her sex, this intrepid young woman followed the Dissident through the dark and winding dockside alleys. And by the very waterside she saw Pertellis meet in a sly and sleekish manner with the captain of our river barge, and saw him offer him a purse of money, and depart with him. Clearly Partridge had some clandestine dealings with Pertellis . . . and perhaps he found out too much for the Vile Radical Conspiracy to let him live.'

'Did she mention none of this before?' The constable's tone was sharp, but he seemed excited, not angry.

'Oh, she did,' Clent answered quickly. 'But of course we were all far too interested in the Floating School to pay the rest of her story any mind, and for myself I had entirely forgotten it until she reminded me. She even went back to the captain's barge herself the next day, so determined was she to uncover all evil doings, but he was not there.'

'Is all this true?' The constable looked directly at Mosca, and raised his eyebrows meaningfully, to show that he expected a response from her and not from Clent. Heat washed upwards from the base of Mosca's spine to the tops of her unconvincing eyebrows.

She nodded just once, and the deed was done.

'Then that's a tale to gladden my heart indeed.' The constable's battered face relaxed into a smile. 'You'll sit and have a tot of Kill-grief? Wait . . .' He left the room, returning a moment later with a jug and three pots. 'The girl will have to identify him now, of course, and again in the trial, but it sounds like she has the right sort of mettle, so I don't think she'll faint at the task.' His eye was far friendlier now when it fell upon her, and his voice was warmer and more confidential. 'You cannot imagine the trouble we've had since we clapped the darbies on Pertellis. So many people seem to see him as some kind of hero, and we get stones thrown at the door of the watch house, or rotten eggs flung at the windows of our homes. And poor folks come by the jail with money they should be using to feed their families, and beg us to use it to make Pertellis a bit more comfortable. It boils me up inside. But once everyone knows he's a murderer . . . well, no one will see him as a hero then, will they? No one will care if he lives or dies.'

Mosca took the offered pot, and sipped carefully. The

 281

gin stole the feeling from her tongue, and left the inside of her nose feeling stripped and cold.

The door opened and three petty constables in Duke's colours entered, supporting a fourth man between them.

The blue-lensed spectacles were long gone, and every button had been pulled from his jacket. He was wigless and his brown hair had curled and matted itself into ingenious shapes. A chain linked the manacles around his ankles, and his arms were fastened behind his back. Red-rimmed, sleepless eyes winced at the dim light of the little room as if it were blazing sunlight. His clothes smelt of damp straw and despair.

'Pertellis, do you know who is speaking to you?' The constable asked coldly.

'Yes, I think so.' Pertellis's face was dazed and deathly white, and he spoke stumblingly. 'I'm terribly sorry but I . . . can't remember your name. I'm not myself right now.'

'You're not likely to be yourself much longer, or anything else for that matter,' muttered the constable with grim humour, and he walked over to stand before the manacled attorney. 'We know all about the barge captain now.' The constable bristled as Pertellis gave a short, mournful breath of a laugh. 'What's so funny?'

'I'm sorry. I'm sorry, but I lose track of all the things I'm supposed to have done. Everyone tells me that I've been running an illegal printing press, and I'm very much afraid I haven't. And all week people have told me that I'm the leader of a radical plot against the Twin Queens, and

I'm really not, you know. And this morning someone ran in to tell me that I've been melting down religious statues to make bullets. Which is quite a clever idea, but I never thought of it.'

'Pity you didn't think of a better way of getting rid of poor Partridge than throwing him in the river,' remarked the constable drily.

Pertellis's eyebrows drew up as he peered intently at the constable's middle button. He seemed to listen for a few more seconds, as if the constable's words were still echoing in his ears.

'I beg your pardon,' he said at last, 'but am I supposed to have killed someone?'

'That won't wash with me,' the constable muttered through his teeth. 'That pious act of yours may fool good and simple people into thinking that you're some saint acting for the greater good, but you don't kid me. I'm not some wide-eyed child you can fill with hellskate ideas about equality and overthrowing rulers . . . poisoning their innocent minds . . .'

'You have children,' Pertellis said suddenly, his eyes widening.

'How do you know?' The constable sounded frightened and suspicious.

'I've only just guessed. You worry for your children, and so of course you hate me.' Hopewood Pertellis looked up at the constable, and attempted a smile. 'How old are they?'

The constable did not answer. To tell the truth, he

looked a little afraid, as if answering the question might give Pertellis the power to flit away from the jail like a genie and steal his children.

'You were seen,' he declared in a steely tone, 'meeting with the said Halk Partridge, speaking with him, paying him a sum of money and walking away in conversation with him, after which time the said Halk Partridge was never seen alive again.'

'Who says so?' Pertellis looked simply perplexed.

It doesn't matter it doesn't matter he's going to be hanged anyway and there's nothing I can do about it . . . Mosca was guided forward by the constable, in a kind but firm manner. *It's too late now anyway because I nodded when they asked and it's done, and now I don't have any choice* . . .

Pertellis peered at Mosca as she stepped forward unwillingly, and a sad dawn of realization swept across his face as he recognized her. She stared back, her eyes wide and helpless with misery.

'There now, child.' Clent's voice, warm and confident. 'He's manacled, he won't harm you.'

'Are you willing to swear on your oath that this was the man you saw? A nod will do.' The constable's voice, calmer now.

Pertellis gave her a faint smile that was sad but kind, almost encouraging. *It's all right*, said the smile. *It's all right. I know you have no choice.*

Mosca suddenly realized that she did have a choice.

'No! You can't make me say it, Mr Clent! It's none of it true, an' you can't make me say it!' Mosca's voice, which had been trapped in her chest for hours, suddenly erupted, as shrill and unstoppable as steam from a kettle. 'Every time I do what you say I tumble a bit further down this well of darkness, an' this here is a drop too deep an' too dark for me. I have to stop falling while I can still see a bit of the sky. Mr Pertellis never killed Mr Partridge. It was Mr Clent – I found him bendin' over the body back at our rooms, puttin' it into the old clothes chest. He told me to help him put the body in the river an' I did, cos I knew he was a murderer an' he would kill me if I didn't, an' I'll swear to *that* if you need me to.' The details of the dreadful night rushed out of her in a shrill torrent, and there was no stopping them.

Clent answered her flashing gaze with a look of utter shock. Behind his eyes stars were falling.

'Beloved above,' the constable muttered in disgust. 'All right, take Mr Pertellis back to his cell – and throw this one into the condemned hold as well, until we can sort out a trial.'

Clent allowed himself to be led away, staring down at his hands as if they held the broken pieces of his perfect story.

'And as for the girl . . . just get her out of my sight.'

Mosca found her own way to the door, and she ran until the river's edge stopped her. A sharp wind was blowing from the distant sea, and she stood and heaved it into her lungs. She felt as if she had forgotten to breathe for a week, and had only just remembered how to do it.

P IS FOR PRISON

What now?

High above Mosca's head, a small kite broke free. The larger, older kites tugged and trembled on their leashes, but they understood that if they did not go where they were pulled, their story would be one long fall with a soggy ending. The little kite only knew that it could not bear the wires any more. Now it was a bird with harlequin plumage rising to steal ribbons of blue from the sky.

Seeing a pale, thin girl squatting on a jetty, observers would not have guessed that Mosca's soul was rising to do battle with the clouds. Her mind was cold and in a place full of dazzling and terrible perspectives, but it was free. She had been sleepwalking, letting Clent lead her every step, and now she could do whatever she liked. She was dabbling her feet in the icy water of the river to prove it.

What now? Staying alive seemed to be the most important thing for the moment. She would deal with everything else later. Mosca's feet were wrinkled, and she was not sure how long she had been sitting there. She pulled them out of the water, and scrabbled for her stockings and shoes.

Word of what had happened would reach the marriage house before long, she suspected. Mosca had to get there before Word did, or her version of events would be lost. But the truth seemed to have rushed out of her too fast and washed away her strength. Her legs wobbled as she clambered to her feet.

Three men were lounging by the watch house, one whittling a spoon, two playing at cards. When a constable left the watch house, they abandoned these pastimes and trotted alongside him, like dogs flanking a chef with a joint. They caught at his sleeve and he relented, tossing them a few sentences like scraps. They looked sharply at one another, clapped the constable on the back, and then sprinted to the jetty.

The Word was already on the move, and it was not weak like Mosca, it was keen and as strong as a deerhound.

Mosca began to run, but the three news-carriers were faster. One piled into a waiting scull and began plying his oars. Another ran to the nearest alehouse, which a moment later spewed out a dozen urchins, all with excited, purposeful faces. The third sprinted to the perilous edge of the jetty, where a coffeehouse was just pulling away, and cupped his hands around his mouth.

'Ahoy and Hear Me – The Murderer of Whickerback Point is Uncovered, the Duke's Men have arrested Mr Pennymouse Clent, for his bloody slaughter of a Riverboat Radical . . .'

The door of the coffeehouse swung wide, and a gentleman with a tight little bob wig appeared in the

 287

gap, steadying himself against the jamb to stop himself tumbling forward into the water. He tossed a pouch of coins to the runner, who was already holding up a hand in readiness. Excited voices were raised inside the coffeehouse, and someone started singing something that sounded like an anthem to freedom.

Mosca realized that the news-carrier in the scull had dropped his oars and was standing unsteadily in his boat so that he could call out to the cluster of little boats touching keels around the Sussuratch pillar. His voice was just audible to Mosca as she hitched her skirts and began to run in good earnest.

'Ahoy and Hear Me – The Body of Whickerback Point Revealed to be a Waterman Spy named Pigeon, Horribly Murdered after Discovering a Reeking Radical Plot . . .'

On the street side a rabbit-featured boy in worn boots flung open the door of the Strangled Bird tavern.

'News from the watch, word straight from the Justice of the Peace himself,' he gabbled breathlessly. 'A Great Radical Plot to Steal Statues from Every Church an' Melt 'em Down an' Pour 'em into Everyone's Ears while they Sleep . . .' He ducked too slowly to avoid the resultant coin shrapnel hitting him in the face, and had to fight off a swoop of other urchins with an eye to snatching his reward from the mud.

By the time Mosca paused for breath at the corner of East Straddle Street, another boy runner was reciting his message to a gaggle of sedan chairmen waiting outside the Simpering Squirrel.

' . . . an' then there was a big battle between the Duke's men an' the radicals, an' they had to call in the Watermen to help, but the head of the radicals was this man called Spinymouse Lint, an' he had this special cannon made so he could put whole statues in it, an' he fired a statue right through the head of this one Waterman called Pilchard an' he died right then and there . . .'

The shutters of the marriage house were fastened although it was mid-afternoon. Unlike Clent, Mosca had no key to the front door, and no one answered her quiet rat-a-tat. She threw pebbles up against the window of the Cakes' room, and eventually one shutter opened just wide enough to let a couple of red ringlets fly free on the breeze.

'We're all closed up today. Out of . . . respect for the solemn festival of Goodman Grenoble.'

'Cakes! It's me! An' besides, Grenoble's the Goodman of Keeping Knots out of Moustachios . . .'

'I can't let you in. Mr Bockerby was in the Tattler's Tale when the news-carrier come by an' told us everything.'

'It's not true!' Mosca bit her lip. 'Well . . . probably not. What colour of everything?'

A thin slice of the Cakes' face was visible through the shutter crack. She had the pale, miserable expression Mosca remembered from the days before the midnight marriage. 'Mr Bockerby, he says any friend of Mistress Bessel's is a friend of his, an' any friend of any friend of Mistress Bessel's likewise, an' Mr Clent's a friend of Mistress Bessel, but you ain't any kind of a friend to Mr

Clent. We heard how you got Mr Clent arrested, what with telling the constable that he'd been smuggling shrine statues into Mandelion hidden in dead partridges . . .'

'Oh – that really *isn't* true . . .' With a warm flood of relief, Mosca at last let the whole truth spill out of her: the discovery of Clent with the body of Partridge, the unspeakable task of moving the body, and the final scene in the watch house. When she had finished, she looked up expectantly.

The Cakes opened the shutter a little further. Her face was peaked and pale, and the corners of her mouth drooped as if something had disappointed her.

'So . . . it was you that shopped Mr Pertellis to the Stationers and the Duke's men?' There had been no easy way to leave this fact out of the story. 'Mosca – it was you?'

Mosca's mouth fell open. She did not feel ready to lie to the Cakes, but even if she had wanted to, she would have been too busy watching a series of memories parade across her vision. A picture of the Cakes carefully writing out each of the names in the marriage register. An image of the Cakes in the midnight chapel, her tearful face almost hidden under the white webwork of a shawl. A vision of a young girl crouching in an alleyway and noting down Pertellis's words in her notebook, her hair hidden beneath a length of white lace . . . It had never occurred to Mosca to wonder where the Cakes had learned to write.

'It was you, wasn't it?' the Cakes said sadly, and started to close the shutters.

'Wait!' There had to be more to say. 'They tried to make me say Mr Pertellis killed the barge captain too, but I didn't—'

'Doesn't help Mr Pertellis much, does it? Your goose is round the back – I led him out with a trail of barley.' The shutters closed with a sad but resolute little click. Mosca stared up at them for a few turbulent seconds before the injustice of it overwhelmed her.

'I'm never telling the truth again! It gets you hanged and locked out and starved and froze and hated . . .'

Then, *I'll get Saracen*, she thought, *and I'll set him on their chickens*.

When she found him, Saracen had finished his barley and was happily chewing at the corner of a sheet that had been spread across a hedge to dry. He had once discovered a tablecloth, and ever since had been optimistic about the effects of dragging cloths off the top of things. The miserable-looking chickens had holed up in a bucket, suggesting that Saracen had pre-empted Mosca's schemes against them.

'Come on, Saracen. The cakes are stale here, an' the rooms are draughty, an' there's no sleepin' with the endless marryin' goin' on.' Mosca was stooping to pick up Saracen when a roughly tied bundle landed in a cloth dollop at her feet.

'Kip the blankt genst the cold' read the little note pinned to the top. Inside the blanket the soft-hearted Cakes had stowed two small loaves and a shilling. Mosca stared up at the windows, but there was no sign of anyone watching to see her reaction so she settled for smiling reassuringly at the chickens.

Back in the street, she noticed that the marriage house was not the only building that had shuttered its windows. Outside a neighbouring building two serving maids were hastily finishing their job of sweeping the front step.

'. . . a huge store of bullets they say the radicals have stored away in a cave, like a squirrel's acorns,' Mosca heard one whisper to the other. 'And no doubt muskets hid under flags in their cellars, all ready to storm the Duke's spire.'

'Will they come to common sort of houses after, d'you think?'

'Most likely. And when they do, master'll go the colour of custard and give them his money and anything else they've a mind to, and thank them kindly for taking it. Don't you wish that we had a gentleman like that Captain Blythe on hand to keep us safe?'

The other serving maid answered with a sigh that spoke volumes.

Around the next corner a horse reared, startled by the flutter of paper amid the cobbles. Walkers recoiled, clearing a little round theatre of space around two curling sheets of parchment. They were printed in heavy, black letters, but they did not bear a Stationers' seal.

'What is it?'

'Get back! Don't look at it!' One young mother scooped up her toddler son, burying his head against her dress so that he would not see the offending papers, and pushed her way through the crowd.

'What do we do, heap earth on it so it doesn't get away?'

'The Stationers! Fetch the Stationers! They'll know what to do.'

The wind picked up, and the paper rolled itself back into a scroll, and tumbled gently towards the kennel ditch of the street, the crowd clearing before it with a scuffle of frightened feet. One larding-pin-seller, bolder than the rest of the throng, stepped forward, one hand shielding his eyes, and kicked a clod of horse manure on to the wicked paper. After this it lay, weighted to the cobbles, but still curled and uncurled its corners in a lazy, beckoning motion.

Five minutes later, a small cart racketed up, with two men in Stationers' livery gripping their hats to their heads and their writing boxes to their chests. They dismounted, and with great care one used tongs to put the dangerous paper on a curious long-handled spade, held by the other. The Stationer with the spade took a moment to clean his spectacles, then surveyed the crowd sternly.

'Did anyone look at it?'

'He did! He did!' The manure-kicker was pushed to the front.

'No I never! Well, not hardly . . . 'sides, I can't read.'

'Ooh, what a lie, I saw his eyes moving from side to side like they was following words . . .'

'We'd better take him along too, then. Come on, sir,

 293

into the cart, don't make a fuss. If it turns out you can't read after all, then you've nothing to worry about, have you? Otherwise . . .' The paper-scooper and the hapless larding-pin-seller were loaded into the Stationers' cart, and the bay mare nodded sleepily at a twitch of the reins and ambled into motion.

The cart had just reached the corner when a rock flew from somewhere in the crowd, and struck one Stationer solidly on the back of the skull.

'That's for Mr Pertellis!' A youthful shout with no apparent owner.

The crowd turned for the source in vain. Amid the gasps of outrage could be heard murmurs of approval.

'Radicals!' bellowed one man, and, 'Locksmiths!' another. Both calls were taken up, but pell-mell, so that it was impossible to tell if they were accusations or rallying cries. The Stationer who had been struck cried, 'Call the constables!'

Soon the rim of the crowd was buckling before a handful of men in the Duke's colours who strode in shouldering muskets.

'A rock . . .'

'Locksmiths! Somewhere in the . . .'

'If so, we'll find them. You! Take off your glove! Let's see your right hand!' The Duke's men barged through the crowd, muskets levelled, forcing each man in their path to strip off his right-hand glove. Mosca knew they were looking for the Locksmiths' key brand.

Not far from Mosca a man in a ragged, brown coat

shoved his way free of the crowd and bolted for an alley-way.

'Stop!' A Duke's man levelled his musket. Footsteps continued to ring out from the alley.

A summer's worth of thunder in an instant, and a surge of musket smoke. A woman standing next to Mosca screamed and clutched a powder-burned cheek. One petty constable sprinted into the alley.

'There's nothing but a thief's brand on the fellow's hand!' came his cry. Amid the crowd, angry whispers fizzed to and fro like water beads on a griddle.

Perhaps the world has always been like this, Mosca thought as she pushed her way through the crowd. Like a broken honeypot that looks whole, but just holds together because the shards are resting in place and are glued together with honey. You just need to prod it a bit, and it all starts oozing apart. And perhaps, when Clent had cackled on her, the world would come oozing after Mosca in a mass of madness and misheard gossip, accusing her of mill-burning and mischief and multiple misdemeanours. She needed to find somewhere to hide.

Kohlrabi.

His favourite coffeehouse was the *Hind at Bay*. When it drew near to its usual mooring place on Merryhell Row, it became clear that a fracas was taking place on board. Two men had hit the wooden wall with such violence that they had knocked a hole in it, and now their upper bodies protruded through the splintered gash, where they struggled over a tiny pistol gripped between their interlocked fists. The ball rolled out of the barrel and hit the water with a sad little *plish*, but the combat continued unabated. A plum-faced lawyer shouted a hoarse diatribe against the Locksmiths, while a young apothecary said nothing, happy in the knowledge that a bitten eyebrow was worth a thousand words.

'Scuse me,' Mosca called out to the two coffeemaidens busy trying to pull the combatants back from the drop, 'but is there a Mr Kohlrabi supping there, please?'

'Not this last hour, me dove,' one called as she wound her fingers into the lawyer's cravat and hauled him back by force. 'Try in the cathedral, I would, dearie. He's often there at this time.'

But this was no easy matter. The road to the cathedral was full of crowds and excitable voices. Mosca's legs were weak and her arms were full of Saracen.

There were other faces in the throng as well, child faces with tight mouths, and eyes that followed her. Word of Mosca's part in the arrest of Hopewood Pertellis had travelled fast. Grim-faced and grimy-locked, the children of the Floating School left their mops and their marbles and followed her to the doors of the cathedral, first at a trot, then at a jog, then at a run.

Darkness was kind to the cathedral, and hid the scars left by flames, war and time. Mosca saw only rich hanging tapestries and pillars of rose-coloured marble, whorled in whisker-fine gold leaf. Until now she had seen the Beloved only in their wooden, workaday faces, but here they were languorous in marble, some indolently holding a sword or a set of scales in a drooping hand. High in the dome above were arches where more Beloved appeared in attitudes of mild surprise, as if they had opened the wrong door by mistake and found themselves above a perilous drop.

In the middle of the main aisle stood a mighty marble font, full of dried rose petals. An inscription on the side explained that this was the last resting place of the Little Goodkin, three children who had been abandoned in the woods and starved to death, but whose skeletons returned to their village church a month later to shame their parents. Even Mosca had heard the tale that when a child was lost in a dark and lonely place the Little Goodkin would come to them and guide them home. The Little Goodkin had doubtless been responsible for keeping countless children from harm, for there is nothing like the prospect of acquiring three well-meaning but skeletal companions to persuade one out of dark and lonely places.

Despite her haste, Mosca took a moment to snatch a handful of the petals and rub them against her face in the time-honoured manner, before letting them fall back into the font.

'Fenfenny,' she whispered, the common corruption of the old prayer 'Friends defend me.'

. . . where is she is that her this way . . .

The whispers were not far behind.

The nearest wall was covered from floor to roof with the arched mouths of tiny shrines which in turn led into other shrines behind them, all part of the same inter-connected warren. Most were too small and inaccessible to be visited easily, and rich worshippers generally paid a priest to carry their offering up to the correct shrine, while those of modest means were reduced to flicking coins up at the little arches that appeared in the front facade and hoping for the best.

Mosca stowed Saracen in a nook beside Goodman Blackwhistle of the Favourable Wind, then scrambled in through the nearest shrine opening, bruising her hands on coins. Some connecting passages were little more than cracks in the masonry, and as she squeezed up through them she tried not to imagine herself getting trapped like a sweep in a chimney kink. Just as the pressing wall of the Warren was stirring panic in her, she saw light ahead and realized that she had reached an empty shrine, set twenty feet above the cathedral floor.

. . . there she is where how did she get up there . . .

For a while Mosca heard scufflings around and below her, and then one by one the children of the Floating School emerged back from the Warren and peered up at her. She had no idea how she had reached her current precarious position, and it was pretty clear that they hadn't either. They stood by the font of the Little Goodkin, and as they discussed her in whispers each reached without thinking into the font to rub a handful of petals against his or her face and murmur the traditional benediction. It almost seemed as if they had gathered to pay their respects to Mosca, and it was a shock when the first flung stone stung her shin.

But a new set of steps rang out across the mosaic floor, and soon the stones ceased to clack against the stonework by her head. Mosca took a few deep breaths, drew her knees away from her chin and peered from beneath the brim of her bonnet

'Hello, little god,' said Kohlrabi. 'What are you the deity of, may I ask?'

'Hiding, and staying alive.' Mosca rubbed at a new tear in her stocking, and felt the edges damp with blood. Someone had a good aim.

'Who are you hiding from?'

'Other children.'

'Is it a game?'

Mosca shook her head.

'I don't see any other children.' Indeed, the children of the Floating School had chosen this time to float elsewhere. 'In fact, I suspect you have been waiting here in ambush to swoop down and crush my hat again. But let's see.'

Kohlrabi paced a few leisurely steps to the main aisle, swept back his cloak and raised both his fists in an exaggerated yawn and stretch. There was a rapid patter of feet, and the cathedral door banged and juddered. 'Well, I was wrong. Lots of children. What did you do to bring such wrath on your head?'

For a moment Mosca thought about lying and telling him that it had been a game after all. But instead somehow she found herself pouring out the truth for the third time that day: the arrest of Pertellis, the murder of Partridge, the denunciation of Clent and the vengeance of the schoolchildren.

'You better go now,' she said when she'd finished, not wanting to look at Kohlrabi's face in case he started hating her as well.

'I bought you something,' Kohlrabi answered, as if he had not heard her. Out of his pocket he drew a long briar pipe. 'It's a little large for you, but I think you'll grow into it. It's been used, so it has the scent of tobacco. But you . . . you'll have to come down for it. I don't want to throw it and risk breaking it. You *are* planning to come down some time, aren't you? Or are you just hoping to live off food offerings in the shrines?'

'I don't think I can come down.'

'Mosca, the world is not as bleak as it seems right now—'

'No . . . I mean, I'm not sure I can find my way down again. I can't really turn round easily neither, without falling off the ledge.'

When Kohlrabi extended his arms, Mosca dropped from her shrine hideaway, and managed not to crush his hat. He caught her under the armpits and set her on her feet, then squeezed her by the shoulders.

'Well done, Mosca. Well done.' Mosca got the impression that he was not talking just about her jump. He polished the pipe with his sleeve and presented it to her. It was a little singed about the bowl, but the wood was glossy and honey-coloured. Mosca chewed at the stem experimentally, and found that another set of teeth had left a little groove into which her own fitted.

'It's a different sort of smell from my father's tobacco, but it's . . .' Mosca suddenly realized that she was going to cry and there was nothing she could do about it. She clenched her teeth on the pipe stem, but the world became misty.

'Is it all right? Can you think with it?'

Mosca nodded, but couldn't speak.

'Come on, I'll take you home.'

Mosca could only shake her head.

'All right . . . not to the marriage house, then.' There was a pause, and Kohlrabi let out a long breath. 'You'd better come with me.'

Saracen had decided he liked being a god, and was coaxed out of the Warren with some difficulty and several breadcrusts. Before leaving the cathedral, Kohlrabi wrapped the Cakes' blanket around Mosca so that she would not be recognized, but when they reached the street there was no sign of the Floating School children. The crowds outside were still tense and unquiet, but calm pooled around Kohlrabi like a cloak. He smiled and whistled under his breath, as if he was carrying a secret; and after a while Mosca felt calmer, as if she knew it as well. They walked into a wigmaker's which seemed to have been squeezed thinly between two larger shops.

'Mosca, this is Mrs Nokes.' A woman in a primrose-yellow cottager's gown and cap tripped forward, her face wearing a vague smile, as if she had just heard the punchline to a joke and was waiting to understand it.

'Mrs Nokes, Mosca will be taking that room of yours on the second floor. Can we have the key?'

Mrs Nokes had to spell out the keys on her chatelaine one by one with great care, and she finally held up the right one with an air of mute surprise and triumph. Kohlrabi folded her hand carefully around a few coins, and held her fingers in place a moment to make sure she did not drop them.

'Mrs Nokes is not one for talking,' Kohlrabi explained as he led Mosca up the stairs, 'but she's an excellent cook. Ah! Here we are. How is this, Mosca? Do you think you can survive here for a few days until things calm down?'

The room had a proper bed, with chocolate-brown curtains and embroidered pillows. There was a dressing table with, Mosca noted in amazement, a mirror two spans high. There were three candlesticks, good, long ones. There was a little hollow in one wall for visitors to place a pocket idol while they were staying. There was a stand for a wig, and a little bone comb. And . . .

'It's got *wallpaper*,' Mosca said in awe.

Kohlrabi reached for the purse at his belt. 'You will be safe here, providing you stay in this room and don't open the door to anyone but myself or Mrs Nokes. Here's a few coins to tide you over. Mrs Nokes will bring you meals, but if you need anything else, ask her to go out and get it for you, and give her the money.'

Mosca did not answer. In reaching for his purse, Kohlrabi had carelessly pushed aside his cloak, and suddenly she knew exactly why the children of the

Floating School had run from him.

Kohlrabi's eyes dropped to discover the object of Mosca's fascinated gaze. 'Oh, that.' He pulled the cloak back to conceal the pistol strapped to his flank. 'There is danger on the streets,' he admitted. 'Danger on the highways as well, or I might have tried to spirit you out of Mandelion. Some villagers have turned to banditry, they say.'

'There's going to be a war, isn't there?' Everything seemed to be unravelling.

'In Mandelion?' Kohlrabi seemed to be considering the question seriously. 'Perhaps a little one, but only a little one. Mosca, things will get worse before they get better, but believe me when I tell you that everything will happen for the best.' He studied her features with a worried smile-frown.

'It's all right,' he said. 'Lady Tamarind is a very clever woman, and has planned for everything. And when the time comes for you to appear in the Assizes to testify against Clent, I will make sure that you get there and back safely, no matter what hurly-burly there may be on the streets.'

'What . . . I got to go back an' tell everyone about it *again*?' faltered Mosca.

'It would be best,' Kohlrabi said gently. 'I can help you write up a deposition, but if you do not turn up at court, there is a chance that Clent may walk free. It is a capital crime, so he will be defending himself, but I hear that he is a gifted speaker . . .'

303

Mosca would have to hobble her way through her story again, in a courtroom this time, with the gaze of a thousand eyes pressing the breath out of her. Perhaps Cakes and Bockerby looking on with cold reproach, or the Floating School watching with eyes like coals. Around her laws and rules would lie like invisible wires, and she would snag and tangle in them blindly with every sentence. When she did, Clent would pounce on her mistakes, for Clent would be there, with his silver voice and cold grey eyes . . .

'All right,' she muttered gruffly.

Over the next few days, Kohlrabi brought her paper and ink, and helped her word her deposition. He also brought books of law, so that she could understand the traps that might be laid for her in the court. He seemed quite confident of her success. This strengthened Mosca during his absences, as she heard the subdued sea-cave roar of angry crowds, and the crackle of distant musket-fire.

Night after night, however, Mosca lay awake in the middle of her great bed between the cool, clean sheets, stroking the worn damask of the curtains to comfort herself. Her stomach kept trying to squirm out of her belly, and her mind wriggled around, looking for reasons to run away before the Assizes. But if she ran away, Eponymous Clent would slide through the fingers of the law, and when he came after her there would be no Kohlrabi to protect her . . .

All too soon, Mosca woke to her breakfast chocolate and realized that the first day of Clent's trial had arrived. Kohlrabi had brought her a clean white dress and apron for appearing in court.

'How do you feel, Mosca?'

'Like I swallowed a dozen live jackdaws what hate each other.' Mosca sat on the edge of her bed, staring at her hands.

'The worst of it is the waiting.' Kohlrabi crouched in front of her. 'Trust me, compared to that, giving testimony will be the easiest thing in the world.'

''S funny,' Mosca said. 'All this time I've been skithered of standing up in court, but that bit of my brain's gone numb now. Now it feels like the worst of it will be walking through the streets, an' feelin' like everybody knows I'm going there to blow the gab on someone, an' wondering if they'll throw stones at me again. I'm turning stag, and nobody likes that.'

'All right,' Kohlrabi said quietly. 'I know a time when the streets will be empty.' He left Mosca alone for a few minutes, then returned with two long scarves draped over his arm. 'We can wrap these around our heads. And these –' he held out a handful of what seemed to be fragments of waxed cloth – 'we can put in our ears.'

'You mean . . . Clamouring Hour?'

'Yes. It starts in ten minutes.'

When they left Mrs Nokes's shop, fifteen minutes later, the scarves swaddling their heads like turbans, Mandelion had pulled itself indoors and shuttered itself against the war of the bells. Even with her ears plugged, Mosca could feel the sound drumming against her skin like rain. The turmoil of the city had made the ringers more zealous and aggressive in their clanging competition.

Mosca felt filled with panic. She was an arsonist, runaway, thief, spy and murderer's accomplice, and here she was of her own free will taking step after weak-kneed step towards the prison. She turned a final corner, and now she could see the prison waiting to pounce on her, crouched behind the watch house like a panther behind a mound. The prison – the 'louse house', the 'tribulation', the 'stone jug', the 'naskin'. It would put out a great paw to pin her, and she would never escape it again.

Perhaps Kohlrabi shared her thoughts because he suddenly halted. But he was staring towards the prison gate, where a dozen scrolls of paper were rolling over lazily like cats so that the wind could stroke them. Spread-eagled on the ground lay three men in the Duke's colours.

Kohlrabi signalled to Mosca to stay where she was, and he sprinted to the watch house. He beat on the door, but there was no response. He had started running back towards Mosca when the prison gates swung wide and three men ran out into the street. Their faces were muffled and they carried muskets.

Kohlrabi reached Mosca, grabbed her wrist and spun her around. The next moment the pair of them were running away from the prison at full pelt, with the heavens clamouring above them.

Q IS FOR QUESTIONING

They returned to the wigmaker's shop at the tail end of Clamouring Hour and had to wait for Mrs Nokes to unfasten the door. Gently but firmly Kohlrabi guided Mosca inside, then ran off down the street again without explanation.

In her upper-room eyrie, Mosca pulled the stoppers out of her ears. One by one the bells lost breath and hushed, until one lone, monotonous bell rang without ceasing. Hugging her knees in the window seat, Mosca listened in an agony of suspense to running feet, shouted queries.

Two hours passed before Kohlrabi returned. Mosca's heart plummeted when she saw his expression.

'What is it?'

'Mosca, I don't want you to be worried or upset . . .'

Mosca was instantly worried and upset.

'What's happened? Something's happened! I'm going to be arrested! You're going to be arrested! Something's happened to Lady Tamarind!'

'No, steady, Mosca, none of those. But . . . there's been a prison break.'

At first Mosca thought of Pertellis, perhaps being carried out by a mob of pistol-wielding children. Then another possibility occurred to her.

'Mr Clent!'

'Yes, it seems he has escaped . . . but that's only a part of the truth. The fact is, the entire prison has been broken out. Every single convict. All of them.' Kohlrabi gave a wry smile. 'That, I suspect, is what comes of trying to keep Locksmiths under lock and key.'

This is what had happened.

Just after the start of Clamouring Hour, when all petty constables unlucky enough to be on duty in the streets had wads of cotton in their ears, a cart parading Stationers' colours had sauntered up to the jail. Because so many pamphlets from the illegal press had been found, the sheriff had ordered a small furnace to be built by the jail, so that they could be burned quickly. The Stationers themselves had taken to bringing little cart-loads of suspicious papers to burn in this furnace, and the guards had grown used to turning their faces away, as if they were plague carts carrying the dead.

The guards at the gate of the jail said later that the driver of the cart seemed to be shouting something to them, and gesturing with a sheaf of parchments, none of them bearing the Stationers' seal. Then the wind rose, the driver gestured too freely, and the papers escaped, capering and spiralling upon the breeze.

The guards had, of course, reacted with horror. One paper wrapped itself playfully around a man's leg, and he had buckled up as if it scalded him. One was chased around the corner of the wall by two tumbling sheets, which seemed to flank him like hounds pursuing a deer. The third man curled into a little ball, and was in no position to stop someone coshing him neatly on the head.

None of these guards had the key to the main gate of the jail, but it seemed that the intruders in Stationers' clothing had. Furthermore, they seemed to have the keys to the holding cells, the Question cells, the Forgotten Fall, and the Vaults of Silence. Meanwhile, when the Duke's men in the nearby barracks finally realized that something was amiss, the door to the barracks remained obstinately closed, and precious minutes were lost kicking it open. When they sprinted to the armoury, *that* door also snubbed them.

One guard inside the building, who was overcome, pinioned and gagged, explained later that when the first musket shot was heard, cell door after cell door had opened from the inside, and the Locksmiths had stepped out, casually kicking off their manacles as they did so. Without bothering to claim the guards' keys, they had walked calmly through the passageways, picking all the locks with combs, spoons and spectacle frames, so swiftly that they scarcely broke stride.

Outside in the courtyard, the Duke's men finally knocked in the door of the armoury and surged inside. They shouldered muskets and blunderbusses, seized pistols and pikes, turned to leave, and discovered that the door was jammed again.

The streets were virtually empty, and those few people who were hanging out of their windows to shake their bells were simply amused when they saw a scattered horde of men and women fleeing through the streets with their hands over their ears. Only when the Hour had ended, and the ears of the observers had stopped ringing, did they become aware of the sad, lonely clanging of the alarm bell.

Needless to say, the intruders were not Stationers at all, and the Stationers had no idea who they were.

'Don't look so alarmed, Mosca. The Duke's men are raiding every rat-hole in the city, and will have rounded up most of the convicts by dawn. If Eponymous Clent is still in the city, he will be run to earth in no time. If he has fled Mandelion, he will be declared an outlaw, and perhaps you will never need to testify in court against him. Either way, I will see you safe, and so will Lady Tamarind. I have spoken with her again – she has an interest in you.'

'Lady Tamarind! What did she say?'

'"I think we must find work for that girl, or she will tear the spires apart with her fingernails, looking for it." And then she laughed to herself. Her Ladyship never laughs. She sees something special in you, Mosca, and I think I understand why. Do you remember the part of the cathedral where the font of the Little Goodkin stands?'

Mosca nodded.

'Perhaps you did not notice, but in that part of the

church the roof is lower and the stone flags more chipped. The truth is, back when Mandelion was little more than a village, a square little church stood on that very spot. It was not pretty; it looked as severe as a fortress – which is exactly what it was. The villagers at that time lived in fear of pirates, and a watchtower stood where the Eastern Spire now rises. When the lookout glimpsed the sails of a cutter, he would ring an alarm, and the whole village would run to hide in the church and hold off the attackers.

'The walls of the church still stand, hidden under the gilt of the cathedral marble. To the west, although you cannot see them, there are spouts so that boiling oil can be poured down into the courtyard. In the southern wall, below the Heart of the Consequence, there are hidden arrow slits facing the river.

'I think that when Lady Tamarind looks at you, she feels as the cathedral might if it suddenly remembered that once it had been a grim little church facing down musket fire and a cruel sea wind.'

That is all very well, thought Mosca after he had gone, *it's all very well me being a grim little church, but what do I do when I don't know who the pirates are, or where they're coming from, and I don't have no arrows anyway?* She amused herself with trying to think of ways to defend her room if she found herself besieged by pirates or anyone else, but even with Saracen as her champion this became boring after a while.

It is all very well being safe, thought Mosca, *but how can I be safe if I don't know what's happening?*

 311

She gave Mrs Nokes money for news broadsheets, but poor Mrs Nokes was easily confused, and brought back improving stories about little girls whom the Beloved blessed because they never swore and worked harder than their brothers and sisters. Mrs Nokes smiled so hopefully that Mosca thought there was little point in complaining.

It was at an early hour on the second morning after the prison break that she turned her attention to the dressing table and mirror. There was a bone comb with nearly all its teeth, a brush with a cracked enamel back, a little pot of face powder, a block of rouge and all sorts of strange little brushes, patches and pincers. There were jars of wig powder coloured white, creamy yellow, lilac and pale peach respectively. She spent half an hour fiddling with her bonnet, and succeeded in arranging the ribbons as the lavender girl had shown her. Then, remembering Lady Tamarind's marble pallor, Mosca dipped one of the brushes into the face powder and dabbed it experimentally on her face. She moved the candles nearer to the mirror and leaned forward so that she could examine her face more closely as she did so.

How strange it was to see her face reflected so clearly in a real mirror! Tiny candle flames were reflected in her eyes, which pleased her. She was even more delighted to notice that her eyebrows were starting to grow through, black at the roots. Saved at last from the Chough water, they were turning the same colour as her hair.

Mosca pulled off her bonnet and cap to extract a lock

of her black hair so that she could hold it against her eyebrows and compare. She lifted a candle to let more light fall on her face, then set it down abruptly with a jolt.

Faint creases ran down each of Mosca's cheeks, as if twin tears had worn grooves in them. They joined in a red crease under her chin. They were almost identical to the marks she had seen on the face of the dead Partridge.

Maybe all dead faces looked that way. Maybe death crumpled you up like a ball of paper. Maybe she was starting to die and hadn't noticed and maybe the creases would become deeper and deeper and her skin would turn blue and . . .

. . . and perhaps there was a quite different explanation.

Mosca fumbled in her pockets for her new pipe and then, gripping it between her teeth, went to sit on the bed. The stem waggled as she chewed on it, frowning all the while into space. Then, still frowning, she swung herself off the bed again, scooped up her bonnet from the top of the wigstand, and went back to the mirror.

She put the bonnet back on her head and fastened the ribbons in the fashionable style that the lavender girl had shown her. The ribbons rested neatly against the creases in her cheek, and the knot rubbed against a red dent under her chin. Yes, there was no doubt about it, the marks on Mosca's face had been caused by the bonnet ribbon. But in answering this small mystery she found herself faced with a larger one.

Why would Partridge have been wearing a woman's bonnet?

The black-eyed imp in the mirror rested its chin on its

hands and stared back at Mosca, champing all the while on its pipe. And then the movement of the chewing jaw slowed, and the black eyes became round, as the mistakes and misunderstandings brushed away like cobwebs, leaving the true shape of things bare before her mind's eye. Suddenly she could see what *must* have happened the night of the beast fight. Which of course meant . . .

'Oh, Saracen!' Mosca exclaimed, wide-eyed. 'What have we done?'

Saracen had just taken a big beakful of feathers from a pillow and was too busy snapping his beak and sputtering to share in Mosca's moment of revelation.

What could she do? Kohlrabi might not call by for days, and she could hardly count upon poor, confused Mrs Nokes to carry a message this important. No, she would have to go back and find the Cakes herself. She would only be gone a little while; she could return before anyone missed her and worried. Saracen would be safe enough in the little room. Providing, of course, he did not become restless and start overturning furniture, and providing Mrs Nokes did not come up to investigate the sound, and providing he did not burst out upon a rampage as soon as the door was opened . . .

'You'd better come with me,' Mosca sighed.

The shop was not yet open, so Mosca could not hope to slip out through a mill of customers. However, Mrs Nokes was busy arranging satin flowers and stuffed hummingbirds in a pale-green wig, and she did not notice as Mosca crept along behind the counter on all fours, Saracen's leash wound around her wrist. At the door, as an afterthought, Mosca caught up a large, dark-red wig box and tucked it under one arm.

'It's only borrowing,' she explained to Saracen when the door was safely closed behind them. 'Borrowing don't count.'

The box's rounded lid slid off easily. It slid on again rather less easily once the box was full of goose, since Saracen was not at all happy about the sky being blocked out, and he kept trying to peer his beak out through the crack.

'You're too recognizable, Saracen,' Mosca explained, pushing the lid firmly into place. There was a leather strap so the box could be tied to luggage when travelling by coach, and Mosca found that it could be slung over her right shoulder and buckled under her left armpit.

The market bell had rung, so the Cakes would be at the market.

The air was chill, but for now the wind had slackened. Mosca had half expected the streets outside to be deserted, while everyone peeped through their shutters and waited for war, but here were dozens of housewives and housekeepers, gripping their baskets and filling the air with the steam of their breath, chattered conversations, and the slap of their slippers against the cobbles.

Ordinary life did not stop just because kings rose and fell, Mosca realized. People adapted. If the world turned upside down, everyone ran and hid in their houses, but a very short while later, if all seemed quiet, they came out again and started selling each other potatoes.

The old marketplace within the city walls had been too far east for the Duke's sense of symmetry, so he had given orders for a new street to be run through it, and the foundations laid for a set of new houses. He had found a nice new site for the marketplace, which was much nearer the city centre. Unfortunately the new site was full of ungrateful and unreasonable people who liked their houses and did not care that knocking them down would make the maps look neater. While the Duke's men struggled to evict these people from their homes, the morning market had moved by unspoken consent to a space of grazing land south of the Ashbridge.

The river was still oozing mist as Mosca walked across the Ashbridge, which was so named because of the sheer number of times it had been burnt by pirates, robber barons and, finally, Parliamentarians.

At the far side the marketplace spread out like a fan, vivid with stalls of fruit and spices.

There was no sign of the Cakes among the stalls. However, the market did not end where the water began.

For the first hour after the market bell rang, the Water Market appeared as if from nowhere. Like a cluster of lily pads, a rocking plain of little boats gathered around the island of Goodman Sussuratch, tethered the one to the other, the furthest indistinct in the mist. Those with a little more money to spare shared a crammed wherry to the island, and leaned over the side to barter and buy. Many chose instead a more precarious route.

Starting at the base of the bridge, and tracing a winding path to the island, a line of boats was strung, each linked to the next by grappling chains. Little gangplanks bridged the gaps between them. The housewives hitched their skirts up and sidled carefully along the planks, their baskets and carrying yokes slung over their shoulders. Sometimes, where the boats were laden low and the mist was thick, they appeared to be walking upon the surface of the river itself.

'Pretty,' said the old woman in the first boat, looping two nooses of scarlet ribbon over Mosca's arm. 'Make you look pretty as a May morning, these will.' Mosca tottered, disentangled herself, and continued along the dipping plank-walk.

The boats nearest the shore sold wares much like those in the market square. One was loaded to the brim with pumpkins and celeriac. Another was heavy with crates of live chickens and rabbits. However, as Mosca drew near to the island of Sussuratch, she noticed a change. The river was the domain of the Watermen, and the usual laws of the land did not apply. Here the other guilds and the Duke had little power, and a different kind of market seller had glided out of the shadows.

Here chymists sold from their little, bobbing stalls without fear of the Apothecaries' Guild. Cat's teeth floating in bottled hyacinth water, toadstones, essence of garden tansy to aid childbirth, whole stuffed badgers as treatment against gout, and ground millipedes as a cure for earache.

The triple ball of the pawnbroker's sign hung from some masts. Mosca saw one such broker haggling with a woman in a tattered black cambric shawl who had spread across her lap a dozen pigtails, all crudely severed. She cast a black look over her shoulder when Mosca paused to peer, and Mosca guessed that she must be one of the notorious scissor-women, who would snip the locks off unguarded children to sell to wigmakers. The pigtails lay like fat, silken ropes, their sad little ribbons still attached.

In the next boat, a seller casually tossed a blanket over three sleeping pistols as she passed, and his conversation with his customer fell into a lull.

Around the island of Sussuratch itself, the boats lay flank to flank. This made it easier to step from one to the next, though no doubt if someone had fallen through a gap, it would also have made it easier for them to drown beneath the boats without anyone noticing.

Not far from the island's jetty, Mosca finally saw the Cakes, the baskets of her carrying yoke laden down with fruit and philtre bottles. When Mosca sidled up to her, the Cakes stiffened, but she continued ladling blood-red juice out of a cauldron into a pot she had brought for the purpose.

'I haven't seen you,' she said, a little primly. 'I'm buying stewed prunes and loveapples and payin' you no mind.'

'All right,' Mosca said with unusual meekness. Paying her no mind did not seem to stop the Cakes talking to her, so she supposed that was good enough.

'Cakes – I got to ask you somink.'

'I ain't talking to you,' the Cakes explained. 'I'm just mutterin' to myself, that's all.'

'Right – but you might just happen to mutter 'bout the same thing as I'm asking? I'm trying to – I'm trying to fix everything that's broken.'

The Cakes made a disapproving little mouth as she pushed the cork into her pot, but she seemed to be listening.

'The day after we married your parents – I remember you sayin' a couple came in with the bride so sloshy she could hardly stand. Can you remember anything about them?' Mosca bit her lip. 'I s'pose you'd need to check the register . . .'

'Course I wouldn't!' The Cakes was so surprised by the suggestion that she turned to Mosca and quite forgot to mutter. 'I could tell you every name on that register for every day this month, right here and now in my clogs. And I remember that day because I was merry as a cricket because . . . oh, you know why. There *was* a bride that had been making good cheer, and had to be propped up every step by her sweetheart – he had to guide her hand across the register to draw her "X" as well, but that often happens, you know. They took a room for the night, and must have left next morning while I was out at market.'

'Do you remember what she looked like?' Mosca had trouble keeping the excitement out of her voice.

'Don't recall seeing much of her face – she had her bonnet pushed forward on to her forehead. Not a lady.

 319

Sunburned and doughty. She had on a yellow stuff gown, I can tell you that much. And a cream-coloured casaque over the top, with blue woollen embroidery at the collar and cuffs, all done like daisies. Oh – and I do remember that she had a little bulging bone under the skin just here.' The Cakes tapped the side of her wrist. 'I remember feeling sorry for her, thinking maybe she drank a lot out of loneliness, and maybe she fell over and broke her wrist that way. So I was pleased for her, imagining her waking up the next morning, and finding herself *married*.' The Cakes beamed.

'What about the feller – do you remember him?'

The Cakes frowned, and shrugged a little.

'Too good for her, I remember thinking. Trim, with a gentlemanly way, and a nice silk stock collar. I remember the name, because it was a queer one. Duplimore Gweed.'

'Duplimore?' Mosca crinkled her forehead.

'Looked it up afterwards.' The Cakes looked pleased, like a fisherman describing a rare catch. 'It's sacred to Goodlady Judin of the Borrowed Face – if a babe's born while the sun's coming up for Goodman Greyglory's day, it's a child of Judin.'

'Cakes,' Mosca said in a small, quiet voice, 'you wouldn't get anybody named Duplimore.'

'Not often, no. I mean, what's the odds of being born just at sun-wake on that particular day?'

'No . . . I mean, even if you *were*. Judin's about the unluckiest Beloved to be born under – *nobody* wants

320

to name their child for her. So they wouldn't, Cakes. They'd squint at the sun and say it was as near up as not, and name the babe after Greyglory. The nursemaid wanted to say *I* was born before sunset, so I'd be a child of Boniface, not Palpitattle, only my father was . . . my father wasn't like anybody else.'

'You mean . . . people might . . . lie about names?' The two girls stared at one another as they grappled with the concept. It was like trying to imagine someone peeling off their own face to put on a false one. How would they put their own name on again afterwards? Wouldn't the Beloved they were born under be angry? The name you gave a child was as indelible as a brand, it was who they would become . . . and nobody, not even the slippery Eponymous Clent, ever lied about their name . . .

'I think somebody has,' Mosca said slowly. 'Did you see where the couple came from?'

'The river, I think. Yes, that was it, I saw them stepping off one of the ragmen's boats when I was out feeding the chickens. I suppose he must have given them a lift out of kindness.' The Cakes' smile faded as she remembered that she was not talking to Mosca.

'I'm going to fix everything,' Mosca promised, without knowing quite what she planned to do. 'Where do I find the ragmen?'

'Most of them are at the market – west side of the island.' The Cakes had withdrawn behind a stony expression once more, so Mosca took the hint and left her to herself.

It was true, then. The revelation that had dazzled her as she sat before the mirror was true. Why had she never stopped to wonder how Partridge had entered the marriage house in the first place? Now she knew.

Partridge had entered the house disguised as a woman, with a full-brimmed bonnet that fell over his face. He had been guided into a chapel, he had been married for a handful of shillings, he had been helped in signing the register, he had been half carried to one of the private rooms. And Partridge had objected to none of this because Partridge had already been dead.

So who was the name-changing bridegroom, the man in the silk stock collar? The murderer, almost certainly. What could such a man be like? He must have had blood like icewater to walk through a public street with his arm around the man he had killed. He must have had nerves of iron to go through a whole wedding ceremony, never knowing if someone might glimpse a male face under the bonnet, or touch the bride's hand and find it suspiciously cold. He must have had a strange, playful, twisted mind even to think of such a plan in the first place.

One further thing Mosca knew about this man without the slightest doubt: he could not possibly be Eponymous Clent. He had been at the Grey Mastiff all evening, and besides, the Cakes would have recognized him immediately.

Until today, Mosca had been haunted by images of Clent coming after her with revenge in mind. Now she was troubled by visions of him being chased over cold fields by men with muskets, trying to hide his plump and trembling bulk in hedges and under barrows. He was probably guilty of a hundred hanging offences, thefts and cheats and lays and lies, so perhaps it did not matter if he was hanged for one crime he had not committed. And yet it *did* matter. Mosca knew that she had to save him, and the only way to do so was to find the real murderer.

The ragmen's decks were not so much laden as littered, scraps and frills and whole garments locked in multi-coloured mêlée. Most of the vessels were simple, square rafts, but there were a couple of small barges with fringed awnings like those on tilt-boats, to keep the dew off the rags. Servant girls, seamstresses and housewives scrambled over the mounds, tugging at this and that like gulls picking at scraps.

''Scuse me.'

Two elderly women on one of the rag barges stopped their stitching and lifted their heads as Mosca raised her voice. They both wore a strangely stitched patchwork of snippets and sequins. 'My uncle got a lift with a ragman a week ago, an' he never come home . . . I was trying to find out where he was heading.'

'You're mistaken, my butterfly,' said the thinner of the two women. Her nose was so crooked that it seemed to have a knuckle in the middle. 'Ragmen don't give lifts – Watermen's rules. That's right, isn't it, Butterbara?'

'That's right,' agreed her plumper friend. 'Isn't that

 323

right, Tare?' A younger man looked up from his little raft and nodded vigorously, but insisted on calling his brother Sorrel to back him up, who in turn called upon his friend Dregly to agree with him. The word passed around all the ragmen, who agreed unanimously that no ragman could possibly have offered anyone a lift.

'Perhaps it was just a scruffy-looking wherry,' Butterbara suggested helpfully.

Mosca narrowed her eyes, but nodded. The ragmen lost interest in her and turned their attention to loosing their chains and casting off. Mosca was about to turn away when something on one of the rafts caught her eye.

Among the torn petticoats and bruised linen dangled a sleeve of cream-coloured linen. The light was still poor, but Mosca could make out a daisy pattern around the edge, embroidered in blue. She clambered down from the barge to the raft, which was small but laden with a rag heap almost as high as her head. As she crouched, she heard the rubbery patter of Saracen's webbed feet from inside his box, as if he was dancing sideways in an attempt to keep his balance. She unstrapped the wig box, and placed it down beside her.

Mosca pulled at the cream-coloured fabric, gingerly at first for fear of toppling the whole rag heap into the water, then more firmly, but still the sleeve resisted. Pushing at the mound with her shoulder, Mosca managed to clear enough of the deck to see that the sleeve was clenched fast in a closed trapdoor set in the deck.

The trapdoor had a ring, and Mosca was able to lift

it and pull the whole length of fabric free. Sure enough, it was a woman's 'casaque', a practical, short-sleeved, flared jacket meant to be worn over a gown. It was made for a woman of ample dimensions; it had blue woollen embroidery around the collar and cuffs, and in every particular it matched the Cakes' description of the casaque worn by the 'bride' during the macabre ceremony. And there, near the stomach – was that a smudge of mud or gravy, or something quite different? The fabric bore the marks of many bootsoles, and it was hard to tell.

Perhaps this was all she needed to clear Clent. Perhaps she did not need to find out why Partridge had been killed, or why this dress was here on the raft . . . or why a rag raft needed a trapdoor.

Mosca lifted the trapdoor and peered down into a darkness punctured only by the occasional gleam of morning light on metal. She leaned as far forward as she dared, and her nose caught something that smelt the way warm metal tastes. The next moment she leaned forward far further than she had intended as the raft lurched into motion, and she showed Goodman Sussuratch the soles of her clogs as she tumbled in through the hatchway.

'Have we struck something?' A voice from above. Mosca was too winded to speak, lost in a blackness where blurred red stars came and went. She could only guess that the trapdoor must have fallen shut behind her.

'Not at this depth. We bumped hips with the *Letitia*, that's all.'

'Tare.' The first man's voice had become lower and

more serious, with a dangerous edge to it. 'What's this doing here?'

'What?'

'The cream casaque – this should have been burned or ripped for scraps long since. We don't want it recognized.'

Mosca, who had drawn a breath to call out to the crew above, let the air out of her lungs slowly.

'I'll take it below and deal with it now, if you're ghaisted about it.' A pale square of sky appeared above, and a ladder of knotted rags tumbled down to brush the floor of the hold with its bottom rung.

Mosca scrambled to a crouch. Beside her squatted an object that to her night-stricken eyes looked a lot like a wrought-iron harpsichord. Mosca's long fingers told her that there were no keys to this harpsichord, but there were two iron shelves. The gap between them was narrow, but large enough to admit a Mosca, so she wriggled in, head first, while the rope ladder swung and jerked. By the time two heavy boots struck the floor of the hold, Mosca was tucked out of sight.

As she listened to the sound of someone ripping cloth with a knife, her curious fingers were still exploring. The shelf above her did not feel like metal. It had a slightly downy roughness, like the hide of a drum, and with a shock she realized that she was stroking paper. She lowered her hand and ran it over the shelf upon which she lay. It was slightly oily, and covered in jutting shapes that felt like row upon row of little teeth. Her fingertips, when she held them in front of her eyes, were stained black as coal.

On the upside, Mosca was now one of the few people in Mandelion who knew where the infamous illegal printing press was. On the downside, she rather suspected that she was in it.

R IS FOR REDEMPTION

At least, thought Mosca, *at least his hand isn't nowhere near the lever. So I probably won't get printed to death when I'm not expecting it.*

Through the crack between the metal plates, Mosca watched the glimmering knife of the ragman called Tare as he rent the cream casaque into little squares and tossed the fragments on to a pile of rags in the corner. He slid the blade through the fabric with a patient and careful pride – obviously a man who enjoyed using knives. When the task was over, his silhouette moved across to the wall, where a dozen or so pale squares hung in the darkness.

'Paper's nearly dry,' he called up.

'Quiet, until we're out of hearing of the town,' was the growled response from above. 'Let's try to make good speed towards Fainbless before the mists clear. The breeze will be rising soon.' The music of gullsong, horses' hoofs and street cries were becoming softer. Somewhere above, a pole churned through the water, and the beams of the raft creaked like the frame of a broken bellows. The river had remembered a lot of deep things it wished to say, and spoke them at length.

From time to time there came a tiny, ponderously regular sound like a whip-crack, which became louder and louder until it was almost deafening, and then was gradually left behind. In between times, curlews and warblers dropped thin spirals of sound into the stillness.

The ragman in the hold grew bored with ripping rags. His trunk of darkness approached the side of the press, and, from somewhere above her, Mosca heard two clicks, like a key turning in a stiff lock. The plate above her jolted and dropped an inch.

'Tare? Come up and take a look at this.'

The dark shape at the side of the press receded, and there followed the sounds of someone climbing the ladder.

'What is it?'

'Take a look for yourself – I'm manning the pole. There, by the hatchway. Do you recall seeing that before?'

'No, cannot say I have. Looks like a wigmaker's box.'

In the darkness of the hold below, two black eyes became as round as sovereigns.

'Well, take a look and see if there's anything in it.' There was a huff of someone stooping to lift something, and then a muffled thump-thump-thump as if they had shaken it to find out if it was empty. 'Careful there, you'll crush the wig – hi, what's the matter with you?'

'Something . . .' Tare sounded shaken. 'Something moved in there, Sorrel. Don't look at me that way. I'll show you – hand me that boathook.' There was a pause, a faint *thwoop* of a lid sliding away from a wig box, and

329

then two men's voices joined in laughter.

'I was expecting a boggling or a snarp at least,' gasped Sorrel after a while. 'You've an admirer, Tare. Someone's left you a present. Well, there'll be goose in the pot tonight, anyway.'

'Wait.' The mirth had died in Tare's voice. 'By my troth, it is the goose from the Grey Mastiff!'

It was happening, the preposterous scene Clent had painted for Mosca in words. The two men had recognized the valiant goose that had defeated the Civet of Queen Capillarie. They were touched, they were awed. They were remembering the exploits of their forgotten soldiering days and feeling noble impulses rekindle in their hearts. Mosca frowned. The kindling of noble impulses should surely involve less scuffling and shouting.

'Tare! What are you doing? Are you mad? Put that pistol away!'

'I tell you, it's the goose from the Grey Mastiff! I've seen it break men's legs like kindling!'

'Fire that pistol, and everyone this side of the valley will hear it. Every farmstead, every Waterman between here and Fainbless. Tare, no!' A mighty thump, a muffled thrashing, a clatter.

'Well, that's torn it. Did you see where that landed? White eyes of heaven, it's coming for us!'

A twin splash. Splutters, swimming strokes receding, and then, a short time later, faint voices in muted conversation.

'The raft'll tangle in that tree ahead. We'll loop a towline and pull her in, then wait . . .'

Mosca's limbs were still tender from her fall, and she hoped that all of the moisture on her hands was ink. Wriggling out sideways was no mean task, and once the print plate chafed her face. As she tried to climb the rag-ladder, it swung foolishly and tried to steal her feet out from under her, but when she kicked off her clogs, climbing became a lot easier.

After the darkness of the hold, the early light seemed like full morning. On a misty bank twenty yards away, two figures sat amid the blackberry bushes, wringing the riverwater out of their hats. Ahead, a fallen tree jutted from the bank and draggled in the water, bearded with dead leaves, foam and flotsam. The pole rested within Mosca's reach, cradled on two metal hooks, but it looked heavy and cumbersome. The paddle seemed a much better bet.

She crouched behind the pile of rags and paddled like fury. At first it seemed she was doing nothing to change the course of the raft, but then, when she looked up, the tree which had been dead ahead had moved a little to the left, and it seemed the raft might just slide past its grasp.

The ragmen had seen her and were running along the bank. One of them, Tare she thought, struggled through the tree's earth-caked fan of roots and scrambled along its trunk on all fours. Just as Mosca was fearing that he might intercept her, he lost his balance sideways and disappeared into the water with a sound like a gulp, leaving his hat bobbing on the surface. By the time he reappeared, huffing and blowing spray, the furthest twigs of the tree were drawing their nails along the boards of the raft. Using all her might, Mosca pushed the boughs away with her paddle, and the raft was caught by the river's current and swung away into the mist, while Saracen stood at the pinnacle of the rag mountain, his neck raised high and wings beating as if he could move the raft with his own wingstrokes.

'But, Saracen,' Mosca whispered to him as the confused cries of the ragmen faded behind her, 'after this we really got to stop stealing boats.'

She was aware that as a loyal citizen she should be taking the printing press back to Mandelion to hand over to the Stationers' Guild, and therefore she was going the wrong way. However, the river seemed to have strong opinions about their route, and it seemed rude to argue with it when it was being so helpful.

The faint whip-crack began again, and had just become a furious *clack-clack-clack* when through the vapour the domed head of a windmill appeared, its aged sails sounding like gunfire. The wind was rising and starting to tug away the mist like sheets from the furniture in an unused house. Beyond either bank lay empty fields and lowlands. At last an autumn sun peered above the grey woods, as bright and cold as toothache, and little golden fringes appeared along the tops of every treeline.

Mosca had watched the ragmen poling up and down the river, and she was fairly sure that the pole was meant to be driven into the riverbed to push the raft along. Her attempts to master the art, however, left her sodden, exhausted and floating far from the bank so that the pole could not reach the riverbed at all.

'Well, s'pose that's just Fate, then,' she said, flinging herself down on the deck. 'We'll just 'ave to be swept to sea an' hope we get captured by smugglers 'stead of pirates.'

Mosca wrung out her skirts, made herself a heaped rag mattress, and lay down upon it with her hands behind her head. Above, the clouds started to peel away like an old poster and show a sky of crystal blue. As she slid away from Mandelion, her heaviness of spirit also seemed to be peeling away. Would it be all that terrible if she did drift away to sea?

She closed her eyes against the aching brightness of the sky, and in a very short time she did drift away, but into sleep. When she awoke, her sky was fringed with rushes, and the feathery fronds of reeds were brushing her face.

The raft had drifted in among a great bank of reeds on the river's edge and tangled there. Perhaps Fate did not want Mosca to run away to sea after all, and suddenly she was fairly sure that this was not what she wanted either.

For a moment, Mosca's mind returned to her fellow-traveller, the grim-toothed press beneath the deck. She could almost imagine spider-letters and mad thoughts pouring from between its plates and chittering in the darkness. And yet, her dread of the press was not unmixed with fascination . . . No, she told herself. She would not let it lure her into its den.

The valley here was almost a plain, and the river had grown broad and lazy. Gleaming flats of mud pushed their faces above the water here and there so that geese and swans could hold conference. Much further downstream an ash-coloured dome seemed to hang unsupported in the morning light, and Mosca guessed that this might be the hill where the ruined city of Fainbless stood.

Plying her pole, Mosca managed to force her raft through the reeds until it nudged against the bank. In the clear morning sun she realized that her hands were dark with more than grime, and that her gown and apron were a smudged mass of printed words.

'Saracen!' She gaped at him in horror. 'Look! I'm all criminally printed!'

Below the rushes, water gleamed, so Mosca pushed them aside until enough water was visible to offer her a little mirror. The disaster was more complete than she had first thought. Her reflection showed her a host of blurry, backwards characters across her forearms and face.

'Well, I can't go back to Mandelion like this,' she muttered. 'I got an illegal nose.'

There was no saving her apron. She had knelt on it when wriggling out of the printing press, and her knees had crushed the cloth against the inky text plate. Mosca took it off hurriedly and paused to stare at a clear, black mark on the left-hand side of her apron. It was about the size of a hand's palm, jet-black and shaped like a playing-card heart.

Where had she seen a mark like that before? After a few moments the memory returned, but it placed her in even deeper perplexity. Back in the Grey Mastiff on the night of the beast fight she had seen a woman in a white dress up in the gallery. A woman who tried to look like Lady Tamarind but had a foolish, flabby face, a dress like Lady Tamarind's but with a black heart just like this one marking the sleeve. Lady Tamarind's dress, another woman's face, a black printed heart . . . it was a dreamlike jumble of oddments that did not seem to fit together.

She would make sense of it later. Cleansing herself of the ink was a more urgent matter. She dipped the corner of her apron into the water and began fiercely rubbing at her skin. After a while the letters on her face started to fade, but the printing on her right forearm was still clear and black. Indeed, it was so clear and black that Mosca was able to make out some of the words as she scrubbed.

'. . . and where the sword and cannon hold dominion keep this heart from trembling . . .' Mosca frowned. She'd been expecting some radical rantings, or political revelations, but this looked very like an old-fashioned 'heart's ease' prayer. In the time of the civil war many soldiers had marched into battle with a prayer of this sort written out on parchment and folded in the pocket over their heart, in the belief that it would bring them luck and courage.

'It's like someone's getting ready for a battle,' she murmured under her breath. Why were the heart's ease prayers being printed, rather than hand-written by a

 335

priest? Could it be that there was too little time to write them out – or too many soldiers to supply?

'. . . the land has sunk into a sickness of the soul . . . a poison that can only be removed by letting blood . . . our figures seem dark for the Light is behind us . . .' Mosca read on with new interest. '. . . our glorious brethren of the—' The next word was hard to read, running as it did across Mosca's wrist. She twisted her arm about and squinted until the smudged ink revealed its secret to her.

She sat back with a crash. The air was suddenly full of birds. They erupted from the rushes on all sides, their wings beating like frightened hearts, the white under-sides of their wings flashing with each beat. The air they left behind them shook and rippled and would not settle.

But they're dead, thought Mosca desperately, *they're all gone, everyone knows that . . .*

With urgent eyes she stared at the smudges on her skirts, skin and stockings, tracing the threads of sooty letters that wound about her like snakes.

'. . . with a sword of fire . . . and even their children . . . purity . . .'

And there again was the word she had found on her wrist. And there, and there . . .

Birdcatchers . . .

The morning air was as golden as ever, the wild rose-hips still bobbed gaily on the hedges, but the breeze had a new taste now, and the cries of the birds sounded like tearing metal.

Birdcatchers . . .

Anything was possible now. Mosca thought she could hear bland hillsides groaning open to release the monsters of the past. The worst of the dead times were rising from their graves, and it would take more than Little Goodman Postrophe and a mountain of mellowberries to stop them coming home.

But no, Mosca realized, the truth was less childish and more frightening. The Birdcatcher army that awaited these prayers would not be a spectral horde. Its soldiers would be flesh and blood, men and women of Mandelion, all waiting through the years for the right moment with a ghastly patience, like the Birdcatcher church attendant in Kohlrabi's story. The Birdcatchers had never been extinguished at all. They had just remembered how to be invisible.

And now they were ready to act. A battle was being planned, and beyond it Mosca seemed to see a world where trees screamed under the weight of hanged bodies, and the fears that still lurked like bats in the eaves of every mind surged out and blackened the sky.

Before her the clear, black heart on her apron burned into her gaze until it seemed to pulse with the heartbeat she heard in her ears. It was the Heart of the Consequence, the essence of purity, the drum of an unseen army. But it was more than that, and as she stared, Mosca started to see a new meaning in the mark.

Seven hours later, amid the crush of Mandelion's main thoroughfare, two young girls huddled by a ragged out-

337

crop of the old city wall and talked in low, urgent voices. The taller of the two had red ringlets too unruly for her cap, and she kept her hands bunched in her apron to keep them warm. The shorter had black hair, caked and clinging with earthy-pink powder, and she wore a patched olive-green dress of a style too old for her. On a strap over her shoulder hung a round, red wig box, and her clogs were caked with mud. Looking at the pair, a passer-by might think they were two shopkeepers' daughters taking a moment out of their errands to gossip. Few would suspect that they were discussing gods, and guilds, and the fate of the nation.

'I'm still not *really* talking to you,' the Cakes insisted for the sixth time. She scanned the crowds in front of the wrought-iron gates of the Eastern Spire. 'Remind me – what does she look like again?'

'Plump and peachy,' muttered Mosca. 'With a flouncety walk, and a nose stuck up like this.' With a fingertip she pushed up the tip of her own nose.

'I never done anything like this before,' murmured the Cakes nervously.

'You just got to throw her apron over her head, and hold on. You won't need to say anything.' Mosca grabbed the Cakes' arm. 'There! There she is! Come on!'

The lavender girl had stopped at the gate to preen the frills at the bustle of her pretty saque-backed gown. She smiled her way past the guards, observing their admira-tion through lowered lashes, then paused to look for a gap in the ebb and flow of bodies and coaches.

This hesitation was her undoing.

The first the poor lavender girl knew of her danger was when she found herself with a face full of linen. Before she could recover or scream, four thin hands gripped her arms, hurried her off her feet into an echoing alley and pushed her against a wall. The Cakes held on to her like a drowning sailor clinging to a beam, while Mosca placed a couple of well-aimed pinches on the prisoner's plump arms.

'Who are you? What do you want? Ow!'

'You weren't supposed to sell that dress, were you?' hissed Mosca.

'What? What dress?' The lavender girl was still too bewildered to pull the apron from her face.

'Lady Tamarind give you a snow-white dress, foaming with lace and all over pearls, with a heart-shaped stain on the sleeve. You was told to burn it, weren't you? But you didn't – that's stealing, that is. They're holding an Assizes right now for people like you.'

The lavender girl gave a whimper.

'Her Ladyship didn't say it *had* to be burned – she said it was all right to sell it, I just had to cut the cuffs off first. But . . . they were such *fine* cuffs, with real Meidermill lace, and I thought she couldn't really mean it. And the lady I sold the dress to said she thought the little heart looked rather pretty – like what poets say about wearing your heart on your sleeve. It wasn't really stealing, it wasn't, really it wasn't . . .'

'All right.' Mosca gave the prisoner one more pinch

 339

for luck. 'You tell nobody 'bout our parley, an' I'll tell nobody 'bout the dress.' She clapped the Cakes on the shoulder, and the red-haired girl followed her out of the alley at a run, leaving the lavender girl quivering under her apron.

'Did we have to do that?' the Cakes asked when she caught up.

Mosca shrugged. 'Don't have much time, do we?'

'I suppose not,' the Cakes answered uncertainly. 'So . . . your 'spicion was right, then?'

'Yes.' Mosca clapped both hands behind her bonnet, and leaned back to stare up at the Eastern Spire. 'Lady Tamarind got everyone running mulberry bush after that printing press: the Duke chasing after radicals, the Stationers chasing after Locksmiths. An' all the time it was *hers*.'

'So . . . that mark on her dress came from the printing press?'

'Yes. It wasn't enough seeing all the hurly-burly she was causing. She couldn't help herself, she had to go and *look* at the press.'

'Why?' The Cakes blinked, nonplussed.

'Power.' Mosca surprised herself at her own certainty. 'The press just sits there grinning at you with its metal teeth, like it's telling you it can turn cities upside down and send dukes mad and cause riots and wars. An' the thing about power is, it makes you want to get close to it, an' breathe it in, an' be part of it.'

She knew now that it was power that had hypnotized

her when she met Lady Tamarind. Lady Tamarind *wore* power, the way other ladies of the court wore jessamine perfume. Mosca had sensed it: a white, glowing, invisible essence that hung in the air around Tamarind, and she had wanted it without knowing what it was.

Lady Tamarind would have been bewitched by the press in the same way. Mosca could imagine her running her hands over the press, wanting to feel a tingle of power from the touch . . .

'She wouldn't know she had to pull out frames and bend them crookways to get the printed page loose,' Mosca added aloud, 'so maybe she just tried to reach inside and pull it out. And so she ended up with a big, black mark printed on her sleeve. She got rid of the dress the way she always did, by giving it to that pinch-nosed maid, only telling her this time to burn it or cut off the cuffs. But the maid was a silly, greedy hoity-toity who thought she could sell it for a better price with the cuffs still on. And so a lady with a flabby mouth and silly laugh bought it, and wore it to the beast fight, and that's where I saw her in it.'

'But why? What would Lady Tamarind want with a printing press?'

'I don't know,' answered Mosca. 'And I don't know why she's been printing all that radical stuff about the Duke's taxes on the starving poor. She's not a radical; I don't think she gives tuppence for the poor. She's a Birdcatcher.'

I must have given her the scare of her life when I told her she

 341

had a Stationer spy in her carriage, thought Mosca with a grim smile. Perhaps Tamarind had never seen anything special in Mosca, only a chance to spy on the Stationers, and make sure they were hunting for the press in the wrong places.

The Cakes shuddered. 'What are we going to do, Mosca?'

Mosca realized suddenly that the older girl would follow her lead. If Mosca chose to keep Tamarind's secret, the Cakes would hold her tongue.

Mosca had never tasted power before. It was a little like the feeling the gin had given her, but without the bitterness and the numbness in her nose. If she went to the Eastern Spire with what she knew, surely Lady Tamarind would do anything and give her anything to keep her quiet.

No wonder Tamarind schemed and spun to garner power, if power felt like this! Perhaps from the lofty rooms of her spire Mandelion always looked small and tame. Mosca imagined Lady Tamarind's long white fingers reaching down from the sky to shuffle the population like cards. Pertellis, shocked and ill, was nothing but a card. Eponymous Clent, ponderous and perspiring, was nothing but a card. Mosca Mye, black eyes alive with rage, was nothing but a card, to be played or discarded at will . . .

Mosca pulled out her handkerchief, unfolded it and shook out the seed-pearl she had wrapped in it for safety's sake. When she held the pearl to the light, it glowed like something eternal, but when she laid it on a cobble-stone and ground her heel against it a few times it crushed like wax.

'We stop her, that's what we do. Whatever she's doing, we stop her. But first I've got to find Mr Clent.'

The Cakes blinked, overwhelmed. 'We'd better find Carmine.'

Carmine, the clothier's apprentice, was no longer to be found briskly billowing silks and damasks outside his master's shop. He was in the cellar of a neighbouring chandler, his forehead as creased as his clothes, as if he hoped not to be found at all. His face brightened exceedingly when he saw the Cakes, and darkened in equal measure when he saw Mosca.

'Dormalise, what's she doing here?'

'Who's Dormalise?' asked Mosca. The Cakes gave her a nervous little smile. It struck Mosca too late that 'the Cakes' was probably not her original name.

'She wants to help . . . She thinks you know where Mr Pertellis is hiding, an' she wants to talk to him about . . .' The Cakes gave Mosca a careful glance.

'Matters of Consequence,' finished Mosca.

'You should never have brought her here.' Although he sounded bitterly exasperated, Carmine was gently patting at the Cakes' hand.

'I know who's been running the printing press. I know where it is. Only if I'm going to tell you, Mr Pertellis has got to help me find my Mr Clent. I know he escaped with Mr Pertellis, and I got to find him.'

 343

Carmine looked surprised, but he immediately dropped his eyes and tried to hide it.

'Oh, so you think finding the crooked printers will make everything better for Mr Pertellis, do you?'

'Yes,' Mosca declared with more confidence than she felt. 'No one cares about anything 'cept the press. The Duke is just angry cos someone was rude about the Twin Queens, an' the Stationers just want to have all the presses to themselves, right? An' when they know who has *really* been running the press, they won't care a bee's pouch 'bout Mr Pertellis or any of you any more.'

'Who is it, then?' Carmine folded his arms.

Mosca leaned forward. She told him, and watched the colour drain from his face.

The *Laurel Bower* coffeehouse was fastened near the Ashbridge when a fifteen-year-old apprentice approached it along the jetty, a few paces ahead of two younger girls.

'No customers!' called out one of the *Bower* deckhands, climbing down the wooden rungs from the roof. 'Lady of the house is ill – we're just stopping to take on food and physick. Oh – hello, Carmine.' His voice dropped to a lower and friendlier tone. 'Didn't recognize you. Since it's you, you can nip right in, but be sharpish about it, and don't let anyone see you.'

Carmine leaned forward to murmur into his ear, and the sailor cast a suspicious glance at Mosca before gripping the apprentice by the arm and drawing him in through the coffeehouse door. Despite a pleading look from the Cakes, Mosca slipped up to press her ear against the door.

It did not sound much like an invalid's house. There seemed to be a lot of people behind the door, all talking at once.

'Dormalise Bockerby says she's flash,' Carmine was saying, 'and I took 'em here the long way by the Scrapes so I was sure we weren't followed. I didn't like it at first, but I think you'll want to hear what she has to say.'

'That girl is clearly a pawn.' An educated, excitable voice that somehow reminded Mosca of a colt's harness bells. 'It little matters whose pawn – we can find out only to our cost.'

'Am I to understand that the poor girl is actually waiting there on the doorstep as we speak?' It was unmistakably the voice of Hopewood Pertellis, tired and patient. 'Then for goodness sake bring her in. If there *is* damage to be done, I would say it has already *been* done – she knows where we are. Bring her out of the cold and give her some chocolate.' There was a ripple of protest. 'My friends, either someone must let her in, or I shall go out and talk to her personally.'

Mosca managed to withdraw a few steps before the door was opened to admit the Cakes and herself.

Inside she had to blink a few times before her eyes grew used to the windowless dark. Daylight bored in through knotholes in the wooden walls, and a candle-holder was fixed to the centre of every table. Between the tables rose two wooden pillars, each the base of one of the masts above. They had been painted in genteel stripes to match the walls.

The lady of the house did not look ill. She was pale, but pale by nature, and perhaps from living in a half-light. Her vivid blue eyes were clear and calm beneath their heavy lids. A few roughly torn linen bandages hung over one arm, and the steaming bowl in her hand smelt of herbs.

Pertellis looked far more like an invalid, although he seemed to have recovered a little since Mosca had seen him in the watch house. He was muffled to the chin in a woollen kerchief, but although he was still pale his skin was less patchy, and he was clean-shaven.

There seemed to be a large number of men in the room, some unshaven, some sporting bandages. If these were Pertellis's radical conspirators, they didn't look like the leaders of a revolution. Mosca could not help notic-ing a smaller group that stood apart from the rest. They all wore gloves and had chatelaines dangling conspicu-ously at their belts. They accepted dishes of coffee from the serving girls with reflexive courtesy, but the wary politeness between the two groups spoke of uneasy alliance rather than trust. They all avoided the seated figure of Eponymous Clent in a corner, his head bowed as if happy to avoid notice. Eponymous Clent, crumpled and crestfallen . . . but seemingly uninjured.

There were a lot of eyes resting on Mosca's face as she stepped forward to breast the wave.

'I am Mosca Mye, and I . . . want to fix *everything*.'

'Really?' Pertellis's forehead crinkled as he smiled ruefully. 'I suppose that makes two of us. Oh, pardon me, about fifteen of us, within this house alone. It's all right, come and sit down. Miss Kitely has brought you up a dish of chocolate.'

Mosca took a dish from the lady of the house in silence. So this was a nest of radicals. She thought a hotbed of sedition would involve more gunpowder and secret handshakes, and less shuffling of feet and passing the sugar.

'I understand you know something about this printing press?'

'I found it. It's in a hidden hold on one of the old rag-men's rafts, only I had to get out again quick.' Mosca pulled a crumpled mass of linen out of one of her pockets and passed it to Pertellis.

'What's this?' He shook it out across the table.

'My old apron.'

Pertellis pulled a chipped monocle out of his waistcoat pocket and held it a few inches from his eye so as to peer at the letters. Then he slowly straightened, and his hand strayed back to his waistcoat, where it made three or four uncoordinated attempts to slide the monocle back into its pocket. His forehead was puckered and he was blinking very fast.

'My word,' he murmured.

'Birdcatchers.' Mosca voiced the unspoken.

There was a hush, and then the word took wing and fluttered, frightened, from mouth to mouth, stirring up questions and exclamations and fear and incredulity.

'I cannot believe it.' There was something in Pertellis's expression like that of a young child understanding about death for the first time. 'Can there really be a man or woman on this beloved earth who would wish those days of horror back upon us? Who would do this?'

'I can tell you that right enough,' Mosca answered grimly. Feeling their eyes pressing upon her, she told the story of Lady Tamarind's dress.

There was an appalled silence.

'I find it hard to believe that a lady like . . .' Pertellis hesitated, and coughed. 'There is something elevated in the female spirit that will always hold a woman back from the coldest and most vicious forms of villainy.'

'No, there isn't,' Miss Kitely said kindly but firmly, as she set a dish in his hand. 'Drink your chocolate, Mr Pertellis.'

'I believe I can perceive the lady's strategy, Pertellis.' One of the Locksmiths spoke with a soft rasp, as if through a mouthful of chalk powder. He was seated in a dark corner of the coffeehouse, and his face was all but lost in the murk. One slender ray of light fell across the tiny, gloved hands that lay, clasped, upon his knee.

Goshawk, thought Mosca. She could just make out light pooling palely where his eyes had to be.

'Ruling Mandelion is a matter of pulling the Duke's strings. That much must be obvious to all of you. And if you know what a man wants most, and fears most, and which lies he tells himself, then you may puppet-dance him for your pleasure until the end of his days.'

Several of Pertellis's companions bristled slightly at these sentiments, but Goshawk continued unabashed.

'Lady Tamarind has twisted her brother around her little finger since she was a child, and she would have done so forever if we had not appeared on the scene. For nearly six months we have been fighting her for control of the Duke – and slowly but surely we were winning.

'His great, mad dream is to see the Twin Queens return to the Realm to rule Mandelion. We encouraged him to believe it could happen. More than anything, he fears men like *you*, Pertellis, dangerous idealists who cannot be frightened or bribed into being sensible. So we stoked the flames of his fear, and taught him to see a great and bloody radical conspiracy in every paltry highway robber, every drunken riot, every rumour of a Floating School.'

'It sounds as if you were so busy trying to frame us, you did not notice Her Ladyship setting out to frame *you*.' The speaker was a young man whose bright brown eyes made him look twice as awake as everyone else, and three times as angry. Mosca recognized the 'colt harness' voice she had heard while eavesdropping.

'Succintly put, Mr Copperback,' said Goshawk, without any sign of resentment. 'Three months ago, the Duke was almost ready to sign any charter we wanted. Her Ladyship must have set up the secret printing press as a last desperate gamble. An inspired gamble, with one important effect – the Stationers' Guild became involved.

She persuaded the Stationers that *we* were running the press in order to manipulate the Duke. Then she made it appear that the Stationers had plotted our arrest. No doubt she has amused herself greatly watching our guilds tearing one another apart.'

'But surely that is a rather short-sighted plan?' Pertellis blinked across at the Goshawk-shaped patch of murk. 'In time, both sides were bound to compare notes and realize they had been tricked. She will be left vulnerable.'

Mosca's blood suddenly ran cold.

'No, she won't,' she said. 'I heard the Duke give her a by-your-leave to bring in a big ship from the coast, all up to its ears in troops for keeping order. That's who the new Birdcatcher printings are for . . .'

'The Watermen would never allow it!' exclaimed Miss Kitely.

There was a murmur of assent from the rest of the room.

'In case you have not noticed, madam,' Goshawk interjected, 'there are currently hardly any Watermen in Mandelion. Most of them disappeared upstream several days ago.'

Mosca looked sideways at the Locksmith leader. 'I heard Lady Tamarind say something about that too. They've been sent to "delay" the Locksmith troops that she knew were waiting upstream.'

'Are you saying that the waterway is clear for a ship full of Birdcatcher troops to sail into Mandelion and take it over?' Pertellis was cleaning his monocle hard enough to push the lens out. 'When does this ship arrive, Miss Mye?'

'She said it would take ten days to get 'ere. An' that was . . . about ten days ago.'

'Beloved above,' whispered Pertellis. 'They could turn up at any moment.'

The conversation became very animated and confusing, so Mosca went and sat next to Eponymous Clent, and kicked her heels against the chair leg for a minute or so.

'So, you just found the barge captain's body in the clothes chest, then, did you?' she asked at last. She was not very good at apologizing.

'On the bed, actually. When you found me, I was trying to, ah, hide it. I fear I was not thinking with my usual crystalline lucidity. I even suspected for a while that you might have been responsible for, as it were, spilling the fellow's claret. You need not look so shocked – younger than you have done worse, and you have a wealth of rage in that reed-like form of yours.'

'But you didn't cackle on me?'

'No.' Clent looked a little embarrassed, as if he had been caught out in a weakness. 'When you denounced me in the watch house I saw myself reflected in your eyes as a monstrous mankiller, and I realized that you truly thought I was guilty. I suppose I could have exposed your petty little crimes and dragged you to the gallows with me, but . . . what would have been the point?'

'I came back to sort it all out,' said Mosca, after an awkward pause.

351

'Ah,' Clent responded without the faintest trace of hope.

'Thought I'd better. No one else cares 'bout you at all, do they?'

'No, I suppose not. Have you been rubbing ashes into your hair as a sign of penitence?'

'That's just powder. I'm in disguise.'

'As a wig-seller?' Clent nudged the wig box with his toe.

'The box is just borrowed,' Mosca explained quickly. 'Had to put Saracen somewhere, didn't I?'

'Of course.' Clent lowered his face into his hands. 'The sad and weather beaten violins of my existence are tuning up for the coda of my life's symphony, my hopes and dreams are preparing to drain into the forgetful sands like so much rain – and my last and darkest hours would not be complete without the presence of The Goose.'

While Pertellis and his fellow radicals tried to make sense of what Mosca had told them, Miss Kitely, who had withdrawn through a little doorway, re-emerged, this time without a coffee-pot.

'Mr Pertellis,' she said, her quiet voice creating a space for itself amid the raised tones, 'I have consulted *him* on the matter, and he would like to speak with the girl.'

'Him?' Mosca looked a question at Pertellis.

'Our leader.' Pertellis beamed with pride. 'But . . . I thought you were the leader!' Mosca exchanged a glance with Clent, who seemed as surprised as she was.

'Oh no, not really. The truth is, we've never really had

a leader.' Pertellis gave the men around him an abashed smile. 'We were just a group of friends who did our best to change things for the better in little ways – and met in this coffeehouse so we could talk safely. I suppose I kept everyone in touch with each other, but I was always ready to step down when a true leader came along. And he did – in our darkest hour. A man of action, of decision.' A number of the Locksmiths were looking curious, and Mosca suspected that perhaps they had not met the mysterious leader either.

Mosca rose a little unsteadily and found that Clent was also on his feet.

'If you have no objection, I shall accompany my secretary. I would be glad to trade a few words with this incomparable leader of yours.'

The leader would be someone with eyes as sharp as glass shards, Mosca thought, a man whose mind cut to the heart of things like a knife through cheese, a man like her father. The leader would be a man calm in every crisis, with a clear gaze and a smile as frank as a handshake.

Pertellis held the door ajar for Mosca and Clent, and he followed them into the room. It had the sick-room smells of vegetable soup and laudanum, but the man seated in a mahogany chair was dressed crisply, not with the slack helplessness of the invalid.

The radical leader was Captain Blythe the highwayman.

S IS FOR SEDITION

Captain Blythe, the highwayman. Captain Blythe in a redingote of good green cloth, with his hair combed back in its pigtail, and cobbled boots on his feet.

'This is the young lady with the printed heart.' Pertellis diligently recounted Mosca's words.

Blythe did not offer him so much as a glance. Nor did he look at Mosca. His eyes were set upon the face of Eponymous Clent, as if he hoped to pin him with his gaze like a butterfly to a board.

'How long has this man been here?' he asked sharply as soon as Pertellis had finished speaking.

'Mr Eponymous Clent was one of many languishing in the jail when your men led the rescue mission using the information and keys that Mr Goshawk gave us. He is . . . not exactly of our party but we took him with us because, well, we were not sure what else to do with him.'

'I need to speak with him. Alone, if you please.' Blythe remembered Mosca and gave her a fleeting glance. 'All right, his familiar may stay if she must.' Pertellis left the room without complaint.

'I must say,' Clent declared, rallying from his shock,

'this is not a total surprise to me. When we, ah, met by the road to Mandelion, even then I noted something of a twinkle in your eye and said to myself, here is a gentleman who is more than he seems. Thievery is a game that he plays to, ah, mislead those who seek the leader of the valiant, freedom-loving radicals . . .' Something in Blythe's glare quelled Clent's flow of words.

The highwayman placed his hands upon his knees, and leaned forward, still piercing Clent with his eyes. 'Are you aware that you and your infernal ballad have ruined my life?'

'Ah . . .'

Blythe erupted to his feet and took a few angry paces down the room and back, gripping his own fist as if trying to crush it.

'I always laughed at those gulls who thought going on the highway was the way to become a gentleman. I saw them riding in darbies to the tree in their velvet lapels, with lasses of the town pretending to weep for them. And I laughed at them – for *I* knew that was not how it was done. It should be blood, and business, and keep your dreams in your head.

'Then your cursed ballad changed everything. All my men started hearing they were my Gallant Company of Merry Rogues, and they took a liking to it. Then one evening, I came upon a big man in a black cap bullying two village lasses. They hailed me as if they knew me – they didn't *ask* me to help them, they beamed and told Black-cap that now I was there they would surely see his crown broken. So he rounded on me, and so I rounded on him, and . . . tapped his claret for him. He ran off with his broken nose, and I found myself with a bundle of rosemary and half a rye cake in thanks. I could hardly peel their arms from round my neck. Well, that . . .'

Blythe looked distracted and waved a finger.

'That bit was not so bad.

'But word got out. Black-cap was a beadle, it turned out, with a turn for bullying extra tax, and by morning the new songs had it that I was defending the poor and helpless against the Duke's men. I was a hero standing between little lowly folk and their oppressors. And the little lowly folk believed it, and so did the oppressors, right up to the Duke himself, His Grace of the Cloven Brain.' Blythe ran a distracted hand over his hair. 'The Duke's men searched every garret and barn for us. But the villagers hid us in cellars, they fed us and lent us their best boots when ours were run to rags, then turned hopeful eyes on us because they knew we had come to help them. So somehow I found myself stopping families being thrown out of their cottages, and beating off taxmen so that villagers could eat that night.

'I was taken sick with an ague after hiding in the heather for three nights, and a family of farmers smuggled me into Mandelion in their market cart to find a physician. I have lain low in this coffeehouse ever since, and cannot show my face for fear of the constables.

'Your damnable way with words has brought me to this pass. I am leader of a valiant resistance, whether I will or nay, and trapped beyond my wits to remedy. Any suggestions?'

Clent cleared his throat. He took some time about it, and Mosca guessed that his feverish mind was searching for words.

'My dear good sir, your story is extraordinary, indeed one that I would be proud to have written, but I cannot see why your anger has turned upon me. You wished to become the stuff of ballads, and that you are. Perhaps you are a little more legendary than you hoped, but you have no one to blame for that but yourself. I fulfilled my part of the bargain, and you needed only to keep a cool head and revel in your glory until some other brisk blade with a good seat on a horse came along to steal your thunder.'

'A cool head? A week ago the Duke's men arrested a young farmer because he would not betray me. His wife rode through dark and storm in nothing but her gown to tell me of it, so that I should rescue her husband before he could be taken to Mandelion to stand trial. What was I to do? Say no?'

'Yes,' Clent replied promptly. 'I would have done, and so would countless other men. If you have weakened to the siren songs of valour and virtue, I hardly see how you can blame me.'

The door behind Mosca opened again, and Miss Kitely put her head around it.

'The boy we sent for Mr Trifish the barber-surgeon is back, Clam. He found a kerchief dropped on the

 357

step – the signal Mr Trifish said he'd leave if the Duke's men had taken him.'

'Cast off, then. Trifish is a milk-and-mallow cove, and will squeak if they prick him. The constables will be here any minute.'

Miss Kitely withdrew, closing the door behind her, and Blythe gave Clent a blazing look.

'You see? They rely on me. Even she . . .' He waved a despairing hand at the door. '. . . she relies on me.'

'A-a-ah . . . I think I understand. There is a charming complication in the matter, a delicate dilemma, a sweet distraction . . .' Clent halted as Mosca elbowed him sharply in the ribs. 'My dear fellow,' he continued more soberly, 'if you have managed to complicate things by forming a sentimental attachment in less than a week, then I doubt there is anything I can do for you. You, sir, are a romantic, and I suspect your condition is incurable.'

There were feet moving on the roof above, and ropes ticked as they were played out. Paintings rattled against the wall as the room lurched, then accepted the river as a dancing partner. Suddenly there was the crash of a crockery catastrophe, raised voices in the next room, and feet thundering above.

Blythe threw the door open, and Mosca and Clent followed him through it.

'What's happening?'

A grimy boy Mosca recognized from the Floating School was recovering his breath.

'The Duke's men, sir – they're searchin' all the

coffeehouses at moorings, sir.'

'Cast off quickly! Cut the ropes if you have to! Have we men still ashore?'

'Only Hamby and Foddle loosing the lines. Here they come!'

The street outside was sliding to the right and a dark mouth of a gap slowly opening between the waterfront and the doorstep. First one man and then a second leaped for the doorway, and each was caught by a forest of waiting arms and pulled to safety. When the doorway cleared, two coffeemaidens knelt on the threshold, bracing a broom and a warming pan against the street's edge to push it away.

'Miss Kitely! We're like to catch our doorscraper in the figurehead of the *Spry Squirrelhawk*!' squeaked the shorter and plumper of the two coffeemaidens, sidling up against the jamb to brace herself.

Miss Kitely snatched up a long mop and beat the handle-end against a trapdoor in the roof until it cracked open.

'Mr Stallwrath, hard-a-chimneyside, if you would.' A harassed-looking sailor above gave a hurried salute.

Mosca pushed her eye against a knothole. She could see a group of Duke's men pushing through the crowd carrying cudgels, and two of them seemed to be shouldering muskets. Their leader was calling something aloft, hailing the sailors up on the deck of the *Bower*. He pointed at the jetty, as if ordering them back to their moorings. As the coffeehouse drifted further away, his mouth shrank to an angry crack across his face. He started to drive his way through the crowd with a new fierceness and resolution.

'Up kites, Mr Stallwrath!'

'But Miss Kitely, we ain't ten paddle-lengths clear of the bank . . .'

'We shall worry about the fine later, Mr Stallwrath.'

There was a squeal of consternation from the coffeemaidens as the first Duke's man reached the jetty side.

'Grab their lines! Stop that coffeehouse!' someone was shouting. 'There are fugitives and cell-breakers aboard!'

'Sussuratch smile!' murmured Miss Kitely. 'She's gathering away – we are finding our pace at last.'

Perhaps they were. Perhaps this was fast for a coffeehouse. Mosca could not help noticing that they were still being overtaken by ducks.

A shout of triumph. One of the Duke's men lifted a dripping boathook with a trailing line looped across the end. Four deputies seized hold and braced their weight against it, the drift of the *Laurel Bower* dragging them towards the brink in stuttering steps. Drawing his sword, Blythe pushed his way to the doorway and swung himself out and to one side. Mosca recollected the rungs set in the outside wall.

A blade flashed downwards once, twice, and the cluster of deputies fell backwards, the severed rope-end flicking back into their faces like a cow's tail swatting flies. Blythe swung back into the room and turned to stand in the doorway, daring anyone on the jetty to leap for the boat. No one seemed ready to take up the challenge.

'We're clearing the *Squirrelhawk* . . . we'll clear the *Donkey Dancer* . . . our stern's three paddle-lengths from the shore, Skipp'am!' The final word, to judge by the confused salute that accompanied it, was a compromise between 'skipper' and 'madam'.

'Gentlemen, we are on the river, and out of the Duke's jurisdiction!' Miss Kitely's declaration was met by a brief burst of cheering on all sides. One radical even slapped Blythe heartily on the back, almost toppling him forward into the water, and earning himself a glare.

There was a violent crack, like a tree bough snapping, and suddenly there was a new knothole in the northern wall, and another in the southern wall.

'Good heavens!' exclaimed Pertellis in consternation, gazing down at Blythe, who was now lying at full length upon his face. 'Are you all right, sir?'

Blythe lifted himself on to his elbows and directed a red-faced, disbelieving glare around the room.

'Weeping Lord of the Bloody Eye, will you all get down? *They are shooting at us.*'

The other men in the *Laurel Bower* obediently lowered themselves, some of them carefully laying down their coffee dishes first, others looking around for the cleanest place on the floor. When a second shot punctured a sampler and gonged off a coffee-pot, the floorboards suddenly looked a lot more comfortable to everyone.

'They cannot be.' Miss Kitely's voice was fragile. 'No one . . . no one would shoot at us on the river . . . The Watermen would never . . . never allow . . .' Blythe grabbed for her sleeve to pull her down. Her skirt ballooned about her as she sank to her knees, then subsided around her with a silken sigh.

Clent and Mosca had crouched scarcely a second after Blythe had flung himself flat, and now they peeped at each other between their fingers.

'Madam,' Clent muttered, 'I owe you an apology. You were correct, and I was in error. The Duke *is* pixelated.'

'Where's the Cakes?' Mosca looked about.

She need not have worried. Carmine had taken it upon himself to save the Cakes. This involved dragging her down to a corner of the floor and wrapping his arms protectively around her. Even the floor must have seemed quite a dangerous place to him, since he appeared to be in no hurry to let her go.

'Dulcet!' A flush was creeping up from Miss Kitely's collar. 'Dulcet, run to the galley and put another cauldron on the boil, then come back here with those three muskets. Shrewlie, go with her and bring back as much shot as you can carry. You other girls, help them carry.' Seeing both the coffeemaidens scampering for the internal door, Mosca suddenly realized that 'you other girls' must mean the Cakes and herself. It did not look as if the Cakes would escape from her saviour at any time soon, so Mosca followed the coffeemaidens.

The galley was blisteringly hot. Heaps of coffeebeans

glistened through the steam like burned-out mountains of some volcanic land. Squat little Moscas of different sizes were reflected in the bowls of a dozen ladles. The table was also a cupboard, the top folded back to show everything stowed tidily on hooks and in lined pockets, ready to be 'battened down when the coffeehouse was underway'.

'Take these.' Dulcet, the tall girl with honey-coloured hair, looped the strings of four heavy leather pouches over Mosca's wrists. 'And some of them snuffbottles. The green ones. Blue ones are snuff, green ones are gunpowder.' The muskets that filled Shrewlie's arms gleamed with a dull oiliness, and smelt of beeswax.

This is more like it, Mosca decided, as she filled her hands with tiny, scarab-shaped bottles. When they struggled back into the main room, the door had been wedged so that it stood open barely the width of a hand. Blythe lay on his belly, aiming a pistol through the aperture. Without the view of the bobbing shore it did not feel so much as if they were in a boat, rather a parlour with hiccups.

Another shot punctured the door and tore apart the head of a stuffed fish that decorated the wall, showering bystanders with sawdust.

'How do you come to have so much lead shot, Miss Kitely?' Pertellis seemed bewildered by the laden appearance of the girls.

'Mr Copperback has been expecting something of this sort for a while. He has been making his own shot, and it

 363

seemed most sensible to hide it on the *Bower*.' Miss Kitely continued to clean out a pistol barrel in a business-like manner.

'But where in the name of goodness did you find the lead?'

Copperback opened his mouth to say something, but forgot what it was when Miss Kitely gave him a meaningful look.

'It is a long story,' Miss Kitely explained coolly, as she took a snuff bottle from Mosca and began trickling the powder into the pan. In Mosca's experience, a 'long story' was always a short story someone did not want to tell. In this case she thought it probably involved stolen shrine icons.

'Um . . . I could swear that this bullet has an eye.'

'A freak of the mould, Mr Pertellis.'

Mosca left the last pouch of shot in the eager hand of Copperback, then ran to press her eye to a knothole in the shoreward wall. She could see a gaggle of Duke's men in black and green standing on the jetty, now a reassuring distance away. There was a downy puff, like a dandelion clock being torn apart by the wind. Only as the smoke unravelled did Mosca glimpse the musket barrel behind it. Just as she was wondering how the gun had fouled, she heard a crack and felt the wall tremble against her cheek.

It was all so odd and unreal, she could not feel any sense of danger. She was marvelling at this when a dun yellow cloth slid across the scene like a theatre curtain. Her cry of surprise was echoed by several others nearby.

'It's the *Catnip*! They've pulled alongside us!' was the call from above.

'Call out to them! Let them know they're likely to be caught in the crossfire!' Miss Kitely called back.

'They're saying nothing, but they're keeping pace and giving us the wave.' Stallwrath sounded bewildered.

It was true. The little lighter with the yellow sail had slowed to hold its place between the *Laurel Bower* and the jetty where the Duke's men levelled their muskets in vain. 'Her mainsail is shaking, but they're making no move to right her. I think . . . she's shielding us from fire.'

From Mosca's knothole she could see nothing but the yellow sail, but a minute later she heard gasps from a couple of the radicals at other spyholes.

'It's the *Peck o' Clams*,' cried Miss Kitely, 'sails close-hauled to hide us, dragging anchor to slow her down to our pace. What are they doing?'

There was no answer to this question. All that Stallwrath could report as he crouched behind the safety of the coffeehouse chimney was that they were suddenly surrounded by a convoy of little boats, whose grimly smiling captains saluted them but offered no explanation. For the moment there was little danger of being shot, and as little chance of firing at their attackers on the bank. Everyone on the *Bower* quickly realized they could get on with the argument they'd been itching to have.

Miss Kitely was sure that if the Watermen knew what was happening, they would rush back to defend the *Laurel Bower*, then charge to the coast to stop the

Birdcatchers. Everyone else thought that the Watermen were unlikely to accept the word of a huddle of outlaws against the word of a duke.

Goshawk wanted to send one of his men on a fast horse to the Locksmith troops waiting upstream, so that if everyone in the *Laurel Bower* perished, 'the Duke would pay the price'. Everyone else thought this sounded extremely dangerous, and they were not at all keen on the bit about everyone in the coffeehouse dying.

Hopewood Pertellis suggested that he should borrow a little dinghy from the convoy and approach the shore under a flag of parley to explain everything 'and stop all this foolishness'. Everyone else was very polite about this idea, then changed the subject completely.

'There is another way,' Eponymous Clent said. In fact, he said it several times without anyone hearing, but Copperback accidentally sparked the powder in his pan, deafening everyone and filling the room with smoke. While they were all still coughing, Clent declared loudly, 'There is another way. Perhaps the Watermen will not listen to us, but they will certainly listen to the Stationers' Guild. The two guilds have been on excellent terms for years.'

'Which does us little good, since the Stationers' Guild will certainly not listen to us,' retorted Copperback, as he primed his rifle again.

'They will listen to me,' Clent declared with simple grandeur. 'Particularly when they learn that someone has tried to trick them into a guild war.'

There was an impressed silence. 'So,' Pertellis said slowly, 'you are saying that we should send you to tell the Stationers about Lady Tamarind's plot against the Locksmiths and persuade them to warn the Watermen about the Birdcatchers?' A hush followed this question while everyone tried to piece the sentence together in their heads. 'Oh dear, this is complicated . . . perhaps if I drew a diagram to make things clearer?'

'Whatever happened to simple plans?' muttered Blythe, still sighting along his gun through the doorway.

'Do you have a better idea, sir?' asked Clent coolly.

'I'm far too confused to have a better idea!' flared Blythe.

Mosca found herself warming to him.

Blythe looked Clent up and down. 'How well do you swim?'

'Ah . . .' Clent dropped his eyes. Most of the radicals and Locksmiths were looking similarly sheepish.

'I can swim,' said Mosca.

Clent raised his eyes to heaven. 'What was I thinking? Gentlemen, this girl was brought up in a drowned village, nursemaided by frogs and swaddled in lilies. She can swim like a Timberline trout, and she is a contracted apprentice of the Stationers' Guild.' He drew Mosca with both hands into the centre of the room. 'She can take a missive from me to the Stationers at the *Telling Word* coffeehouse. Miss Kitely, do you have a small boat of any sort?'

'I fear we do not, Mr Clent, but there is a wooden

367

washing tub in which we sometimes lower one of the girls when we need to look to the hull.'

Mosca had flushed bright red and suddenly couldn't understand anything that was being said, although the fog of faces was smiling at her. She seemed to have volunteered, and things were happening so quickly she could hardly keep her feet. Out of the corner of her eye she saw Goshawk beckon Clent over, whisper to him, and place two keys in his hand.

'Miss Mye –' Pertellis was looking into her face with his usual expression of dazzled concern – 'no one will blame you if you choose not do this.'

'That isn't true, is it, Mr Pertellis?' Mosca whispered back gently.

Miss Kitely took control. While Clent wrote his letter, Mosca was to eat a little supper in the back room and compose herself. Mosca was glad of the privacy, but she had no stomach for the apple pie that was brought to her. She had just pushed it aside when Blythe entered, stifling a cough. He looked embarrassed to find himself observed, and settled for staring at an ornamental anchor hanging on the wall. Blythe reminded Mosca of the civet, trapped in a battle it did not understand, its eyes reflecting images of its lost freedom.

'So, do you want to marry Miss Kitely?'

'If she'd have me.' Blythe looked as if he would like to be angry at the question but had too much to think about. If Mosca said nothing more, he would start thinking about the heath again.

'She's got strange eyes.'

'She has very fine eyes.' The highwayman sounded affronted. 'She's . . . like no one I've met before. A real lady. And . . .' A dreamy look crossed his face. '. . . she can clean, load and present a pistol in twenty heartbeats.'

Mosca thought this a much better reason to be in love with someone. But Miss Kitely seemed so unlikely in every other way, so prim and high-collared. Then she remembered the gentle way the coffee mistress had said the highwayman's name, Clam . . .

'Were you born under Goodman Sicklenose—'

'He Who Lures the Shelled Fish into the Hungry Net. Yes.' Blythe peered at her. He mouthed the name 'Mosca' to himself, then raised an eyebrow. 'Palpitattle?' Mosca nodded, and they exchanged a smile of grim sympathy.

'It would have been my twenty-ninth nameday two weeks from now.'

'It would have been my thirteenth in eleven months.'

This seemed to be all that needed to be said.

'All right,' growled Blythe. 'Let's go. Our friends need Black Captain Blythe to be a hero, and you have a washing tub to catch.'

T IS FOR TRIAL BY COMBAT

When Mosca emerged from the back room, Clent placed a sealed letter in her hand, but seemed reluctant to release his end of it.

'You . . . you *do* swim well, I trust?'

'Like a Timberline trout,' Mosca replied promptly.

'Ha. Hum. Mosca, when you have delivered this letter, make your way to the Ashbridge. If our dice fall ill, leave Mandelion with all dispatch. If you see smoke rising from the river, assume the worst.'

'If the worst comes . . . you'll let Saracen out of 'is box, won't you, Mr Clent?'

'I swear it upon my muse.'

Mosca knew that, like Clent, she wore the expression of one who has heard a trickle above become a rumble, and is waiting for the avalanche. They did not know what was happening in Mandelion, but they were fairly sure it would end up happening to them.

'They're . . . they're like a sack of kittens chucked in a river,' Mosca whispered as Clent accompanied her through the crowd of radicals. He slowly lowered his lids once in silent agreement.

Fear made everyone look very alive in a strange and fragile way, like the last flare of a candle before it dies. *It cannot end well*, said a leaden weight in Mosca's stomach. *Some of them will die, perhaps all.*

Mosca wanted to say goodbye to the Cakes, but the older girl was still being saved by Carmine. Indeed, the Cakes seemed to be so very, very safe that Mosca began to wonder if marriage might not rub off on her after all.

In the galley, a trapdoor had been opened in one wall, and a large, sturdy-looking cedar washing tub was being fastened to lines from the ceiling.

'Madam, take some care climbing in, you are blessing the company with sight of a generous extent of your stockinged . . . oh, painted smirk of a hopeless dawn, the child is still wearing her breeches . . .'

Miss Kitely slid a bracelet over Mosca's wrist, and Mosca saw that tiny wooden figures with carved skeletal faces dangled from it. They were the Little Goodkin, and she realized to her surprise that Miss Kitely thought of her as a child.

Many hands hauled on the ropes. They guided the tub's giddy ascent towards the hatch, and suddenly Mosca was in the open air, steam from the galley surging out around her, the skin of her face feeling stripped and cold. The tub lowered in jolts, banging against the side of the coffeehouse all the way to the waterline. Under the 'coffeehouse' was an ordinary hull, against which water cast dancing hieroglyphs of light.

Mosca loosed the hooks that held the tub to the lines,

 371

and a sudden plunge left the tub lolling in the lap of the river as it fell quickly astern of the *Laurel Bower*.

'Ahoy! Catch hold there, we'll haul you in!'

A line end stung Mosca's cheek, and she grabbed at it automatically. A little bumboat of the sort that sold provisions to large ships in dock was bobbing in the wake of the *Catnip*. Over the gunwale peered two burnished faces. The two girls wore their plaits down and, like most gypsies, they wore rich waistcoats over their workday clothes, with the meandering of the River Slye embroidered across their chests.

As water was seeping in between the slats of the tub, Mosca made the line fast to one of the handles. The gypsies hauled it in, arm over arm, and then reached over the side to pull her into the bumboat.

'Is everyone hale in the *Bower*?' was the first question after they had recovered their breath.

'Not holed yet, as I saw. The Duke's men just shot a fish and killed a kettle,' replied Mosca, feeling her arms where the gypsies' strong fingers had left tender places.

'What about Him?' asked the younger of the two.

'Him?'

'It's no secret,' explained the older. 'When he swung out and cut away the mooring ropes with his sword, Mr-Woolnough-the-Physician's-youngest-daughter-Tinda caught a sight of him, and couldn't stop herself squealing out his name. The Duke's men and everyone else heard her, and the constables started shouting that Black Captain Blythe was aboard, and if the *Bower* didn't pull to they'd run to the Western Spire, drop a carcass in the cannon, and burn 'em to the waterline.' Mosca had read enough of piratical battles to know that a carcass was a can of oiled rags that could be used to set fire to buildings or ships. 'Well, we couldn't be having with that. Not a coward trick like that against brave Captain Blythe.'

'Brave and handsome Captain Blythe,' the younger added. 'Is he as handsome as they say?'

'Three times as handsome,' Mosca answered without hesitation. 'An' . . . he got a commandin' eye which makes him look six times as handsome.'

'What colour are his eyes?'

Mosca paused. She had no idea what colour Blythe's eyes were.

'Well, they sort of change like the sky when the clouds are skittish. When he's starin' down a foe, all undomitable, they're all silvery grey like stone in moonlight. And . . . when he smiles they go a merry sort of blue. And other times they're all sorts of other colours.'

'But sometimes they're green?'

Mosca could not mistake the note of hope in the younger gypsy's voice.

'Oh yes. Course. *Most* of the time they're green.'

'I *knew* it. Didn't I say Captain Blythe would have green eyes?'

The musket-wielding deputies on the bank paid the little bumboat *All-awry* very little heed as it detached itself from the convoy surrounding the *Laurel Bower* and made for the bank. After all, there were only three gypsy

373

girls aboard, and youthful ones at that. So what if one of them seemed a good deal paler than her companions? Her eyes were as black as theirs, if not blacker.

'The *Telling Word* is moored at Whitherwend Street until the next bell,' the eldest gypsy whispered as Mosca climbed out, ignored by the waterside throng.

The cathedral bell rang when Mosca was halfway down Witherwend Street, and the Stationers' coffee-house was still distant. The *Telling Word* had, it seemed, been searched, along with the other coffeehouses, and outside its fantastical collage walls a number of be-wigged and bespectacled gentlemen waited with patient belligerence, many still holding their coffee dishes. As the bell rang, however, they started to file back along the gangplank. The crew on the roof was readying the sails and preparing to cast off.

Everyone in Mandelion seemed to have seethed to the waterside to watch the drama on the river – cooper and cockle-seller, weaver and wheelwright. The carriages could find no way through, nor did they seek it, and dozens climbed onto the motionless wagons for a better view of the water. Facing a wall of fustian fronts and woollen backs, Mosca realized that she was going to miss the coffeehouse.

With trembling hands, she pulled her printed apron from her capacious skirt pocket, and flung it over her own head. She emitted what was meant to be a blood-curdling shriek, but which came out sounding more like the battle cry of a militant shrew. However, the screams that ensued all around her were a lot more convincing and impressive.

'It's print! Print! Hide your eyes!'

Suddenly there were no bodies pressed against her. She ran forward, praying to the Palpitattle in her head, to the Little Goodkin around her wrist, and to any Beloved who might be skilled at preventing young girls running blind off the edge of jetties. Just as she was thinking that she must be nearing the *Telling Word*, someone snatched the apron away from her face, and she found herself staring up at the red-headed constable from the jail. Fortunately he busied himself with flinging the apron into a herring barrel full of brine and lunging at it with his sword to make it sink, so she sprinted the last few steps to the coffeehouse and jammed her clog in the door as it was closing.

'I got an important message for Mr Mabwick Toke, from Mr Eponymous Clent!'

Two minutes later she was standing in the *Telling Word*, watching as Mabwick Toke broke the seal on Clent's letter. He unfolded it, shaking out the two small and elaborate keys Mosca had seen Goshawk give to Clent. Toke read quickly, drawing the side of one long finger to and fro against his tongue, as if sharpening it.

'Your employer tells me,' Toke said at last, raising his eyes to Mosca's face, 'that he has secured a wealth of evidence against Lady Tamarind as a traitress, dissident and queen of a poison press, all of which he promises to place in my hands in the fullness of time if I act against her now. Is any of this true?'

375

Mosca nodded.

'He says that you carry proof of the . . . old enemy's involvement?'

The printed apron was drowned in the herring-barrel, so there was nothing for it. Mosca rolled up her sleeve and showed her forearm, bending back her hand to smooth the creases on her wrist.

"Fraid I got no Stationers' seal,' she remarked, her Chough accent thickening the words in her mouth like dry oats. 'You goin' to burn me?'

'Not while your skin is evidence, girl.' The corners of Toke's mouth dragged sharply down in what seemed to be a curious sort of upside-down smile. Then he sat in silence, his eyes flitting, unseeing, from one side of his desk to the other, as if Mosca had passed him a secret thread and he was following it to find out how it twisted through a mighty web.

'What a mind that woman must have!' he said with admiration. It was the hushed tone of a jeweller studying the largest and finest diamond he will ever see. 'Where did you find the press?'

'Ragman's raft, down under a trap.'

'Of course . . . rags . . . no wonder we could not trace them through their paper, they were making their own . . . That explains the wool threads mixed in with the cotton, and the poor pulping . . . clever rats, clever rats. But we have our own clever rats, don't we, girl?' He gave her his upside-down smile again. 'Where is the press now?'

'Still in the raft, most likely. I 'ad to skip out quick. Didn't want the ragmen findin' me.' *The press is mine mine mine mine . . .*

'No, of course.' His pale, unblinking eyes were fixed on her face. 'Let us hope those devils have left the raft tethered far downstream – if I read the wind aright, the next high tide in the estuary will rush the river and cause wild water for miles. The river can tear loose all but the strongest moorings when it's in that mood, and chew boats to pieces.

'Now, I trust that you can leave more quietly than you arrived . . .'

As soon as the coffeehouse had made fast to the shore and the door had shut behind Mosca, Toke's yellow head snapped up like the lock on a pistol.

'Wove! Take two men, and do not let her get out of sight!'

'Who, sir?'

'The ferrety-looking girl with the unconvincing eyebrows, of course! The world is full of liars of different humours. Coy liars drop their eyes. Bold liars forget to blink. I saw that girl bite a truth into silence, and that's a lie in another coat. I'm sure she knows where the press is. She believed my fairy story about the estuary tides, so she'll soon be running to the press to make it safe. Follow her long enough and she will lead you to it – go!'

Wove left with two stout men. Toke took paper from

 377

his writing box, penned a hasty letter, then folded and sealed it.

'Jot! Ride upstream until you find a Waterman – deliver this letter to them and bid them take it to their leader. There is a river battle the Watermen must halt before too many lives are lost. And there is a ship coming from the coast which must be stopped before it reaches Mandelion. Find a fast horse and teach it to fly – go!'

As Jot ran from the room, Toke exhaled and went back to studying the invisible web.

'What a pity I will never play cards with Lady Tamarind.' And yet he did feel that he was playing cards with her, trying to read signs in her implacable, snow-like countenance. 'Do you know what courage is? Not a willingness to fling oneself into danger without proper thought – that is nothing, nothing. There is cowardice in all impulse. Real courage lies in thinking things through, seeing all the risks, and taking them anyway. Lady Tamarind has courage. The question is, do I? I think she has misplayed her hand, but dare I gamble our lives upon it?' For a few seconds he shook the two keys in his palm like dice, then came to a decision.

'Caveat, you will need these where you are going. They are the keys to the inner door of the Eastern Spire.'

Caveat was lost in a flutter and a stutter.

'How. Did we come. By . . .'

'Provided with the Locksmiths' compliments. Haul that jaw back up to your face, man. Is that how you wish to be seen when you walk in to arrest Lady Tamarind?'

'La . . . la-la-lady-Tama-ma-ma-rindledindle . . .'

'Here.' A sealed parchment was slapped into Caveat's hand. 'The Duke has given us a warrant to search any room or house we please, and arrest all within if we find a trace of the printing press. Be sure you find something, or we shall all dry in the wind after this Assizes. Take three men, and a brace of pistols.'

Some. Kind of boat race probably, thought Caveat, noticing the large, excitable crowd jostling on the jetty. *How very foolish and. Dangerous.*

Mr Toke always knows exactly. What he is doing how cold. It is I shall have Martha tell the girl. To patch those old curtains and. Hang. Them after all. But no one else is shivering so. Perhaps I am sickening for something. Mr Toke always knows. What he. Is. Doing.

The crowds parted before men in Stationers' livery, as they always did. The guards at the gate of the Eastern Spire glanced at the Duke's seal on the parchment, then stood aside.

How shabby I must. Seem next to these fine ladies and gentlemen I wish. I had been. Given time to fetch my. Silk cravat and good bag-wig.

'Duke's business!' he snapped crisply, waving the warrant in the face of the footmen at the door to the spire. Before they could protest, he pulled back his great cuffs and flourished the little silver keys, then turned them in the locks with all the confidence he could muster. The uniform, the keys and the air of confidence were enough.

379

Someone ran off to report, but no one stopped him.

Halfway up the stairs he passed a young man with a warm and open face who gave him a look of guileless curiosity but did not question him. Caveat climbed the stairs, his pistol barrel chilling him through his shirt.

Lady Tamarind sat at her dressing table, mending her face. A tiny crack in the powder had appeared at the corner of one eye. The blemish was so small that it would probably have been invisible to any eye but hers, but she plied a tiny cat's hair brush dipped in powder and smoothed her skin back to perfection.

How had her mask of powder cracked? Had she winced at something, crinkling her eye? What was there to wince at? Her Birdcatcher spies had informed her of the stand-off between the *Laurel Bower* and the Duke's men. She was sure that the Duke would soon lose patience and rain fire upon the coffeehouse, and let the little convoy burn or scatter. Soon the highwayman Blythe, Pertellis's radicals and the Locksmiths on board would be nothing but a sad and sooty memory. Soon the ship carrying her Birdcatcher allies would slide into Mandelion, ready to take control.

On the dressing table lay two letters, which her forgers had written in the handwriting of the Twin Queens, just like the others. She had sealed them with the false signet ring she had brought back with her from the Capital. The letters thanked the Duke for his faithful service. They also included a list of men and women who should be arrested immediately. It was a short list, for Tamarind was patient. Later letters would contain longer lists.

There was no need to falter or fear now. Her plans were perfect.

In the glass she surveyed the face that she had made hers, looking for any hint of a flaw. Perfect.

Lady Tamarind reached out to lay her brush next to her powder tin, and stayed her hand. The smooth white perfection of the powder in the tin was marred by a struggling blackness, battered black armour, dull shards of wing-glass. It rucked and ravaged the creamy surface, scrambling a trail. It was a fly.

There were footsteps on the stairway outside her door, and a pulse fluttered beneath the scar on her cheek.

Through ear-slits like buttonholes in its leathery hide, the crocodile heard the silvery chuckle of key in lock. It heard the swish of skirts as Lady Tamarind stood up hastily. As the door opened to let in four men, the crocodile's mouth opened to let in the taste of the air. The men brought smells that meant nothing to it: ink, pipesmoke, by-the-way mud. But they definitely smelt of strangeness and of fear, and the crocodile was fairly sure that this meant it was allowed to eat them.

Its belly scales rasped against the mosaic floor as it slithered from its basking place.

Linden Kohlrabi had been surprised to see four men in Stationers' uniforms hurrying up the stairs with a look of furrowed purpose, but not enough to halt his step.

 381

There was no point in following them. You were likely to learn more from finding out where they had just come from. At the entrance to the Honeycomb Courtyard the guards were showing their nervousness by questioning everyone sharply before opening the gates. Kohlrabi, however, slid through easily on the grease of remembered tips, and learned in a few quiet words the direction from which the Stationers had arrived. With swift strides he headed towards the river.

On the jetty he paused to put on his gloves, and he drew deep breaths. Here the air braced him with its chill, the dry scent of a distant storm, and the rousing smell of gunpowder.

In one part of the street the crowd was hushed and huddled. An emergency of some sort had taken place. He strode to the centre with quiet confidence and the crowd parted, assuming that he had come to solve the problem. Kohlrabi had delved his cane into the barrel of brine and hooked out part of the sodden apron when the red-headed constable laid a hand on his arm.

'Printed matter, sir,' he whispered urgently. 'No Stationers' seal.'

'I can see that. This is a child's garment – I hope she is not still in it?'

'No . . . she threw it down and ran.'

'Did you get a good look at her?'

'Good enough,' muttered the constable. 'Ferrety-looking girl with pink hair and unconvincing eyebrows. She boarded the *Telling Word*.'

To the constable's consternation, Kohlrabi bent to peer at the wet folds of the apron more closely.

'Oh, Mosca Mye, what dangerous games you play. I had better find you before anyone else does,' he murmured under his breath.

The constable's attention was quickly diverted from the young man with the unassuming smile who had vanished back into the crowd. People were pushing forward so keenly to watch the river battle that those in front were in danger of being pitched into the water.

'Sir . . .' A petty constable tugged at his sleeve.

The constable turned to find the crowd parting in awe and consternation before a sedan chair decorated in whorls of gold and blue. There was no mistaking the heraldic device emblazoned on the side.

Oh Beloved Above, not now . . . The constable had often daydreamed of meeting the Duke, perhaps by catching a thief with one of His Grace's rose-silk gloves, or by besting a burly footpad within sight of the ducal coach. But here and now the constable wished only that the Duke was away in his spire, having his teeth powdered, or his eyebrows scented, or some equally aristocratic activity.

He used his sleeve to clean the sweat from his face, and hurried to the side of the sedan. He was not sure when to bow, so he started bowing halfway to the chair, and trotted the rest of the way stooped, as if passing through an invisible tunnel.

At first glance the chair appeared to be entirely full of an enormous wig, powdered pale lilac and cunningly shaped to resemble a sultan's turban. On second glance the constable discovered a long, handsome face beneath it, with beauty spots carefully painted in the same place on either cheek. The face was smiling, but the smile looked out of place, as if the Duke were holding it for someone else.

'Why,' asked the madly smiling, richly rouged mouth, 'are none of your men on the river?' The Duke's voice was pitched higher than the constable had expected. 'I am told that the highwayman Blythe and the seditious rabble responsible for every ill in Mandelion are mocking you from the waters with impunity.'

'Begging your pardon, Your Grace, but no boat will take us.' The constable could not prevent desperation and frustration creeping into his voice. 'All the skippers say that it's against the Watermen's rules – only the Watermen's wherries can take passengers . . . I swear it, Your Grace, I all but clapped a pistol to their heads, but they wouldn't say different.'

'Then call a wherry!'

'Your Grace . . . there aren't any. They've all vanished upstream . . . searching for the highwayman, some say . . .' The constable licked his lips. 'There's the coffeehouses, of course, but you have to hand in your weapons when you enter them . . .'

'They will not ask me to disarm,' the Duke declared. 'Feldspar! My hat and my walking wig.' He ducked out of the enormous, turban-like wig, which remained exactly where it was, hanging from great pins that jutted out of the walls of the sedan. The Duke's valet slipped a silky, flowing wig in the 'natural' style on his master's head, and perched a triangular hat trimmed with peacock feathers on the top.

The crowd on the waterfront hushed as the Duke stepped out of the chair, resplendent in sapphire and kingfisher-blue, his silk waistcoat shimmering beneath his full-skirted velvet coat. The raised heels of his crimson shoes turned him from a tall man into a gleaming giant out of a court painting. Staring across the water, he treated his people to the sight of the famous, handsome profile of the Dukes of Mandelion.

'See!' He suddenly pointed upwards. High above hovered a great kite, decorated with two female heads that faced one another and seemed to smile a secret. 'The owners of that kite honour Their Majesties, and so in turn they shall be honoured with our custom.'

The kite belonged to a coffeehouse known as the *Queens' Heads*. The balding proprietor was clearly taken aback when he opened the door to find the glittering figure of the Duke bearing down on him, heralded by a constable, flanked by armed deputies, and followed by a middle-aged valet laden with boxes, muffs and spare wigs.

'We are honoured . . . beyond honour . . . Your most gracious Graceness . . .' This coffeehouse was a favourite haunt of persons who were fiercely loyal both to the

 385

Avourlace family and to the Twin Queens, and as the Duke strode in through the door the customers showed this by choking on their coffee and throwing themselves into a series of elaborate and possibly dangerous bows.

'You may all be of the greatest service to Their Majesties,' the Duke declared to the room at large. His long hand seized a curtain and tugged it down with one motion. He pointed a trembling finger out through the window towards the *Laurel Bower*. 'Follow that coffeehouse!'

'The *Queens' Heads* is casting off again,' remarked Miss Kitely. 'Curious –she should be at her address on Mettlemonger Street for two more bells.'

'Another for our convoy?' Pertellis tried to focus on the distant coffeehouse through his borrowed monocle, but quickly gave up.

'I doubt it somehow, Mr Pertellis. Most of her customers are Royalists of the old school, who will take a birch to a serving girl if she spills their tea, and will ride over a poor child rather than risk their carriage wheels in the kennel ditch.'

A rope ladder had been lowered from the trapdoor in the roof, and Blythe stood on the upper rungs, high enough to peer across the deck towards the other coffeehouse.

'There are men taking positions at her windows,' he called down. 'Duke's men – I see their colours.'

'That is what I feared,' murmured Miss Kitely. 'It will

take some time for her to gather away while she's beam-reaching, but even if she cannot head us off, she will fall in behind us and try to take the wind out of our sails. She will press us hard – her master-kite is much bigger than ours, and she has eight dog-kites to our six. Take her a little to port, Mr Stallwrath.'

The pursuing coffeehouse was painted spring-green. It was lower and faster than the *Laurel Bower*, and at its stern was a little veranda for riverside supping. On this veranda two deputies now crouched, using an over-turned table for cover. They disappeared behind a flower of smoke, and a sharp crack echoed across the water.

'What was that, a shot across our bows to ask for surrender?'

'No! Look at the *Catnip*!' The helmsman of the lighter had slumped across his rudder, a dark patch spreading over his coat near the hip. As his fellow crewmen dragged him below, the prow of the *Catnip* began to wander. 'Her mainsail's taken the wind – she's pulling away despite herself.'

'I hope they've seen that aboard the *Dry Spell* and the *Peck o' Clams*,' whispered Miss Kitely, 'or they'll ram her as she turns.'

From within the *Laurel Bower* it was impossible to see past the struggling lighter, but from astern came a grinding crack that set everyone's teeth on edge.

'The *Dry Spell* has steered clear,' Stallwrath called down, 'but they're standing a-luff now. The *Peck o' Clams* has ploughed into the *Catnip*, and I think she'll be tangled

 387

there for a time. The *Queens' Heads* is going about, and her crew is whisker-poling the jib. Skipp'am, she's goose-winged and bearing down on us.'

The pursuit was all the more tense owing to the fact that both coffeehouses were going rather more slowly than the average oyster barrow. A race run through treacle is very hard on the nerves.

'We could go faster straddling a cat,' Captain Blythe was heard to mutter.

Another shot was fired, and one of the little bumboats rowed away for the shore, water spewing in from a hole beneath its waterline. When those on the *Laurel Bower* could make out the pattern on the curtains of the pursuing coffeehouse, the pistols came into their own, and soon the main coffeeroom of the *Bower* was lost in a fog of gunsmoke. Still the *Queens' Heads* gained, and as the *Bower*'s sails sagged the remaining gap closed all the more quickly.

'What was that?' A loud rattle above, from the neighbourhood of the chimney.

'Boarders! It's a grappling iron!' Blythe's legs disappeared as he scrambled up the ladder to the deck. 'I think it's meant to be, anyway,' his voice continued more faintly. 'It looks like part of someone's grate . . .'

'Girls! To the galley!' Miss Kitely looked around her for the nearest set of ready arms. 'You too, Mr Clent.' Clent was not to be trusted with a pistol, but Miss Kitely was willing to place a ladle in his hands.

In the galley, Miss Kitely swung open the hatch to

reveal the startled face of a petty constable, clinging to a rope with one hand and holding a pistol in the other. Concerted blows from three fiercely wielded ladles convinced him to release the pistol, and a faceful of boiling coffee persuaded him to relinquish the rope. He disappeared downwards with a shriek.

Destiny is overtaking us upon wings of canvas, thought Eponymous Clent as he sagged back against the wooden wall, mopping his brow, *and it seems I am to die armed with nothing but a spoon.* Until now he had remained quiet and cowed, hoping only to escape the wrath of everyone else on the *Bower*, but his mind had noticed everything as it scurried to and fro like a rat looking to escape a burning room. As he wandered back from a room full of blinding steam to a room full of blinding smoke, his foot struck a rounded something. It answered the blow with a sound like the flutter of wings. *Wings of destiny. Wings of destiny . . .*

'Tell me, young sir, how well can you throw?' Carmine looked up from loading Copperback's pistol.

'Well enough to knock chestnuts from a tree.' His expression was a question.

'Could you throw this,' Clent lifted the wig box into his hands, 'through one of the windows in the coffee-house yonder?'

There was a long and prickly pause.

'I would need to be outside.'

'I know.'

'Would it help?'

 389

'In truth, I cannot say. It might.'

'Give me the box, sir.'

With the wig box slung over his shoulder, Carmine paused at the bottom of the rope ladder. It did seem hard to be doing something heroic while everyone was too busy to notice. Almost everyone – the Cakes had seen him and was staring up at him in surprise. On impulse he stooped and kissed her on the cheek, clumsily, so that her forehead knocked against his eyebrow.

When he reached the top of the rope ladder the wind blew his collar into his mouth and his short pigtail beat at the base of his neck. Brave Captain Blythe was crouching behind the chimney, cleaning out his pistol. The crew of the *Bower* ducked low to the deck or ran at a crouch from point to point when the lines needed trimming.

Carmine lay flat on his stomach near the edge of the deck and let his arm dangle over the side, the wig box hanging from his fist by its leather straps. As he began to swing it back and forth, Carmine kept his eye on a window below on the other boat, where a man in a plum-coloured surcoat was beating a playful curtain out of his face and levelling his pistol at Captain Blythe's hiding place. *A swing, and a one, and a two, and a . . .*

The man at the window took the wig box full in the face and staggered backwards. The box bounced against the sill, then tumbled down inside rather than out. The men at the other windows of the *Queens' Heads* pulled back, as if eager to find out what had landed in their midst.

'Pull yourselves together, men!' someone was bellowing. 'You dolts! You . . . you squirrels! It's a goose, nothing but a goose. Just a distraction. Here, I'll show you . . .'

The sounds that followed greatly resembled those that might be caused by locking half a dozen farmyard animals into a dresser and then pushing it downstairs. Somewhere in the confusion someone discharged a rifle. To judge by the edgy, hot-coals dance that the crew on the *Queens' Heads* were suddenly performing, they had just seen the bullet hole appear through the deck upon which they stood. The street door flung wide, and someone dived into the water and began swimming to the shore, leaving a cocked hat bobbing behind him.

Carmine scrambled to his feet and ran back to the trapdoor. He paused only for a second at the top of the rope ladder, but suddenly he was staring up at the sky. The deck had charged him from behind like a bully, and something seemed to be gripping his upper arm fiercely as if he might escape upwards into the sky. A wet heat was spreading across his shoulder, and as he tried to sit up the world raised its voice in a chorus of pain and pushed him down again.

Something was pulling at his leg. Looking down the length of his own body, Carmine could see the frightened face of Eponymous Clent, who had pushed his head up through the trapdoor and taken hold of Carmine's ankle. Carmine wondered dully if Clent was trying to steal his boots, and whether anyone would notice. However, he let himself be dragged inch by painful inch, and at last

391

felt someone grip him under the arms and lower him down through the trapdoor, where he seemed to sink into darkness like a drowner, amid a crowd of supporting hands. He was laid gently on to the floorboards. Voices echoed oddly in his ear, and there were red ringlets trailed across his face.

Blythe saw the young apprentice fall to a pistol shot but was too far away to do more than watch as Clent crept from cover to drag the boy to safety. *What a world this is*, he thought. *Children put us to shame with their pluck, and are shot in the back for it.*

The highwayman's mind was filled with a terrible, aching clarity, for he had no doubt in his mind that he would be dead by evening. He hid this belief from his comrades, just as he hid the fact that his recent influenza had left his throat rough as bracken, and that from time to time his head became so light that the objects around him seemed to glisten darkly. The men who depended upon him needed to see him strong and able.

But they need more than Captain Blythe the hero, they need a dozen more men and as many guns . . . no, they need a miracle. On the other coffeehouse, Blythe could see men hanging off the outside wall rungs, or perched on sills, or skulking on deck and veranda – anything rather than face whatever it was that was breaking furniture in the main coffeeroom. Carmine's strange attack had bought the *Bower* time, but it would not be long before the *Queens' Heads* recovered from the crisis.

'Ahoy the *Laurel Bower*! The Duke himself commands you to pull to and surrender yourselves to him and his men!' The cry seemed to come from the veranda of the *Queens' Heads*.

Blythe thought again of Carmine's face as the shot had torn through his arm, and his chest exploded with anger.

'This is Captain Clam Blythe, and I challenge Vocado Avourlace, called Duke of Mandelion, to a test of pistols. I stand for the rights of the people he robs and oppresses, and will risk my body for my cause. I call upon him to stand against me for the Queens he claims to honour, and let the Beloved decide the Right of it.' Blythe could hear his own words echoing long after he had spoken them. He realized that little sculls were bobbing not far from the shore, and that the men on them were bellowing his words to a listening multitude on the waterfront.

'The Duke accepts.'

Praise be to Goodman Varple of Thieves and Vagabonds, and bless his ugly dog, thought Blythe. *The Duke truly is mad.*

'Mr Hind, captain of the *Queens' Heads*, shall be my second.' It was the Duke's voice.

Blythe gave Stallwrath a questioning glance, and received a nod.

'Mr Stallwrath shall serve as mine.'

While the crew of the *Bower* hurried to clear the deck, Blythe stood up, so that he could be seen by the men of the *Queens' Heads*, the crew of the little boats bobbing nearby and the throngs at the riverside. *If they shoot me*

 393

like a dog now, it will be remembered . . .

His heart beat as a tall man in jewelled blues and golds climbed on to the roof of the *Queens' Heads*, the wind splaying the locks of his pale gold wig until it seemed to circle his head like a halo. With a throb the highwayman remembered that, as the man challenged, the Duke would be allowed to take the first shot.

As Blythe willed himself to stand firm, the Duke carefully polished a slender, girlish pistol with a flared muzzle, then turned to regard his enemy shoulder-on, and brought his pistol down to bear. The other coffee-house was close enough for Blythe to see the flash of the powder before the surge of smoke. There was a bang so loud it seemed as if someone had slapped their palms hard against the highwayman's ears. He took a deep breath, and found that his lungs were still whole. The Duke had missed.

Blythe raised his own pistol and slowly lowered it, until he stared down the barrel at the figure of the Duke, bright as a damselfly. With a single shot he could take the Duke's madness out of the world. But on either side, hundreds watched, and he felt the bating of their breath like the silence before thunder. Their eyes and hearts were full of Captain Blythe, the hero for whom villagers had risked the scaffold and the stocks, for whom the radicals would fight to the last man, for whom skippers of little boats would hazard fire and musketball. If he took mean advantage of a now unarmed man, the Duke of Mandelion would die, but so would the Hero.

Blythe raised his gun to aim far above the Duke's head, and pulled the trigger, sending a bullet through the string of the pursuing coffeehouse's master-kite. As he lowered his smoking gun, Blythe heard a roar of applause erupt from the banks. There were cheers nearby from the lighters and dugouts, the dinghies and sculls.

He was turning away from his opponent when the applause changed to a gasp. Blythe saw shock on the faces of the *Bower*'s crew, and turned to see the Duke pulling from his coat a second pistol, identical to his first, and levelling it with one smooth gesture. The beating of Blythe's heart suddenly seemed too loud for one chest, as if he were hearing the heart of every watcher pounding for his peril. There was no time to throw himself flat. There was time only to think, *so this is how it feels to be a hero . . .*

Then the frozen second ended, and from the skies swooped the severed master-kite, its canvas juddering with a sound like a mighty wingbeat. It struck the Duke on the back of the head with a chopping-block thud and tumbled him overboard. After the splash, nothing rose to the surface but a seethe of bubbles and the Duke's three-cornered hat.

Why have his men stopped firing at us? Blythe wondered, as he leaned against the chimney for support. A glance over his shoulder answered his question. The sky was thick with kites, all bearing the Watermen's insignia. The swift wherries had slipped in among the other river traffic, only now throwing up kites to declare their

395

presence. There would be no more gunfire on their patch.

Skin me, thought Blythe, *that girl must have got her message through to the Stationers after all.* The far cries of the crowds were as shrill and gleeful as gull calls over a ploughed field, and Blythe looked about him, dazed, as distant hats were hurled into the air, and little boats ran up flags of celebration.

Among the figures thronging the Ashbridge, Blythe thought for a moment he saw a short and slender figure in an olive-green dress, a point of stillness amid the jubilation. But a fit of light-headedness came over him again before he could be sure whether it was Mosca, and by the time it cleared the figure was gone.

U IS FOR UNDEFENDED

So this is what living honesty is like, Mosca thought as she waded through bristling, rustling plants. The thick green seedpods that patted the skin of her arms were as cool and rough as the pads of cats' paws. The riverside paths had been easy enough to follow in daylight, but now the light was starting to dim. Her only hope of finding the ragman's raft again was to follow the river, so she struggled along within sight of the water even when the bank became overgrown.

Ugly Mr Toke had told her that the high tide would cause wild water. The ragman's raft was tethered by just one mooring pin in the soft bank. She needed to moor it more safely so that the river would not drag it loose and chew it to pieces, the way he had described. And she needed to find a better hiding place for it so that the Stationers did not find it.

No, she did not want the Stationers to find it; she knew that now. She had realized that while she was staring into Toke's clever little eyes. The Stationers would cage the press like a wild animal, and break its spirit. Suddenly she had known that the printing press should be hers and hers alone.

There was a terrible excitement in the thought of the press lurking in its darkened lair with its iron grin and ink-stained teeth, ready to whisper forbidden secrets to her. *If there is paper, there may be books*, whispered a voice in her head. *Dangerous books, gunpowder books, books that could burn away the castles of the mind and change the colour of the sky.*

Of course it was madness to be out alone in the woods, let alone at such an hour. Mosca had read of Wry Petchers, the Manhandler of Scumpy Bank, not to mention countless other footpads, cut-throats and gangs preying through the waysides and wild places. Even an ordinary pedlar might snatch the chance of robbing a small and solitary girl. But somehow these thoughts and the tingling scratches left by the briars only made her more determined. Besides, woods made sense. Woods were home.

On two occasions Mosca noticed a convoy of Watermen boats sail by, kites high. The first convoy was a flotilla of small, fleet boats. The second was a glide of larger tideboats and barges, flanked by wherries. Each time, she hid in the undergrowth until they had passed.

By the time a nibbled moon was climbing the treeline, Mosca's clogs were heavy with black mud and her stomach was a blank, demanding hole.

The river's voice changed, and Mosca realized that it was struggling with a foaming tangle of boughs which chafed in the drag of the current. Her heart somersaulted as she recognized the dead tree where she had narrowly escaped the Birdcatcher ragmen. But surely it was foolish to imagine that they would still be waiting here in such a desolate place?

Using the ripple of roots as rungs, she climbed up on to the trunk of the fallen tree, and kicked her heels against the bark to knock off the mud. She pulled a few blackberries from the nearest bush, but they were still hard and bitter to chew, and she could feel their tiny hairs tickle her tongue and throat as she swallowed them. She was just thinking of climbing further up the fan of roots to reach a dark spray of elderberries when a firm hand was placed over her mouth and she was pulled backwards off the trunk. Despite her shock, Mosca made hearty use of her elbows until her attacker set her on her feet and released her. She turned, fear hammering in her chest.

'Mr Kohlrabi!' Mosca was flooded with relief. 'I looked for you an' couldn't find you an' lots of things 've 'appened an' you weren't at your coffeehouse where you said to look an' Mrs Nokes couldn't say . . .' Mosca's voice dropped to a whisper as Kohlrabi shook his head and raised a finger to his lips.

'Hush . . . Mosca, you are being followed. You have been followed all the way from Mandelion. And I do not think you wish to lead them to the printing press, do you?'

Mosca shook her head silently.

'Let's see if we can lose them, then, shall we?'

Kohlrabi seemed to know the paths of the wood where

 399

moss would silence their steps. He appeared much taller in the dark, or perhaps, Mosca's tired brain wondered, perhaps he wore daylight in a way that made him seem shorter and more ordinary.

'Who are they?' whispered Mosca when they had been creeping in this way for some time.

'Stationers.' Kohlrabi's whisper was a little louder than hers, as if he thought Mosca's pursuers had probably been left behind. 'Little god, you have been crashing through the undergrowth like a wounded boar, and they have been following the sound. I in turn have been following them. They were quite worried when you stopped walking, and they started arguing about which one of them should creep forward and get a sight of you. I thought I would try and reach you first.'

'An' how did you know I was goin' after the printing press?'

'A little guesswork, based on an apron in a herring-barrel. The Stationers must have suspected as much to trail you like that, and I trust them to know their job. So – where is the press?'

'In the hold of a ragman's raft. Ihid it in the rushes an' made sure I'd know the place again. I can take you there.' Mosca paused and swallowed mournfully. 'Are you going to take it away?'

'Mosca –' Kohlrabi's voice was kind and patient – 'look at all the hubbub this one printing press has caused in Mandelion. You must see that it is far too important a thing to have it falling into the wrong hands. Now, the

Stationers would break it apart, or use it to print dull essays, and I think that would be a waste, don't you? And other people might use it to print all kinds of stupid things and get themselves in trouble. Someone has to make sure it is used properly and fulfils its destiny.'

'If there are books there with the press . . . can I read them?'

Kohlrabi mulled this over for a few moments, his face invisible in the darkness.

'Perhaps,' he said at last. 'Yes. I think, when we take the raft downstream, it would be best if you came with us.'

'We can't go downstream, Mr Kohlrabi! That's what I wanted to tell you about! There's people comin' from the coast, an' they mustn't catch us. And listen, listen, Mr Kohlrabi, I got to warn you about Lady Tamarind . . .'

As Mosca's voice rose in pitch, Kohlrabi turned to stare back through the trees behind him, hushing her. One of his hands slid to his belt, and she remembered his pistol. He held up a hand for silence and spent a few seconds quite motionless, before beckoning to her sharply, and creeping on stealthily as they had at first.

Almost stifling with unspoken words, she followed him as the woods thinned and gave way to fields. She followed him at a crouch along ditches and through hedge shadow, across streams and over drystone walls. By the time they reached the darkness of the woods again, she had taken her new pipe from her pocket and was chewing at the stem while she fended the briars from her face.

'I think that pipe is twice as loud as our steps,'

Kohlrabi whispered at long last.

His only answer was the sound of wood clicking against the teeth of his companion.

'You must be hungry, if you are willing to devour wood.'

Mosca said nothing, but continued her champ, champ, champ in the darkness.

'At this rate you will chew your way right through the stem. I would probably not have given you the pipe if I had known that you would think so hard with it.'

'I can believe that,' Mosca muttered.

An opening in the trees allowed the moon to fall upon Kohlrabi's face. He strode in silence for a few moments, then turned a puzzled smile upon his companion. At least, he would have done so if that companion had still been at his side.

'Mosca?' Kohlrabi's expression see-sawed between a smile and a frown as he looked about him. Then both expressions faded like smoke and he wore only the wide-eyed look of one who is listening very intently.

Hidden behind a fringe of ferns, Mosca lay flat, her cheek against the clammy softness of the dead leaves.

'Mosca?'

In a Mandelion street, Mosca would have been at the mercy of its flurry and flow, the hurried weaving of stride and barrow. But this was the freckled woodland, where you needed a different set of tricks. Be still where you can, be as silent as you can, let other small sounds drown your steps. If you cannot fool the eye, then fool the brain – stand where you are not expected and you will not be seen. Keep to the highs, keep to the lows, and avoid eye level if the terrain lets you. These were tricks that Mosca knew.

She had abandoned her gleaming white bonnet and cap on the path as she slipped away. Her dark hair was now pulled forward to mask the pale skin of her face. She waited for Kohlrabi to take a few steps in the wrong direction before rising to a crouch. While he turned his back, a light figure beam-balanced its way along the trunk of a felled tree, arms spread for balance, stockinged feet silent on the dank green velvet covering the bark. By the time he looked back, the figure had dropped out of sight with a faint sound like a chestnut falling.

These were tricks that Mosca knew better than Kohlrabi.

Her skirts scooped over one arm, the pipe clamped silently in her mouth, Mosca slipped to the thicket's edge, and found a feathered sea of reeds before her, shivering moonlight like shot silk. Where was the rag-man's raft? Mosca found a gash in the mud where she had anchored the mooring peg, and she knew that the raft must have pulled loose and floated away. But no – there was a strange, squarish clearing among the reeds. The raft had floated, but not far.

Wading through the reeds, Mosca found the ground growing treacherously moist and cloying, the mud wel-coming her feet eagerly and giving an annoyed cluck of its tongue each time she drew them out for another step.

At last the unseen ground surpassed itself by suddenly becoming river. Mosca found herself up to her hips in icy water, her descent slowed only by her skirts, which spread about her, the muslin seething with bubbles like egg white in a poaching pan.

Mosca grabbed fistfuls of the reeds and used them to drag herself towards the raft. She reached it just before her skirts became sodden enough to drag her down, and she heaved her torso on to its planks. Using her legs to kick, she pulled at the reeds to drag the raft out towards the river. Only when she reached the very edge of the reed-forest and pulled herself up on to the timbers did Mosca realize why the raft had not floated away. The mooring rope had pulled taut. Somewhere among the reeds the trailing end with the mooring peg had caught on something.

Almost in tears with desperation and cold, Mosca gave the rope several violent tugs, but it held. The mooring rope was fastened to a metal ring on the raft with a knot that made no sense to her, and her fingers were so numb the bristling rope was painful to twist. She was still struggling with it when she looked up and saw that Kohlrabi was standing on the bank.

He was out of breath, as if he had reached the bank at a run. The moon was full on his face, and he still wore an expression of slight puzzlement. He took a step towards Mosca, before looking down at his feet, up at the raft, and then searchingly at the reeds separating him from the raft. Perhaps he had worked out that he was near the brink. Mosca was fairly sure he did not know how near.

In his left hand he carried his hat, as if he had snatched it off in order to run without losing it. He held it casually, but in such a way that it hid his right hand.

'Little Mosca,' he called out at last, 'do you really want to keep the press so much?'

'I don't think I want the future we was talkin' about.' Mosca did not move a muscle, but stayed crouching with her hands around the knotted rope. 'I don't want to work for Lady Tamarind.'

'To tell the truth, I never intended that you should.' Kohlrabi smiled, and looked rather relieved. 'She is a very clever woman, but her aims are rather tawdry.' A touch of embarrassment crept into his smile, as if he had been caught buying Mosca a nameday present ahead of time. 'I'm afraid I was always planning to steal you away from her. It's probably time I explained things properly but, Pale Fates, can you bring the raft in first? If we keep shouting like this we will have the Stationers or worse to deal with.'

'I'm sorry, Mr Kohlrabi, but I got all these bits and pieces of thoughts. An' most of 'em are just little, an' none of 'em proves anything, but they stick into my mind like pine needles in my socks. An' there's only one way of lookin' at 'em all that makes sense.'

Looking at his carefully hovering hat, Mosca knew exactly what Kohlrabi was holding in his hidden right hand.

'It all makes sense if you're a Birdcatcher, Mr Kohlrabi.'

Kohlrabi still wore a look of slightly concerned attentiveness. It seemed to Mosca that he was staring at her hands. He could not know if the mooring rope was still fastened, or if Mosca had already loosed it and was simply holding the rope. For all he knew, if she let go, the raft and the printing press would float away down the river and be lost to him.

'You never swear by the Beloved, never. I mean, I seen you in the cathedral . . . but in the bit which is still the old church really, with its Heart of the Consequence still there under the shines an' shimmers.' Mosca paused, but the figure on the bank remained silent and motionless. 'An' you work for Lady Tamarind, an' Lady Tamarind is working with the Birdcatchers. An' then there's you followin' Mr Clent all around the country, an' sayin' it's cos he's dangerous an' got blood on his hands, when all the time he's a fat, skittered old tomcat with long claws an' no teeth. *That* only makes sense if it was you what stole the letter Mr Toke sent to Mr Clent – the second one, asking him to come to Mandelion. You found out the Stationers had sent for a special agent to find the printing press, and went out to stop him 'fore he even got here. They just brung him in cos they didn't want to risk one of their own, and didn't care if the Locksmiths killed him, but *you* thought they must be sendin' for someone really special and clever and dangerous. An' when you . . .' Mosca paused, wondering if she was going too far. 'When you told me that story 'bout the night your father died, when that church got blasted to smithereens by a Birdcatcher spy . . . the spy *was* your father, wasn't he?'

'The bravest man I have ever known,' Kohlrabi said simply.

Mosca's waterlogged petticoats clung to her legs, and her teeth were starting to chatter. She realized suddenly that she had wanted Kohlrabi to laugh at her, and deny everything, and show her where she had been stupid. Instead, he continued to smile as if everything was still a game, and a game that Mosca was playing rather well.

'You're a Birdcatcher,' she said in a small, stifled voice.

'Birdcatcher is a word,' said Kohlrabi. 'The whole country is frightened of a word. Mosca, the word has no poisoned bite. It has never smothered a baby. You cannot fire it out of a cannon. And yet, say "Birdcatcher" to a company, and they will scatter like rabbits at the scent of a fox. You are better than that, Mosca. You are not a rabbit.'

Mosca sniffed, and wrinkled her nostrils, very much like a rabbit. An icy tickle plagued her nose, but she dared not move her hands to scratch it.

'Will you let me tell you what the name Birdcatcher means? A Birdcatcher knows that there is something higher and better in this world than the dirt and darkness which surrounds us. Not the Beloved, sitting in their little shrines like wooden shopkeepers, with everyone trying to buy their favours with gold and flowers and turnips. No, something else, something pure, something so bright that its light could enchant everything

407

else, like sunlight through a stained-glass window. Now, are you going to shun someone just because they believe the world has meaning?'

Mosca shook her head slowly.

'Then can we please bring in the raft?' Kohlrabi still wore an expression of tender good humour.

Mosca shook her head again, and snuffled out a single word.

'I didn't hear that.'

'Partridge,' she repeated, with muffled fierceness. 'The barge captain. He was a crotchet an' a bully an' he left bruises on my shoulders, an' he was stealing the Beloved out of their shrines, but . . . then someone stuck a knife in him 'fore I'd decided what I thought of him. An' maybe there was a story to the way his wrist was broken, and the way his smile looked like he was suckin' crab apples, an' nobody will ever care enough to find out. But leastways, someone ought to care 'bout the last bit of his story, the bit where he died.

'It's funny, I mean, everyone thought he got killed cos he was a Waterman spy, or cos he was blackmailing radicals, or cos he went after Mr Clent wantin' money. But it wasn't really 'bout any of that stuff. He died cos of a goose. And . . . cos of me.

'All he wanted was his barge back, the one my goose Saracen sort of stole by mistake. An' so when he saw me, he chased me cos he needed me and Mr Clent to take Saracen away. An' then, right in front of a coffeehouse, I disappeared an' he couldn't find me. So I 'spect he searched up and down, an' then someone took his penny and said, "Yeah, we seen the ferrety-looking girl. Popped under a gentleman's cloak, she did." So he got a description of the gent with the cloak, an' started asking to find out where he'd gone.

'Sooner or later he tracked him to a ragman's raft. Maybe he even spied the gent comin' up out of the hatch. Then . . . I think I see how it went. He pushed his way past the gent and climbed down through the trapdoor, thinkin' I was hidin' below. But I wasn't. An' suddenly there Partridge was in the dark, and in front of him was the printing press an' lots of pages of Madness and Mayhem drying on racks . . . and behind him there was *you*, Mr Kohlrabi.'

Kohlrabi's face had no expression at all, and suddenly Mosca could barely recognize him. His face had always seemed so honest, like an unshuttered window through which emotions shone without disguise. Perhaps his expressions had always been a magic-lantern display, a conjurer's trick.

'You had to get rid of the body, an' you wanted to scotch Mr Clent, so when we was out you dressed Partridge up in women's togs, and brought him to the marriage house. I can just imagine the marriage, Partridge lollin' and saggin', you sayin' he's drunk and dippin' your ear to his mouth so you can pretend he's talkin' to you, Mr Bockerby nippin' through all the versadiddle cos a pot of porter is waitin' for him by the hearth, an' the Cakes throwin' honesty pods over you, with her eyes too tear-fogged to take a good, hard look at the bride . . . an' you carry the bride off to the private chambers with your pockets full of wedding cakes, strip off the bonnet and gown, an' leave the body sitting up straight an' smart on Mr Clent's bed . . .'

'Halk Partridge was a pillager and thief of the lowest sort,' Kohlrabi said quietly. 'He had an ugly temper, and would have ended up bleeding his thoughts into a tavern's floorboards sooner or later. The river runs more cleanly without him riding its back.'

'Yeah, but you didn't know all that when he had his back to you, did you?' Perhaps Kohlrabi's face had worn just this mask-like look when Partridge had turned in bewilderment from the printing press, his lips ready with a question that was never asked.

'What if it had been *me*, Mr Kohlrabi? Would Mr Clent have rolled in from the tavern an' found me sitting up on his bed, periwinkle-blue an' cold as a lawyer's heart?'

'Do you really believe that?' Kohlrabi tilted his head a little, and his eyes were bright with something that might have been hurt, and might have been moon. 'Little god, you see the world through such black eyes.'

'Got no choice. My father give 'em to me.'

'I think he gave you more than that, Mosca.' Kohlrabi's tone set something jangling in the depths of Mosca's soul like a bucket in a well. 'I told you how I worshipped Quillam Mye when I was growing up. My own father was dead, and your father became my hero. He spoke out against the Stationers when they were trying to burn

410

all books touched with our philosophy. It inspired me. I became certain that he must secretly be a member of our faith. The Stationers destroyed nearly all his books, but I found a few copies and read them. Mosca . . . down in the hold is a copy of one of his works. It is called *On the Popular Superstition and Delusion Commonly Called the Beloved.'*

'No! I don't believe you!' *He wasn't a Birdcatcher he wasn't he wasn't he wasn't . . .*

'The hatch is right there. Take a look below for yourself. Or if you are afraid that I might leap on to the raft in a single bound, cast your mind back. Did it never seem to you that your father's views were . . . uncommon?'

For the hundredth time in her short life Mosca conjured up a remembered image of her father. In her mind's eye she set his desk halfway between herself and Kohlrabi and saw him writing there busily, despite the reeds tickling against his calves and the feeble light offered by the moon. A moth blundered through his head, but he did not even look up in annoyance. *I know you're busy but this is really really important an' I need to ask somink . . .*

'Mosca, your father wrote that the Beloved were no more real than the dolls that children give names and squeaky voices. Do you know what he said of them? He said, "They are best used as poppets and toys for green young minds while they are learning to understand the world, and it is the most miserable thing that our grown men cannot bring themselves to lock away the Beloved with their hoops and wooden soldiers."'

411

The imagined Quillam Mye dipped his pen, and wrote eagerly, silently mouthing the very words the Birdcatcher was speaking. Mosca's eyes misted. The manner of speaking was all too familiar.

You should have told me, she shouted silently to the heedless figure of her father, *and I should have broke your pince-nez, and hid your pipe from your blind, old, black-pebble eyes* . . .

'He was right, Mosca, can you not see that? The Beloved, with all their nursery-rhyme names, just distract everyone from the Greater Truth, the Brighter Light. Mosca, I believe that in your deepest heart you hunger for that kind of brightness. You looked at Lady Tamarind and thought you saw it: something shining, beautiful, pure, raised above the rest of the world. Of course she disappointed you, for she is only a human woman. She believes in nothing really – except power, in the same way that a pike believes in feeding. You need something sacred.'

'I don't think I like sacred very much,' Mosca called back. ''Cept maybe Palpitattle . . . an' he's not *very* sacred.'

'If nothing is sacred, then we are all left to crawl through the mud, and there is no meaning to anything. Since the Heart of Consequence was ripped out of the churches, even the stars shine crooked in the skies. Everyone goes to church to gossip and envy each other's hats, but the *heart* has gone out of it. This country is like an old mother dying, and nobody cares enough to save her because they are too busy going through her purse.

Every city is a snake's nest of pillagers, pickpockets, anglers, cheats, cardsharps, harlots, forgers, smugglers, charlatans, footpads, highwaymen, blackmailers, pettifoggers, hedge-robbers and drunkards – you have seen all this for yourself. How can their soul survive when they have ripped out their Heart?'

The phantom Quillam Mye had paused, pen poised, but she could not tell whether he was re-reading his own words or waiting for hers. The wind shifted, and carried Mosca a whiff of remembered pipesmoke.

'And yes, amid this poison smog of the soul that is trying to choke out the light of sun, moon and stars, we are trying to rekindle a light. It is a harsh light that will dazzle some and burn others, but it will take the world out of this terrible darkness of Disbelief.' So this was Kohlrabi's true face, pale and strange, older than his years, as if his father and countless others were speaking through him. 'I am content to be hated, and bloody, and outnumbered. For in this sickened world, it is better to believe in something too fiercely than to believe in nothing.'

Words, words, wonderful words. But lies too.

'No, it isn't!' shouted Mosca the Housefly, Quillam Mye's daughter. 'Not if what you're believin' isn't blinkin' well True! You shouldn't just go believin' things for no reason, pertickly if you got a sword in your hand! Sacred just means something you're not meant to think about properly, an' you should never stop thinking! Show me something I can kick, and hit with rocks, and set fire to, and leave out in the rain, and *think about*, and if it's still standing after all that then maybe, just maybe, I'll start to believe in it, but not till then. An' if all we're left with is muck and wickedness and no gods, then we'd better face it and get used to it because it's better than a lie. Which is what *you* are, Mr Kohlrabi.'

Mosca's voice had become fierce and loud, and the low hills passed her words to and fro, marvelling at them. Kohlrabi's face softened and took on the gentle, rueful smile with which he had always wished her farewell. The tricorn dropped from his left hand, and Mosca threw herself forward, bruising her chest against the iron mooring ring. Kohlrabi's smile vanished behind a wreath of smoke. She felt a wind stroke her cheek, as if an invisible dog had licked her face with a long, cold tongue.

The pistol shot shocked Mosca's ears into white, whistling deafness. Her trembling fingers forced the rough cords of the mooring rope to loosen. On the shore Kohlrabi would be advancing, testing his ground with a careful foot . . .

But there were other figures on the bank now, sprinting along the paths with swords drawn, calling words that made no sound. Kohlrabi drew his rapier and stepped forward. The foremost of his opponents slithered to a stop too slowly, and took a wicked kick to the kneecap. He staggered and fell to one knee, and the Birdcatcher aimed a vicious cut down towards his face. The stricken man flung up a parry too late, and fell back with a scream.

As Kohlrabi turned and ran, one of his attackers raised

and levelled a pistol. Smoke gasped silently out of the gun, and then wind sucked it up greedily and swallowed it. Kohlrabi spun as if to face his pursuers, but somehow the motion did not end, and he kept on spinning right around, toppling sideways at the same time. Mosca saw him break the moon-gilded mirror of the river without making a sound, and then the current took pity on her and drew the ragman's raft away.

Mosca was sure that the men on the bank would be calling to her, but she huddled herself in a nest of rags, and shivered in silence. It was only after she had drifted for an hour that the ringing faded from her ears. A low, soft booming seemed to sound from the hills like gunfire, but she could not be sure if it existed inside her head or out. At last she raised her head to look at the imagined figure of her father, whose desk was now perched up on the rag-mountain.

'You weren't much help,' she murmured bitterly. 'Why didn't you tell me anything about all this?'

'If you want someone to tell you what to think,' the phantom answered briskly, without looking up, 'you will never be short of people willing to do so.' There. She had it at long last, his voice and manner exactly. Quillam Mye paused to polish his pince-nez, and then squinted at his daughter through them for a long while, as if mildly surprised that she had grown up so much while his attention was elsewhere. 'Come now,' he said at last, 'you can hardly claim that I have left you ignorant. I taught you to read, did I not?'

V IS FOR VERDICT

As Mosca found out later, the distant booming she had heard reverberating between the hills was not a buzzing in her stricken eardrums. It was cannonfire.

On receiving Toke's warning, the Watermen had sent all available boats downstream in two flotillas, one made of swift-skimming vessels, the other of larger, slower vessels, to intercept the ship carrying Lady Tamarind's troops.

In the short term this meant that a boatload of highly disgruntled Locksmith troops, who had been trying to act upon the orders of their guildmaster in Mandelion to reach the city with all speed, were finally able to sail on without being stopped at every bend in the river by good-natured Watermen who insisted on 'searching the boat for Captain Blythe'. They reached Mandelion, and found the city in a state of celebratory riot. Disembarking, they were mistaken for reinforcements of Duke's men, were overwhelmed by the jubilant crowd, and stripped of their weapons and clothes.

The fast Watermen flotilla, meanwhile, reached Fainbless before the moon rose. There was barely time to put men ashore on the bank and a mid-river island before a solitary ship was spied, a three-masted lugger with eight cannon. She flew no colours.

From a tower in Fainbless, the Watermen hailed the unknown ship, waving brands to signal her to shore. Their only answer was an echo, and the crack of gunfire.

Three Watermen were lost as the tower collapsed, and their comrades were not slow to touch off their cannon. The crew of the strange ship knew nothing of the Watermen hidden on the island until a flaming 'carcass' arc'd from among the trees and landed mid-deck.

The little Watermen boats flitted and slipped around the great ship like dogs at a baiting, but her muskets and riflemen were too numerous to risk a close approach. Even at long range her cannon ripped their sails.

Just as it seemed that nothing could be done to stop her passing out of range of the Fainbless cannon, the second Watermen flotilla arrived. In desperation a boat was fired and the flaming vessel sent towards the lugger, which steered wildly from its path and grounded itself in unsuspected shallows.

Pelted with carcasses, the lugger slowly burned to the waterline. There was no call for aid from on board, however. No boats were lowered, no survivors were fished out of the water. A superstitious fear settled, and some whispered that the the unknown ship might as well have been crewed and captained by the dead.

It was during the journey back to Mandelion that a

sharp-eyed sculler spotted a chilled and feverish Mosca Mye huddled on one bank in the middle of a nest of rags.

Two days later, in a secret antechamber of what had once been the Duke's Western Spire, Mosca and Clent found themselves standing before a group of quietly insistent men in very clean but well-worn overalls. Some of them wore pince-nez and ink-spattered cravats, and had thick pen-callouses on their third fingers. Some wore gloves and chatelaines of keys, and their colourless eyes watched the world narrowly, like oysters peeping from their shells. Some were tanned brown as conkers, and wore sashes bearing the design of a silver pond skater against a black background.

'What amazes me,' declared Mabwick Toke in a wormwood tone, 'is that two human beetles of this sort should have played such a large part in creating this diabolical mess.'

Mosca used her free hand to wipe her nose, which was still sore and runny after her recent cold. Her right arm was being held captive by Aramai Goshawk of the Locksmiths' Guild, while he tried to make out the faint print on her skin.

'How did this child come by so many bruises? I can hardly read the words.'

'As I hear it, she has been clambering into, over and under anything that would permit it.' Toke barked a laugh. 'Count yourselves lucky you have not found her hiding in your writing desks or frolicking in your afternoon stew.'

Eponymous Clent gave a warm gust of laughter, which cooled when everyone else in the room remained stony.

'We have little enough to laugh about, Clent,' Toke commented coldly. 'A few weeks ago, Mandelion was a stable and thriving city, with one problem – an illegal printing press. The Stationers' Guild called you in to find this press, in exchange for overlooking your past misdemeanours. We did not order you to fling bodies in the river, throw in your lot with radicals, release savage animals in popular alehouses, or investigate the Duke's family.

'The Duke himself is stone-cold dead, and with him a decade of our careful diplomacy down the drain. His men have completely lost control of the city, and Mandelion is being run by a common highwayman whom *your ballad* has turned into the darling of the people. Thanks to you, the people of Mandelion will not be ruled by anyone but their famous Captain Blythe and his gang of radical reprobates.'

'*We* might have controlled the Duke, once he had reached an understanding with us,' Goshawk remarked quietly.

'From what I seen,' muttered Mosca, 'the Duke din't have much of an understanding at all.'

Clent cast a beseeching look in Mosca's direction.

'The Duke was mad,' Toke conceded, 'but we knew

 419

where we were with him. This man Blythe is another matter.'

'Ah now, I quite understand your concern, but I can assure you that beneath that burly, boorish, black-dog exterior lurks a dapper wit and—'

'Clent!' Toke's voice slammed Clent into silence like a gavel. 'You have talked quite enough already. I hear from my counterpart here –' he gestured towards the head of the Locksmiths – 'that you showed every willingness to join his guild when he caught you listening in on his meeting at the Grey Mastiff. Furthermore, the constables tell me that when you were arrested, you happily answered all their questions about our guild secrets, and a few more they lacked the wits to ask. And finally, there was the letter in which you promised me evidence linking Lady Tamarind Avourlace to the printing press and the Birdcatchers. What if we had arrested her on your word, and then found ourselves explaining to the Duke that our only evidence was a black mark on an apron, blurred beyond recognition by a sojourn in a herring barrel?' Toke's mouth closed itself into its cold little V. 'You may count yourself lucky that my men *were* able to find evidence of forgery and treason in Lady Tamarind's chambers. Two letters forged to look like the Twin Queens' handwriting, and a copy of their signet ring, no less.'

'Of course it may be argued that the lady's behaviour is evidence enough,' Goshawk added.

'What did she do?' Mosca could not help asking.

'She set her crocodile on my men,' Toke snapped. 'It shook one man around like a sheaf at threshing, then grabbed a second by the ankle. My man Caveat put a bullet in its skull, but by then the lady had her own pistol to his head, and he was forced to escort her to a fast horse. She could be sipping wine in the Capital by now.'

. . . sipping pale golden wine with the late light in it, pouting her mouth carefully so that the paint on the lips could not wrinkle, pale and perfect as porcelain, with a snow-white guinea pig on a leash at her feet . . . Part of Mosca's heart was glad that Lady Tamarind was still free, though something in her soul still roared with hate like a forest fire.

The head of the Watermen turned to Mosca.

'That other Birdcatcher.' His tone was low, almost confidential, as if they were the only people in the room. 'The one who killed the barge captain. Coldrabble?'

'Linden Kohlrabi,' Mosca said quietly. Perhaps it had not been his name at all. She supposed that a Birdcatcher would care nothing for the wrath of his nameday god. Maybe he had put names on and off like gloves.

'Dead, you said?'

'Yes.'

The Waterman sat quietly nodding, his eyes on her face. His expression was not unfriendly. After all, what was it to the Watermen who ruled Mandelion? They were river-kings, and the Slye still flowed.

'We might know more of this Birdcatcher plot if we had the printing press,' Toke continued. 'The press that *you* discovered and concealed from the proper author-ities. Do you have anything further to say on this?'

'I told you.' Mosca met Toke's gaze boldly and blackly, without blinking. 'I sunk it.'

'Sunk it?' The head of the Watermen cast a question-ing glance at Toke.

'The raft 'ad these little barrels strapped under the planks, for keepin' her afloat, I've seen the kind of thing b'fore. So when I got scared, with me out in the wilds an' the press just sittin' there, full of wickedness, I sharpened a stick an' poked it in the barrels, an' they bubbled a lot an' the river sucked up the raft like a mouthful of dry bread.'

A sigh settled upon the room, a sigh of disappointment mixed with relief.

'Clent, you will stay here and answer more questions,' Toke dictated crisply. 'The girl must be taken away and washed – her skin is an incitement to treason.'

Mosca spent the next two hours being scrubbed red and raw by two muscular matrons until not a trace of Birdcatcher doctrine smudged her skin. Just when she felt there was no skin left, she was bundled back into her stolen olive-green dress and brought out into a corridor, where Clent was waiting amid bags and bundles, fret-ting the ends of his cravat to feather-wisps. His ears were bright red as if they too had been well scrubbed.

Toke emerged, his parchment-yellow face older than ever beneath his glossy, caramel-coloured wig.

'You, girl.'

Mosca obediently drew closer.

'Who was your father?'

'Quillam Mye.' Mosca could not help speaking his name with pride, as if she expected everyone to know it.

'I thought so.' Toke peered at her. 'I knew him. I knew him well. Your father had a brilliant mind – I have never known a keener. The hardest thing I ever had to do was to give the order for his books to be burned.' He barked his laugh. 'And the second hardest was persuading the Guild that they should not burn him as well as his books. Did he ever mention me?'

Mosca shook her head.

'During the Years of the Birdcatchers, he was the only man I truly trusted. We worked together, fighting the Birdcatchers. I found new recruits for the Resistance, and he wrote tracts that were circulated in secret, giving the people the hope and courage to rise up against the Birdcatchers.

'I only found out how wild his opinions were once the Birdcatchers were overthrown. He thought that letting the people worship the Beloved freely again would be only the first step. He had fantastical ideas of letting everyone adopt whatever crazed and treasonous views they pleased, and print their own books without limit. He told me that if the Stationers burned books, we were no better than the Birdcatchers and their shrine-burning.

'He would not be silent, and he would not flee Mandelion. One half of Mandelion called him a

423

monster, the other half a hero. The Guild disowned him, and the Duke sent men to arrest him for spreading sedition. Do you know what happened? An infatuated mob overpowered the Duke's men, untethered the horses and pulled the carriage themselves through the streets as if he was a war hero, shouting, "Mye and a Free Voice".'

Mosca could picture this, but in her imagination her father looked embarrassed and annoyed.

'The Duke ordered his men to fire into the crowd. Dozens were injured, and ten killed outright. That very night I had Quillam kidnapped, and spirited from Mandelion in my personal carriage. It saved his life, but I did not expect him to thank me for it. I think he would have returned to Mandelion if he had not seen the crowd that followed him falling to the Duke's muskets that night. He did not appear in Mandelion again, but his books did, each wilder and more seditious than the last. We burned every copy we found, but we couldn't stop men like your friend Pertellis smuggling them in, or copying them by hand, or learning chapters by rote and teaching them to others.'

Toke stared at her, using the knife of his gaze as if he wanted to prise her apart like a walnut shell.

'Quillam is dead, isn't he?'

Mosca nodded.

'I knew that he had to be. I have not seen a new work by Quillam for four years, and only one thing on earth could have stopped him writing.' Toke looked briefly annoyed, as if the walnut shell was proving more difficult to open than he expected. 'Tell me, do you have any brothers?'

'No, nor sisters neither. I'm all there is of him left.'

'Good. If Quillam had sons, they would grow up too much like him, and cause no end of trouble.'

Mosca Mye said nothing, and Mabwick Toke looked into her smoked-glass eyes and saw a mind full of nothing he could understand.

Toke started to turn away, then paused. 'Caveat!'

The quiver-cheeked guildsman entered the corridor. From his hand trailed a leash. At the end of the leash a leather muzzle was fastened about a beak the colour of pumpkin peel. Saracen had lost a few feathers around the shoulders, and there was a black bar across one wing which looked like a powder burn, but he was as puffed and pugnacious as ever.

'Do not *think* of leaving without your goose,' Toke said crisply, and his mouth set once more in its poisoned triangle as he left for the antechamber.

Mosca took the leash and, following Clent's lead, hefted one of the bundles on to her shoulder. It seemed to be stuffed full of Clent's coat and her borrowed blanket. An empty place in her heart swelled full as Saracen swaggered beside her, trying to match her pace.

'What's it mean?' she hissed as she followed Clent to the door.

'It means that against all the odds we have a small but palpable chance of surviving this whole adventure, providing we leave the city now. Keep walking.' The guards at the gates to the spire opened them without looking at their faces.

A spirit of carnival had seized Mandelion. Clamouring Hour had broken its banks like a river after rain, and many people hung out of their windows to ring their god-bells with gleeful abandon. Upon the railings that surrounded the Western Spire, turnips and beets had been impaled. They had crudely carved faces and wigs of straw, and Mosca guessed that they were meant to represent the Duke.

There were traces of past riot as well as present revelry. A couple of boys in battered, broad-brimmed hats dawdled by houses that were freckled by musketfire, and used clever little knives to pick out the shot when no one was looking. In the old marketplace a burned-out sedan chair tilted on a pile of blackened timbers, and Mosca's heart lurched as she saw what seemed to be a charred human figure inside. As she passed, however, she saw that beneath an enormous, singed wig shaped like a wasp's nest, the white face was chill and unmarred, except for the chin, which the flames had tiger-striped in bars of soot and sallow. It was a marble statue of the Duke that had been clumsily dressed and given to the pyre.

'Mr Clent? We fixed everything an' prevented a war an' stopped the Birdcatchers, din't we? How come everything's suddenly our fault?'

'The privilege of the weak, I fear. People must have someone to blame. If you live to be older and wiser, you will look back and wonder not that we were turned out of the city, but that we were allowed to walk away. Keep walking.'

Mosca thought about the sullen, heavy-wigged guildsmen fretting that their power had been taken away and given to a highwayman, and knew that she did not feel at all sorry. In fact, she felt fiercely pleased about it.

'Mr Clent . . .' Mosca remembered the discussion in the antechamber. 'Lady Tamarind had a pocket watch shaped like a pistol, didn't she?'

'The same thought had occurred to me.'

'But you don't think we should tell . . .'

'No, madam, I do not propose to tell the Stationers that one of their best operatives was probably held at pocket-watch point long enough to let an arch-criminal escape. I do not think they would take the news well.'

'S'pose not. You got bits of cotton stuck 'tween yer teeth, Mr Clent.' It looked as if he had been nervously chewing the ends of his cravat.

'Yes . . . a rather trying interview, what with seven of Mandelion's keenest minds all trying to fillet me like a fish. If I were a vain man, I might have taken offence at how many of their questions were about you. They seemed particularly eager to know whether you had read any of the infamous Birdcatcher books. Fortunately, I was able to put their minds at rest.' Clent cast Mosca a twinkling glance. '"She is as sharp as a hornet's breeches," I told them, "and keen to learn, but her education has been sadly lacking. She can scratch out her letters, but she has no particular way with words."

'Curiously, I am not convinced that they believed either of us. The Stationers will probably have us followed out of the city and beyond, to see if we lead them to the press.' Clent gave Mosca one of his sharp, questioning looks. 'Of course . . . you really did send the press to drink deep of the Slye, did you not?'

'Course,' answered Mosca without hesitation.

'Naturally. Though . . . sweet petals of Goodlady Aesthelia the Flower-faced, I could not have done so,' Clent murmured with feeling.

'It was tricky,' admitted Mosca.

'All those books unborn, waiting to spring out of it,' added Clent.

'Stories of genies an' songs about kings with their heads cut off,' said Mosca. They exchanged guilty, hungry smiles. 'So, s'posing someone jus' let the raft with the printing press slide off down the river – what do you think would happen to it?'

'Well . . . if it was not found by the Stationers or nests of waiting Birdcatchers . . . I rather think it would float right out to sea to haunt the visions of late-night helmsmen and perhaps wash up against an exotic shore to cause more mischief.'

'Good,' muttered Mosca. When she had released the rope and watched the ragman's raft float away down the river, she had felt much as she had watching the lantern fall from her hand into the gorse stacks on her last night in Chough. It occurred to her that perhaps, just perhaps, a part of her really *had* decided to set fire to her uncle's mill, so that she would have no choice but to run away. 'Some kinds of places need some kinds of trouble,' she finished gnomically.

Mosca and Clent trailed their way along the Drimps, laden like two pedlars, and won hardly a glance from the shopkeepers, who were decorating sills and eaves with every ribbon, kerchief and stocking they could find to serve as flags. Many boats on the river had run up the silver swallowtail flag of celebration, and the kites of the coffeehouses danced and spiralled instead of hauling their strings in a workaday fashion.

'I suppose,' Clent asked casually, 'I suppose there were no ready-printed books lying around the press? Not that I am saying you would sully your eyes with Birdcatcher books . . .'

They walked in silence for a few minutes.

'Y'know what, Mr Clent? I don't think books make you mad at all. I mean, I started readin' 'em really slow, an' stoppin' now and then to see if I felt any more inklinged than before. Once I was feelin' all fuzzy and light in my head, an' I thought maybe that was me startin' to go mad. But then I realized that I was just bored. The Birdcatcher books were mostly just boring, and a bit silly.' Mosca wiped her nose up the length of her sleeve. 'My father's book was much better.

'It was this funny story 'bout how all these people up in the Capital was arguing 'bout how they had to have a king or queen, and they had to choose right, cos the Beloved

429

knew who should get the crown and you couldn't wish it different without being sinful. They argued so loud, the Beloved heard, an' started tryin' to decide between 'em who should rule. They held a big, old meeting in the horizon-halls but they couldn't agree to anything. Syropia wanted to crown the meanest and maddest to show her forgiveness, an' Cramflick wanted someone with an 'ead like a potato, an' Sussuratch wanted a sailor, an' while they were arguing Palpitattle an' Varple stole all the food for the meeting. An' while they was all cooin' an' squeakin' an' boomin' an' shriekin' like six winter winds trapped in a chicken coop, each of 'em thought of a sudden that if they ran back to the world of men, they could get their word in first.

'So all the men praying for the Beloved's advice felt a great big wind about them which swivelled their wigs an' blew their garters right off so their stockings came down. They run out of the cathedral with Beloved swarming all over 'em, like bees over a beekeeper, all buzzin' their wishes at once. The men run straight to the river an' jumped in, but the Beloved hung on. When the men was almost goin' mad with the sound of thousands of voices, they covered their ears and yelled for the Beloved to leave 'em to decide everythin' for themselves. The Beloved said they were needed there to keep the moonblot beetles out of the lanterns, an' peel the skin from the milk, an' stop the snarps stealin' children. But the men told 'em to leave the world anyway . . . an' the Beloved did. And nothin' changed at all, cos there never *were* any Beloved, just people making their voices up in their heads, the way I often do with people.'

'That is a very charming story, Mosca. Never tell it again.'

'My father didn't believe in the Beloved, but he didn't believe in the Heart of the Consequence either – he wasn't a Birdcatcher. Mr . . .' Mosca had been about to say, *Mr Kohlrabi worshipped him but he'd got him all wrong*. But she was not ready to think about Kohlrabi yet. When she thought of his name she felt nothing, but she felt nothing in a way that hurt.

'No, from what you say your father was an atheist, an out-and-out unbeliever. Atheism will see your head spiked on a church spire just as soon as Birdcatchery.'

Mosca was silent for a few moments.

'But, Mr Clent,' she said at last, 'what if he was right? What if it's *true*?'

'I think we will have to leave the clerics and scholars to decide that.'

'Why?' Mosca slowed her pace.

'Who else should?' Clent gave her a sideways glance. 'You perhaps? Ah, I foresee frightful things when you are old enough to work your will on the world. Cathedrals torn down, mention of both the Consequence and the Beloved banned from the common speech, and children brought up to believe in an empty, soulless heaven . . .'

'No, I . . .' They were passing a cluster of shrines. As she watched, a troop of grateful citizens trooped past the shrines, dropping different thanksgiving offerings

 431

before each icon. A biscuit for Goodman Blackwhistle. A mackerel for Goodman Sussuratch. A shiny coin for Goodman Greyglory. The little gods looked so good-humoured, sitting side by side, none of them fighting to have all the worshippers to themselves, and Mosca felt a rush of weary tenderness for the Beloved. It was so different from the cold, inhuman zeal of Kohlrabi. Perhaps, as her father had thought, the Beloved were toys that a childish world needed. Perhaps, too, the world was growing up, and even now was starting to put them aside, affectionately but forever.

'Beloved are all right,' she murmured gruffly. 'Wouldn't want to go burning 'em.'

'Not even in the service of truth?'

'That's not serving truth!' Mosca thought back to what she'd already said to Kohlrabi, and tried to make sense of her scattered thoughts. 'I mean . . . if I told people what to believe, they'd stop thinking. And then they'd be easier to lie to. And . . . what if I was wrong?'

'So . . . if *you* may not decide what is true, and the men of letters may not, who may?'

'Nobody. Everybody.' Mosca looked up at the windows where the jubilant people of Mandelion swung their bells. 'Clamouring Hour – that's the only way. Everybody able to stand up and shout what they think, all at once. An' not just the men of letters, an' the lords in their full-bottomed wigs, but the streetsellers an' the porters an' the bakers. An' not just the clever men, but the muddle-headed, and the madmen, and the criminals, an' the children in their infant gowns, an' the really, really stupid. All of 'em. Even the wicked, Mr Clent. Even the Birdcatchers.'

'Confusion, madam. The truth would be drowned out and never heard.'

'Maybe.'

'People would close their ears and beg to be told what to think.'

'Maybe.'

'Terrible ideas would spread like wildfire from tongue to tongue, and nobody would be able to stop them.'

'Maybe.'

Clent was right, and Mosca knew it. Words were dangerous when loosed. They were more powerful than cannon and more unpredictable than storms. They could turn men's heads inside out and warp their destinies. They could pick up kingdoms and shake them until they rattled. And this was a *good* thing, a *wonderful* thing . . . and in her heart Mosca was sure that Clent knew this too. Mosca recalled the words she had heard Pertellis reading to the Floating School – words that she now knew had been written by her father, Quillam Mye.

. . . there is one thing that is more dangerous than Truth. Those who would try to silence Truth's voice are more destructive by far . . .

In Suet Street, currant-scented steam eased through a gash in the diamond-paned window of a baker, lighting a flame in Mosca's stomach and a concern in her mind.

'What 'appened to the Cakes, Mr Clent?'

'She lives and thrives, though I fancy she will be busy for a time, tending to that young admirer of hers until his shoulder recovers.'

. . . the Cakes piling Carmine's bedside with cinnamon treats and brandy-apple pies, open treacle pastries covered in flourishes of cream, and all the while wearing the pink-faced, bright-eyed look that made her seem less pert and pointed . . .

'What 'bout Mr Pertellis an' the radicals? They won't be arrested, will they?'

'I think not. The radicals have spoken with the guilds, and I fancy an uneasy truce will be struck. Neither side will be happy with it, but Man is born to walk this world in misery.'

'So . . . really, the Locksmiths an' the rest will be taking over the city after all?'

'Ah no – Blythe and his radicals would never allow that, and at the moment he has the backing of the whole city. And I think even when the hubbub has died down he will do well enough with Pertellis and that alarming ladle-wielding ptarmigan to advise him.'

. . . Blythe sitting uncomfortably in the Duke's spire and scowling his way through sheaves of papers, while Pertellis patiently leans over his shoulder to point and explain, and Miss Kitely frowning at a map of Mandelion as if it were the pattern for a smock that needed adjusting for a new owner . . .

'Hopewood Pertellis asked a great deal about you while we were in the coffeehouse,' Clent added in a deliberately casual manner.

'You didn't tell him I was dragged out of a burning

building by a goose, or kidnapped by gypsies, or any of those things?'

'I was the model of candour. I told him that you were an inscrutable little animal and never told me anything, but that I believed your parents were dead.'

They were crossing the Ashbridge. Unexpectedly, Clent slowed and halted.

'Mosca, give me the leash for a moment.' She obeyed, compelled by the unusual seriousness in his manner. 'The Guildmasters may have banished us, but their displeasure lies chiefly on my shoulders . . . and perhaps that of the goose. The truth is, they care little where you go. Pertellis has an interest in your welfare, and if you went to him I have no doubt he would take you in.'

It was true, Mosca felt it. And as if she were riffling the years of her life like the pages of her book, she saw in a very few seconds what would happen and how it would all go. Pertellis's spring-blue eyes would brighten and he would take her in without hesitation or reproach. Miss Kitely would pick out some clothes for her, and she would find herself taking dictation in the Floating School, then teaching the younger children when it was noticed how well she read. In a hundred quiet little ways she would become trusted, and appreciated, and finally necessary. One day Pertellis would look up at her as she marshalled his library, and he would realize that she was not twelve now, she was twenty. And she would marry him, or someone very like him . . . as her mother had done.

'No,' said Mosca.

'You have a chance of security here – food, shelter, friends, prospects . . . books . . .'

'No.' Mosca bit her lip and shook her head firmly. Books no longer seemed quite enough. *I don't want a happy ending, I want more story.*

'Mosca . . . I am not even certain whither I am wending. What can I offer a secretary but a life of sleeping in hedges, chicken-stealing, and climbing out through midnight windows to avoid paying innkeepers in the morning?'

Nothing, except . . . loose strands of possibility snaking like maypole ribbons. Roads fringed with russet bracken, roads sparkling with frost, hill roads split with the rising sun, forest roads livid with fallen leaves, the Crystalcourt with its million windows throwing tiaras of rainbow colour upon the floor, ladies with legends of days past embroidered along their trains, wine dark as blackberry juice sipped under a green-fringed canopy, accents as strange as a walking cane worn by another hand, estuaries bold with man-o'-war ships, and perhaps beyond it the shimmering, much-dreamed-upon expanse of the sea . . .

'You need someone to look out for you, Mr Clent. You're a rotten liar. Good liars lie only when they need to. 'Sides, if I left you with Saracen you'd just eat 'im.'

Mosca held out her hand for Saracen's leash, and after a moment's hesitation Clent gave it back to her, with a small but ceremonious bow.

DISCLAIMER

This is not a historical novel. It is a yarn. Although the Realm is based roughly on England at the start of the eighteenth century, I have taken appalling liberties with historical authenticity and, when I felt like it, the laws of physics.

ACKNOWLEDGEMENTS

I would like to thank the following people: Maureen Waller for her fascinating and colourful book, *1700: Scenes from London Life*, from which I learned about marriage houses, 'a fair mark' and countless other fascinating details of eighteenth-century life; the Duelling Association, for showing me a historical world full of wit, wickedness and panache; Colin Shaw of Roving Romania, who showed us around the wild countryside of that bruised and beautiful country, with its tiny shrines, name-day celebrations and 'weddings of the dead', and the denizens of Zehazel for all their support over the years.

ABOUT THE AUTHOR

Frances Hardinge spent a large part of her childhood in a huge old house that inspired her to write strange stories from an early age. She read English at Oxford University, and then got a job at a software company. However, a few years later her first children's novel, *Fly By Night*, was snapped up by Macmillan. The book went on to publish to huge critical acclaim and win the Branford Boase First Novel Award. She has been nominated for, and won, several other awards, including being shortlisted for the prestigious CILIP Carnegie Medal for *Cuckoo Song* and winning the coveted Costa Book of the Year Award for *The Lie Tree*.

Read on for an extract of the sequel to *Fly by Night*

TWILIGHT ROBBERY

FRANCES HARDINGE

THAT CLOCK'S A LOT LIKE THE TOWN, SHE
DECIDED. *IT'S ROTTEN AND BROKEN RIGHT DOWN
INSIDE WHERE ITS HEART'S COGS MEET.
THAT'S TOLL.*

As dusk approaches, the good people of Toll-by-Day slam shut
their doors and tremble. For, as the shadows lengthen, the city
of Toll-by-Night emerges from the darkness – a city full of
scoundrels, brigands and murderers.

Stuck in this wicked underworld, orphan Mosca Mye and her
conman companion Eponymous Clent find themselves embroiled
in a dark and treacherous kidnap plot, with only a midwife,
a wayward goose and a war-crazed knight to help them . . .

GOODMAN SPRINGZEL,
BRINGER OF SURPRISES

'Read the paper for you, sir?'

One small voice strove against the thunder of rain, the shuffle and huff of the passing mules, the damp flap of canvas as the last sodden stallholders gave up their fight against the dismal weather. Market day was coming apart like a biscuit in coffee, fragments of it running for cover with trays and baskets held over their heads.

'Oi! Gentlemen! Read the paper for you?'

The two farmers that had been hailed hurried on, without looking up to see where the voice came from. And so they did not notice a small figure that had found, if not shelter, at least a place where the rain simply pelted her instead of pummelling her. The upper storeys of the courthouse, debtors' prison and magistrate's house all jutted themselves forward like three frowning foreheads, and beneath this the figure hunched against the wall, bowing so as to shield a crumpled, sodden copy of a much-travelled *Pincaster Gazette* from the worst of the rain. Small wonder that the poor *Gazette* drooped so forlornly. Even in the cities reading was a rare talent, and here in the little sheep-farming town of Grabely none of the inhabitants could read the tiniest tittle.

The rain washed people, stalls and barrows from the market square, leaving only that one figure like a particularly stubborn stain. Drips fell from the tip of a pointed nose. Beneath a drooping bonnet with a frayed brim, hair spiked and straggled like a tempest-tossed blackbird's nest. An olive-green dress two sizes too big was hitched at the waist and daubed knee high in thick yellow mud. And behind the clinging strands of damp hair two large black eyes glistened like coal and gave the marketplace a look that spoke of coal's grit, griminess and hidden fire.

This shivering, clench-jawed scrap of damp doggedness had a name, and that name was Mosca Mye. 'Mosca' meant fly, a housefly name well suited to one born on an evening sacred to Palpitattle, He Who Keeps Flies out of Jams and Butterchurns. It was a name that would have been recognized in her home village, where a number of people would have had questions to ask about the burning of a mill, the release of a notorious felon and the theft of a large and savage goose. In Mandelion, a city port to the west, a well-informed few would have known her name, and how it fitted into the tale of conspiracy, murder, river battles and revolution that had turned the city upside down and shaped it anew.

Three months had now passed since the gates of Mandelion closed behind Mosca. Those three months had brought in winter, eaten the soles of her shoes to a paper thinness, pinched her cheeks, emptied her purse and, most importantly of all, used up her last ounce of patience with her travelling companion.

'Mosca?' A faint, querulous voice sounded behind her,

rather like that of a dying great-aunt. 'If you do not wish me to perish from want, you might try to use a little charm. The flower girls manage to coo or sing their wares – they do not shriek like an attacking hawk.'

The voice came from a narrow, barred window set in the wall of the debtors' prison. Peering in, Mosca could just make out a ponderous figure lying in its shirtsleeves upon a bed of straw. The man in question had allowed a tragic and injured expression to settle upon his plump face, as if it was he and not Mosca who was braving the elements. His coat, wig and pocket-watch chain had all been sold, leaving his much-patched waistcoat on display. Eponymous Clent, poet extraordinaire, word-wizard laureate and eternal bane of all those mean-minded enough to expect him to pay his bills. Once upon a time Mosca had thought it a good idea to continue travelling with him instead of settling in Mandelion. They shared a love of words, a taste for adventure and a dubious relationship with the truth, but such common ground can take two people only so far – and it was starting to seem as if it would take them to Grabely and no further.

'What's your charm done for us, Mr Clent?' snapped Mosca through her teeth. 'Why don't you charm your way out of that cell? Why don't you charm us some dinner?'

'She mocks me,' murmured Clent with a maddening air of stoic forgiveness. 'It is her nature. Those of tottering intellect and meagre spirit always turn against their best friends and protectors as soon as they face real hardship. She cannot help it, Fates.' He sighed. 'Madam, you might reflect upon the fact that you at least have your liberty.'

'Yeah, it's lovely out here.' Mosca glared up at the louring sky of her liberty. 'If I was any freer, I'd have influenza already.'

'Or,' Clent continued with a hint of bitterness, you might reflect on the reason I find myself thus incommoded. After all, you would insist on bringing *him* into this accursed town.'

Mosca made a crab-apple face, but here sadly Clent had a point. If it had not been for her, Saracen would not have been with them. For a good deal of her childhood Saracen had been the orphaned Mosca's only friend and ally, and so she had taken him with her when she fled her damp and miserable home village. Since then she had resisted all Clent's attempts to sell him, lose him or lure him into a pie-case. Mosca usually kept Saracen on a muzzle and leash, but on their first night in Grabely a laughing ostler had made the mistake of assuming that if something waddles it is funny, and that if it is funny then it is harmless, and that if it is harmless there is nothing to be lost by removing its muzzle . . .

Clent had been thrown into the debtors' prison due to his inability to pay for the resultant damage to the inn. The ostler, who was somewhat damaged himself, was carried off demanding that Saracen be put in the stocks (into which his wings would hardly have fitted) and that he be publicly flogged (which nobody seemed willing to attempt). And by the time the townspeople had collected their courage and an array of long sharp objects, Saracen had escaped into the countryside.

Since that time Saracen had been making a name for

himself. That name was not 'Saracen'. Indeed the name was more along the lines of 'that hell-fowl', 'did-you-see-what-it-did-to-my-leg', 'kill-it-kill-it-there-it-goes' or 'what's-that-chirfugging-goose-done-now'. Every time Mosca begged, stole or earned almost enough to pay off Clent's debt, another bruised and bleeding farmer would limp into town to report a shattered roof or a stunned mule, Clent would be blamed for Saracens doings and they would find themselves right back where they started.

'Naturally I would earn our way if I could,' continued Clent in the same dolorous tone, 'but since the Stationers stopped buying my poetry . . . what am I to do?'

Although nobody usually admitted it, everybody knew that between them the powerful guilds that represented the main professions and crafts of the land held the country together. The formidable Guild of Stationers controlled the printing of all books in the Realm, and burned any book they considered dangerous. Most people were glad to leave them to this, for it was believed that reading the wrong book could drive you mad. The Stationers appeared the lesser of two evils, albeit one with a tendency to correct your grammar while burning your neighbours. Clent had once worked as a spy for the Stationers, and it was on their orders that he had travelled to Mandelion with Mosca at his heels. The Stationers had not, however, ordered him to help overthrow the city's government, and had been unamused by Mosca and Clent's involvement in Mandelion's revolution. Over the last three months they had shown their lack of amusement by refusing to buy any of Clent's work, not so much as a limerick.

'Why do you not cut off my hand if you will not let it write?' Clent had railed at them. 'Why not cut off my head if you will not let it dream?'

'Don't think it wasn't considered, Mr Clent,' had been the curt response.

Remembering all this did nothing to improve Mosca's mood. At the moment the most marketable commodity Mosca owned were her eyes – and the fact that she and Clent were the only people in Grabely who knew how to read. Newspapers sometimes washed up in Grabely, declarations and wanted posters were pinned to the door of the courthouse by the decree of the nearest cities, but they might have been covered in bird footprints for all the sense the inhabitants could make of them. And so every day for the last two weeks Mosca had been standing in the square offering to read newspapers, letters, wanted posters and pamphlets to anyone who would pay her a penny. Mosca had always felt a passionate hunger for the books everyone else feared, but right now most of her waking thoughts were taken up with a far more ordinary sort of hunger.

Most people were interested in the copy of the *Gazette*, of course, wanting to hear more of the strange rebel town of Mandelion that had overthrown its duke and, with a reformed highwayman as its leader, still held out against the disapproval of its neighbours. Unfortunately after the first week there was nobody in town who had not heard every word in the newspaper, so Mosca had started making up more stories, and she was afraid that people were beginning to notice.

'Try calling out again, this time in a sweeter manner . . .'

'There's nobody here!' exploded Mosca. 'There's nobody on the blinkin' streets! Nobody wants to know how the world's going! I'm sellin' the news to the bleedin' pigeons! There's nobody – oh, hang on . . .'

A serving man had just come out of the courthouse, staring in confusion at a poster in his hand, before pinning it against the door, upside down. When official declarations and bills were sent to Grabely, the local magistrate always ordered them to be posted outside his courthouse in the approved fashion, despite the fact that even he had no idea what they said.

'Mister! Mister! Do you want me to read that for you? Mister! Only a penny!'

The man looked at her, then swept his wet hair out of his eyes.

'All right.' He tossed a penny. 'Just the gist. Make it snappy.'

Mosca tilted herself so her head was almost inverted, gripping her bonnet as she did so.

'It's a . . .' Unlike every other ounce of Mosca, her mouth was suddenly dry. 'It's . . . It's an announcement of a . . . new . . . tax . . . on . . . table legs.'

'Table legs!' The man swore, and turned up his collar. "Twas only a matter of time, I suppose,' he muttered as he clipped off down the street.

Mosca turned back to the poster and gaped at it white-faced. What it actually said was this:

 9

Eponymous Clent – Wanted for thirty-nine cases of fraud, counterfeiting, selling and circulating lewd and unlicensed literature, claiming to be the impecunious son of a duke, impersonating a magistrate, impersonating a horse doctor, breach of promise, forty-seven moonlit flits without payment of debts, robbing shrines, fleeing from justice before trial, stealing pies from windows and small furniture from inns, fabricating the Great Palthrop Horse Plague for purposes of profit, operating a hurdy-gurdy without a licence. The public are advised against lending him money, buying anything from him, letting him rooms or believing a word he says. Contrary to his professions, he will not pay you the day after tomorrow.

Eponymous Clent was known in the debtors' prison by his real name. That had been unavoidable.

Nobody ever did lie about their name, not least for fear of angering their patron Beloved. The Beloved were the little gods everybody trusted to take care of running the world, keeping clouds afloat, hens laying and dust out of babies' eyes. There were far too many Beloved for each to have a whole day of the year sacred to them, and so instead every little god had to make do with a fraction of a day or night. If you were born in an hour sacred to a particular Beloved, it became your patron god, and you were given one of the names linked to that god. Everybody agreed that your name was who you *were,* your destined, god-given nature. Lying about it was as unthinkable as slapping a god in the face or trying to glue a new soul into your body.

Clent had been named 'Eponymous' because he had been born under Phangavotte, He Who Smooths the Tongue of the Storyteller and Frames the Legendary Deed. While he was shameless enough to impersonate anything from a High Constable to a hedgehog, even Clent would not lie about his name. And so, sooner or later, somebody else who could read would turn up in Grabely and look at the poster, maybe read it aloud . . .

'Oh muckbuckle,' muttered Mosca. 'We're sunk.'

And then, not for the first time, it occurred to her that only Clent need sink, and that she did not have to be aboard when it happened.

The thunder of the rain hid the clatter of clog on cobble as she ran along this wall and that, making her way towards the easterly road. It did not take long. The town was tiny, and soon her clogs were squishing into mud. The houses fell back, and she was gasping and sneezing and gazing out along a barren dirt track ribboning across the grey heath.

Ranged along the road like a rough-cut welcoming committee were Grabely's statues of some of the Beloved. These particular Beloved were hacked and hewn from wood, which the water glossed to a slick, dark red. Greyglory with his sword, Halfapath brandishing a sextant, Tombeliss beating on his drum.

The morning had been sacred to Goodlady Emberleather, She Who Prevents the Meat from Becoming Chewy and Unwholesome. The hours between noon and dusk on this day of the year, however, were devoted to Goodman Springzel, He Who Tips Icewater Down the Collar and Hides the Pearl in the Oyster, the Beloved in charge of surprises both good and ill. Somebody had placed a crude wreath of leaves around his statue's neck to show that this was his sacred time.

Like everybody else, Mosca had been brought up worshipping the Beloved. Every habit of her mind told her that she *needed* to perform little gestures of respect to these miniature gods, in order to ward off disasters great and small. *But,* wondered her fierce, rebellious, practical mind, *what happens if I don't?*

Mosca's mother had died in childbirth, and thus the only parent she had ever known had been her father, the studious and uncompromising Quillam Mye. He had died when she was eight, leaving her an orphan. Some remembered him as a great thinker, and a hero in the fight against the murderous Birdcatchers, who had ruled the Realm for a few bloody years. However, the wild and radical views on equality that filled his later books had seen him exiled, spending his last years in the miserable backwater village of Chough, where his daughter was born and raised. Mosca's childhood had always been tainted by the villagers' suspicion of her father. Had they known the full truth of his views, the people of Chough would probably have burned him when he first set foot in the village . . . for Quillam Mye had secretly been an atheist.

Ever since discovering the truth of her father's atheism, Mosca had discreetly stopped nodding to the Beloved's statues, reciting prayers to calm them or leaving offerings in their tiny shrines. In spite of this it did not seem that rain made her any wetter, or that her milk curdled any faster, or that she was any more prone to attack by wolves.

And thus she felt no particular qualms about sitting down upon the wide flat head of Goodman Springzel to consider her situation. She took out a wooden pipe and chewed angrily at the stem, but left it empty and unlit. It was a habit she had developed long ago, whenever she needed to clear her thoughts.

I'm done with Mr Clent – done for good this time. All I need to do is find Saracen, then I'll leave that ungrateful old bag of lies to stew in his own juice.

But where could she run? To the west, back towards Mandelion? It was not that easy. She had friends there . . . but after the revolution a number of powerful and dangerous people had made it clear that she, Clent and Saracen should leave Mandelion and never come back. Besides, even if she did strike out for the city, she might never reach it. The land around it was starting to sound like a warzone in the making.

A month ago all the big cities within spitting distance of Mandelion had passed hasty new laws decreeing that nobody was allowed to trade with the rebel city. The idea was to starve them out, but what it really meant was that suddenly all the little towns like Grabely that needed their trade with Mandelion to make ends meet found themselves with meagre market stalls and dwindling granaries. And so some people had decided that life might be better in Mandelion itself and had tried to flee to join the rebels. Now many of the local towns and cities had beadles and other lawmakers patrolling the moors in search of such refugees, ready to drag them back to a worse cell than Clent's.

Could she last the winter in one of the nearby towns or

 13

villages to the north or south? Unlikely. Soon there would be no more apples to tug off the trees, any hint of good humour and charity would be pinched away by the cold and nobody would pay to have a newspaper read to them. Knowing would become less important than eating.

Where did houseflies go in the winter?

'They don't,' muttered Mosca with her eyes full of water. 'They jus' die. Well, squash that for a start.'